Jupiter's Shadow

Jupiter's Shadow

David M. Drury

FIVE STAR
An imprint of Thomson Gale, a part of The Thomson Corporation

THOMSON
GALE

Detroit • New York • San Francisco • New Haven, Conn. • Waterville, Maine • London

THOMSON
GALE

Sequel to: All the Gold of Ophir.
Five Star, an imprint of the Gale Group.
Thomson and Star Logo and Five Star are trademarks and Gale is a registered trademark used herein under license.

Set in 11 pt. Plantin.

LIBRARY OF CONGRESS CATALOGING-IN-PUBLICATION DATA

Drury, David M. (David Michael), 1951–.
Jupiter's Shadow / David M. Drury.
p. cm.
Sequel to: All the Gold of Ophir.
ISBN-13: 978-1-59414-607-7 (hardcover : alk. paper)
ISBN-10: 1-59414-607-1 (hardcover : alk. paper)
1. Gold mines and mining—Fiction. 2. Space stations—Fiction. 3. Private investigators—Fiction. 4. Murder victims—Fiction. I. Title.
PS3604.R87J87 2007
813'.6—dc22 2007011922

First Edition. First Printing: September 2007.

Published in 2007 in conjunction with Tekno Books and Ed Gorman.

Printed in the United States of America on permanent paper
10 9 8 7 6 5 4 3 2 1

This book is dedicated to all the people who bought my first novel, *All the Gold of Ophir.* Without them, the publisher would never have bought *Jupiter's Shadow.*

Chapter 1

Michael Flynn jogged twice around Jupiter Station every day. He jogged on level one, where the circumference of the Station was over three kilometers and the gravity was five percent greater than Earth standard. He jogged on Eighth Street, because of its interlevel ramps, early in the morning, just as the lighting increased to simulate daylight and the streets were quiet and empty.

That Tuesday, however, the streets were neither quiet nor empty. Emergency vehicles with flashing blue lights clogged Seattle Avenue, a block up station from Eighth Street. Behind the yellow tape stretched across the avenue were the blue uniforms of U.S. marshals and the blaze-orange coveralls of Company security guards. Station Manager Ed Warshovsky and Security Director Silvanus Drake were there, too.

The presence of such important people at that early hour aroused Flynn's curiosity. Michael decided to investigate. That, after all, is what private investigators did.

A deputy that Flynn knew moved to the tape to intercept him. "Sorry, Flynn. This is a potential crime scene. You'll have to go around." He pointed to his right, toward Chicago Avenue.

Flynn didn't like Silvanus Drake and suspected the feeling was mutual. He was surprised when the security director said, "Let him through, Deputy. Maybe Flynn can ID the guy."

The deputy lifted the tape and Flynn ducked under it. Michael followed Drake to an ambulance. Drake nodded at the ambulance driver, who pulled back the tarpaulin covering a body bag and unzipped it. "Recognize him?" Drake asked.

The man in the bag had dark hair, white skin, and a deep gash in his right cheek. His eyes were closed.

Flynn ran his tongue along the inside of his lower lip. "Looks familiar. I probably have seen him around, but I can't say where and I can't say when."

"You don't know his name?" Warshovsky asked.

Michael looked at the Station manager. Warshovsky was as tall as Flynn, but he was twenty years older, and youth drugs hadn't been invented in time to keep his hair from turning gray at the edges. His suit hid his stomach, but his rounded jowls showed that he ate well. The right side of his face pulsed blue in synchronism with the lights on the ambulance.

"Don't you?"

Warshovsky hesitated. "There was no ID on the body."

Flynn examined the deceased. "His face isn't that bunged up." Nobody stopped him as he reached out and peeled back an eyelid. "Retinals intact."

Warshovsky opened his mouth, then glanced at his security director. Drake was shorter than Flynn, with brown eyes, dark hair, and a dark, almost gray, complexion. Drake's expression and eyes, as blank as a robot's, revealed nothing. They never did.

"He's not in our database," Drake said.

Drake was lying. Everybody on the Station was in his database.

The lie did not surprise Flynn, who would hesitate to believe Drake if he had said that today was Tuesday. "Where was he found?"

The security director gestured with his head toward the open deck hatch behind the ambulance. "Night shift discovered him in a bin beneath a recycling chute."

Flynn reflexively looked at the hatch. "Did he die before or after he entered the chute?"

For a moment Flynn thought that Drake wasn't going to answer the question. He finally said, "Yes."

Someone called, "Hurry up down there! I want to be out of here before the news people wake up!" Flynn looked at the deck hatch and saw U.S. Marshal Devon Hathaway emerge from the basement. Hathaway's dark brown hair was much shorter than it had been in the photos that had preceded her to the Station. She was of average height and had a stocky build, and looked like she could take care of herself in unarmed combat. Her eyes scanned the scene, then stopped on Flynn. She put her hands on her hips.

"Michael Flynn. I've been looking forward to meeting you."

"If it's to thank me for the career opportunity that brought you here, you can forget it. It was nothing, really."

The corners of Hathaway's mouth turned down slightly. "Rustin said you had a smart mouth."

Flynn smiled. "Thanks. A mouth is no smarter than the brain driving it."

Hathaway pressed her lips together and took a deep breath. She pointed her finger at the detective. "You got away with disrespect for authority before, but things are going to be different now that I'm in charge."

Flynn couldn't pass up that straight line, either. "So honesty and integrity in the Marshals Office will now come from the top down instead of the bottom up?"

The marshal had dark, heavy eyebrows, which lowered ominously as she glared at Flynn. She turned to Warshovsky and asked, "What the hell is this comedian doing here?"

Drake answered for his boss. "We thought he might be able to identify the deceased. He couldn't."

"Then there's no need for him to stay here. Get lost, Flynn.

This is a potential crime scene."

"Potential?"

"What part of 'get lost' did you not understand?"

Flynn walked away, knowing that he had learned all he was going to learn.

Warshovsky watched the detective return to Eighth Street and resume jogging. He said to Drake, "Even Flynn can't ID him. So who the hell is he? One of those neoluddite terrorists?"

Drake waited for Flynn to disappear around the corner. In a voice too soft for anyone but Warshovsky to hear, he said, "I think we have finally found the babysitter."

Flynn's apartment was on Ninth Street on level six. It opened onto a balcony that was connected by a ramp to Ninth Street on level five. Flynn jogged up the ramp to the apartment door. The lock recognized his retinals and the door slid open when he twisted the latch. He heard the shower running. As Flynn closed the door he spied a black cat on the kitchen counter.

"Furrball!" The cat adopted an expression of innocence, as though it wasn't doing anything wrong, then thought better of it and jumped to the floor. Flynn waved his finger at the animal. "If Wendy caught you up there, she'd cut off your tail right behind your ears!"

The apartment was a perquisite of Wendy's position as director of the Company's legal department on the Station. It was larger than most apartments on Jupiter Station and had its own laundry facilities. The cleaning robot came twice a week instead of only once. Flynn reached the bathroom doorway just as the shower stopped and his wife stepped out.

"You started without me!" Flynn complained.

"You were late!" Wendy liked her routines and her schedules. She started drying herself, showing her displeasure at her husband's tardiness with the forceful strokes of the towel. "I told you I had to get to work early this morning to get ready for the staff meeting!"

Flynn peeled off his jogging clothes and pitched them into the bedroom. "Well, your meeting's going to run longer than scheduled. Another item's been added to the agenda."

Wendy stopped drying her legs and looked at her husband. "What happened?"

"Night shift found a body in one of the recycling bins."

Wendy closed her eyes. "Damn it! And Dr. Liao's coming today!" She opened her eyes, but the scene hadn't changed; she hadn't been dreaming. "Anybody we know?"

The bathroom, palatial by the standards of Jupiter Station, would have been considered tiny on Earth. Flynn squeezed passed his wife and stepped into the shower. "I didn't recognize him. Nobody can. He's not in Drake's computer." Flynn turned on the water. Wendy had it too hot again.

Wendy stood on her toes and looked over the top of the shower door. "Everybody's in Drake's computer! Even the construction workers from the Asian station who come here on R and R! Silvanus Drake violates civil rights regardless of gender, race, creed, color, or national origin!"

Michael shrugged. "Drake was there. So was Warshovsky. They claim they can't ID this guy."

Wendy made a face. "Maybe the security cameras missed him. The way they cram people onto those shuttles from the Asian station . . ."

"Maybe, but this was a white guy. Most of the workers from the Asian station are . . . Asian."

Wendy slowly lowered herself from her toes and turned away. Her red hair was wet and she rubbed it with her towel. She paused in the bathroom doorway. "Please tell me this wasn't a homicide."

Flynn massaged his hair with shampoo. "The deceased had a

deep gash in his cheek that hadn't bled, and the tissue around it wasn't bruised, so he got it after he died. Unless the gash was caused by something falling on him in the recycling bin, he probably was dead before he entered the chute. There was no ID on the body, so it might have been a mugging that got out of hand."

Wendy turned away. "The Station's original designer is making his first trip to Jupiter, and some idiot chooses this moment to commit murder!"

"The victim managed to get onto the Station without getting into Drake's computer. His death just before Liao's visit is a huge coincidence. I'd bet that Liao's visit is the reason for the murder."

Silvanus Drake had an extremely suspicious mind. Michael guessed that Drake would make the same bet.

Flynn's office was on Butte Avenue on level two, where the gravity was stronger than Earth normal and the rents were lower than they were on higher levels. The office had been Wendy's idea. In the good old days, bachelor Michael Flynn had worked from a desk in his apartment. But that was before his fame had given him more work than he could handle and had left his competition without enough work to survive. Now Flynn subcontracted most of his investigations to the other four private detectives on the Station.

The office was barely big enough for a desk, a chair for Flynn, and two chairs for visitors, but it featured a glass front wall that gave Flynn a splendid view of Butte Avenue. Flynn left the door open to accommodate clients and stepped behind the desk. He sat down and was startled to see Peter Chow sitting across the desk from him.

Flynn winced. "I asked you not to do that anymore!"

"Sorry, Mike." Chow was short and slender and he moved

liked a ghost. He claimed to have high-degree black belts in nearly every form of martial arts, which Flynn couldn't confirm because he had never seen Chow fight. Pete was wearing a dark green turtleneck under a lightweight leather jacket. From the pocket of the jacket he produced a memory fiche and slid it across the desk. "My report on the Trudell investigation. If that woman was ever on the Station, she didn't work for anyone, she didn't talk to anyone, and she wasn't seen by anyone."

Alivia Trudell had become engaged to a man who wanted to know exactly whom he was marrying and who was rich enough to hire investigators all over the solar system to find out. The case, subcontracted to Flynn by Pinkerton's in New York, was typical of his work.

Flynn took the fiche in his fingers. He looked at the man on the other side of the desk. Pete was a poor detective—people wouldn't talk to him, even when offered large financial incentives. "Pinkerton says she came to Jupiter."

Chow shrugged. "If she did, she didn't stay very long. She changed her name a couple of times before she came here; she might have changed her name again and departed on the next ship."

Trips to Jupiter were expensive as well as time-consuming. Alivia Trudell would not have gone there from planet four just to catch another ship back to the inner solar system. Flynn tapped the memory fiche against the desk top. "Expenses?"

Chow nodded at the fiche in Flynn's hand. "In the report."

Flynn nodded. "I'll credit your account."

"Have any more work for me?"

Flynn checked the office computer. Job-protection laws that made it difficult for employers to dismiss employees—even dishonest, lazy, or otherwise unproductive ones—had created a huge demand for private investigators. Four requests for preemployment background investigations had come from Earth overnight. Meditech Hospital on the Station also wanted a potential employee checked out. “There are five cases here. Give me a couple of hours to sort through them.”

Chow stood up. “Thanks, Mike.” He left as quickly and silently as he had appeared.

Edwin Warshovsky, general manager of Conglomerated Mining and Manufacturing Company’s Jupiter Station, met with his department directors every Tuesday morning at ten in the Executive Meeting Room. Silvanus Drake always sat on his right and Wendy Chadwick on his left. Marvin Chalmisiak, director of accounting, sat at the opposite end of the table from Warshovsky, a symbolic expression of his opposition to almost everything that Warshovsky did. The construction of Jupiter Station had put the Company deeply in debt. Warshovsky had saved the Company from financial disaster by turning the Station—a huge factory complex surrounded by free raw materials—into the most automated, most productive, and most profitable manufacturing facility in the solar system. Chalmisiak, however, thought that Warshovsky defrauded Company stockholders by reinvesting profits in grandiose schemes, and felt that it was only Warshovsky’s good luck that those schemes earned the Company even more money. Company CEO Ricardo Kung was retiring next year and everybody knew that Warshovsky would replace him. Warshovsky’s good luck couldn’t last forever. Chalmisiak dreaded what would happen to the Company’s price-earnings ratio with Warshovsky in control.

Warshovsky scanned the people seated around the table, their computers open to record the meeting. He could tell from their eyes what was on their minds, but he would make them wait. He would run the meeting according to his agenda.

Warshovsky smiled. “First, the good news. As soon as the signal gets here from Earth, everyone on the Station will know that half an hour ago, Attorney General Marianne Archuleta announced that the contract to build the orbiting prison was awarded to the Conglomerated Mining and Manufacturing Company."

The reaction did not disappoint Warshovsky. Kevin McSheridan, operations director, got downright boisterous, slapping Engineering Director Luke Timchenko on the back and shouting, "A ten *billion* dollar contract! Ten *billion!*"

Lisa Reisbach, manufacturing director, said, "We can start rolling steel for it by Friday." She tossed her head back, as though trying to get her black hair out of her eyes.

Chalmisiak eyed Reisbach suspiciously. "What about our other contracts? We're operating close to capacity."

"We have two big ones with delivery dates that are eighteen months off," Wendy said. She didn't like Chalmisiak. None of the department directors did. "We can postpone work on those."

"We can't take on any more big projects, though," Reisbach warned. "When we deliver that prison—built here, in Jovian orbit—to Earth orbit, on schedule and for less money than any Earth-based manufacturer could do it, people are going to stop dreaming about putting cities in orbit and start construction. They'll want us to build them, and we'll be short of rolling capacity. That will create a big opening for the competition."

"We'll be short of construction workers, too," Clarisse Jackson added. She was the Company's human resources director at Jupiter. "The contracts of almost three hundred of our structural-assembly people expire in the next year." The workers were to go back to Earth on the new prison, completing it during its twelve-month journey.

Chalmisiak didn't like to hear arguments in favor of bringing more workers to Jupiter Station. "We don't have any competition! The Brazilians haven't even started construction. The Asian station is behind schedule and is going to go way over budget.

They'll probably run out of money before they finish it."

"They brought Dr. Liao out here to get the project back on track," Warshovsky pointed out.

"Liao won't help," Timchenko said. He had short black hair that was almost hidden behind thick black eyebrows. He didn't like to support Chalmisiak, but in this case he agreed with the accountant. "The problems with the Asian station are his fault. He designed it just like he designed this station fifteen years ago and repeated every mistake. He hasn't learned a damned thing from what we've done here. He's made it too small, the plumbing's inadequate, he's using those damn balancing weights without the mods we had to do to keep them from jamming, he's got aluminum *everywhere* so when they expand with cheaper steel they'll have the same interface problems we had. When our ex-employees—who were hired for their experience—tell them what they're doing wrong, they're ignored."

Chalmisiak was not mollified. "Did we invite Liao over here to show him the error of his ways?"

Warshovsky tried to keep his temper. "Satellite Kilo is nearly finished. Dr. Liao won't see anything here that he hasn't already seen in *National Geographic.*"

"Well," Chalmisiak said, "we picked a hell of time to invite him, right after another murder." The accountant not only changed the subject to the topic that had been on everyone's mind, but made it sound like the death had been Warshovsky's fault.

Warshovsky glanced at Drake. The security director rarely spoke at the weekly meetings, but he took the hint. "The cause of death has not been determined."

"Mr. Drake, would you commit suicide by jumping down a recycling chute?" Having made his point, Chalmisiak turned his attention back to the general manager. "Was the victim one of our employees?"

Warshovsky shook his head. "Definitely not. And since the marshals have taken charge of the investigation, we can concentrate on other matters, such as the reception for Dr. Liao this evening." He looked at his human resources director. "Ms. Jackson, is everything ready?"

Clarisse was the most fashion-conscious of the directors, and was wearing an iridescent light-red business suit that nicely complemented her black skin. She gave the thumbs up. "Bill Renny at the hotel is laying out the most opulent buffet the Station's ever seen."

"Liao is supposed to have a thing for scotch," McSheridan said.

Ms. Jackson smiled. "And seafood. We've taken care of it."

Chalmisiak scowled. Bourbon was distilled on the Station, but scotch and seafood had to be imported from Earth, at considerable expense.

"You and your spouses will attend?" Warshovsky said, scanning the faces at the table. He paused when he got to Wendy. Warshovsky didn't like the fact that she had married the private detective who had nearly brought down the entire Company. Wendy guessed that Warshovsky was hoping that her husband wouldn't show up. She smiled and nodded. Warshovsky looked away. "I can't overstress the importance of making a good impression on Dr. Liao," he continued. "He has direct connections to the hard-liners who control the Chinese government. Our government is trying to improve relations with China. Liao can help achieve that, and if we help to persuade Liao we gain ammunition to use against our critics in Washington, who would love to impose the same regulations on us that stifle our Earth-based competitors. So let's make sure Liao has a good time while he's here."

The rest of the meeting was spent discussing the negotiations with the Brazilians. The Company had offered to build their station for them. The Brazilians wanted their own workers to do the construction, under the guidance of Company engineers. Marv Chalmisiak was adamantly opposed to "training the competition." Lisa Reisbach pointed out that the Brazilians had planned a station too small to be economically viable. Warshovsky wanted another customer for the food that would be grown on Satellite Kilo. The directors could not reach agreement, which meant that Warshovsky would do whatever he thought best—which he would have done in any case.

The directors were still congratulating each other for the prison contract when they filed out of the meeting room. Wendy lingered to talk to Warshovsky. So, to her disgruntlement, did Silvanus Drake.

"My husband tells me that we can't identify last night's fatality."

Warshovsky hesitated, as though he wasn't going to respond. Then he said, "That was true at six-thirty this morning. We have since learned that his name was Helmuth Manstein, a manufacturer's representative."

Wendy glanced at the security director. "I thought he wasn't in your database."

Drake didn't reply, so Warshovsky said, "Mr. Drake had the morning Security shift show the photo around. Manstein's neighbor identified him. He lived in that block of apartments near the hotel that we rent to long-term residents who are not Company employees. His name is still confidential—the marshals have not yet informed his next of kin back on Earth."

When Wendy had come to Jupiter, Warshovsky had been almost a father figure to her. He had mentored her and made her the director of the Legal Department despite her youth and lack of experience. But then Wendy had learned the hard way that the general manager could be as underhanded and untrustworthy as Silvanus Drake. Now, as she eyed Warshovsky's face, she got the feeling that she wasn't being told the whole truth. "Why couldn't the computer identify him?"

"I'm looking into that," Drake said.

Wendy glanced from Drake to Warshovsky and back to Drake again. She was being given the runaround. "Does he show up in any of last night's Security videos?"

Drake said, "He was in our casino, a couple of elevators, several streets. Nothing suspicious and no clues to his demise."

"Do we know where he entered the chute?"

"The marshals are trying to find out," Drake replied. "They are inspecting the inside of the chute for tissue samples."

Chadwick wearied of prying loose information with a crowbar. "If Manstein was knocked off in a part of the Station for which we, and not the marshals, provide security, the courts will hold the Company liable for civil damages. I'm the head of the Legal Department. Please inform me of any developments."

"There is a door to the recycling chute not far from Manstein's apartment, out of sight of any security camera," Drake said. "I'd guess he entered the chute there. The door's on a public street, in the marshals' area of responsibility, so I wouldn't worry about Company liability yet, Ms. Chadwick." He paused. "I'll see you at the reception tonight."

"Mr. Flynn?"

Michael looked up. A woman was standing in the office door. She had flawless black skin and the kind of figure that men's magazines paid money to exhibit undraped. The woman was dressed in the garish European fashion that had spread like corn blight across the solar system in the preceding two years: form-fitting silver blouse over silver tights, a tiny silver skirt that didn't reach anywhere near mid thigh, and a silver coat that extended below the bottom of the skirt and was topped with square, masculine shoulders. She had tinted her hair and eyebrows to match the outfit. Despite Flynn's dislike of her attire, he still thought she looked fantastic. He was looking for a wedding ring before he remembered that he had taken himself out of the game the year before.

The woman didn't look threatening. "Yes?" Flynn admitted.

The woman bit her lower lip. "I, ah . . ."

"Come in. Sit down." Flynn pressed the key on his computer that closed the office door and polarized the glass wall opaque. "What can I do for you?"

The woman kept her hands in her lap where Flynn couldn't see them. "I, um . . . I've never hired a private investigator before." The fact that this particular investigator was handsome enough to be a movie star increased her unease.

"Most of the people in the solar system can say the same thing."

The woman managed to smile. Her teeth were even and sparkling white. "I'm . . . Francine Cross." She was committed now; Flynn knew who she was. "I . . . I think my husband is having an affair."

"With whom?" There were twice as many men as women on Jupiter Station. Flynn knew a dozen guys who would have hocked half their family jewels to time-share Francine Cross. Her husband had the good fortune to have exclusive rights to her. Flynn couldn't believe that Mr. Cross would want to have an affair, even if he had been lucky enough to find a woman to have one with.

Francine didn't take Flynn's question that way. "I don't know!" She blinked back a tear. "That's what I want you to find out!"

Flynn suppressed a sigh. He didn't handle cases of marital infidelity. "My services will cost you eighteen hundred dollars a day plus reasonable expenses."

Ms. Cross's urge to cry disappeared. She swallowed.

"Eighteen hundred a *day?*"

"Plus expenses."

Francine opened the small silver-gray purse that was slung by a strap over her right shoulder and took out a sheaf of currency. "Would a two-day retainer be enough for you to get started?"

Flynn's strategy for getting rid of Ms. Cross wasn't working. "A one-day retainer would be enough to start, but I can't predict how long it will take to finish." Michael leaned back in his chair. "All I'm going to do is follow your husband around to see if he meets another woman. That could take several days. Weeks, maybe."

Francine counted out thirty-six one-hundred-dollar bills and pushed them across the desk. Cash wouldn't leave a record the way a debit card would. "I think he's seeing her more than once a week."

"Jeremy Kuchek charges only eight hundred a day." Jeremy was the most inept investigator at Jupiter; Flynn rarely subcontracted work to him. Kuchek had cut his rates, trying to get more business.

"I've never heard of Jeremy Kuchek. Everyone on the Station has heard of you."

Flynn had been done in by his own fame. He took the money. "What makes you think your husband's having an affair?"

Ms. Cross ran the tip of her tongue along her bottom lip. "He's been acting . . . strange for the last month—aloof, preoccupied . . . nervous. We haven't . . . you know, in a month. And I've taken three phone calls in the last few weeks where the caller hung up as soon as I said hello."

Flynn raised his eyebrows. "Did you check the caller ID?"

"Not the first two times—I wasn't suspicious enough then. But the last time it was a public phone."

"Do you remember which one?"

"Ah, it was on Fourteenth Street someplace."

In his mind's eye Flynn could see the densely packed apartments at the new end of the Station. Most were inhabited by blue-collar workers. "Does your husband work for the Company?"

Ms. Cross nodded. "Leron's a cowboy."

"Is he at work right now?"

Francine shook her head. "He's working nights this week." She looked at her watch. "And I have a class in fifteen minutes." She looked up at Flynn. "I teach fifth grade."

That made Francine Cross a Company employee, too—the Company operated the Station's only school.

"May I see your ID card?" Flynn asked.

Cross squinted. "My ID card?"

"Privacy laws keep you from investigating just anybody. You must have what's called an 'investigatible interest.' If you really are Francine Cross, you have an investigatible interest in your husband."

Francine reopened her purse, extracted her ID card, and handed it to Flynn. The computer vouched for its authenticity and downloaded her address and contact codes from the Station database. "You have a photo of your husband?"

Ms. Cross hesitated, then reached inside her coat and removed her computer from an inside pocket. "There's one in here."

There were several photos of Leron Cross in Francine's computer. His skin was dark brown and his eyes were large. Flynn copied all of the photos to his machine. "I'll tail your husband when he leaves your apartment this afternoon. I'll hire another investigator to pick him up after his shift and follow him home. If he talks to any women, we'll find out who they are. If he doesn't talk to any women, I'll have to start asking questions. He might find out he's being investigated."

Francine's fingers squirmed on the clasp of her purse. "When will that start?"

"When you get tired of paying eighteen hundred a day without results."

Francine nodded. "Please contact me through my computer—Leron and I have separate accounts."

Flynn nodded. "Okay, I'll do that." Ms. Cross stood up and opened the door. She peeked into the street to see if anyone she knew was there, then slipped through the doorway. Her silver tights gave Flynn a good idea of what her legs looked like. They were almost as good as his wife's, and that was saying a lot. Flynn unpolarized the glass wall, wondering why Mr. Cross's supposed girlfriend had tried to reach him on the family telephone instead of through his private computer.

Flynn could limit his involvement in the Cross investigation by subcontracting it to Peter Chow—Pete had an unremarkable face and could follow people without attracting attention. He sent the particulars of the case, including the photos, with a priority alarm to Chow's computer.

Thinking of Chow prompted Flynn to access the report that Pete had submitted that morning. Chow couldn't investigate but he could write, which was more than Flynn could say for the other three detectives on the Station. Pete had left no stone unturned. Unfortunately, he couldn't tell when the creatures that crawled out from under the stones were lying to him. He had expended twenty-four hundred and fifty dollars in bribes but no one had admitted to knowing Alivia Trudell. Flynn studied the photos of the subject. They gave him the same feeling that he had had when Silvanus Drake had shown him the body from the recycling bin. He had seen Ms. Trudell someplace, probably on the Station. If no one had been willing to talk to Pete about her, Flynn could guess what that someplace was.

Flynn took the memory fiche containing the Trudell report

and put it in the top drawer of the desk. The office door locked behind him as he turned right on Butte Avenue.

The Station's red light district was on Fifth Street, between Chicago and Tucson Avenues on level five. It was bustling with people who worked weekend or evening shifts. Flynn walked past the Company casino, where Conglomerated Mining and Manufacturing took back a lot of the money it paid to its employees, and headed straight for the Pussy Kat Klub. The garish display above its door proclaimed

ALL LIVE GIRLS!
ABSOLUTELY NO ROBOTS!
NO HOLOGRAPHIC PROJECTIONS!

Inside the door a bar stretched along the right wall. On the stage against the back wall three women attired only in makeup and artificial smiles were gyrating in time to the music but not in time with each other. One of the women was good-looking. All of the tables in the room were occupied.

The man seated behind the bar near the door had a short, neatly trimmed beard. He got to his feet when he saw Flynn. "Michael Flynn!" he said, smiling. "It's about time!" He crooked his finger at the robot that tended the bar.

Flynn raised his had to stop the bartender. "Thanks, Arlen, but I'm working."

Arlen Hoffmuller had shortened his name to Hoff when he had moved to the Station. Since the last time Flynn had seen him he had gone European—he was wearing the male version of the gaudy fashion that Flynn loathed. His coat and tights were iridescent yellow and his shirt and shorts were green. "Work never stopped you from drinking before," Arlen said. "Besides, this is on me. Your money isn't good in here anymore." The robot poured two fingers of whiskey into a glass and pushed it across the bar to Flynn.

"My wife doesn't like me drinking on the job."

Hoff looked over Flynn's shoulder at the door. "Huh. Looks like your wife didn't come in with you." He gave Flynn a conspiratorial wink. "Go ahead. She'll never know." Flynn still hesitated. "Come on, Mike. I owe you. The whole Station does."

"The debt was paid in full last year." He looked longingly at the drink, then his resistance failed and he took it. "Mustn't let it go to waste."

"I haven't seen you in here since before last year's unpleasantness. Did you get married or did you join a monastery?"

"Is there a difference?" Flynn took his computer from his coat pocket, opened it, and positioned it so that Hoff could see the display. "This girl used to work for you." The computer was displaying six versions of Alivia Trudell, with different combinations of hair length and hair color. Flynn indicated the image in the middle of the top row. "This one, here, with the jet black hair that's much too dark for the pale complexion, looks the most familiar to me. But I'll be darned if I can remember her name."

Hoff nodded at the computer. "There was another investigator in here a couple of days ago with the same pictures. I didn't recognize her then and I don't recognize her now."

"Arlen, she must have worked for you. Look at her: if the Hot Spot had dancers who looked that good, Papandreou wouldn't have had to bring in that robot."

Hoff shrugged. "Sorry, Mike, but she never worked for me."

"Michael Flynn!" The attractive blonde who had been dancing on the stage made her way to Flynn's side. She had donned a robe that was too short and too transparent to conceal anything. She batted her centimeter-long eyelashes. "You never come to see me anymore!"

"Hi, Mona." The name was as false as the eyelashes.

Mona leaned against Flynn's shoulder. "Are you going to buy

me a drink?"

"Oh, I'll buy you lots of drinks." Flynn took a hundred-dollar bill from his wallet and held it between his fingers. "If you can tell me what her name is." Flynn showed his computer display to Mona.

Mona opened her mouth, but hesitated. "Sorry, Mike. I've never seen her before."

Flynn took another hundred from his wallet. "Maybe a few more drinks will help you remember."

Mona glanced at Hoff, then shook her head.

Not all exotic dancers who went on to bigger and better things wanted that work experience on their résumés. Apparently Alivia Trudell had been liked well enough by her coworkers for them to keep her past a secret. Michael put the bills back into his wallet. He shook his head. "I sure would like to know what the hell she did to you for you to ruin her chance at a better life."

Mona blinked her big eyelashes. "Huh?"

"It takes a rich man to commission a premarital background check way out here. She marries him, the Spouse Protection Act has her set for life." Flynn folded his computer and slipped it into his coat pocket. "Now there'll be a big hole in her history that will make her fiancé very suspicious." Flynn finished his whiskey. "I suppose she can get another dancing job."

Mona swallowed. "You think her fiancé would marry her if he knew that—"

"Maybe she already told him," Flynn suggested. "Then you're making her look like a liar. He'll start wondering what she was really doing while she claimed to be an exotic dancer."

Mona swallowed again and looked at Hoff. Arlen sighed.

"She called herself Alma Thames, like the river," Mona confessed.

Flynn smiled. "That's better." He took his computer out of

his pocket and turned to Hoff. "But that's not the name under which you withheld her taxes."

"Trudell. Alivia Trudell." Hoff produced his own computer and opened it. "She worked here for . . . fourteen months. Left a little over two years ago." Arlen made a face. "Want her Social Security number, too?"

"Just transfer that employment record to my computer. Do you know where she went when she left here?"

"She took a ship to Earth," Mona said. "The *Sunflower.* I went with her when she boarded."

Flynn nodded. "A Company ship—nice accommodations. Where did she stay when she was here?"

"Ah, she roomed with Bridgette Floss—she's not here anymore—and Kari Ashe and Lisa Luz." Mona glanced over her shoulder at a brunette still gyrating on the stage.

Flynn put his computer away again, took the two hundred-dollar bills, and handed them to Mona. "A rich man can afford to buy a lady a few drinks." He turned toward the bar. "Arlen, thanks for the help. I won't forget it."

Hoff grunted. "Yeah, well, don't be such a stranger in the future. Drop in more often. Bring the new wife."

Flynn glanced at the girls on the stage. "Great idea, Arlen. She'd love it here."

Out on the street, Flynn used his computer to access the shipping records. Passenger manifests were confidential, but the *Sunflower* had departed from Jupiter Station at the time Mona had indicated and had gone directly to Earth. Pinkerton's could pick up Ms. Trudell's trail there. Flynn wondered if he should talk to Lisa Luz about her former roommate, but decided not to take the time. If Pinkerton's wanted more information on Trudell's activities on Jupiter Station, they would let him know.

The street was more crowded than when Flynn had entered the club. He thought about Chow's detailed, carefully written, and incorrect report. He wondered how many other reports that he had sent to Earth were similarly erroneous. Flynn had the uneasy feeling that his profession was going to make a lot of lawyers rich. He decided to increase his liability coverage.

Michael looked at his watch. The day shift had ended, but he could still rewrite the Trudell report and get home in time to join his wife for the Liao reception.

CHAPTER 2

"Just how formal is this reception?"

Wendy looked away from the closet and toward her husband, who was standing in the bedroom doorway. "Oh, ah, Dr. Liao and his assistants didn't bring any formal attire. That sport coat is fine."

"I think I'll change this shirt," Flynn said. Wendy was looking from one end of the closet to another. "Don't tell me, let me guess. You have nothing to wear."

"I don't!"

"Wendy, half the *bedrooms* on this station are smaller than that closet, and three fourths of it is filled with your clothes."

"My *old* clothes." Wendy took a party dress from the closet, looked at it, and sighed. "This is fossilized. A dinosaur was wearing it when they went extinct."

"Liao won't know. Engineers are notorious for their lack of fashion knowledge."

"Liao won't be the only one there. Clarisse Jackson spends more on clothes than the state of Arkansas spends on education. She'll know."

"What about one of those outfits in the corner there?"

Wendy looked at Mike and made a face. "You hate those new fashions!"

Flynn was running late and didn't have time to argue with his wife. A concession was in order. "Just because I wouldn't be caught dead in one doesn't mean you can't wear them."

In a year of dating and marriage, Wendy had heard only disparaging remarks from her husband about the new fashion. She looked at him as though she expected to see signs of brain damage. "Are you sure you don't mind?"

"Wendy, you're so gorgeous that you look fantastic no matter what you wear." Flynn gazed at his wife's figure. "Or don't wear."

Wendy hesitated, then put the party dress back into the closet and took two shiny ensembles from the rack. She held them up for Flynn to see. "Should I go as female professional or as woman?"

Flynn went through the motions of appraising the outfits. "Woman—there's less of that nauseating bright fabric."

Michael had obviously not suffered brain damage. Wendy wrinkled her nose, but she put the suit back on the rack and kept the party outfit. "The dead man has been identified. His neighbor recognized him from a photo: Helmuth Manstein, a manufacturer's sales representative from Munich, Germany. His name is being withheld until the marshals can notify his next of kin, so you didn't hear that from me. You didn't hear that, period."

"How long has he been here?"

"Good question. There's no record of his arrival. And it's definitely murder: The ME found three hard blows to the skull with a blunt instrument—a big wrench, maybe—delivered around twenty-two last night."

Wendy sat on the edge of the bed to pull on her tights, letting Flynn get to the closet and extract a shirt. "I assume I didn't hear that, either. Did I ever tell you how great you look in tights?"

"Ah-hah. Several times, the first when you were in the process of peeling them off." Wendy stood up and pulled on the form-fitting, sleeveless minidress with thin straps that went with her tights.

Flynn put his sport coat back on over the new shirt. "You say Manstein claimed to be a manufacturer's rep?" He shook his head. "A real manufacturer's rep would have visited Company engineers, trying to sell products he represented. He'd have been in and out of Company offices and would have shown up on Drake's radar. Since he didn't, I'd guess that he was actually a spy. By the way, I won't tell you what to wear, but if you tint your hair to match those clothes I will immediately file for divorce."

"I never tint my hair. By 'spy,' you mean industrial espionage?"

Flynn shook his head. "I mean political espionage. Manstein's murder coincides with the visit of a dedicated communist with connections to the top people in the Chinese government. It might be a coincidence, but I'll bet you dinner at the Martian Nugget that when the Munich police try to notify Manstein's relatives of his demise, they will discover that either there is no Helmuth Manstein, or that he looks nothing like the victim found this morning."

Wendy examined her appearance in the mirror, then picked up a small, bright-yellow handbag that matched her ensemble. "Let's go. We're going to be late."

Flynn eyed the iridescent yellow shorts with blue vertical stripes that Wendy had left on the bed. "Forget something?"

"This outfit is two years old. Shorts were in style then. They aren't this year. If I don't wear them, maybe I can fool some of the people tonight into thinking this is new."

Flynn used his computer to summon a taxi. At nineteen o'clock the evening commuter rush had dissipated, and he and Wendy reached the Jupiter Hotel, on the Main Plaza on the opposite side of the Station from Company Headquarters, five minutes after leaving their apartment. The hotel ballroom was one of the few spaces on the Station big enough for the Station's curvature to be visible. The buffet had been set up at the far end of the room, in front of a large holographic display that was disguised to look like a window. The "window" was showing Jupiter, a quarter of a million kilometers away. Either the display was generated from a despun camera or it had been processed digitally, because the image of Jupiter wasn't rotating with the Station.

All of the people in the room were near the buffet. Some were seated at tables and the rest were standing in small groups. Wendy counted them and moaned, "We're late. Only twenty-five people and their guests were invited, and they're all here." She nodded at the guest of honor. "That's Liao Chu, standing with Ed and Mary Warshovsky." Flynn recognized the doctor—his photo had been on Station news broadcasts for two weeks. "Those are two of his assistants over there on the right . . . and those are the other two on the left."

Flynn took in the scene with a practiced investigative glance. He recognized nearly everyone except for Liao's assistants. "His assistants don't seem to like parties. They're standing by themselves, not socializing."

"Well, you're going to like this party. Liao has a taste for scotch. The hotel manager broke out four bottles from the Company stockpile."

Flynn's mouth started to water. "Irish is better."

Wendy looked at her husband out of the corner of her eye. "Then why is that bottle of Irish whiskey that Betty O'Brien gave us for a wedding present still almost full?"

So you won't accuse me of drinking too much, Michael thought, but he said, "Whiskey that good should be saved for special occasions."

Kevin McSheridan and his wife were standing with Dr. and

Mrs. Luke Timchenko near the bar. Half of the women in the room were wearing iridescent clothes, but Kevin was the only man so attired. His coat and tights were bright red, as was the curly, normally black hair on his head. Red was not a good match for his complexion. Flynn thought he looked like a circus clown.

"We're going to get another memo from Warshovsky tomorrow," Wendy said under her breath.

"Hmm?"

"He hates these modern fashions even more than you do. He's already sent us two memos on appropriate attire for business executives."

"You're not here as female executive tonight. You're here as woman."

"Are you going to get 'woman' a drink?"

Flynn stepped to the bar. Warshovsky was serving champagne in honor of Liao's visit. Champagne was the only alcoholic beverage that Wendy couldn't resist. Flynn guessed that his wife wouldn't object if he got a glass of Warshovsky's single-malt scotch for himself. Wendy had joined the McSheridans and Timchenkos. He handed her the champagne glass.

Luke Timchenko said, "Liao was looking forward to seeing the waterfall, to see if photos did it justice. I was right behind him when the elevator door opened. He stopped dead in the doorway and stood there with his mouth agape, just like any newcomer."

"I don't think he can admit how far we've taken the Station beyond his design," McSheridan said. "Did you see him in the shuttle, coming over from Kilo? The Station just kept getting bigger and bigger and bigger . . . Bet he was realizing that he's making the Asian station much too small."

Flynn looked around the room. Marvin Chalmisiak was the only Company employee without a guest—he had left his wife on Earth, so that Company profits would not be reduced by the cost of transporting her to Jupiter. “Who’s the guy with Clarisse Jackson?” Michael asked.

The others in the group looked in the direction of Flynn’s gaze. “Dr. Dumas Gupta,” Timchenko said, “one of Lou Cheng’s lead brains. He’s the genius behind the robots running around here picking up empty glasses.” The Station had been making its own housekeeping robots for three years, using technology developed for robotic mining and smelting operations.

Clarisse noticed the heads turned in her direction. She was wearing a bright blue outfit and had tinted her hair, eyebrows, and fingernails to match. McSheridan nodded at her.

Warshovsky chose that moment to introduce Dr. Liao to Wendy. Liao was one hundred and seventy centimeters tall, thin, and clean-shaven. He smiled, revealing teeth stained from cigarette smoke. Wendy’s first impression of the doctor was similar to her impression of the scientists and engineers she knew on the Station: clothes that lacked style, an aura of intellectual competence, none of the reserved aloofness of a diplomat. Nor was there anything to reveal that Liao was one of the greatest engineers of the twenty-first century.

When Liao had been young, the Chinese economy had been booming under the leadership of the “market socialists.” Liao had invented the engineering specialty of designing and constructing large space structures for the aggressive space program the market socialists funded from years of trade surpluses. Then the Chinese had run out of resources (they had nearly run the entire planet out of resources) at the same time as the newly prosperous population had demanded higher wages, health care, and retirement plans. The economic advantages that had fueled the boom had vanished and the boom had collapsed, leaving Liao unemployed and embittered.

He had eagerly supported the hard-liners who took over from the market socialists, but their economic policies were unable to generate the wealth needed to support a space program big enough to use Liao's talents. Liao had spent his career designing stations for other countries. His firm had been employed by the Company to design the original Jupiter Station, and Liao had consulted on its first expansion. Liao had remained loyal to the hard-liners even when economic stagnation had brought the market socialists back to power. Unfortunately for them, China had limited families to one child for almost a century, so its population was top-heavy with old people. The market socialists' inability to support so many retirees had put Liao's hard-liner comrades in charge again. Liao, with his international reputation, was their top technology advisor.

Liao spoke good English. He greeted Wendy politely but showed more interest in Flynn. "You are the private detective. The gumshoe." He leaned conspiratorially close and whispered, "Carrying a gat?"

Flynn didn't know if Liao was trying to be humorous, so he resisted the urge to chuckle at the anachronisms. He patted his empty pockets. "Darn it. Left it in my other coat. Enjoying your first trip to Jupiter?"

"I never expected this station to become so grandiose! This room was originally intended to be twenty hotel suites! The Station corridors have become as wide as superhighways! There is a park, with trees in it! And when I designed the Station, I had to calculate the amount of water vapor that would be lost every time an airlock was opened to vacuum. Now there are more swimming pools per person than in Beverly Hills!"

"When we expanded the Station, we added apartments for long-term guests," McSheridan explained. "That freed this space for other uses. Our advanced automation reduced the number of people required, which made wider corridors and the park possible—the psychologists told us we needed more open space. We found all the water we needed in icy moonlets; the swimming pools are water reservoirs for fire fighting."

Liao's fingers danced on the whiskey glass. McSheridan's explanations sounded like typical capitalist self-indulgence. "Wouldn't it be simpler and safer to furnish the Station with fire-resistant materials?"

Before McSheridan could think of a response, Flynn said, "Is your suit fire resistant, Dr. Liao?" When Liao didn't answer the question, Flynn asked, "How's your new project coming along?"

"Ah! Your wife's employers have hired you to pump me for information!" Liao grinned at the people standing around him. They didn't smile in return. "Badly," he confessed. "The Consortium offered capitalist incentives for fast work, inducing the workers to take risks. They are being killed in foolish accidents, which slow the work instead of speeding it up. And this isn't India or Africa; there aren't swarms of laborers available to take the places of men who die."

"We offered to sell them robots," Timchenko said. "They could do the most hazardous work and increase productivity in the bargain."

Liao barely nodded. "They would also make us a target of those neoluddite terrorists who blow up your factories."

Everyone but Liao glanced at Silvanus Drake. As long as Drake directed Station security, no terrorist could get a bomb bigger than a firecracker onto the Station.

Liao emptied his glass and glanced at the bar. "Excuse me."

One of Liao's assistants glided from the edge of the crowd to the buffet table and began piling a plate with food. Flynn nudged his wife to get her attention. "See the way that guy moves?"

Wendy watched the man return to his companion. "Like a ballet dancer. His feet hardly touch the deck."

Flynn nodded. "Peter Chow, self-proclaimed martial-arts expert, moves like that. And Darin Hamashita moved like that."

"Who's Darin Hamashita?"

"A civilian employed by the Marine Corps at Parris Island to teach unarmed combat. With his bare hands, he'd take on a squad of Recon wannabes armed with knives and leave them all on the ground and disarmed. Whenever I thought I was getting good at unarmed combat he'd take me to the mat and show me that I didn't know squat."

Ms. Timchenko was wearing a glaringly white skin-tight jump suit with thin shoulder straps that was cut nearly to the navel in front. She didn't have the hips or thighs to do it justice. She peered at Flynn over her champagne glass and asked, "Is there a point to this story, Mr. Flynn?"

Flynn addressed his reply to her husband, McSheridan, and Warshovsky. "You were with them all afternoon. How many technical questions did Liao's assistants ask?"

Timchenko shook his head. "You don't understand Oriental society. They let their boss do the talking. Even when we questioned them, they deferred everything to Liao."

Flynn's nose wrinkled. "Oriental deference, my tush. Look at them: standing in pairs, watching everyone, only one in the pair eating or drinking at any moment. And they all move like they've been studying martial arts their whole lives." Flynn shook his head. "They asked and answered no technical questions because they couldn't. They're not Liao's assistants, they're his bodyguards."

"Bodyguards?" McSheridan snorted.

"We have their résumés!" Timchenko protested. "We know where they went to school, the degrees they earned, the projects they worked on . . ."

"And from where did you get those résumés? The Chinese government?"

Flynn noticed that Warshovsky wasn't looking at him. The Station manager was looking at Silvanus Drake, who was standing nearby, close enough to overhear. Drake was looking back. He took a sip of champagne, then turned away.

"Why would Liao need bodyguards?" Ms. Timchenko asked.

"He has close ties to the Chinese government," Flynn answered. "Right now his hard-liner friends have the upper hand. They took control by promising to seize the assets of China's market socialists to pay the pensions of China's retired people. The market socialists would love to weaken them, and Liao's death would do that."

Ms. Timchenko said, "You're saying that the Chinese government thought Liao might be assassinated way out here?"

"Well, the man who was murdered last night got onto this station without being noticed by Security."

Luke Timchenko sipped his gin and tonic while looking at Flynn. "You don't think he was the manufacturer's rep he claimed to be?"

Flynn glanced at Warshovsky, to see if Timchenko would be rebuked for revealing what was supposed to be confidential information, but Warshovsky seemed to be waiting for Flynn's answer. "Do you?"

Kevin McSheridan looked at Liao from beneath his dyed hair and said, "If the Chinese thought Liao might be in danger here, why didn't they ask us for security help?"

"Maybe they were afraid the Company would help the assassin." Beyond Timchenko and his wife was the buffet table. "Is that crab?" Flynn handed his glass to his wife. "Hold on to this."

It was crab—shipped frozen from Earth, of course. There were two kinds of shrimp, too—frozen again; the shrimp tanks on Satellite Kilo were not yet in service. Wendy loved shrimp. Flynn took two plates and loaded them with seafood. He ignored the Chinese entrees on the table—he could get those any time.

When Michael returned with the plates, the Warshovskys had introduced Dr. Liao to Silvanus Drake and his wife. Flynn handed one of the plates to Wendy in exchange for his whiskey glass. "Let's grab a table," he suggested.

The McSheridans joined them. Timchenko and his wife elected to do their good deed for the day and keep Marv Chalmisiak company. Flynn kept his eye on Dr. Liao, who tried in vain to get Drake to discuss the murder. Drake's wife, a short, not unattractive brunette who was wearing a strapless black party dress, rarely attended social functions and took no part in the conversation. Her complexion was more brown than her husband's, but her features suggested that her background contained a smorgasbord of Earth's ethnic groups. Michael tried to remember her name, then realized that he had never known it.

"What's Drake's wife's name?" he asked.

"Hmm?" McSheridan said. He had been looking elsewhere.

"Mrs. Drake's first name."

McSheridan's wife—whose name, Michael remembered, was Melissa—wrinkled her forehead. "I don't think I've ever heard it."

"Megan, I think," Wendy offered. "It's on Drake's form nine."

Clarisse Jackson and her escort approached the table. "Mind if we join you?" She sat down next to Kevin McSheridan before anyone could respond. "Love the outfit, Wendy. Without the shorts, it almost looks new."

"Our private investigator here thinks that Dr. Liao's assistants are actually bodyguards," Ms. McSheridan said.

Clarisse looked over her shoulder at two of the people in question. Her friend Dr. Gupta said, "Really? That would explain a lot! I've never seen four engineers—supposedly experts in space-station design—less interested in space-station technology."

"He also thinks that the man murdered last night was the assassin the bodyguards are protecting Liao from," Ms. McSheridan went on.

"I didn't say that," Flynn corrected. "Although I would like to know if any of Liao's bodyguards came over from the Asian station with the R and R crowd yesterday."

"If they did, Drake would know," Gupta surmised.

"But wouldn't tell anybody," Wendy muttered.

"How's the crab?" Clarisse asked.

"Delicious, considering it's been frozen for a year," Flynn said.

Clarisse turned to her escort. "Dumas, could you get me some? And another glass of champagne?"

Dr. Gupta smiled. "Your wish is my command." He crooked a finger at a robot, which rolled to the table. "A plate of crab for Ms. Jackson, and a glass of champagne."

"Yes, sir," the robot said, and turned to carry out its instructions.

Wendy watched the machine in disbelief. "The robot knows what crab is?"

"We enhanced their programming last week," Gupta explained.

Clarisse did not look impressed. Melissa McSheridan, on the other hand, did. "When can I get one of those robots for my apartment?"

"When Mr. Warshovsky puts them into production," Gupta replied.

"Which won't be anytime soon," Kevin McSheridan said. "We don't have the space to produce them. When the food production facilities from Delta are all moved to Kilo, Delta will be converted to steel production, and the factories on the

Station are busy fabricating the new steel-manufacturing equipment. Besides, there's no real profit for the Company in mass production of robots. They'd be obsolescent before we could get them to planet three. We'll probably recover the development cost by licensing the patent rights to a robotics company on Earth. You should be able to order a housekeeping robot with that technology in a year or so."

Ms. McSheridan gave the robot a last, fond look, then changed the subject. "Allie Cheng seems bored already."

"Allison *is* bored already," Kevin said. "Her husband gets to run the best corporate R and D lab in the solar system. She only gets to work there. And she would much rather be working on Earth."

The robot returned with the crab and champagne for Clarisse. "We should do something to make her happier," she said. "If she goes home and takes her husband with her, it will cost the Company a fortune to replace him."

"You're starting to sound like Marvin," Kevin McSheridan said, smiling. Clarisse made a face at him.

The evening went by quickly. Flynn had three helpings of crab and, since his wife was freely imbibing champagne, lost track of the amount of whiskey he consumed. He tried to engage Liao's assistants in conversation, but they feigned poor English and pretended to be interested only in technical matters. Wendy was happy to see her husband acting like his premarital self, socializing and drinking. Silvanus Drake and his wife left early, which surprised no one. Mary Warshovsky said she had a headache, and she and her husband left soon after the Drakes, leaving the guest of honor in the care of Luke Timchenko and Louis Cheng. Everybody got a chance to talk with Dr. Liao, who consumed even more scotch than Flynn did and became merrier with each glass.

Liao intercepted Michael and Wendy when they were leaving.

"Gumshoe! I suggested to Mr. Warshovsky that he should hire you to find out who killed that man last night. The murderer could be the first inmate of that new prison the Company will build for your capitalist overlords."

"The marshals are investigating the crime."

Liao smiled and took a drink of whiskey. "They don't have your track record. What if they fail?"

Flynn smiled in return. "Then Drake will succeed."

"Will you be staying on the Station, Dr. Liao?" Wendy asked.

Liao shook his head. "Only for a couple of days. Being this far from the new station is almost as bad as being on Earth. I have established an office in its pressurized section. But I hope to visit here again before I return to Earth." He looked over his shoulder. "Doctors Cheng and Timchenko are taking me to the observatory. I want to see the new station through your telescopes before it passes into Jupiter's shadow."

"Make them show you the digitally processed images and not the raw data," Flynn suggested. "You can almost recognize the faces of the workers."

Liao laughed and emptied his glass. "I'll be able to see how many of my secrets the Company is learning!" he said, as though he didn't know that the Asian workers who visited the Station talked freely about what they were doing.

Flynn and Wendy took a taxi home. Wendy leaned back in her seat and said, "That was a wonderful reception. What did you think of Dr. Liao?"

Flynn clasped his hands over his knee. "I think he was very well briefed—seemed to know everything about everybody there. And he would make a great diplomat or politician—he talked all evening, while consuming a large quantity of mind-altering fluid, without actually saying anything. Very impressive."

"He's supposed to be a genius."

"Genius of an engineer, perhaps, but if he was that smart all around he wouldn't be a communist. A bank in Hong Kong provided part of the financing for the Asian station. Hong Kong is the stronghold of China's market socialists. It's ironic that they hired one of their political opponents to design their station. How long have Kevin McSheridan and Clarisse Jackson been having an affair?"

Wendy turned abruptly and stared at her husband. "Who told you that?"

"It was obvious. Kevin and Clarisse ignored their partners all evening. They talked mostly to each other. And have you seen Kevin in one of those silly—in one of those stylish outfits before tonight?"

Wendy shut her eyes. "Ed Warshovsky is going to be very unhappy. He'll be more upset about one of his directors committing adultery than he was about a director marrying a private detective." The taxi slowed to turn the corner onto Ninth Street, but Flynn couldn't help leaning into his wife. "I want to hire you, Michael."

Flynn grinned. "For you, I work for free."

Wendy poked him playfully in the ribs with her elbow. "I mean, your professional services. I want you to find out what happened to that man last night."

"Ask Drake."

"I did! And Warshovsky! They're covering up something again! You know what they were into the last time they wouldn't tell me everything!" Wendy paused to get herself under control. "You were right about Liao's 'assistants.' As soon as you said they were bodyguards, Warshovsky looked at Drake, who was eavesdropping. Drake looked him right in the eye and then turned away. That's his way of saying, 'I told you so.' So Drake knew and he had told Warshovsky, but there wasn't a hint of it in Drake's daily security reports. No, they're hiding something, and I want to know what it is."

The taxi slowed to maneuver around six boisterous drunks, who managed to take up most of the street. They looked Oriental, and were probably from the Asian station.

Flynn knew he had been right about Liao's assistants: he had shaken hands with each of them, and they all had the calluses that karate experts developed by breaking bricks with their hands. "You don't think the marshals will solve the case?"

Wendy snorted. "I think Drake can keep the marshals so far in the dark that they'll conclude that Manstein hit himself over the head three times."

"What do you think the Company is covering up?"

Wendy shook her head. "I don't know, Michael. But I think you're right about Liao being involved in some way—he was very interested in the murder. Raised the topic with everybody he talked to, like he was trying to find out what we knew." Wendy bit her lip. "The Company can do without a diplomatic incident. This station is so profitable only because we're exempt from most of the laws that reduce productivity in the United States. There are a lot of people in Congress who'd love to extend those laws to cover us, and a diplomatic tiff with China would give them an excuse. Especially now, when President Mendez is trying to improve relations with the Chinese."

"Maybe Warshovsky and Drake are trying to prevent a tiff with the Chinese."

Wendy took a deep breath. "Maybe they are, but I don't know what they're up to and they aren't telling me. So I need you to find out. I have some discretionary funds in the Legal Department budget."

"Wouldn't hiring your husband be considered rank nepotism?"

"My husband is the best private investigator on the Station. Hiring anybody but him would be a waste of Company resources. Will you do it?"

Flynn hesitated. More requests for background checks would come from Earth overnight, and there was the Cross case . . . "I'll have to tread carefully—I can't interfere in an ongoing police investigation."

"No, but you don't have to be as careful when you're working for an officer of the court."

Flynn sighed. "Okay. You can help me by getting the Security videos from yesterday afternoon and evening."

Wendy shook her head. "The murder didn't show on the video records. The marshals already checked."

"I know. I want to see if any of Liao's assistants visited the Station."

Wendy felt that she was already getting her money's worth. "Ah. Okay. Anything else?"

"Find out how Manstein was paying for his apartment—there's no record of his being here, so he didn't have a bank account. And write me a letter on official Company stationary, authorizing me to conduct the investigation and to enter Company premises—it might help loosen a few tongues."

"It will also get me summoned to Warshovsky's office."

"You'll get summoned to his office as soon as he learns you've hired me, which Drake will know before noon tomorrow."

The taxi dropped them at the foot of the ramp leading to their apartment. Two deputy marshals were standing in front of the apartment door. There were no bars on Ninth Street; the deputies should have been someplace else.

One of the deputies stepped forward. Flynn knew him; his name was Juan Salazar. "Mr. Flynn, Marshal Hathaway would like you to come to the Marshals Office and answer a few questions about the murder."

Flynn was not in the mood to go anywhere except to bed with Wendy. "You have a warrant? I'm not going anywhere with you if you don't have a warrant."

Salazar rubbed the palms of hands against his slacks. "Please, Mike. Hathaway's been looking for a way to make your life unpleasant since she got here. You can do yourself a world of good if you cooperate. It won't take more than half an hour."

"It won't take more than half a minute. I don't know a damn thing about yesterday's murder. And I have a perfect alibi for it." He pointed at Wendy. "I was with her."

Salazar shook his head. "We're not talking about yesterday's murder. We're talking about this afternoon's."

Wendy's jaw dropped open and anguish creased her face. "There's been *another* one?"

Salazar nodded. "Company employee named Leron Cross."

Chapter 3

Flynn closed his eyes. It never rained on Jupiter Station, but it poured.

"Are you going to cooperate, Mike?" Salazar asked.

"How can I cooperate? I don't know anything about Cross's murder! I didn't even know he was dead!"

Salazar shrugged. "The boss wants to ask you some questions. That's all I know."

"Then why isn't she here instead of you?"

"It doesn't work that way, Mike. You know that."

"Look: I've been with my wife all evening. In front of dozens of witnesses at the hotel. If Marshal Hathaway doesn't believe us, have her ask Ed Warshovsky or Silvanus Drake. If that doesn't satisfy her, and she still wants to question me, she can come here, because I'm not going to the Marshals Office at—" Flynn glanced at his watch. "Twenty-two forty, to be questioned about something of which I have no knowledge, unless she gets a warrant. And before she does that, she should consider all those alibi witnesses of mine and what a suit for false arrest would do to her career. Now, if you will excuse us, deputies . . ."

Flynn took Wendy by the arm and stepped past the deputies to the apartment door. The deputy with Salazar made a move toward them, but Juan stopped him. Flynn ushered his wife into the apartment and closed the door.

Wendy stared at him from beneath lowered eyebrows. "Who

is Leron Cross?"

Flynn took a deep breath and let it out slowly. "A cowboy. His wife hired me to find out if he was having an affair."

"When?"

"This afternoon."

The legal circuits in Wendy's brain began seeking loopholes. "So you hadn't actually started working on the case yet?"

"I don't like infidelity cases. I subcontracted it to Peter Chow."

"Why didn't you tell the deputies that?"

Flynn looked at his wife as though the answer was obvious. "They didn't ask." Flynn took his computer from his pocket, opened it, and established a video link to Peter Chow.

Pete started talking as soon as he recognized Flynn's face on his display. "Mike! Have you heard? There's been another murder! The marshals haven't released his name yet, but—"

"Yeah, yeah, I heard. Did you start on the Cross investigation?"

"Oh, sure. Picked him up at his apartment and followed him to where the cowboys suit up. I couldn't follow him in there—employees only. But he didn't talk with any women while I was watching. I'll pick him up when he comes off shift."

"No, you won't. He was the second murder victim."

Chow's excited appearance was replaced with one of stunned bewilderment. "But . . . it's not possible! I followed him all the way to work! I . . . how did you know who it was?"

"Two deputies were waiting for me when I got home. Ms. Cross probably told the marshals that she'd hired me."

Chow frowned. "Did you tell them that you'd passed it to me?"

"Not yet, but I'll have to, soon. If you want to get on the marshal's good side, go to her office and volunteer the information. Did you see anyone else showing interest in him?"

Chow hesitated. "Sorry, Mike, I wasn't looking."

Flynn couldn't get upset about that. He wouldn't have been looking, either. "Have you heard where the murder occurred?"

"People are saying that it was on the new end of the Station."

That's where the cowboys suited up. Flynn nodded. "Thanks. I'll keep in touch."

Flynn broke the connection and tried to establish a video link to Francine Cross. He wasn't surprised when that proved impossible—Ms. Cross probably didn't feel like facing anyone at the moment. He had to settle for an audio link.

"Ms. Cross? Answer, please. It's Michael Flynn."

Flynn waited several seconds before Francine's voice came through his computer. "Mr. Flynn! Have you heard? Leron's dead." She paused, as though making that statement had taken all of her energy. "Somebody killed him. The marshals came and . . . Did you see who did it?"

"I wasn't working the case tonight. I had another obligation, so a colleague covered for me. He followed your husband from your apartment to his workplace. He didn't see anything happen."

There was a pause. "I see." Francine sounded like she had been crying. "I had hoped . . . I told them that you might have seen something."

"Did you tell them why you had hired me?"

Flynn heard a sniffle. "I had to. They were insistent."

"I'm sorry for your loss. I'll return your second day's retainer tomorrow."

"Oh, there's no rush."

Flynn remembered Francine's preference for cash instead of a money card. "Oh, there is. You had a joint account with your husband? If it wasn't what bankers call a survivor account, it will be frozen as soon as the bank learns he's dead. I'll give your cash back tomorrow." Flynn shut off his computer.

Wendy wasn't paying attention to Michael's conversation. She was seething. "Headache, like hell!"

"Hmm?"

"Mary Warshovsky's 'headache.' Hah! First Drake left, and then Warshovsky—not together, so they wouldn't raise suspicions. Security let Drake know about the murder as soon as it was discovered, and he told Warshovsky, so they left the reception to see to it. Without a word to the head of the Legal Department! Damn it! They don't tell me anything!" Wendy stopped ranting and stared out of the living-room window. It was a real window, and overlooked the swimming pool in the courtyard of the apartment block. Her forehead wrinkled and her eyebrows drew closer together.

Flynn recognized the look on her face. "Wendy . . ."

"Where's my computer?" Wendy had left the machine on the table when she had come home from work. She had a one-key shortcut to establish the desired connection. The face that appeared on the display belonged to Silvanus Drake.

"Ms. Chadwick. What can I do for you tonight?"

"You can enlighten me about the latest murder."

Drake didn't even blink. "The marshals have preempted us again. I am not investigating it. I'll put what I know in the morning security report."

"I don't feel like waiting until morning!"

"Then ask your husband. I understand he knows something about it."

Wendy saw an opening and jumped on it. "I'll make a deal with you, Mr. Drake: Tell me what you know right now, and I'll tell you what my husband told me, before you get it secondhand from Marshal Hathaway."

Flynn waved his hands to get his wife's attention, but Wendy was focused on her computer display. Drake's eyelids lowered slightly. He nodded. "Deal. What did Mr. Flynn tell you?"

"Ms. Cross suspected Leron was having an affair." Wendy didn't look at Michael. "She hired my husband this afternoon, to find out whom he was cheating with. Michael subcontracted the case to Peter Chow. Chow followed the victim from his apartment to his workplace but saw nothing of interest."

Flynn closed his eyes and sighed.

Drake said, "Mr. Cross reached the cowboys' locker room at seventeen. His ship had been docked by another pilot, Andy Deltoro, ten minutes earlier. Deltoro was removing his pressure suit in the locker room when Cross came in. He saw Cross get a phone call. Cross left the locker room through the corridor that leads to the ship maintenance shops, to take the call in private. Deltoro left the locker room and didn't see Cross again. Two hours later the cowboy controller, having trouble handling the incoming rocks, told the cowboy supervisor that he was one ship short. The supervisor went looking for the missing ship. He found Cross's ship docked to the Station but couldn't find Cross and was unable to contact him by phone or computer. He went to the maintenance shops to see if someone was working on Cross's ship, and found Cross's body around twenty. He informed me. I summoned Dr. Williams, the medical examiner on call, and notified the marshals, as required. Dr. Williams found multiple stab wounds in Cross's abdomen—through the diaphragm and into the heart. Hathaway arrived shortly after Williams had made his preliminary examination and exercised her prerogative to take over the investigation, even though it occurred in an area of the Station for which we are responsible for security since it is not open to the public."

Wendy glared at the image of Drake in her holographic display. "Murder isn't covered by Workmen's Comp! The courts will hold the Company liable when Cross's wife sues us for zillions of dollars! Why wasn't I informed immediately?"

Drake almost looked amused. "His wife won't be suing us

tonight, Ms. Chadwick. Cross's name has not yet been released to the press, so trial lawyers have not begun pounding on her door, offering their services."

Wendy clenched her teeth. "If I can get to her first, I might be able to negotiate a settlement before she even thinks of hiring a lawyer!"

Flynn finally got his wife's attention. She read his lips and asked Drake, "What about the security cameras?"

"There are no security cameras in the corridor where the body was found."

Wendy wanted to scream. "We have thousands of security cameras on the Station. Why don't we have any in places where people get murdered?"

"Careful murderers."

Wendy was angry enough to kill someone in full view of a security camera. "Please inform me immediately of any developments." She shut off her computer.

Flynn was rubbing his chin thoughtfully. Wendy looked at him. "What's wrong?"

"The only time I made a deal to swap info with Silvanus Drake, I told him everything I knew and he told me absolutely nothing in return."

Wendy closed her computer and pushed it away from her, across the table top. She looked at Michael. "Do you think he lied?"

Flynn shook his head. "The facts he gave you are too easy to check." He rubbed his chin again. "Maybe he has a soft spot in his heart for redheads."

Wendy made a face. "You don't believe that any more than I do."

Flynn stumbled across no murder scenes on his Wednesday jog. The surprise that morning was waiting for him when he returned to his apartment.

Wendy was wearing her exercise clothes but was not working out on her machine. She was sitting at the table with Francine Cross.

Even though Ms. Cross was backlit by the simulated daylight seeping through the living-room window, her makeup didn't conceal her reddened eyes. Flynn guessed that she hadn't slept at all.

"Good morning," Michael said politely. There was a coffee cup on the table in front of Ms. Cross. "Your retainer is locked in the desk in my office. I'll get it for you as soon as I've showered."

Francine shook her head. "Keep the retainer, Mr. Flynn. I want you to find out who killed Leron."

Flynn glanced at his wife. Wendy did not look surprised; Ms. Cross must have already informed her of the reason for the early-morning visit. Michael said, "The marshals will do that for free."

Ms. Cross stared Flynn right in the eye. "You proved last year that they sometimes do things for money—dirty money. And there are only twenty-five of them on the Station. That's not enough to patrol the areas for which they are responsible under normal circumstances. They now have two murders to investigate. I don't think they have the resources."

"They have more resources than I do. More than both of us combined. You could go broke before I solve the case."

"Then I'll sign another five-year contract. That's a hundred-thousand-dollar bonus for teachers."

Flynn glanced at his wife. Ms. Cross hadn't mentioned the possibility of suing Conglomerated for zillions of dollars to finance the investigation. "And five more years away from your family on Earth."

Ms. Cross drew erect in her chair. "The family that I cared

most about was murdered last night! And it was my fault!" A tear escaped from her left eye and trickled down her cheek. "I jumped to the conclusion that Leron was having an affair. I was afraid to discuss it with him without proof, and it took me a week to work up the courage to hire you. But he wasn't cheating on me; the phone calls and his behavior were connected to whatever and whoever killed him. If I had had more faith in my husband, I would have talked to him about what was bothering him. We could have gotten help, before he was killed. This is my punishment for doubting him. His death was my fault, and I have to make it right."

From the look on Wendy's face, Flynn knew that he couldn't turn down Ms. Cross without exiling himself from the bedroom for a month. "I'll give you progress reports periodically, and accountings of expenses."

Francine stood up. "Thank you, Mr. Flynn." She turned to Wendy. "Thank you for the coffee, Ms. Chadwick."

"Company Medical provides support for survivors—"

"The only support I need is to see my husband's killer in jail. Good day, Ms. Chadwick, Mr. Flynn." Francine showed herself out.

Wendy gave her husband a disapproving look. "You acted like you didn't want to take the case."

"I didn't."

"But, it's a real investigation! A murder! It has to be more interesting than background checks!"

"Background checks are the bulk of my business. Most of them are subcontracted to me from Earth. If I disappoint those clients, that business goes away, and I don't think I'll have enough murder investigations to take up the slack."

"You can subcontract the background checks to the other investigators on the Station."

"Peter Chow botched one of those investigations yesterday. I had to finish it myself. I should be checking the information the other PIs give me before forwarding it to Earth—sending bad info to my clients is an excellent way to lose them. And I recall agreeing to investigate a different murder last night. I really don't want to disappoint that client."

Wendy hesitated. "You've juggled investigations before."

"Yeah, background checks. I've never tried to do two murder investigations at the same time." Michael shook his head. "I can start on the first murder. The authorities usually don't accuse a PI of interference if he's following behind them. Besides, on that one I'm working for an officer of the court. On the second murder, I'd be ahead of them, because the first person they'll investigate is my client—a large percentage of murder victims are done in by their significant others."

Wendy's forehead wrinkled. "Francine? How could they possibly think she murdered her husband right after hiring you to follow him?"

"What better way to avoid suspicion than by hiring a detective to follow the intended victim? No, I'll have to go slowly on the Cross investigation until the marshals are convinced she didn't do it." That way Flynn would avoid having to investigate Francine himself. "She didn't sound like she was planning to sue."

"Give the trial lawyers awhile. Her husband was killed in a secured Company work area. Only Company employees can get in there. They'll invoke the law of agency—we should have known we had a murderer working for us, and it's our fault that her husband was killed."

Furrball leaped onto the table and used the strategic position to nuzzle Flynn's hand. Michael glanced into the kitchen. Only the coffee maker was operating; Wendy hadn't started breakfast. "What do you want first, breakfast, or shower?"

Wendy stood up. "Shower. The stall's so small, if we eat first both of us won't fit in it at the same time."

"Two murder investigations." Flynn bit his lip. "We won't be spending quiet evenings together for awhile."

Wendy didn't reply. It was during those quiet evenings together that she felt that there was something wrong with her marriage.

Chapter 4

Flynn selected his gray sport coat from the closet, checked his appearance in the mirror, headed for the doorway, and stopped. He would be hunting dangerous game—murderers. Wendy might worry . . . Wendy wouldn't have to know. Michael stepped to the bedside table and took out his stun pistol, a Smith and Wesson Model 20456. He ejected the energy cell from the grip. It was fully charged and good for ten shots. He snapped the cell back into place and slipped the pistol into the pocket of his coat.

Only three background investigations had been subcontracted to Flynn overnight. Two of them were straightforward preemployment checks. He could subcontract them to anybody. The third was a premarital investigation—a prospective bride wanted to know how her fiancé had spent his spare time while he had been employed by the Company five years before. Doug Sanchez was the only PI besides Flynn who had been on Jupiter Station that long; he was the only colleague who would know whom to ask for five-year-old information. He was also drunk half the time. Flynn would have to do that investigation himself. Fortunately, it wasn't a rush job. Reports on two investigations that Flynn had subcontracted the previous week had been submitted that morning. Both were poorly written and Flynn would not send them to his clients over his signature. He had to edit them extensively before forwarding them to Earth. He was rewriting the second report when his wife called.

"I just sent your letter of employment to your computer. It authorizes you to enter Company property to conduct the investigation for which you were hired."

Flynn accessed the letter with the lower half of his holographic display while keeping video contact with his wife on the upper half. The letter didn't specify what he would be investigating. A copy had been sent to Company Security. "What did Drake say about it?"

"I didn't send it to Drake personally. I sent it to Security Control, so they wouldn't dispatch goons to roust you as soon as you tried to enter private Company work space. I don't know if the shift commander will call it to Drake's attention right away."

Flynn nodded. "Thanks, Wendy. Was there anything of interest in the morning security report?"

"Very little that Drake didn't tell us last night. The marshals found blood splatters on the walls of Manstein's apartment, so he was probably killed there and carried to the recycling chute." That piece of news had spoiled Wendy's whole day—Manstein's apartment was in the Company's area of responsibility, not the government's. Manstein's next of kin could sue Conglomerated for inadequate security. "They didn't find any money in the apartment—curious, for a man with no bank account or plastic. They have no new leads. The Cross autopsy is being done this morning. He was killed in a Company work area, so we'll get a copy of the autopsy report.

"I checked Company financial records," Wendy continued. "The rent on Manstein's apartment was paid to Company HQ on planet three by a bank in Zurich. The bank did not indicate on whose behalf it was acting."

Flynn didn't have the connections or the resources to penetrate the secrecy conferred by Swiss banking laws. Maybe Drake did—he was certain to follow the same line of inquiry.

"Are you sure that Manstein didn't have any debit or credit cards?"

"As far as I can tell. The Company owns the First National Bank here on the Station, and I just discovered that my executive privileges enable me to check the bank's records. There is no account or safe deposit box for anyone named Manstein."

Flynn was not surprised. "I doubt Manstein was his real name. He might have been banking under another one. Can you cross-reference the names on the bank accounts against the names in the Security computer?"

Wendy hesitated. "I suppose. Won't do any good if he was banking at Second National—we don't own that one."

Flynn shook his head. "Serious oversight on the part of the Company. Tell your boss to get on the ball and buy up the competition. Did you get the security videos from the day before Manstein's body was found?"

Wendy nodded and smiled. "Those records would have been deleted by now if the marshals hadn't ordered them retained. I saved you some time and checked them myself. That was an interesting search. None of Liao's bodyguards were here, but the search took very little time. Either it was short-circuited, or somebody else had already done it so the computer only had to check its log files for the results."

Flynn turned that information over in his mind. "Do your executive privileges allow you to determine who did the earlier search?"

"I tried, Michael. If I have the privileges, I don't know how to use them."

"It's no big deal. It was Silvanus Drake—I don't think Marshal Hathaway has linked Liao's visit to Manstein's demise. Oh, that picture of Manstein that Drake's goons were showing around: Can you send me a copy of it?"

"Ah, yeah. It was in the security report."

"Thanks, Wendy. I'll let you know if I'll be home for dinner."

Flynn finished editing the reports, e-mailed them to Earth, then locked his office door and walked up Butte Avenue to Seventh Street. He took the ramp down to level one, where an airlock hatch protruded from the deck. Below level one was the basement, the outermost pressurized level of the Station and home to sewer mains, water lines, circulating pumps, and recycling bins. The basement was kept at a lower pressure than the rest of the Station so that air leaks from the inhabited regions of the Station could be detected by an increase in basement pressure. The hatch that Flynn opened was the only basement entrance that wasn't kept locked. He closed the upper hatch, waited for the airlock pressure to drop, then opened the lower hatch and climbed down the ladder to the basement deck.

An old desk sat in the cone of light from an overhead lamp. The chair behind the desk was empty. Rows of equipment racks and bins surrounded the desk and faded away into the dark recesses of the basement. Flynn heard footsteps and a mustache poked around the corner of one of the racks. Attached to the mustache was the face of Joe Aguirre.

Joe had opened his recycling business before Conglomerated Mining and Manufacturing had realized that the Station was becoming a small city that would need many such businesses. There had been no Company policy for renting Station space to outside interests at the time, so Aguirre had been granted a small area of the basement at very low rent. Now there were many non-Company businesses on the Station, but Joe had stayed in the basement rather than paying the high rents the Company charged for more desirable locations.

"Huh. Michael Flynn. You never drop in for a visit unless there's something to investigate."

Flynn put on a pained expression. "Joe! Did I, or did I not, buy you a beer just . . . two months ago?"

"That was in the Moonshine Bar, and you bumped into me on the street. You didn't come down here."

"Since I bumped into you on the street, I didn't have to come down here."

Aguirre wrinkled his nose. "Well, since you are here, I'm willing to bet that you're investigating one of the murders, and not that you feel the need to slake my thirst."

"I don't see why we can't do both. You tell me what you know about the death of the man found in the Dumpster, and I'll buy you a beer."

Aguirre had a long, sloping forehead above bushy black eyebrows. He rubbed his forehead and said, "Make it a shot of tequila. Two shots."

"Joe, if you're going to do me a favor, why would I want to poison you?"

Aguirre nodded. "Okay, since you put it that way, three shots."

"You drive a hard bargain."

"I have to. I'm a poor working man. And what makes you think that I know anything about the Manstein murder?"

Flynn started to ask a question, then stopped. "I thought his name hadn't been released."

Aguirre shrugged. "As far as I know, it hasn't. I heard some of the deputies talking. They told me to keep my mouth shut about anything I overheard." But the cheapskates hadn't bribed him to keep quiet.

Flynn grinned. "I knew that nothing happens down here that you don't know about."

"But Manstein wasn't killed down here." Aguirre knew that Flynn could be trusted not to tell anyone where he got his information. "He was switched off on level eight, where his apartment is—er, was. His body was dumped into a recycling chute and wound up in a bin near Seattle Avenue yesterday morning."

"Deputies were talking about that, too?"

Aguirre nodded. "They were climbing up and down that recycling chute most of yesterday and didn't find any blood traceable to Manstein above level eight, and since the access hatch to that chute on level eight is just around the corner from Manstein's apartment, the marshals think he was terminated there. They asked me to keep an eye out for big wrenches, with at least four centimeter apertures, so they probably think he was killed with one."

Flynn mulled over that information. "That means the marshals haven't found the murder weapon."

"Oh, but they tried—emptied every recycling bin looking for it. And while they were at it, they sent the contents of the bin he was found in to the lab. I was talking to a technician in the Moonshine last night, and he said they got so much stuff dumped on 'em that they're all earning overtime."

The only government laboratory on the Station was run by OSHA. The security agreement between the Company and the government required the Company to provide the laboratory facilities necessary for criminal investigations. Now Lou Cheng's R and D people on Satellite Charlie and the lab technicians in the Company hospital were pretending to be forensic scientists, looking through the garbage of hundreds of people for potential clues. Marshal Hathaway was not endearing herself to Company management.

"Manstein was supposed to be a sales rep," Flynn said. "Did you ever meet him?"

Aguirre shook his head. "Never heard his name before yesterday. Was he really not in the Security database?"

"So I was told."

"Remarkable. Even the workers from the Asian station who come here to blow off steam are in the database."

"Well, maybe that means he didn't come here from the Asian

station." Flynn pointed at Aguirre. "After work. Moonshine Bar. Tequila."

Aguirre nodded. "I'll be there."

Flynn climbed back through the airlock to level one. The street was quiet; Flynn unfolded his computer. He had to dig through his personal address file to find the contact code he wanted. A female face framed by a mane of black hair appeared on the display.

"Laboratory—Michael Flynn. I haven't heard from you since . . ." The woman's eyes narrowed. "Since before you got married!" She made the wedding sound like a crime of which Flynn was guilty.

"I've been busy, Sheri."

"Doing what? Keeping your wife satisfied?"

"Sheri, we only dated, what, two or three times? What did you do before you met me? There are twice as many men as women on the Station. You are in a target-rich environment."

Sheri's pleasant features distorted into a frown. "Yeah, rich in jerks! Half of those men are water-conservation zealots—they haven't taken a shower since coming here."

Flynn shook his head sadly. "You must be looking in the wrong places. I never meet any guys like that."

"Then you meet the other half—the drunks. You wouldn't be calling me with good news, would you? Like, your wife kicked you out?"

"Not yet, but if she catches me talking with attractive brunettes she probably will. No, I was just wondering if you could tell me anything about the Manstein autopsy."

Sheri winced. "That's confidential information, Michael! You know that!" She lowered her voice. "And how did you learn his name?"

Flynn ignored the question. "Nobody'll know you talked to me except the two of us, and I don't plan on telling anybody about our conversation."

Sheri hesitated. "What's in it for me?"

"You wouldn't want me to forget your name, would you? In case my wife kicks me out?"

"Oh, like that's going to happen any time soon!" Sheri stared at the detective. "My contract's up in two months. I've already booked passage to Earth on the *Southern Star.*"

Flynn tried to look hurt. "Sheri! The Station won't be the same without you!"

"Huh! You wouldn't even know I was gone if I hadn't just told you!"

Flynn moistened his lips. "How would you like the name of a guy who takes showers once in awhile?"

Sheri opened her mouth for a snappy retort, but changed her mind. "Like, at least once a day?"

"As far as I can tell."

That sounded promising, but . . . "What's his alcohol consumption?"

"Below normal. I'm surprised he's not dehydrated."

"Is he . . . reasonably good-looking? At least, not ugly?"

"Well, he's not ugly. Rather muscular—no body fat."

Sheri glanced around to make sure she was alone. "Manstein was killed by three hard blows, possibly delivered with a big wrench, to the back of his head. They weren't love pats; the killer was very strong—any one of the three blows would have killed him. All other marks and contusions are compatible with being dumped down a recycling chute. He'd been dead about seven hours when his body was discovered. That puts the murder around twenty-two Monday night. The marshals found blood splatter on the walls in Manstein's apartment. The DNA was Manstein's."

"Did you get a DNA match with the European Union database?"

Sheri glanced around again, and leaned closer to her display. "*That* was really weird. The marshals asked us to sequence it again, like we hadn't done it right the first time. Didn't tell us why. Rumor around here is that his DNA didn't match any on file anywhere."

That information started Flynn thinking. People from the European Union—or most of North America, most of South America, and lots of places in Southeast Asia and southern Africa—had their DNA sequenced and recorded at birth. If Manstein's DNA wasn't in a database, his records must have been deleted on purpose.

"That's not all," Sheri continued. "He *didn't* have a microchip implanted in his brain. Nearly everyone his age from Europe or North America had one implanted at birth or during childhood."

Flynn reflexively rubbed the back of his skull. He had been born too soon to have a microchip implanted at birth. The advances in nanotechnology and neurology that had permitted a microcomputer to be interfaced directly with a human brain had not occurred until he was in elementary school. The advantages of having a computer attached to the brain—as well as the prospect of replacing a hugely expensive educational system with cheap information downloads—had been considered so enormous that the U.S. government had paid for the procedure for everyone who wanted it. Flynn's parents, afraid that he would be severely disadvantaged if he didn't have a built-in computer to store facts, do arithmetic, and communicate almost instantaneously with the rest of the solar system, had wanted it. Flynn had been in the seventh grade when a surgical team had come to his school and implanted a chip in his skull and in the skulls of most of his classmates. He had been a tenth grader when scientists had become alarmed over how quickly people—especially children—became dependent on their implanted chips and how severely the brain's normal cognitive functions degraded from disuse. Civil libertarians had worried that governments could download into the chips what they wanted people to think and how they wanted them to vote. Almost overnight, the implantation of microcomputers into human brains had stopped. Flynn's chip was still in the back of his skull, but it, like most of them, had been deactivated electronically—also at government expense.

"So he probably didn't grow up in Europe?"

"No," Sheri said, "he probably did. He'd had the microchip removed when he was an adult—we found the scar. That's almost unheard of. Most of the microchips were deactivated electronically."

The microchips, Flynn knew, had all carried unique serial numbers. Manstein had gone to extremes to make sure he could never be identified against his will.

"Any DNA evidence on the body?"

Sheri took a deep breath. "Very little. We found three human hairs that weren't his. From two different people—we sequenced the DNA. Both were from Company employees. We matched the sequences with their medical records."

"Is an arrest imminent?"

Sheri grunted. "Do you have any idea how many stray hairs you have on your clothes at the moment? In addition to red ones, I mean."

"So the hairs are probably a dead end?"

"Can't answer that, Michael. You'll have to ask the marshal."

Flynn didn't want to talk to the marshal. "Any other crime-scene DNA?"

"Oh, tons of it! The marshals vacuumed Manstein's apartment and the street next to the recycling chute and had us check it. They also dumped all the garbage from the bin where the body was found in our lab. We've generated sequences on over a hundred people so far."

"Sounds like a plethora of dead ends. Thanks for the info."

"Hey! What about the name you promised me?"

Flynn smiled. "I'm old fashioned. I'll have him call you."

Flynn took an elevator to level eight. The streets in the block where Manstein had lived were narrow, barely wide enough for an electric vehicle. Flynn had no trouble finding Manstein's apartment—it had yellow tape with *CRIME SCENE—DO NOT CROSS* in big black letters stretched across the doorway. The nearest circumferential corridor was Fourth Street, just four doors up from Manstein's. Only twenty meters along Fourth Street was a recycling hatch, crisscrossed with more yellow crime-scene tape. Flynn looked both ways along Fourth Street but couldn't see a security camera. Michael walked back to Manstein's apartment. It was on Seattle Avenue, and there was a security camera fifty meters away. At that moment the camera was pointing in Flynn's direction, but since it was on a public street it didn't have to show a red light when it was active.

One of Manstein's neighbors had identified the deceased from a photo. Flynn selected the apartment across the avenue from Mainstein's door and pressed the door bell. He heard a soft chime from the interior, then nothing. He was reaching for the button again when the door slid sideways. There stood a diminutive brunette with blue eyes and hair that barely covered her ears. Even in a baggy sweatshirt and sweat pants, she looked small. She couldn't have massed much over forty kilos. Her feet were bare and she had rings on two of her toes. Flynn's impression that he was facing a teenager changed when he looked closely at her eyes. They were too old for a teenager's.

"Yes?"

"My name is Flynn. I'm a private investigator." Flynn took a business card from his coat and handed it to the woman. "I've been hired to look into the untimely demise of your neighbor."

Flynn indicated Manstein's apartment with his thumb.

The woman took the time to read every word on Flynn's card. "Do you have any formal ID?" Her accent had been polished in London and she sounded more curious than suspicious. Flynn took his license from his coat and showed it to her. She read that thoroughly, too. "I'm Beryl Wylie, European Space Agency." She extended her hand for Flynn to shake.

Flynn raised his eyebrows. "Going to Pluto?"

Beryl nodded. "As soon as the Company gets our ship finished. My husband's over there now, discussing some changes the engineers want to make. They claim they can reduce the cost even more and get it done farther ahead of schedule."

"Will that help? I thought planet positions were critical for a trip that long."

"They are, but everything else is over budget and behind schedule. My radiometric spectrometer is going to cost twice its original quote, and it might not be ready in time—if it doesn't ship from Earth next month, it won't be here before we leave."

"Would you have anything else to do?"

Beryl nodded emphatically. "Lots. Keeping an eye on my husband for one thing—a year out and a year back, plus the time on Pluto, and half the crew are female."

Flynn nodded. "About Mr. Manstein . . ."

"Tragic. The marshals think he was killed in his apartment." Beryl nodded at the taped door.

"Did you know him well?"

"I didn't 'know' him at all. None of us did." Beryl indicated the other apartments on the street. "I've never been in his apartment and he's never been in ours. I'd exchanged greetings with him a couple of times. That's how I recognized his photo when the security guards were showing it around." She cocked her head. "Why are Company security guards called 'goons'?"

"The Company got its start in mining. It needed security

guards who could overpower burly, drunken miners and break up fights. So the guards were big, strong, and adept at hitting people over the head."

Beryl nodded. "I see. Well, when the two 'goons' came around with his photo, I said it looked like Mr. Manstein from across the hall."

Flynn pondered his next question. "Did he sound German to you?"

Beryl squinted. "What makes you say that? Because his name was Manstein?" She shook her head. "I know a lot of Germans. Manstein and I always conversed in English, which he spoke quite well, but he didn't speak it with a German accent."

"Care to hazard a guess as to what kind of accent he had?"

Beryl bit her lower lip. "Finnish?" She shrugged.

"Did you see him get any visitors?"

Beryl shook her head so vigorously that her short hair swung away from her head. "I saw him go in and out a few times, always alone. But Diego Garza from right down the hall—er, street—there said he saw him in the Company casino the night he was killed."

"Is Señor Garza in his apartment?"

"*Doctor* Garza went to the ship with my husband."

"Did *Doctor* Garza say what time he saw Manstein in the casino?"

"Oh, it couldn't have been very late. Dr. Garza goes to bed early."

Flynn nodded. "Thanks for the help, Ms. Wylie." He started to turn away, had a sudden thought, and stopped. "Or is it Dr. Wylie?"

Beryl smiled. "Dr. Wylie. I'm an astrophysicist."

"Good luck with your radiometric spectrometer, Doctor."

Flynn took the elevator to level six, where Seattle Avenue was much wider and had a moving sidewalk. He rode the sidewalk to the new end of the Station and took the elevator to the hub, where the satellite shuttles docked. His watch told him that he had missed lunch. He had to wait twenty minutes for the next shuttle that would stop at Satellite Foxtrot.

The shuttle at that time of day was a work boat, and Flynn had a scenic view through the forward ports. Six spaceships were under construction around Foxtrot. The ESA ship looked ordinary—a habitation ring that would rotate to provide artificial gravity and a central core containing engines and life support. It had two engines—where they were going, the ESA astronauts could not expect anyone to help them if an engine failed. The engines, from the hydrogen reactors to the exhaust nozzles, were the first ones designed and built by the Company instead of being purchased from outside vendors—Conglomerated Mining and Manufacturing couldn't have underbid the competition if it had paid another firm to build the engines and ship them to Jupiter. The ESA ship was much smaller than the others the Company was constructing, since ESA was sending only twenty astronauts on the first manned expedition to Pluto. (The European Union had more welfare programs and a higher percentage of retired people than did the United States, and was in even greater financial straits.)

The ESA ship's airlock was functioning. The shuttle docked to it.

The ship was a Company work site not open to the public. The shuttle pilot raised his hand to stop Flynn when he tried to board the ship. "Sorry, buddy. Company employees and ESA personnel only this stop."

Flynn removed the hard copy of the employment letter Wendy had given him and handed it to the pilot.

"What's this?"

"Read it."

The man scanned it quickly. "You're Mike Flynn? Sorry.

Should have recognized you." He handed the letter back. "What are you investigating?"

"Sorry. Company confidential."

The airlock from the work boat to the spaceship had been opened and workers were moving shipping crates from the back of the boat into the ship. The ship wasn't rotating so everything and everybody was weightless. Shipping crates in free fall obstinately followed Newton's first law of motion, but the workers were experienced and kept the crates from colliding with hatch coamings. Flynn drifted along behind the crates through the coupled airlocks and into the ship. The workers wore Company coveralls and ID badges. Inside the ship, an orange-suited security guard with black hair, a square jaw, and even squarer shoulders took one look at Flynn's clothes and reached out to stop him.

"Mike Flynn!" The guard drew back. "What brings you out here?"

Flynn didn't need to use his authorization letter; he had been getting along well with Company guards for an entire year. "I'm looking for Dr. Garza."

The name tag on the guard's coveralls was inscribed *Duane Dieffenbach.* He nodded, and pointed along the corridor that extended aft from the airlock. "He's in life support with Dr. Timchenko. The hatch is marked; you can't miss it."

Flynn used the handholds welded to the bulkhead to pull himself aft. He was nearly to the point where the corridor ended in a pressure hatch labelled ENGINEERING when a hatch in the side bulkhead opened and Luke Timchenko drifted through, leading four men that Flynn didn't recognize. One of the men said, "We specified the low-energy life support only because energy pollution is such a hot topic in Europe. We had to cater to every political group to get the mission funded, even though energy pollution is of no consequence out here. Now that nearly every part of this mission is over budget, we shouldn't have too much flak if we switch to high-energy recycling—especially if we can get primary and back-up systems for the price of one low-energy system." The man looked around the narrow corridor. "Will you have any trouble getting them in?"

"We'll cut through the exterior bulkhead," Timchenko said, before he noticed the detective in their midst. "Mr. Flynn! How did you get in here?"

Flynn was the only person in the group not wearing coveralls. "Camouflage clothing. Drifted right by the security guard without being noticed." He took Wendy's letter from his coat and handed it to Timchenko. "Which one of you gentlemen is Dr. Garza?"

The man who had been speaking with Luke Timchenko said, "I am Dr. Garza."

Garza was a big man, with wide shoulders and a large head. He had black hair and a small black mustache. "Dr. Garza, my name is Michael Flynn." He showed Garza his investigator's license. "I'm investigating the murder of your neighbor."

"The marshals told us not to talk about him until his name is officially released."

"Don't worry—I already know it. I understand that you saw him in the casino the night he was killed."

Garza nodded. "It was around twenty, maybe twenty-thirty."

"Did you see him talk to anyone?"

Furrows appeared on Garza's forehead. He shook his head. "He was at the crap table. I was playing blackjack."

"Did you speak with him often?"

"I said hello to him a couple of times when we met in the street. I didn't even know his name until the police told me he was dead."

"Did his accent sound German?"

Garza hesitated. "He could have been from anywhere. Not

Spain—I would have recognized a Spanish accent."

Manstein had been a perfect spy. Even when people noticed him, they didn't really notice him. "Thank you, Dr. Garza."

Timchenko handed back Flynn's letter of authorization. "Your wife hired you to investigate the murder? Why didn't she just ask Silvanus Drake?"

"She had some extra money in her budget. You know how the Company works—use it or lose it."

Flynn had to wait fifteen minutes for a shuttle back to the Station. He rode back with Dr. Garza and a man who turned out to be Beryl Wylie's husband. The two scientists discussed the possibility that their trip would be extended from Pluto to planet ten—an extension would help justify the cost overrun, but would add two years to the expedition. Satellite Foxtrot was only five kilometers ahead of Jupiter Station in its orbit, but the shuttle stopped at Echo, Delta, Charlie, and Bravo, so the trip home took almost an hour. Flynn wasn't back aboard the Station again until after fifteen. He took the elevator from the shuttle-docking area in the hub to level four, and used the moving sidewalk on Denver Avenue to get to the other end of the Station.

The Moonshine Bar was on level two. Like all of the Station's watering holes, it was crowded due to the influx of construction workers from the Asian station. Joe Aguirre was standing at the bar, sandwiched between two men Flynn didn't recognize. The bartender was dressed in a bright purple shirt, tights, and a long purple coat. He had tinted his hair to match his attire. Flynn wedged himself between Aguirre and the man to his left and got the bartender's attention. He put thirty dollars on the bar and indicated Joe with his elbow. "Keep this man supplied with tequila."

"What kept you?" Aguirre asked.

"I was off Station."

"How's the investigation going?"

"I have so many clues I don't know how to sort 'em out."

Aguirre grinned. "That bad, eh? Well, maybe you'll get lucky, like the marshals."

"The marshals got lucky?"

"In finding the body so soon after the murder. That recycling bin is normally emptied on Thursdays. They emptied it early in preparation for Dr. Liao's visit, just in case the great doctor wanted to see our recycling system. By Thursday that body would have been buried under a couple of tons of trash and probably wouldn't have been discovered until it hit the separators. Then they wouldn't have known what bin it came from. And by then all the security videos from the day of the murder would have been deleted."

The bartender returned with a shot of tequila and a shot of whiskey. He put the whiskey in front of Michael. "On the house, Mr. Flynn."

Aguirre shook his head. "You live a tough life, my friend." He put the tequila to his lips, tilted his head back, and emptied the glass.

"You don't know how tough. My wife frowns on drinking, except a glass of wine with dinner."

Joe banged his glass onto the bar to get the bartender's attention. "Grounds for divorce."

Michael drained his whiskey. "I go forth to seek more clues. Let me know if any bloodstained wrenches show up."

Aguirre tapped his chest. "You expect me to work for free?"

Flynn took out his computer. "For you, my friend, I have compensation that is difficult to come by on the Station." He found the contact code he wanted and sent a copy to Joe's account.

"What's that?"

"Brunette." Flynn smiled. "Lonely brunette."

Aguirre eyed Flynn suspiciously. "Good-looking?"

"I used to date her."

"Why did you stop?"

"Her hips bring to mind healthy childbirth. Ah, go easy on the sauce, Joe. I told her you don't drink too much."

Second Street was cooler and quieter than the interior of the Moonshine Bar. Flynn checked his computer and found a message from Wendy. She had attached a copy of the autopsy report on Leron Cross, with a note saying that Francine had approved its release to him. Cross had been stabbed three times in the upper abdomen, just below the ribs, but not with a knife. The murder weapon had been a long, thin instrument, probably a Phillips screwdriver. The entrance wounds had been grouped inside a circle only two centimeters in diameter. That sounded like a professional hit. But it was the number of wounds that started Flynn thinking.

Chapter 5

Wendy didn't slow down as she passed the desk of Warshovsky's office manager. "I'm expected," she said. The manager announced her over the intercom as Wendy opened the door to the inner office.

Ed Warshovsky, dressed in a gray suit, was sitting behind his desk. In a chair across from him was Silvanus Drake.

Wendy thought of smiling, but decided it wouldn't be worth the effort. She knew why she had been summoned. She looked Warshovsky in the eye. "You wanted to see me?"

Warshovsky blinked. Wendy was wearing a fashionable business suit with shiny red coat and tights. He thought he had cured her of wearing the distasteful style to the office. "You used Company funds to hire your husband to investigate the Manstein murder."

Wendy phrased her reply carefully. "I already knew that. You didn't have to call me here to tell me. You didn't even have to send me an e-mail."

Warshovsky sighed and leaned back in his leather-covered executive chair. He closed his eyes. "She's starting to talk like him."

"Like whom?" Wendy asked, as innocently as she could.

Warshovsky rubbed the back of his neck. The muscles there were tense; he was getting a headache. "Like your husband!"

"Really?" Wendy clasped her hands behind her back. "Anything else you want to tell me?"

Warshovsky leaned forward and rested his forearms on the desk. "I want *you* to tell *me* why you hired your husband!"

"Because he's the best private investigator on the Station."

Warshovsky took a very deep breath and glanced at Drake. There was a hint of amusement on the security director's usually expressionless face. Warshovsky let his breath out slowly. "Why do you think you need to investigate the Manstein murder?"

"Because you aren't telling me everything about it, which leaves me unprepared to do my job. I work for the Company, Mr. Warshovsky, not for you. If you were forthcoming about the Manstein case, I would not need an outside source of information to help me represent the Company's legal interests."

"We've told you everything we know about the Manstein case!"

Wendy raised an eyebrow. "Really? You mean, it's a mere coincidence that Manstein was shut off just as Dr. Liao was making his first visit to Jupiter, accompanied by four bodyguards?"

"We don't know that they're—"

"Like hell you don't! When Michael mentioned it at the reception, you looked at Mr. Drake, and he gave you an 'I told you so' look!"

"I had no information that Dr. Liao's assistants were actually bodyguards," Drake said. "I had informed Mr. Warshovsky only that I could not confirm certain information on their résumés."

Wendy stared at Drake. "Like their engineering degrees?"

Drake returned the stare. "Among other things."

Wendy looked back at her supervisor. "But do you bother to tell me, the head of your Legal Department, that the Chinese government is so concerned about Liao's safety that they pay to send four bodyguards with him all the way to Jupiter? The Chinese are *broke,* Mr. Warshovsky, almost as broke as the

United States. And the Company has money. If something happens to Dr. Liao while he's on this Station, they will *sue* us. Not raise a diplomatic protest with Washington—there's no money in that. *Sue* us. That's my department. I should have been informed, and wasn't. And since I don't know what else I haven't been told, I hired the best investigator I could find to look into the matter."

"You're wasting Company money," Warshovsky said. "There's no known connection between Liao and Manstein."

"The important word in that statement is 'known.' Manstein was on the Station for who knows how long without our knowledge. He's not in our database. He wasn't doing anything—"

"He was doing lots of things," Drake corrected. "He visited the casinos at least twice a month, never losing more than five hundred dollars. He frequented restaurants. Bartenders in many saloons recognized his photo. He's been seen at airball games."

The unexpected information made Wendy pause. "And he always paid in cash. Right?"

Drake's eyes were empty, like they were windows on a soul he didn't have. "Right."

"So he left no record of what he did or why he was here." Wendy shook her head. "I think he was some kind of spy. And just as Liao arrives, the spy gets his head bashed in." Wendy put her hands on Warshovsky's desk, leaned forward, and looked her supervisor right in the eye. "Tell me what's going on!"

Warshovsky shut his eyes, breathed once, and opened them. "Speculation on our part cannot be used by a lawyer in court."

"It can prepare me for what I might face in court!"

"This isn't going to wind up in court," Drake said.

Warshovsky looked at him sharply. Drake was resting his elbows on the arms of his chair and tapping the tips of his fingers together.

"How do you know that?" Wendy demanded.

Drake continued to tap his fingers together. "The marshal's wrong: Manstein's murder wasn't a robbery that went too far—even though he paid cash for everything, and the marshals found no cash in his apartment. They found no computer, either. They found nothing that a manufacturer's sales representative would need to do his job. He wasn't taking prospective customers to dinner, like a sales rep should do. You're right: he was a spy. And when spies get killed, nobody sues. The governments involved disavow all knowledge of the incident."

Wendy looked at the security director, surprised by his candor and wondering if he was telling the truth. "Whom was he spying for?"

Drake, his fingertips still touching, said, "Perhaps your husband's investigation will reveal that."

Flynn rode a moving sidewalk back to the new end of the Station, where Leron Cross had been killed. The glowing name above the entrance to the High Vacuum bar was fancier than it had been when Flynn had frequented it in his bachelor days. Business was probably good—the High Vacuum was close to the airlocks where the shuttles bringing the Asian workers docked.

Flynn stepped through the door. Business was more than good. Every chair was occupied and there was a solid row of patrons at the bar. Half of the faces were Oriental. Flynn squeezed through the crowd to the right end of the bar, so naturally the bartender was at the left end. A sign was taped to the mirror behind the shelves of intoxicants:

I'M NOT A FAST BARTENDER.
I'M NOT A SLOW BARTENDER.
I'M A HALF-FAST BARTENDER!

Flynn tried to get the bartender's attention. He suddenly recognized the man next to him.

"Chad Kowalski! I thought your contract expired years ago!"

The man turned and looked at Flynn. He had sandy hair with just a tint of red. "Well, Mike Flynn, of the Boston Flynns! Hell, yes, it did, and not a moment too soon!"

"I recall you saying something about never leaving planet three again."

"The Asian consortium offered me a three-hundred-thousand-dollar signing bonus, and I'm getting fifty percent more than most of the workers because of my experience. Hah! They don't give a damn about my experience!" Kowalski's breath smelled strongly of beer. "I thought the Company was screwed up, but they're a model of efficiency compared to my new employers. I got so tired of telling 'em that they were doing things the hard way, the long way, and the just plain wrong way that I shut up and don't tell 'em anything anymore. We work twelve-hour shifts six days a week. And they have no safety regulations. The Company pairs people working in vacuum, so they can look out for each other. On the Asian station, we're on our own. We lost two guys the day after we spun up the station: One fell off an inner girder and tumbled toward the outside, where he collided with another guy, helmet to helmet, and knocked him off the station. Both faceplates cracked. They were breathing vacuum before we could get to 'em. Here, let me get you a beer."

The bartender had worked his way to Flynn's end of the bar. He acted almost as surprised to see Flynn as Kowalski had. "I don't believe it! Michael Flynn! I'd heard you got married, but it's been so long, I thought I must have gotten it wrong and that it was your funeral I'd heard about!"

"Hi, Dinky. Nice seeing you again."

Kowalski looked at Flynn, eyes wide with disbelief. "You got married? Who to?"

"A redhead."

"The Company's top lawyer redhead," Dinky added. "Why don't you quit the PI business and live off her money?"

"I tried that, but my cat wouldn't let me sit around the apartment all day doing nothing." Flynn glanced around to make his next point. "Did you make this place smaller than the last time I was here?"

Dinky was shorter than Flynn and shaved his head. He smiled. "Seems like it, don't it? And yesterday a bearing goes out on my new bartending robot. Fat lot of good the warranty will do me out here." He shook his head. "If I could get Xing Tao beer instead of the Company swill, I'd be rich enough to retire." He held up a finger. "Here, I got something better for you."

"Ah, Dinky . . ." But it was too late; Dinky's back was turned.

Dinky took a bottle of Irish whiskey from the top shelf, slammed a glass onto the bar, and poured a stiff jolt into it. He pushed the glass across the bar to Flynn. "On me."

Flynn pressed his hands against his legs. "My wife doesn't like me drinking on the job."

Dinky wrinkled his nose, then scanned the patrons at the bar. "Huh. You're in luck. None of these people look like her." He pushed the glass closer to Flynn.

Michael jerked his thumb at the security camera in the corner behind the bar. "She has access to security videos."

Dinky looked at the camera. "The lens on that camera doesn't take in the whole room at once. Wait for it to pan away . . . Now!" He picked up the glass and shoved it under Flynn's nose.

Flynn drank. He was out of training, and couldn't empty the glass in one swallow. He put the glass on the bar and asked,

"Did Leron Cross ever come in here?"

Dinky's shoulders sagged. "That was sad. He was a hell of a nice guy. Just got married last year—after you did—to a really nice lady. Great looking, too."

"Was he a ladies' man?"

Dinky squinted. "If he was, he picked the wrong place to work! Go ahead, count the women in this room!"

Flynn looked down at his glass, and absent-mindedly downed the rest of his whiskey without checking the security camera. "Did he have a tab here?"

Dinky shook his head again. "Always paid cash or with a debit card."

"So as far as you know, he didn't owe anybody money?"

Dinky shrugged. "As far as I know, but I didn't know him that well. I don't think he gambled, and that's about the only way you can get into debt out here. But why don't you ask the guys at the table there? They're all cowboys. They worked with Leron."

Four men, hunched over their beers, crowded around the indicated table. Michael reached for his wallet and slapped twenty-five dollars onto the bar. "Get me a pitcher of beer."

Dinky pushed the money back to Flynn. "Keep it. Any drinking you do in here is on me."

Flynn pushed the bills back to Dinky. "I'm working. This is a business expense. My client's paying."

"In that case . . ." The money disappeared into Dinky's shirt pocket as he went to fetch the beer.

Kowalski, leaning on the bar with his elbow, looked at Flynn. "How the hell can Dinky afford to stay in business if he's giving you free drinks?"

"I don't drink as much as I used to."

Dinky brought a pitcher of beer and Flynn carried it to the table. One of the men there was dressed in the red coveralls worn by pilots. The other three were in civilian clothes. Flynn surprised them when he plunked the pitcher on the table in front of them.

"In memory of Leron Cross," Flynn announced.

The men looked at him with a mixture of suspicion and curiosity. The man to Flynn's right said, "You a friend of his?"

The man in the red coveralls, across the table from Flynn, said, "Don't you watch the news, Silas? That's Michael Flynn, the private detective."

The suspicion vanished, leaving only the curiosity. "You investigating Leron's death?" one of the other men asked.

"His wife hired me to look into it. I was told you were friends of his."

"We all worked with him," the man in the red coveralls said. He had a Company ID badge, bearing the name *Russell Murrow,* on his chest. "I undocked fifteen minutes before he went on shift last night, when he was killed."

Flynn glanced at his watch. "If you're working evening shifts, shouldn't you be out in space?"

"I would be, if my forward thrusters were working." Murrow threw up his hands. "She worked perfectly yesterday, but Jonny here," he nodded at the man on his left, "nearly drove her into the aluminum smelter earlier today. Had to bring her in for repairs and had a hell of time docking, didn't you, Jonny?"

"Damn near killed myself." Jonny refilled his glass from the pitcher Flynn had provided.

"Techs are still working on it, so I'm sitting here, drinking Coke, waiting for it to be fixed." Murrow gestured with a glass that had just a trace of brown liquid at the bottom.

"Maybe with you on the case, it'll get solved," Jonny said.

"Maybe, if I can get people to talk to me. I heard Leron was a ladies' man."

Disbelief flashed across the four faces around the table

looked. "Leron? Leron Cross?" Murrow said. "I never saw him date anybody but Francine!"

"Me either," added the man to Flynn's left.

Flynn shook his head. "You see the problems I have? When people do talk to me, they make up information."

The man to Flynn's left pointed his finger at the detective and said, "I'll tell you what I told the marshals: Investigate Big Bill Gorkov. I saw Leron talking to that fat scum just two weeks ago."

Murrow shook his head. "Willy, think for a change! Gorkov couldn't get into the murder site! Only authorized Company employees can get in there!"

"He could have bribed somebody!" Willy argued.

Murrow squinted. "You, maybe?"

Flynn said, "Did Leron owe money to Gorkov?"

"Leron didn't owe money to anybody," Murrow said. "He didn't spend; he saved. He re-upped just before he met Francine, but her contract's over next year. Leron was trying to get enough money to pay the penalty for leaving early, so he and Francine could go back to Earth together."

"So you don't know of any reason why someone would have wanted to kill him?"

Murrow shook his head. Willy said, "Everybody liked Leron. He had no enemies. Which is why it had to be Gorkov. He's supposed to have killed ten or twelve guys on Mars. He probably did it just to keep his hand in."

Murrow leaned across the table and stared Willy in the face. "Willy, which one of us let Gorkov in there?"

Before Willy could answer, Murrow's telephone beeped. He took the instrument from the chest pocket of his coveralls and held it to his ear. "Murrow . . . okay, thanks." He folded the phone with a flip of the wrist and put it back in his pocket. "I'm off shift. The techs won't have the ship fixed before midnight."

He refilled his glass from Flynn's pitcher and took a long drink. When he put the glass down on the table it was half empty. He wiped his lips on his sleeve, then made a face—his coveralls were nonabsorbent. "I can't drink in this!" He emptied his glass and stood up. "I'll be right back. Don't let anyone take my chair."

Flynn seized the opportunity. "Going back to your locker? Could you show me the murder scene?"

Murrow hesitated. "We're not supposed to let nonemployees in there . . . What the hell, you're trying to solve the murder of a Company employee—and a friend of mine. If they object, I'll tell them to snort vacuum. Come on."

The round-up ships docked on the new end of the Station on level one. Murrow led Flynn along Sacramento Avenue almost to the end of the Station, then zigzagged down five ramps. The cowboys' locker room was on Eighteenth Street. The door lock read Murrow's retinals and allowed him to open the door.

"What's down there?" Flynn asked, looking down the corridor to his right.

"My supervisor tonight; day-shift supervisor and office manager during the day; women's locker room—we have two female pilots. Men's locker room's in here." Murrow led Flynn through a doorway. "Shower's there on the left. Over there's the airlocks to the ships. And down this corridor here is where they found Leron."

The corridor was straight and only fifteen meters long. There were two doors on the right, the side facing the end of the Station, none on the left, and one at the end of the corridor. There was no crime-scene tape and no sign of blood.

Flynn followed Murrow into the corridor. The doors on the right were open. Both led to maintenance laboratories. A technician in yellow coveralls was sitting at a workbench in the second room. He looked up when he heard footsteps.

"Russ! Didn't the super tell you? Your ship's down for at least the rest of the shift."

"Hi, Stan. Yeah, he called a few minutes ago. I just came back to shuck these damn coveralls." Murrow eyed the equipment that was torn apart on the workbench. "Is that the problem there?"

"No, this is not the problem. Everything tests to specs. I'm putting it back together." Stan gestured at the bulkhead behind him with his head. "Mary and Kurt are outside, even as we speak, pulling the arms off the ship so we can get at the thruster feeds. We'll be damn lucky to have the ship running in time for the next shift." Stan's eyebrows lowered as he noticed Flynn standing behind Murrow. "Who the hell are you?"

Flynn opened his mouth to respond, but Murrow beat him to it. "This is Mike Flynn, the private detective. Mike, Stan Grunemeyer. Francine hired Mike to investigate Leron's murder."

The explanation didn't make Stan any happier. "You're not supposed to be in here."

Murrow put his hands on his hips. "You want us to do nothing while little Ms. Marshal tries to find the killer? She's been on the Station less than four months. She can't even find the bathroom by herself yet. And have you forgotten the last time a U.S. marshal tried to solve a murder out here?"

Stan glanced up at the security camera in the corner of the lab. It was on the same wall as the door and couldn't view the corridor. "You're going to get us in trouble, Russ. Only authorized Company employees are permitted in this area."

Flynn's authorization letter didn't specify what Wendy had hired him to investigate. Michael took it from his pocket and handed it to Grunemeyer. "Was Leron really killed right out here?"

Stan read the letter, slowly, as though he was more accustomed to reading schematic diagrams. He handed it back, and pointed around the corner of the door. "Just to your right there."

Flynn looked where Stan had pointed. "There's no blood."

Stan shrugged. "I was told that the marshals finished last night and the robot cleaned it this morning. Suits me fine. I wouldn't want to have to walk around Leron's blood every time I go to the can."

Flynn could agree with that. "Were you working last night?"

Stan nodded. "Yep. I prefer evenings." Then the implication of the question dawned on him. "But I didn't see anything. There were no squawks yesterday and no scheduled maintenance, so I got tasked to upgrade security cameras on Second Street. Found out about the murder when it made the late news."

"You weren't in here at all yesterday?"

"For about two minutes. I reported to work at sixteen, was told I wasn't needed here, and was sent to Second Street. Leron's shift didn't start till seventeen. I never saw him."

"Were any technicians working in here yesterday?"

Grunemeyer shook his head. "At the time of the murder? No. Kurt went off shift at sixteen, and Mary got tasked to help with some life-support upgrades in the basement."

Flynn took a moment to digest that information. "This Kurt person normally works days? What's he doing outside now?"

Grunemeyer grinned. "Making copious overtime, the lucky son-of-a-bitch! Time and a half for overtime, and one and a half times that for working outside!" He gestured at the electronic equipment on the workbench. "As soon as I get this back together and reinstalled, I'm suiting up and joining 'em!"

Flynn nodded. "Thanks, Stan. You've been a big help."

Grunemeyer blinked. "I have? Well, I hope you catch the guy who did it. Losing Leron is too much to pay for a new set of screwdrivers."

"Hmm?"

Grunemeyer gestured at the workbench. "These manual screwdrivers are all brand new. I asked Kurt where they came from, and he said the marshals took the old ones away—evidence, I guess."

"I guess." Flynn stepped back from the doorway and looked at the deck where Cross's body had been found. In the opposite bulkhead, not two meters from where he stood, was a recycling hatch. Flynn pulled the lever that opened the hatch and peered down the chute. "Do you know when the bin beneath this chute is scheduled to be emptied?"

Murrow shrugged. "Hey, Stan: When do they empty the bin under this recycling chute?"

"Not often enough. Yesterday the chute was filled all the way to the top of the hatch."

Flynn walked to the other end of the corridor. The door there was not locked from the inside, so that people would be able to escape in case of fire. He opened it. There was an electronic lock on the outside. The corridor—the end of Sacramento Avenue—was empty. The closest security camera was over fifty meters down the avenue toward the center of the Station.

"See what I mean?" Murrow said. "You can't get in here unless you're an authorized employee."

Flynn nodded. "Yeah, I see what you mean. And since these fancy locks inform Security of who opens them from the outside, the marshals know which authorized employees were here last night. None of them have been arrested, so I assume they all have alibis."

"Or no motive. I told you: everybody liked Leron."

Flynn took out his wallet and handed Murrow twenty-five dollars. "Here. Buy yourself and your friends another pitcher." He stuck his head into the lab and gave Grunemeyer a ten.

"Have a drink when you go off shift."

Flynn followed Murrow back to the locker room. "Hope you get back into space tomorrow."

"Aw, I can afford a missed shift now and then," Murrow admitted. "I don't really do it for the money. I enjoy the job." He looked at the investigator out of the corner of his eye. "Have you ever had a ride in a round-up ship?" Flynn shook his head. "How would you like to come out with me sometime?"

"Sounds like fun. Give me a call when your ship's fixed."

Michael let himself out into the corridor. He unfolded his computer and called his wife. "The electronic locks on the cowboys' locker room, where Leron Cross was murdered: Do they inform Security Control when the doors are opened from the inside?"

Wendy hesitated. "Let me check. It's a level-three security area—Company employees only, but not sensitive. No, they don't. Why do you ask?"

"Just wanted to be sure. I have a couple more leads to check out on the Cross investigation. I won't be home for dinner."

"I figured out that you wouldn't be home for dinner an hour ago. What about the Manstein case?"

"You can help me with that. Manstein was seen in the Company casino a couple of hours before he got cancelled. Can you check the Security database and see if he talked with anyone?"

"Ah, just a second . . ." Wendy checked something in another display window. "Yeah, I was afraid of that. Michael, there's only one security camera in the casino. It has to scan the floor and might not show—"

Flynn cut off his wife with a wave of his hand. "Wendy, Manstein didn't seem to have many friends. If he talked with anyone at all, it might be significant. Shoot me a photo of anybody he talked to." He squinted. "Why are you sitting at your desk in your office, instead of waiting for me at home like a good little wife?"

"I'm reviewing outstanding contracts to make sure there's nothing stopping us from starting construction of the new prison on Friday. And I lost half an hour when I got jerked into Warshovsky's office this afternoon to explain why I was wasting Company funds by employing you."

"This afternoon? What took him so long?"

"I wondered about that myself. Turns out he was giving Dr. Liao a tour of some of the satellites."

"What did you tell Warshovsky?"

"I told him I thought he was holding out on me and I wanted to know what was going on."

"Did he tell you anything?"

Wendy summarized her meeting with Warshovsky and Drake. Flynn was impressed by how much Wendy had learned with so little effort. "That's unusually loquacious for Drake. It would have taken me days to check out all those restaurants and bars to find out what Manstein's been doing. Any idea why he's being so helpful?"

"Maybe he's trying to mislead you again."

"Or maybe he's getting desperate. Rumor has it that Manstein's DNA isn't in any database on planet three."

"But . . . all industrialized countries record DNA at birth! To detect genetically based diseases and for identification in case of an accident!" Wendy thought about what she had just said. "So he wasn't from an industrialized country."

"Not necessarily. He'd once had a microchip implanted in his brain, but it had been surgically removed."

Wendy had also had a microcomputer implanted in her brain when she was a child. "I thought they were deactivated in place, electronically."

"They were. But they all had serial numbers. No chip, no serial number that can be traced to the person in whom the chip was planted."

"Wow." That information had important implications. "No wonder the marshals can't inform his next of kin. He really was a spy—identity completely concealed by his government."

"Completely concealed by somebody," Flynn said. A government could have replaced Manstein's chip with another one, or altered the medical records.

"Any idea when you'll be home?"

"Probably won't be for a couple of hours yet. I have to touch base with Francine Cross, and then I have to see a man about a loan."

Chapter 6

Francine Cross lived on Eleventh Street, one block from a children's playground on Denver Avenue. Eleventh Street was wide enough for two electric vehicles to pass each other. The apartments opened directly onto the street, where the institutional-green walls were decorated with bold diagonal stripes of yellow and orange. If fun was proportional to sound level, the kids on the playground were having a great time. Flynn pressed the door bell. He couldn't hear it over the noise of the children.

Francine opened the door. She was dressed in light metallic blue with matching hair and nails. Her attire clashed with her eyes, which were red. "Mr. Flynn!" She sounded surprised. "Have you—oh, ah . . ." She looked over her shoulder. Two people sat in her living room. "Why don't you come in."

Flynn stepped through the doorway and Francine slid the door closed behind him, reducing the racket from the playground to a tolerable level. She swallowed. "Mr. Flynn, this is Dr. Schellenburg and his wife, Dora." The couple rose from their chairs and Michael stepped forward to shake their hands. "Dr. Schellenburg is our school principal. Dora teaches seventh grade."

Schellenburg was as tall as Flynn but had a larger belly and a short, neatly trimmed beard. He squinted at Flynn. "Aren't you a private detective?"

Before Flynn could plead guilty to the charge, Francine said,

"I hired him to investigate Leron's murder. Did you learn something already?"

Flynn had to choose his words carefully with witnesses in the room. "I might have a lead. I need to ask you a couple of questions. Can we speak in private?"

"Oh, sure. Follow me." Francine turned to the Schellenburgs. "Excuse me for a moment."

The apartment was as small as the bachelor pad that Flynn had vacated when he moved in with Wendy. The kitchen was barely big enough for one person at a time and the bathroom was even smaller. Francine led Flynn into the bedroom, which was nearly filled by a double bed with a dark blue bedspread. The bed was neatly made and Flynn had seen a blanket carelessly folded on the couch; he guessed that Ms. Cross couldn't bear to sleep in the bed she had shared with her husband. If she had had him killed, she was either regretting it or was a very good actress.

Francine switched on the light, slid the door closed, and looked expectantly at Flynn.

"First of all, Leron wasn't cheating on you. I couldn't find anybody who'd admit to ever seeing him with anyone but you. And if they had been so discreet that no one ever saw them together, the woman wouldn't have called here when you were home."

"I'd already figured out that Leron wasn't having an affair."

"Did he owe money to anyone?"

Francine blinked. "No. We don't owe anybody. But he didn't have anything saved, either. His father is a pilot. A cropduster. Has his own business in Pennsylvania. Several years ago, he accidentally let his medical insurance expire. Then he had a crash and . . . He spent a month in intensive care, and then he needed several operations. Leron only came out here because of the high salaries. He was sending everything he could back home to help pay his father's medical bills. But he hadn't borrowed anything."

"Have you *tried* to borrow money lately?"

"We looked into it. Leron re-upped just before he met me. He has over three years to go on his contract, but mine is up next year. We wanted to go back to Earth and start a family. The penalty for breaking his contract is two hundred and eighty thousand dollars. I have only fifty thousand saved. We have . . . had no collateral. Nobody but the credit union would loan us a dime, and they'd loan the money only if we stayed with the Company, in which case we wouldn't need the loan."

Flynn nodded thoughtfully. "That's what I needed to know, Ms. Cross. I spent half of today on your case; that's nine hundred, plus another sixty for expenses."

"Expenses?"

"Bribes, Ms. Cross. Alcohol loosens people's tongues."

Wendy left Company headquarters through the front door on the Main Plaza. She walked around the waterfall that cascaded from three levels above and then along the Plaza until she came to Denver Avenue. She turned left and went one block down Station to Fourth Street. On the corner of Fourth and Denver was Betty's Bar. The door opened as Wendy approached and three intoxicated Orientals stumbled through, laughing loudly. The construction workers from the Asian station worked six-day weeks, but their days off were staggered so there were boisterous visitors on the Station all the time. Betty's was full of people. Wendy spotted an opening at the far end of the bar.

Betty had seen Wendy come in and was waiting for her when she got up to the bar. "Wendy Chadwick! Long time no see!"

"Hello, Betty. Have you seen . . . has my husband been in here lately?"

Betty also had red hair, although it wasn't nearly as bright as

Wendy's. The brow beneath the red hair furrowed. "Michael? From what I hear from colleagues, he hasn't been in *any* bar lately, except when working. You have really managed to ground him." She jabbed the index finger of her right hand at Wendy's chest. "You should write a book! A lot of wives would like to know how you did it!"

Wendy put her handbag on the bar. She looked at the bag instead of Betty.

"What's wrong?" Betty asked.

Wendy took a deep breath. "I . . . don't know. Michael . . . he's just not himself. Not like he used to be."

Betty cocked her head. "How not like he used to be?"

Wendy hesitated. She wished she had thought of what to say before she had entered the bar. "You know the way he was, partying all the time. He used to practically live here. Now, he's home every evening that he's not working. He sits in his chair with his cat on his lap and reads, or watches the Red Sox or the Bruins. We go out to dinner a couple of times a week, but that's it. He doesn't even drink at meals anymore!"

Betty put her hands on her hips. "Wendy, I have been tending bar for over thirty years, and this is the first time I've heard a woman complain because her husband was drinking too little!"

"I'm not complaining. I'm . . . worrying. He's not enjoying himself the way he was when we were dating. I thought he might be coming here during the day, but if he hasn't . . ."

"Are the two of you having other problems?"

Wendy shook her head. "Mornings are great. We meet for lunch—he's fine. He brings me flowers nearly every week. He usually makes dinner—I'm a terrible cook. But after dinner, during the evening, he just . . . sits there."

"By evening, you mean . . . all the way through bedtime?"

Wendy gave Betty a sharp look. "No, bed is fine. Bed is outstanding." She had to suppress a smile.

Betty patted the back of Wendy's hand. "Then you have nothing to worry about."

"Betty, he's different. He called me, half an hour ago, to say he'd be working late. He sounded excited, the way he was before we were married."

"Hey, Betty!" someone called from the other end of the bar. "How about another pitcher?"

"What do you do during those quiet evenings at home?" Betty asked.

"Read. Sometimes Michael asks me to play the piano."

"What did you do during the evenings before you were married?"

"On the Station? Read, mostly. Or played my piano."

Betty nodded. "Does he know that?"

"I told him."

"Did you tell him anything else?"

"What do you mean?"

"Do the two of you ever just . . . talk?"

"All the time," Wendy said. "About politics and what the Company's developing and our families and the latest Station gossip. He tries to talk about sports sometimes but I don't follow anything and he knows it bores me."

"But you don't talk about staying home in the evenings."

"Ah . . . no."

Betty rubbed her chin with the tip of her forefinger. "He might be staying home at night because he thinks that's what you want to do."

"We went out all the time when we were dating!"

"That was dating. You weren't living together then. Mike went out a lot because he likes being around people. Now you're living together. He doesn't need those people anymore—he has you. Every night."

"You mean, he's actually *happy,* sitting at home with me?"

Betty nodded. "I'd bet a bottle of Irish whiskey on it. If you'd rather go out at night, tell him."

"Betty!" the voice called again. "Do I have to go down the block to get a refill?"

"I have to go." Betty smiled. "Talk to Michael. I look forward to seeing the two of you in here again one of these evenings."

The Gold Dollar Casino had been competing with the Company casino for the Station's gambling business for over two years. It was on the Government Plaza, at the opposite end of the Station from its competition. Its operator, Jorge Allesandro, had gotten a good deal on the premises. The government had received fifty percent off the usual rent on all the space on the Government Plaza as a condition for making the Station United States territory, but budget shortfalls had kept the government from sending as many people to Jupiter as originally planned and the excess space—like the Gold Dollar—had been subleased for less than the Company normally charged.

The waterfall on the Government Plaza was much smaller than the one on the Main Plaza, and the Gold Dollar was similarly smaller than the Company casino. But it had a more pretentious sign over its portal, and with a steady stream of recreation-starved Asian workers it had plenty of business. Flynn found the gaming tables surrounded by people throwing away money for which they had worked so hard. Electronic displays on the walls advertised the products available at the bar. Four barely attired cocktail waitresses rushed between the bar and the tables, keeping the gamblers fully fueled. The bouncer at the door was watching the crowd and scarcely glanced at Flynn. Michael stepped up to the bar and ordered a beer.

Big Bill Gorkov was the closest thing to a mobster that could be found on Jupiter Station. He had come from Mars ten months earlier, reportedly leaving planet four just before the

FBI could indict him for racketeering. Gorkov wanted to be a full-service gangster, extorting money from businesses and supplying the usual assortment of illegal drugs, weapons, and prostitution, but Silvanus Drake had the Station so tightly controlled that Gorkov had to be content with blackmail (carefully selected blackmail victims rarely went to the police) and loansharking (charging usurious interest rates wasn't illegal). Rumor had it that Drake permitted the loansharking because debt-ridden Company workers were more likely to renew their contracts and save the Company the cost of shipping them back to Earth. Because of his lack of illegitimate income, Gorkov had his thugs work as bouncers in the Gold Dollar in exchange for the use of one of the offices behind the casino. Gorkov had brought five henchmen with him from Mars, but one had been caught trying to bribe a security guard so he could smuggle drugs onto the Station, and another had beaten a prostitute when she had refused to let him be her pimp. The drug smuggler had been sent back to Earth to serve his sentence, and the would-be pimp was serving a year in the Station jail, so Gorkov was down to only three thugs.

As Flynn sipped his beer the door at the end of the bar opened and a short, thin man with dark hair and a small mustache came out. He moved into the crowd around the gaming tables with the rapid, furtive steps of an animal that was low on the food chain. His name was Hector Rivera, but someone had called him Weasel when he had been in middle school and the nickname had stuck. He was the smallest and least harmful of Gorkov's thugs. Weasel had the IQ of a grapefruit but could be vicious if he felt he was in no danger. He was a complete sycophant and Gorkov kept him around because Weasel never ceased flattering him.

Flynn turned his back to the bar. The bouncer at the door was another of Gorkov's pets, John "Knuckles" DiGeorgio. He looked like what central casting would supply if a movie director asked for a thug. His curly blond hair reached to his collar and his nose had been broken at least once and not repaired. He was built like a gorilla but wasn't as good-looking or as smart as one. Flynn had never seen his résumé but had no doubt that under *Hobbies* it listed drinking beer, watching football, and inflicting pain.

The bartender was a petite and good-looking blonde who, like the waitresses, was wearing little more than the exotic dancers in the Pussy Kat Klub. Flynn emptied his glass and put it on the bar to get her attention. When she came over to him he took two hundred-dollar bills and placed them next to his glass.

The blonde's hair was as short as her body but her eyes were big and blue. She eyed the money and asked, "What can I get you?"

"Information."

She pushed the money toward Flynn. "You don't need money to make me tell you what I like to do in bed." Her blue eyes were sparkling.

Flynn guessed that the blonde was one of the women who had come to Jupiter Station on a husband-hunting expedition, attracted by its two-to-one male-to-female ratio, only to discover that the male residents had either brought wives with them or weren't the marrying kind. Most such women lacked the technical skills that were in demand at Jupiter and quickly went through the cash they had brought with them. Those without round-trip tickets were forced into jobs that required little investment in wardrobes. Flynn shook his head. "My wife makes nine hundred thousand dollars a year. Do I look that stupid?"

The sparkle vanished from the blonde's eyes. "Damn it! All the cute ones are taken!" She sighed. "What do you want to know?"

"You know Bill Gorkov?"

The blonde wrinkled her nose. "I know who he is."

"Was he in here last night?"

She nodded. "He came out of his office around, oh, twenty or twenty-one o'clock, used the restroom, then went back to his office."

"You didn't see him come into or leave this establishment?"

The blonde shook her head. "He must have been here before I came on shift at sixteen and gone home after I left at midnight. But he would have had to come through that door because there's no back way out."

Flynn nodded. "How about his personal assistants?"

The blonde automatically looked toward Knuckles. "He wasn't working the door last night. I saw him and Lavalle come in right after I did, at sixteen. They went in back." She gestured with her head toward the door at the end of the bar. "Left around . . . twenty-two or so."

"Could they have left and returned while you were on break?"

She shrugged. "I suppose. You want me to ask around?"

Flynn hesitated. "Better not. They're the kind of people who don't like having questions asked about them." He took her hand and placed it on the hundred-dollar bills. "Thanks. You earned it."

The bartender smiled again. "Men as good-looking as you don't have to pay me to answer questions. Not even about Big Bill." But she kept the money.

Michael boldly walked around the end of the bar and opened the door through which Weasel had come. A corridor paralleled the back wall of the casino. Across from Flynn was another door with *Proprietor* embossed on it in black letters. Five meters farther down the corridor was a door without any lettering. The carpeting on the floor was soft and light blue and wasn't the industrial-strength material that the Company installed in the areas they controlled. Flynn walked to the unmarked door and rapped on it lightly.

The door was opened by a thin black man who was three centimeters taller than Flynn and nearly as handsome. His hair was close-cropped and he wore a shiny gray suit and tights. His name, Flynn knew, was Pierre Lavalle. He was the most dangerous of Gorkov's thugs because he was the only one with a multidigit IQ. Pierre was smart enough and ruthless enough to lead his own gang some day.

Lavalle stood in the half-opened door and eyed Flynn coldly. The detective didn't look like a customer. "What do you want?" he said, making Flynn feel unwelcome.

"I want to see your boss about a loan."

Lavalle sneered. "And you are . . . ?"

"You disappoint me, Pierre," came a voice from within the room. "You should recognize Mike Flynn, Jupiter Station's most famous private detective."

Lavalle stepped back as he looked over his shoulder, revealing Bill Gorkov sitting behind a large desk at the back of the room. "Come in, Mr. Flynn." Gorkov gestured at one of the chairs in front of his desk. "Sit down. Can I offer you a drink?"

"My—" Flynn began, then realized that Gorkov would not be impressed by an admission that Flynn's wife didn't want him drinking so much. "Sure." Flynn took a seat. The chair had arms and leather upholstery.

Gorkov was as tall as Lavalle but had much broader shoulders. He had dark brown hair and a large, square face. He wore a conservative blue suit, complete with vest. He looked at Lavalle. "Pierre, no bourbon for Mr. Flynn. Get him a scotch." He turned his attention to Flynn. "I'm sorry I can't offer you Irish whiskey; I have none in stock."

Lavalle handed Flynn a glass containing three fingers of amber liquid, then took a position behind Flynn's chair. "I drink almost anything," Flynn said.

"You want to borrow money from me, Mr. Flynn?"

Flynn sipped his whiskey. It wasn't as good as the drink Dinky had given him in the High Vacuum. "I don't want to borrow money from you."

Gorkov's thick eyebrows edged downward. "You were standing in that door not two minutes ago, saying you wanted to see me about a loan. Forget already?"

Flynn shook his head. "I didn't forget. The loan I want to talk to you about is the one you gave Leron Cross."

Gorkov lowered his eyes and looked at his hands, which were folded together in his lap. "I assume you are speaking of the Leron Cross who got himself on the news last night." Flynn nodded once. "I didn't loan Mr. Cross any money."

"You were seen speaking with him."

Flynn heard Lavalle shift his feet behind him. Gorkov gave his lackey a look to let him know that he had the situation under control. "Mr. Cross asked me about a loan. He didn't like the interest rates that I'm forced to charge to people with no collateral."

Flynn nodded. "I can understand. Ten percent a week is a might steep."

"I have horrendous overhead."

"Did Cross tell you why he wanted the money?"

"He wanted to buy himself out of his contract so he could go back to three with his wife next year. I had to quote him a higher rate because of that—I'd have to pay someone to collect for me on Earth."

"He didn't like it here?"

Gorkov shrugged. "Not everyone appreciates the opportunities presented by Jupiter Station. But I didn't get his business, although now I wish I had."

"Hmm?"

"If he owed me money, I'd have an excellent motive for not

killing him. Dead people are notorious for not paying their debts."

Flynn feigned incredulity. "You mean, someone suspects an honest, upright businessman like you of shutting down Mr. Cross?"

Gorkov chuckled. "This morning, Marshal Hathaway sat in the very chair you're using and asked me to account for my time yesterday evening. Fortunately, I had unimpeachable alibi witnesses."

"Let me guess: Weasel, Knuckles, and Pierre?"

"And Mr. Allesandro."

"And you, in turn, alibied Weasel, Knuckles, and Pierre?"

Gorkov held his hands with his palms up. "They were here with me until after Mr. Cross's body was discovered."

Flynn shook his head. "Must have greatly disappointed Marshal Hathaway."

"She made thinly veiled threats but she was shooting in the dark, just like you are. And speaking of shooting, do you have a permit for that stun pistol in your coat pocket?" Flynn nodded. "How did you get the marshal to approve it?"

"I didn't," Flynn said. "I got it in Massachusetts. That's one of the states whose concealed-weapons permits are accepted by the Feds." But the permit was invalid whenever Flynn's blood-alcohol level exceeded point oh five, and he was on his second drink in fifteen minutes.

"How much do you want for the pistol?"

"It's not for sale. There are no sporting-goods stores out here; I couldn't replace it." Flynn tried to look puzzled. "What would an honest businessman like you do with a stun pistol?"

"Some of my customers become very unreasonable when they can't make their loan payments."

Flynn finished his whiskey, put the glass down firmly on the desk—an expensive, genuine-wood desk—and got to his feet.

"Thank you for your time, Mr. Gorkov."

Gorkov flashed a smile. "Perhaps we can do business another day."

Flynn walked back to his apartment. He eschewed the moving sidewalks so that he would have more time to think. He would have been disappointed if Leron Cross had borrowed money from Bill Gorkov—like the man had said, it would have given him a motive for not killing Cross. Anyone on the Station who wanted to hire a hit man would think of Gorkov first. Whoever had hired Gorkov to shut off Leron Cross would have an airtight alibi for the time of the murder. Flynn couldn't help but wonder what Francine Cross had been doing then.

Chapter 7

Four requests for background checks were in Flynn's e-mail file on Thursday morning. So were three reports on completed investigations that Flynn had subcontracted to other detectives. Two of the reports, both from Doug Sanchez, were so badly written as to be incomprehensible. Sanchez must have been more drunk than usual when he had written them, which he denied when Flynn called him for the explanations he needed to rewrite the reports before forwarding them to Earth. Sanchez also denied that he didn't know how to use the grammar corrector in his word processor. Flynn did not believe either denial. He delegated three of the new investigations to colleagues and kept one for himself, which he thought he could do simultaneously with the premarital background check that had come in the day before. Flynn would not have been so optimistic, however, if he had known that his wife was not going to cooperate.

"Hi, gorgeous," Flynn said to the red-haired image that looked back at him from his computer display. "How's your morning going?"

"Hectic. Eight of our employees got into a brawl with ten Asians late last night. Mitch Habruch's handling most of them, as usual, but I got the overflow. I want to get everything cleaned up today so I'll be free over the weekend."

"Are you so overworked that you can't check the security videos for me and see if Francine Cross shows up in any of them at the time her husband was knocked off?"

Wendy hesitated. "I can't do that."

"What do you mean, you can't do that? You have access to the videos! And they will not have been deleted because there was a homicide at the time!"

"They're also Company confidential and available only to authorized Company officials and to law enforcement personnel."

Flynn stared into his display with one eye. "Wendy, I'm working for the Company, remember? You hired me!"

"To work on the Manstein case, not the Cross murder. So unless you can convince me that Francine was involved in Manstein's death, I can't give you access to the security videos."

"Wendy, you're the one who persuaded me to take the Cross case!"

"True, but you're working for Francine on that case, not for me and not for the Company. I can't let you see the security videos. And you said you were going to let the marshals clear Francine. If you're not going to wait for them, I'm sure you can find plenty of witnesses who will say that Francine was nowhere near that work area when her husband was killed."

"Lover, the only suspect I have for Leron's murder was probably hired to do it. If Francine hired him, she'd have an ironclad alibi for the time of the killing. If she has no alibi at all, then she probably wasn't involved."

"Reminding me of your award-winning performance in bed last night will not make me change my mind. If you could just get the goods on this suspect of yours, I'm sure he'll tell you that Francine was not involved."

Flynn conceded defeat. He would presume his client was innocent until the marshals proved otherwise. "Did you check the security videos of Manstein in the casino, like I asked you to do last night?"

Wendy stared at her husband, trying to decide if she had convinced Michael that Francine Cross was innocent. "He gave the croupier at the crap table cash in exchange for a pile of chips, but I couldn't tell if they said anything to each other."

Flynn winced. "Is that all?"

"Michael, if he was a spy, wouldn't he have been trained to avoid contacting anyone unless the security camera was pointed in another direction?" Flynn didn't respond, so Wendy said, "How about lunch today?"

"Ah . . . let me get back to you on that, Wendy. I might be busy."

Flynn broke the connection and called Joe Aguirre. Flynn could see from the display that Aguirre wasn't in his workshop in the basement. "Taking the morning off?"

"Hardly! I'm on my way to Charlie to pick up some surplus lab equipment. You wouldn't want to do me a favor for a change and help load it, would you?"

"Sorry, Joe. I'm juggling four investigations at the moment. I was just wondering if you knew if the hatches to the recycling chutes can be opened from inside the chute."

His expression revealed that Aguirre wondered why Flynn would want to open a recycling hatch from the wrong side. Joe shrugged. "Beats me. I probably have the specs on the latching mechanisms somewhere in my computer here, but why don't you ask your friend Sid Feldstein? He was crawling up and down that chute the other morning looking for evidence of where the body was dumped into it."

"Feldstein got stuck with that? He's in charge of the night shift!"

"And the marshals are investigating two murders and there are more than the usual number of drunks on the Station these days. All the deputies are pulling double shifts."

Flynn rubbed his chin. The government was facing another

huge budget deficit and Marshal Hathaway was spending money on overtime like she owned her own mint. If she didn't solve the murders quickly she was going to attract the kind of attention from Washington that would get her fired in place with no money to transport her home. "Thanks, Joe. I'll give Sid a call."

Sid was not happy to see Flynn's face on his computer display.

"Michael, old friend, you caught me at a bad time. I'm questioning a guy who has access to the place where Leron Cross was killed."

"Sorry to interrupt, Sid. One quick question and I'm out of your hair. Do you know if the hatches on the recycling chutes can be opened from inside the chutes?"

Feldstein gave an exasperated sigh. "I should have guessed. You haven't bought me a drink in six months, yet you call me up to ask a favor."

"I'm married now, Sid! I don't get out as much as I used to!"

Feldstein tapped his chest. "I've been married fourteen years, Michael, and I get out as much as I used to! Even with an eleven-year-old son!"

"Okay, Sid. Betty's Bar . . . eighteen or so?"

Feldstein made a face. "I'm running the night shift at that time!"

Flynn took a deep breath. "Then call me when you're free and I'll meet you someplace."

"That's better. Yes, you can open the hatches from inside the chute. It's an OSHA requirement. Why did you want to know?"

"Because it means that someone not authorized to be in the area where Leron Cross was killed could have gotten there through the recycling chute."

The look on Feldstein's face was worth the price of a dozen drinks. "Aw, hell. We never thought of that." Sid looked away from his computer toward someone who didn't show on Flynn's display. "Excuse me for a moment." Flynn watched the change of scenery as Feldstein stepped through a door. "You're playing a dangerous game, Mike. You made Hathaway really mad the other night when you wouldn't come in for questioning about the Cross murder. You're damn lucky that Peter Chow came in the next morning and gave us the info we wanted. Hathaway knows that you've been asking questions about both murders. She'd love it if you did something that would let her charge you with interfering with an official investigation. So far she's been unable to because you've been coming along behind us. But where the hell did you find out that the murderer got in through the recycling chute?"

"I didn't 'find out,' Sid, but it's the easiest way for Big Bill Gorkov and his thugs to have gotten in there without help from someone inside."

"Gorkov didn't do it."

"Just because no one at the Gold Dollar saw him or his thugs leave—"

"Gorkov didn't do it!" Feldstein insisted. "He was our number-one suspect—he was seen talking to Cross a couple of weeks ago. Rustin and Hathaway spent all yesterday morning investigating him. But then we got the word from Washington: Gorkov was not responsible."

Flynn squinted. "Washington, District of Columbia?" Feldstein nodded. "On planet three?" Feldstein nodded again. "Sid, how could Washington know what Gorkov was doing at the time of the murder?"

"They wouldn't tell us. We're guessing that the FBI was so annoyed when Gorkov slipped out of planet four before they could get the goods on him that they sent an agent—probably several agents; one person couldn't keep twenty-four-hour watch on Gorkov and his gang—here to keep him under surveillance."

"Why didn't they just have you guys keep an eye on him?"

"Because the FBI doesn't think anybody else can keep

suspects under proper surveillance. Hathaway is thoroughly p.o.'d that they didn't trust us to do the job. She's even more upset that they didn't inform us of what they were doing."

Flynn didn't want to believe that Gorkov hadn't killed Leron Cross—Michael had no other suspects besides his client. "I assume you've already cleared the widow," he said hopefully.

Sid hesitated. "Well, Gorkov was our primary suspect . . . She's a schoolteacher, Michael. Can you see her shoving a screwdriver three times into her husband's heart?"

"No. But she could have hired Big Bill Gorkov."

Exasperation showed on Feldstein's face. "Michael, the FBI—"

"Yeah, yeah. Any clues as to whom these FBI agents might be?"

Feldstein shook his head. "There are twenty-one thousand adults on this station. Pick three or four."

Flynn picked only one. "How about a guy with a funny accent and the name Helmuth Manstein?"

Feldstein's mouth dropped open. "Damn! If Gorkov had realized he was under surveillance . . . Where are you getting this stuff?"

"Sid, I'm not getting anything anywhere. I'm trying to come up with possible lines of investigation."

"Well, Manstein didn't hang out with any particular person or persons. You'd think that if he was FBI, he'd have associated with the other members of the surveillance team. Besides, he's been on the Station for several years. Got here way before Gorkov did."

"Maybe that means the FBI has had people out here for several years." Before Feldstein could digest that, Flynn added, "Could Gorkov be a federally protected witness?"

Sid shook his head vigorously. "The Marshals Service runs the Witness Protection Program. We would know if he was."

"You mean, you *should* know if he was. That story of Gorkov leaving Mars because the FBI was investigating him might be nothing more than his cover. Washington has a conniption whenever one of their protected witnesses goes bad. Might be easier for them to deny Gorkov's guilt than to admit they let him walk away from felony charges in exchange for testimony." Flynn left Feldstein to ponder that possibility.

The two background checks that Flynn had kept for himself were easy ones. He had the preemployment investigation done by noon and had a good start on the premarital check. He was about to call Wendy for lunch when he got an unexpected call on his computer.

"Gumshoe!" Dr. Liao's face smiled at Flynn from the display. "I hear that the Company took my advice and hired you to investigate the first murder! How's it going?"

"Oh, like most, I guess."

Liao hesitated. "I called you to ask if I could accompany you on your investigation. I would love to see a real private detective at work."

Flynn chose his words carefully. "I'm afraid I can't let you do that. I'm a *private* investigator. What I learn stays private unless my client chooses to make it public. If you accompany me, you'll learn everything I do, and the party paying my fee might not like that."

Liao lost his smile. "I understand. But I will never again have the opportunity to participate in a murder investigation. We don't have many murders in China."

Flynn raised an eyebrow. "Oh? Then why was there a mass execution of almost five hundred convicted murderers in Beijing a couple of months ago?"

Liao's face hardened. "Five hundred executions is insignificant in a country with over a billion inhabitants. Besides, some of them were rapists."

Flynn shook his head. "They must not have had the true socialist spirit." Flynn's computer beeped. "Sorry, Dr. Liao, I've got another call. I have to go."

"I wish you luck with your investigation, Gumshoe."

"Thanks, Dr. Liao. I might need it."

Flynn switched to the second call and the image of Bill Gorkov, seated in his expensive leather chair, appeared. "Mr. Flynn, are you making any progress on the Cross investigation?"

Flynn sighed. "I don't know what's happened all of a sudden. I've never had as many people interested in my work as I've had today."

"No progress, eh? How much are you willing to pay for the name of the guilty party?"

Flynn eyed the gangster. He was still Flynn's prime suspect, no matter what Sid Feldstein had said. Michael suspected that Gorkov was going to offer up a sacrificial lamb. "I think I can go two thousand without checking with my client."

Gorkov snorted. "The number I had in mind was more like twenty thousand. Cash."

Flynn wondered if Francine Cross was desperate enough to put up that much money. "You'll throw in enough evidence that the Federal attorney can get an indictment?"

"I know who did it and I know how it was done. With that as a starting point, it shouldn't take you or the marshals very long to get enough evidence to convict."

Flynn considered the implications of Gorkov's offer. It could be dangerous—*very* dangerous—but it was a chance to wrap up the Cross case almost overnight. "Okay. Where and when?"

"Twenty-thirty tonight. My office. Come alone. I don't want to get the reputation of being an informer."

Flynn shook his head. "I'm not bringing twenty thousand in cash into your office alone at any time of the day or night.

Someplace public."

Gorkov leaned back in his chair. "Then how about . . . level ten, Fifteenth and San Diego?"

The address was in a residential district; it might be nearly deserted at that time of the evening. Flynn nodded once. "Twenty-thirty, Fifteenth and San Diego, level ten. Twenty thousand in cash."

Gorkov smiled briefly, then his serious countenance returned. "Alone! If I even get the feeling that you brought someone along, the deal's off!"

"That's the deal."

"And don't tell anybody about this! I told you: I can't afford to become known as an informer!"

"Bill, I'm a *private* investigator. Don't worry. Your secret's safe with me."

Wendy wouldn't have been able to have lunch with Michael—she was invited to lunch by Ed Warshovsky.

Warshovsky had taken Wendy to lunch only once since she had come to the Station, on the day he offered her the position of director of the Legal Department, so under any circumstances the invitation would have aroused her curiosity. But since Warshovsky had accused Wendy of wasting Company funds just the day before, this invitation made her suspicious. When Warshovsky showed up with Silvanus Drake, Wendy's mood went beyond suspicious to defensive. They were going to butter her up, to try to persuade her to do something she wouldn't normally do. She resolved to resist them.

The restaurant was just down the Main Plaza from Company headquarters. Warshovsky had reserved a booth in the corner, where they would not be overheard. Silvanus Drake took a seat with his back to the wall so he could keep an eye on the other people in the restaurant. Warshovsky offered Wendy the seat next to the window and slid into the booth next to her. He flipped the switch on the edge of the table and the menu was projected onto the tabletop.

"Order whatever you want," Warshovsky said. "On me."

Wendy was not impressed. "On you, or on your expense account?"

Warshovsky glanced across the table at Drake, who didn't bother returning the glance. "I'll have a cheeseburger of real beef, with french fries," Drake said to the intercom.

"Anything to drink, sir?" the computer asked.

"Just water."

Wendy shook her head in disapproval. "You could have fresh soy protein from Satellite Kilo, and you choose to eat freeze-dried beef. I'll have the lettuce salad. Low-calorie ranch dressing. Small glass of pineapple juice."

"Steak sandwich—real steak—and a glass of beer," Warshovsky ordered. He switched off the menu. "Any legal fallout from last night's fight?"

"Nothing to worry about," Wendy assured him. "Asians don't sue people the way Americans do. I'm worried only about what Richie Soames will do when he gets out of the hospital. He is really upset that our guys lost that fight. He's talking like he wants revenge, and I'm not sure he cares which Asians he takes revenge on."

"Normally, eight of our guys could have beat up on ten Asians," Warshovsky said.

"That big Indonesian knows some karate," Drake explained. "He's the one who broke Soames's arm and the reason they won the fight."

Warshovsky scowled. "We have to clamp down on these brawls. The Asian station will be much too small to have sufficient recreational facilities. There's a lot of potential business for the Station in hosting Consortium workers, but they won't keep coming over here if they get beat on all the time."

"They will have nowhere else to go," Drake pointed out.

A robot rolled up to the booth with the food. Warshovsky passed Wendy's plate and glass to her.

"A fight in a bar is scarcely reason for us to have lunch," Wendy said. "What's this really about?"

Warshovsky looked at Drake, who picked up a french fry and bit the end off of it. "Mr. Drake has a very high opinion of your husband. I don't know why he thinks so much of him, but I trust Mr. Drake's opinions concerning security matters, so, even though your husband's service record indicates that he doesn't deal well with people in authority, I agreed to go along with this idea."

Wendy stabbed a cherry tomato with her fork. "Which is?"

"We would like to put your husband on retainer," Warshovsky said.

Wendy paused with the tomato halfway to her mouth. She looked at her boss. "Is this an attempt to stop him from working on the Manstein case?"

"I said retainer, Ms. Chadwick. We don't need him to do anything for us at the moment. I hope he'll never have to work for us. But if a special job comes up—"

Wendy ate the tomato. "Any particular 'special job' you have in mind?"

Warshovsky looked at Drake, who was devouring his cheeseburger. He lowered his voice. "If for some reason Mr. Drake is unable to continue in his position, we want Mr. Flynn to be security director."

Wendy almost dropped her fork. She stared at Warshovsky. "What about Dettweiler?"

Warshovsky didn't answer the question. Drake did. "Werner Dettweiler is a competent subordinate. He is well organized and follows orders. But he is of no more than average intelligence and lacks both imagination and initiative. If someone takes me out of the picture, Dettweiler is not the person to regain control of the situation."

Wendy's palms were suddenly moist. "Who is going to take you out of the picture? What's going on? Does this have something to do with the Manstein case or the Cross murder?"

"Your husband has been reluctant to work for the Company in the past," Drake continued. "We were hoping you could persuade him to accept this offer." He ate a french fry. "Did you know that some researchers think that soy protein is unfit for human consumption?"

Wendy looked from Drake to Warshovsky and back to Drake. "There is no way I can persuade Michael to buy this pig in a poke! Not even by performing sexual favors or by kicking him out of the bedroom altogether! You have to tell him what's going on!"

"If he has to take over Security, all will be explained to him," Drake said.

Wendy shook her head. "That's not good enough."

"The retainer is fifty thousand dollars per year," Warshovsky said. "Plus Mr. Drake's salary if he has to take Drake's place."

Wendy poked at her salad. She shook her head again, slowly. "You really don't know my husband."

"But you do," Warshovsky replied. "We're counting on you to persuade him to accept our offer. This is very important to the Company, Wendy. Please help us."

Wendy looked at Drake. "The soybeans on Satellite Delta have been genetically engineered for human consumption."

The expression on Francine Cross's face was a mixture of shock and surprise. "Twenty *thousand* dollars?"

"Think of it as eleven days of my time," Flynn said to his computer display. When Francine's expression didn't change, he added, "Can you get that much by tonight?"

Ms. Cross bit her lower lip. "You were right about the bank—they froze our joint account. We didn't check the box on the application to make it a survivor account—at the time, we weren't thinking of dying." She sighed. "But I should be able to get a loan from the Company credit union. Are you sure this informant can be trusted?"

Flynn shook his head. "I'm sure he can't, which is why I'm not going to give him the money until I've heard what he has to say."

Francine nodded once. "Okay, Mr. Flynn. I'll get the money. Do you want me to bring it to your office?"

"I might not be in my office. I'll come to your apartment."

Flynn folded his computer. As he slipped it into his pocket, he remembered Dr. Liao's call. Liao had reached him through his computer, not his phone. Flynn took his computer out of his pocket and checked his communication log. Liao's call had been placed through the computer network, not the phone network. But Liao had been on Jupiter Station. He shouldn't have been able to access the Station computer network without a Station account. Michael had just finished a background check at the old end of the Station, near the Company Operations Center, so he decided to investigate his hunch.

Missy Adamly was sitting in front of her computer, pounding furiously at the keyboard. She was wearing a tee shirt, blue shorts, and sneakers. Flynn stood in the open office doorway and said, "Casual Thursday?"

Flynn's voice startled Missy and she turned around abruptly, causing her black hair to fly away from her face. "Well, if it isn't the invisible man! Where the hell have you been?"

"Around."

"We haven't seen you anyplace in months!"

"I got married, remember? I don't get out as much as I used to."

From the expression on her face, Flynn could tell that Missy did not like to be reminded about his marriage. "Does she chain you to the furniture?"

Flynn shook his head. "Nothing so kinky. You were working pretty hard there a moment ago. Why do computer professionals insist on using keyboards instead of menus or voice activation?"

Missy rolled her eyes. "Because if you know the commands the keyboard is faster, and this is a big Security flap. Silvanus Drake had a brain glitch and got the idea that someone has hacked into the security videos. We have to check the entire system—including the video records—for signs of tampering."

"Why can't Drake's programmers do that?"

"Because it has to be done by yesterday, and there aren't enough of them."

Flynn nodded. "I was wondering if you could do me a favor—"

Missy glanced at the painting on the wall to Flynn's left. Flynn knew that Drake had installed a microcam there. Missy decided that she didn't care if Drake knew what she was about to say. "You marry that long-legged redhead, and still expect me to do you a favor?"

Flynn had several arguments that he could use in reply. He selected the one that had worked for him before. "Missy, did you or did you not marry Jack six months before I even met Wendy? In a ceremony to which I was not invited. We invited you and Jack to our wedding." He knew he'd won, so he added, "I just need to know if Dr. Liao Chu has an account on our computer network."

Missy glanced at the painting again, then back at Flynn, as if to ask him if he really wanted her to get into trouble.

"I'm working for the Company on an investigation," Flynn said. He took the letter Wendy had written and handed it to Missy.

Missy skimmed the letter, then read it carefully. "Your *wife* hired you?"

Flynn shrugged. "She wanted the best investigator on the Station."

Missy brandished the letter. "This only gives you access to Company premises, not to our computer files."

"And to interview Company employees on Company time." Missy wasn't convinced. "Go ahead and call the Legal Department. Wendy will tell you it's okay." Wendy might have done nothing of the sort, but Flynn knew that Wendy was one of the last people in the solar system Missy wanted to talk to.

Missy hesitated, then turned back to her terminal. She typed a string of commands, read the response on her display, and shook her head. "Nope. No account for Dr. Liao." She turned back to Flynn.

"Then how could he contact me via computer if he's somewhere on the Station?"

Missy made a face. "Is that all you wanted to know? General delivery."

"Huh?"

"It's a service for transients. You can log into general delivery without an account, place video calls, surf the Station Web . . . if you come out here on business, you can send and receive e-mails via general delivery."

"What keeps other people from accessing your general delivery e-mail if you don't have a separate account?"

"Message encryption, in a cipher known only to you and the people sending you messages, or public-key encryption."

Flynn grunted. "I learn something new every day." He had another pertinent thought. "Did Helmuth Manstein have a network account?"

Missy stared at Flynn from beneath lowered eyebrows. "The guy they found in the recycling bin with his head caved in? Is that what you're investigating? What the hell does he have to do with Dr. Liao?"

Flynn leaned against the door jamb. "That's what I'm trying to find out."

"Well, the marshals already asked that. No, he didn't. The name Helmuth Manstein was nowhere in our records."

"So, if he had been sending and receiving e-mails, it would have been through general delivery?"

Missy nodded. "Every other account corresponds to a known Station resident. But the e-mail logs show nothing under his name."

Flynn tapped his chin with his index finger. "Could you check for general-delivery e-mails—incoming and outgoing—under any name that doesn't exist anywhere else in Station records?"

Missy leaned back in her chair. "You mean, like he was using an alias?"

"Manstein was probably an alias. He might have been getting e-mail under his real name."

"A search like that will give a lot of false positives," Missy warned. "You should see some of the names that hotel guests get e-mail under."

"Limit the search to the month before he died."

"We only save e-mail logs for two weeks."

Flynn shrugged. "Even less work for you."

Missy started to turn toward her computer, stopped, and looked at Flynn. "I can't do it right now. I *have* to finish this system check for Security."

"Any time in the next day or two will be fine. And I'll give Jack a call. It's about time we got together again."

Chapter 8

The computer displayed an unusually somber image of Flynn's wife. "When will you be home?" she asked.

"Probably sometime tomorrow," Flynn complained. "I can't get any investigating done. People keep calling me."

"We have to talk. Soon."

Flynn took note of Wendy's countenance. "What's wrong?"

"I don't want to discuss it on the network."

"Network transmissions are encrypted."

"By the people I don't want to overhear us!"

Before Flynn could respond, his computer beeped at him. He clenched his teeth. "Hold on, Wendy, somebody else is after me."

The somebody else was Russ Murrow. "Hey, Flynn! They finally fixed my ship! Found a small metal flake across a valve throat—valve checked out okay, but the gas wouldn't get through. Ready for that ride? It will be a short one—I have to bring the ship in after an hour so the techs can make sure nothing they worked on is coming loose."

Michael hesitated, then cocked his head. "Will that ship of yours hold two passengers?"

Murrow's eyebrows drew together. "One of 'em would have to squeeze behind the seats."

"I'm an expert squeezer."

Murrow nodded. "I go on shift at sixteen-thirty. Meet me at the locker room. Who else is going?"

"The head of the Legal Department. See you in . . . an hour and a half."

Michael switched back to his wife. "Ever been for a ride on a round-up ship?"

Wendy was not enthralled by the suggestion. "No. Why would I want to? Why would *you* want to?"

"Because the ships dock where Leron Cross was killed. I'll meet you there at sixteen-thirty."

"Michael, cowboys do eight-hour shifts! We'll be out there till midnight!"

Flynn shook his head. "He's working a split shift today. We'll be back in an hour. And then, we can talk."

Flynn had time to finish the premarital check, time to call Peter Chow and give him a new assignment, and time to call Jack Adamly and arrange to meet him that evening, before he headed for the cowboy docking area. He arrived five minutes early and was annoyed that Wendy wasn't waiting for him at the locked door. Then the door was opened from the inside and Wendy poked her head through.

"Ah! There you are!" she said. "I was beginning to think that you were going to be late."

Flynn made a show of consulting his wristwatch. "I'm five minutes early."

Wendy held the door open for Flynn to enter. Russ Murrow was standing there, too. "Normally, I wouldn't take a lawyer out in my ship," he said, "unless I was planning to jettison her on a collision course with Io. But redheaded lawyers are reputed to bring good luck."

Murrow's attempt at charm did not impress Wendy. "Reputed by whom?"

Murrow grinned. "By me! Come on. Let's get the two of you into your suits." He led the way to the women's locker room. "There shouldn't be any ladies in there this afternoon, but why don't you check to make sure before I go in?"

The locker room was empty. Murrow walked to a rack of spare pressure suits on the far wall and selected a suit that looked like it would fit Wendy. The suit was white to reflect light—even at Jupiter, direct sunlight was harsh—and thick with radiation shielding, but its controls were standard and Wendy had worn pressure suits before. Murrow made certain the suit had sealed and was working properly before he led Flynn into the men's locker room and picked out a pressure suit for him. Flynn had long legs but a short torso and he knew that only a custom suit would fit him well. The suit that he pulled on smelled faintly of the last person to wear it and pressed uncomfortably against the stun pistol in his pocket. He closed the faceplate and made sure the suit was airtight and had a full supply of oxygen.

Flynn waddled after Murrow and Wendy to the airlock. Wendy's suit fit better than Flynn's did, or maybe Wendy could move gracefully even in a pressure suit. The airlock leading to Murrow's ship was barely big enough for the three of them. Flynn had to close and secure the inner door. The ship was pressurized; Murrow didn't have to pump down the airlock. He opened the outer door and led the way aboard. He used an overhead handhold to hoist himself over the back of the left seat, then helped Wendy do the same in the right seat. He watched Flynn close and secure the hatch, thick with radiation-absorbing material, then opened his faceplate. "Ship's pressurized." Murrow's voice was crystal-clear in the headphones in Flynn's helmet. "Breathe the ship's air while you can and save your suits' supplies for emergencies. Your faceplates should close automatically if a meteorite pokes a hole in the cabin." He showed his guests how to plug into the ship's communication and air supply. "Even if the cabin's holed, it's best to save your suit supply," he explained.

"Are we breathing air or oxygen?" Flynn asked.

"Air from the ship. Almost anything will burn in a pure oh-two environment. But your suit's supply is oxygen—its storage capacity is limited, so none of it is wasted on gases you don't need to live."

Murrow and Wendy strapped themselves into their seats. Flynn wedged himself between the seats and the aft bulkhead. The forward viewports were large but were made of dense, transparent ceramic to reduce the radiation reaching the crew. Through them Michael could see the end of the Station and the rotating star field. In front of Murrow's ship another vessel was docked. It was five meters long, with a circular cross section almost three meters in diameter. Boots from a pressure suit protruded from alongside its engine nozzle.

"Somebody else have trouble with his ship today?" Flynn asked.

Murrow looked up from his preflight checklist. "Uh-uh. Scheduled maintenance."

"That wouldn't be Stan Grunemeyer, would it?"

Murrow nodded, the gesture going unseen within his pressure helmet. "Ah-huh."

"How did he get out there?"

Murrow pointed up and to his left. "There's an access hatch to a catwalk above the ships."

"Wouldn't a catwalk below the ships be more convenient?" Wendy asked.

"Not when we launch." Murrow had completed his checklist. A heads-up display was projected on the viewport in front of him. "Reactor starting . . . now. Goody. Uncoupling from the airlock . . ." Flynn heard a metallic clank. "All set. Ah, don't talk while I'm transmitting; the transmitter input is taken off the intercom. Cowboy Control? Cowboy One Four ready to launch."

"Cowboy One Four, you set the right squawk code this time?"

"Yes, Control, I set the right squawk code! Dammit, that was two months ago! When are you guys going to forget about it?"

"We could forget about it right now if we knew you weren't going to. One Four, cleared to launch."

"Thanks, Control. One Four launching." Murrow turned toward Wendy. "Ready? Here we go!"

Murrow pushed the launch button and the ship disengaged from its trapeze. The rotation of the Station flung the ship away from Jupiter; to the ship's occupants it felt like they were in free fall. From level one they didn't have far to fall before they cleared the Station, and suddenly nothing showed through the viewports except the distant stars.

"Cowboy One Four, your first rock is bauxite."

"Ah, roger, Control. I got its ephemeris." Murrow punched a button on a panel marked *Autopilot.* Flynn heard the maneuvering thrusters fire and the star field slid across the viewports from right to left. Then the main engine fired and Flynn felt himself pushed against the rear bulkhead.

When the Station had begun mining operations, cowboys had operated the ships that roamed the radiation belts close to Jupiter, rounding up ore-bearing rocks from the planet's sparse rings and launching them into orbits toward the Station. Those ships had since been automated, saving the cowboys from exposure to radiation levels that had limited their careers to two years. Cowboys still manned the ships that met the rocks at the Station because a living, thinking pilot provided an extra margin of safety as the rocks were maneuvered into the smelters. The Station's orbital radius, the thick hulls of the ships, and the heavy pressure suits reduced radiation exposure to a level within OSHA regulations for lifetime employment. The cowboys endured rumors that advances in robotics would soon make human pilots unnecessary around the Station and that the

Company would let their contracts expire.

Murrow's ship dropped behind the Station. A robotic cargo ship, its slow journey from the inner solar system at an end, followed the Station by half a kilometer. Cargo shuttles plied between it and the Station. Murrow's main engine fired again, driving the ship below the Station. The rocks flung out from the radiation belts were on paths that peaked just beneath the Station's altitude—a safety precaution in case one wasn't intercepted in time. The rock Murrow was chasing was undetectable against the backdrop of stars.

"I don't see the rock," Wendy said.

"Oh, sorry." Murrow flipped a switch and another heads-up display was projected onto the viewport in front of Wendy. "It's centered in that circle there."

Wendy leaned forward and squinted. "I still don't see it." Flynn couldn't see it, either.

"They're hard to spot with untrained eyes." Murrow pointed to the radar display. "It's right in front of us, about two hundred meters, and slightly above."

Suddenly, there was the rock, a pitted, dark-gray object the size of a dump truck, tumbling slowly. The ship's computer fired the maneuvering thrusters and the ship closed on the rock. To Flynn, it looked like the rock was coming at the ship, and would crash through the forward viewports. Murrow kept his hands on the controls, ready to take over from the computer if an emergency developed. The forward thrusters fired to slow the ship. An invisible hand pushed Flynn against the back of the seats. The grappling arms on the front of the ship opened, and just as the nose of the ship was about to hit the rock the arms clamped shut. The tumbling rock tried to tip the ship; thrusters fired again, stabilizing it.

"Control, Cowboy One Four's got a load."

"Roger that. You're first in line for Echo."

The main engine fired and the ship, still controlled by its autopilot, headed for the aluminum smelter on Satellite Echo. The Station passed overhead, and four of its satellites, and then Murrow, Wendy, and Michael were staring into the open maw of the smelter on the axis of Echo. The satellite was rotating slowly, just fast enough to create sufficient gravity to keep molten aluminum under control. As the ship neared Echo, the rate of closure seemed to increase. Flynn knew that was an optical illusion, but he found himself gripping the backs of the seats in front of him and almost breathed a sigh of relief when the forward thrusters fired.

Flynn heard a warning beep in his headphones and a red light began flashing on the heads-up display.

"Dammit to hell!" Murrow said. He assumed manual control. At least, he tried to.

"What's wrong?" Wendy said.

"Forward thrusters crapped out again! Close your faceplates!"

Traffic Control knew there was a problem from the ship's telemetry. "Cowboy One Four, I'm showing a forward-thruster failure."

Satellite Echo loomed in the forward viewports. "I know! I know! Stand by!" Murrow tried to turn the ship but only the aft thrusters responded. The satellite began drifting to the left, slowly because the rock had increased the ship's moment of inertia and the forward thrusters weren't functioning. "Come on, baby," he pleaded.

Unsolicited advice came through the headsets. "Dump the rock, Russ!"

"I'm too fast! It'll go right through the satellite!"

Flynn knew that alarms were ringing on Echo. Wendy braced her arms against the control panel.

The thrusters kept firing. Satellite Echo seemed to be rushing toward the ship. But the bow of the ship was no longer pointing at the satellite. Murrow fired the main engine. He leaned forward, against the engine thrust, to keep an eye on the satellite through the corner of the viewport. The maneuvering thrusters kept firing and the ship's rotation rate increased. "Come on, come on . . ."

Flynn couldn't see the satellite from his position behind the seats. He wanted to climb on top of Wendy and shield her from the imminent crash, but the right side of his brain was still working and it convinced him that Murrow could do without the distraction of a pressure-suited body climbing into the front seats at that moment. Michael crouched behind the seats, bracing himself as best he could. He couldn't help Wendy after the crash if he didn't survive it.

"Cowboy One Four, you're clear. Dump the rock and come back to the barn."

Flynn peeked over the seats, between Murrow and Wendy. Nothing showed in the viewports but stars.

"Control, I can get it in without the forward thrusters."

"One Four, you know the regs: no forward thrusters, no deliveries. Dump the rock; we'll send Cowboy Six after it. Show us what a great pilot you are by docking safely without the thrusters."

"We already have one ship down for maintenance!"

"Now you'll have two. Lots of overtime for the techs. Maybe they'll buy you a beer out of gratitude."

Murrow muttered some dirty words, but he released the rock and stabilized the ship. "Damned technicians. Did a piss-poor job of fixing the ship last night; now they're going to get paid more to fix it again. Whoever signed off on this job needs to be roasted slowly over a smelter until the fat is melted out of his butt."

"The legality of that suggestion is dubious." Wendy didn't sound like a female frightened into helplessness by staring death in the face. "You might as well chuck him—or her, as the case might be—right into the smelter."

Murrow roared with laughter. "All right! Mrs. Flynn, you can ride with me any time!"

"It's Ms. Chadwick, and I've had enough excitement to last awhile."

"You're going to have more," Flynn warned, remembering that cowboy Jonny had had trouble docking the same ship when the thrusters had failed the day before. "Can you dock this ship without the forward thrusters?"

"Piece o' cake," Murrow answered, without the enthusiasm with which he had been laughing.

They were in luck: The axis of the Station was parallel to its orbit, the easiest docking situation. Murrow maneuvered alongside the Station and matched orbital velocity with it. Then he turned the ship toward the Station and fired the main engine to bring his transverse velocity up to the speed of the docks on level one, which were rotating with the Station. The ship's orbital velocity kept it safely ahead of the Station, but Flynn could see that it wasn't moving fast enough transversely. Murrow, lining up the first empty dock in his heads-up display, fired the main engine again. The ship accelerated, its docking latch locked onto the trapeze, and the engine stopped. "Cowboy Control, One Four is docked."

"Roger docked."

Murrow leaned back in his seat. "Told you, piece o' cake." He threw the switch to couple the ship's airlock to the Station's, then opened the faceplate on his helmet. He twisted in his seat and grinned at Flynn. There were beads of perspiration on his forehead. "Want to let us out?"

Stan Grunemeyer and Murrow's supervisor were waiting just inside the airlock. The supervisor was short, overweight, and not wearing Company coveralls. The ID badge on his white shirt bore the name Jerry Paloukis. He stared incredulously at Flynn and Wendy. "You had unauthorized passengers?"

"I authorized it," Wendy said.

Paloukis put his hands on his hips. "And just who the hell—Ms. Chadwick?"

"Can you really fix it this time?" Murrow said to Grunemeyer.

"I fixed it last time!"

Murrow disagreed, and the pair started arguing. Paloukis joined in, not helping the situation. Flynn tapped Wendy's arm to get her attention, then led her down the corridor past the airlocks.

"Where are we going?" Wendy asked.

Flynn nodded toward the stairs at the end of the corridor. "Bet that leads to the catwalk above the ships."

It did indeed. Michael and Wendy stepped into the airlock, closed their faceplates, and pumped the pressure down to vacuum. Flynn opened the outer hatch and stepped out.

The Station was on the sun side of Jupiter and the satellites gleamed in the light. The star field was moving—Flynn's frame of reference was fixed to the Station and to his mind the entire universe was revolving about him. The catwalk was a steel grating and Flynn could look straight down. As he did so Jupiter passed beneath his feet.

"Ah, Michael, I should tell you . . ." Wendy swallowed. "I have a thing about heights."

Flynn stared at his wife. She had had a sheltered childhood that could not possibly have prepared her to face death in an out-of-control spaceship, but seemed unperturbed by her brush with eternity. It was the relatively safe prospect of having nothing but a railing between her and a long fall to nowhere that made her uneasy. "Don't let it bother you. Falling never hurt anyone—it's the abrupt stop at the end that does the damage.

They'll come and pick us up before we run into anything."

"If they can find us."

"These suits have transponders." Flynn turned and looked at the hatch from which he had exited. He nodded. "Just as I suspected. Unlocked."

"All airlocks through the hull are unlocked. It's a safety precaution, so people can get back into atmosphere."

Flynn looked up at the towering wall that was the end of the Station. That close to such a massive structure, Flynn thought that he should hear or feel something—the rumble of ventilating fans, the vibration of machinery—that would convey power and vitality. But there was only the soft hiss of his suit's life support system. Five hundred meters above, a work boat exited its dock in the Station's hub and twisted about. Flynn could see the jets from its thrusters but no sound reached through the vacuum to his ears. The boat headed for the satellites. "It also allowed Leron Cross's murderer to enter what was supposed to be a secured work area without authorization."

Wendy squinted at her husband through the faceplate of her suit. "Is that how he got in? You said he climbed in through the recycling chute."

"This is another possibility."

Wendy shook her head. "Every time an external airlock is accessed, that fact is displayed in Security Control."

Flynn looked along the catwalk. Just beneath it were the trapezes to which the cowboy ships docked. Murrow's ship hung from one thirty meters away. "Technicians come out here all the time to service ships. I doubt Security Control gives it a thought when this particular airlock is used."

"But it will be in the Security log."

"There will be a lot of entries concerning this airlock in the Security log. Of greater interest will be the entry for the airlock through which the murderer left the Station to climb down here."

Wendy carefully braced herself against the catwalk's guardrail, then leaned back to look up at the Station. "There can't be many people on the Station capable of doing that."

"It only takes one. Come on. Let's go back in."

Wendy stared at him. "Is this all you wanted to see? I could have told you that this hatch was unlocked!"

Flynn had wondered how his wife would take revenge for being subjected to a near disaster. "Leron Cross was a cowboy. The motive for his murder might have had something to do with his job. I had to see what cowboys do."

"They round up rocks!"

"What if a cowboy also rounded up contraband?"

"Security scanners would spot it when he came back aboard."

"You mean, all of these airlocks—"

"Silvanus Drake leaves no entrances to the Station unguarded."

Flynn shrugged. He let Wendy enter the airlock in front of him.

Murrow, Grunemeyer, and Paloukis were still arguing. "I just want to get back in space!" Murrow complained. "I don't fly, I don't get paid! How long can it take to get at that valve?"

Grunemeyer shrugged. "Two hours, if I get help. But if the valve has the same problem—"

"Of course the valve has the same problem!" Murrow's temper was stretched to the limit. "Haven't you heard a word I've said? It's exactly the same symptom that Jonny Duncan had in that ship yesterday!"

Grunemeyer took a deep breath. "If the valve has the same problem, I'm not signing off on the repair! We've never seen plating flakes foul a valve before! Something is causing the plating to flake off the inside of those gas lines! We need somebody from Engineering to take a look at it!"

"He's right," Paloukis agreed.

Murrow clenched his fists. "Engineering will 'look at it' for weeks!"

"I'll get you another ship to fly," Paloukis promised.

"We'll be going now," Flynn interrupted. "Thanks for the ride."

"Yeah. Sorry for the excitement," Murrow said.

Michael and Wendy climbed to level four, where Sacramento Avenue had a moving sidewalk that they could ride to the other end of the Station. Wendy told her husband about her lunch with Warshovsky and Drake. Flynn stared straight ahead, eyes narrowed, lips pressed together. "If I'm retained by the Company, can I legally investigate the Company?"

"Not if you're working for someone else, unless you return the retainer before undertaking the investigation. But," Wendy added with a grin, "you *can* investigate the Company if you're employed by them."

Flynn had been hired by Wendy with Company funds, so he was working for Conglomerated. "Then this can't be an attempt to get me off either investigation."

"I know," Wendy agreed. "And if Drake really thinks his life is in danger . . . What the hell is going on, Michael?"

"Whatever Helmuth Manstein, Leron Cross, Dr. Liao, and Bill Gorkov have in common. That's what's going on."

Wendy looked at him out of the corner of her eye. "You think the two murders are related?"

Flynn nodded. "Yep."

"What does Liao have to do with it?"

Michael shrugged. "If I knew that, I'd probably know everything. He tried to invite himself along on the Manstein investigation today. He's very curious about who killed Helmuth."

"Is he curious about Cross?"

Flynn shook his head. "He doesn't know that Cross and Manstein are connected."

Wendy looked at her watch. "How about dinner? There's a restaurant just around the corner down here." She gestured at the cross corridor that was Sixth Street.

Flynn shook his head. "Sorry, lover, but I don't have the time today. I have to get over to Francine Cross's and pick up twenty thousand dollars in cash."

"Twenty *thousand?* What for?"

"If all goes according to plan, in a couple of hours I'll trade it to Big Bill Gorkov for the name of Leron's killer."

Chapter 9

The gravity on level ten was three percent lower than Earth normal. It gave Flynn an extra spring in his step, even after twenty o'clock after a long day. He walked along San Diego Avenue and turned onto Fifteenth Street. Its cream-colored and undecorated walls were spaced just wide enough for two electric cars abreast. Apartment doors opened directly onto the street. The lighting had dimmed to simulate evening. The scene was quiet. Flynn guessed the area was one of the child-free zones that the Company reserved for residents who didn't like noise.

There was no security camera. Flynn had not expected one.

Pierre Lavalle and Weasel entered Fifteenth Street from Portland Avenue and walked toward Flynn. Both were attired in the yellow coveralls, complete with shoulder patches bearing the logo of Conglomerated Mining and Manufacturing, worn by Company technicians. Bill Gorkov was nowhere to be seen. Neither was Knuckles DiGeorgio.

Flynn stopped walking. Weasel and Lavalle approached to within three meters and stopped, too.

"You guys get new jobs?" Flynn asked.

Lavalle fingered his coveralls where he had left the zipper open below his throat. "These are wonderful duds. Almost impossible to stain, easy to keep clean. You should try a pair."

"Where's your boss?"

"Busy elsewhere," Lavalle said. "Where's the money?"

"Like your boss—elsewhere. Until you've given me the

information. If it sounds reasonable, you get the money. If it sounds fishy, I check it out first, and then, if it's true, you get the money."

Weasel laughed—a high, shrill, giggle—and almost doubled over. "What a sense of humor!" He forced himself to stand upright but had trouble maintaining his composure. He slapped his companion on the back. "Ain't that the funniest joke you've heard in months, Pierre? He thinks we're going to give him the info before he pays us!"

Flynn said, "I *know* you're going to give me the info before I pay you."

Lavalle stared at the investigator from beneath half-closed eyelids. "Then we don't have a deal. What guarantee do we have that you'd pay up?"

Flynn tried to look incredulous. "You guys are professional collectors! How the hell could I *avoid* paying up?"

Weasel poked Lavalle in the ribs, to Pierre's annoyance. "I bet he's got it on him," Weasel said. "I say we take it and forget about giving him what he wants."

Lavalle's expression suddenly changed. So did Weasel's. "Look out!" Lavalle shouted.

Flynn didn't turn to see what was behind him—Marines were trained to trust their comrades to do their duty. He didn't see Jack Adamly grab Knuckles's arm just before DiGeorgio slammed a hammer into the back of Flynn's head. Knuckles hadn't expected interference and hadn't heard Adamly tip-toe up behind him. He recovered quickly from his surprise, though, and spun around to jab his left fist three times in rapid succession into Adamly's midsection. Knuckles had broad shoulders and most of that breadth was muscle. Lesser men would have been felled by one such punch, but Jack, who was twenty centimeters taller than Knuckles, still had the physique of a Force Recon sergeant. He groaned and almost doubled over, but he absorbed the blows and pulled his massive fist back behind his ear. DiGeorgio was so amazed that his jabs hadn't flattened Adamly that he did nothing but stare as Jack's fist gathered speed. Knuckles got his nose broken again.

Weasel had seen enough. He turned and headed for Portland Avenue as fast as his legs would carry him, which was close to Olympic speed when he was frightened. Lavalle, acting on reason rather than instinct, realized that the plan had failed and turned to follow Weasel.

"I'll get him!" Pete Chow shouted as he dashed past Flynn. Chow really did know karate: His flying kick hit Lavalle in the kidneys and sent him sprawling on the street. Chow leaped on his quarry and twisted his arm behind his head.

Flynn turned to see how Adamly was doing, but Jack needed no help. His blow had knocked Knuckles against the wall, and DiGeorgio was slumped on the street, blood streaming from his broken nose. Jack was holding his left arm across his stomach.

"You okay?" Flynn asked.

Jack nodded. "Yeah. I'll live." He looked at Knuckles. "He packs quite a punch. Now I see why you thought you'd need help."

Knuckles had dropped his hammer. Flynn picked it up with his handkerchief to avoid smudging any fingerprints, even though Knuckles was wearing gloves. He slipped the hammer into his coat pocket. "Come on." He walked to where Chow had Lavalle pinned to the street. From the look on Pierre's face Flynn could tell that Chow was twisting his arm very hard.

"He keeps trying to squirm away," Chow said.

"He's not going anywhere now." Flynn jerked his thumb at DiGeorgio. "Go keep an eye on Knuckles. If he tries to get up, break his nose again."

"Right, Mike."

Flynn and Adamly stood on either side of Lavalle, who rolled onto his back and stared up at the pair.

"What do you want to do with him?" Adamly asked.

"Marine interrogation technique number five." Flynn reached down and seized Pierre's left arm. "Grab his other arm."

They dragged Lavalle to the wall, where a hatch to a recycling chute was conveniently located. Flynn opened the hatch. Jack grabbed Lavalle's legs and boosted him, head first, into the open hatch, holding onto his legs so that he didn't fall ten levels to the recycling bin in the basement.

"Hey!" Lavalle protested. "What are you guys doing?"

"Having a polite conversation," Flynn said. "Pierre, why did your boss have Knuckles switch off Manstein and Cross?"

"Get me out of here!"

"Manstein was dead before you dumped him down the recycling chute. You were going to chuck Leron Cross down a chute, too—there was one right next to where his body was discovered, but it was filled with trash. And now there's a recycling hatch right next to where your boss wanted to meet me. I get the impression that Big Bill wanted me to wind up like Manstein and Cross."

"We didn't kill anybody!"

Jack said, "You know, this isn't a very good way to interrogate people. During the drug wars, I heard of guys who held out so long that the people holding 'em got tired and let 'em slip." He shook his head. "After a guy's fallen a thousand meters from a helicopter, there's not a whole lot left to interrogate." He let Pierre slide another ten centimeters into the chute to emphasize the point.

"Help!" Pierre bellowed.

Flynn winced. "Ooh! He said a dirty word!"

There was no security camera on that stretch of Fifteenth Street, but Pierre's cry must have reached one someplace, and "help" was one of the words that would draw an automatic response from Security Control. Either security guards or marshals were probably on the way.

"Pull him up," Flynn said reluctantly. "Marshal Hathaway will have the fun of interrogating him."

An apartment door slid open, revealing a man in his underwear. He had a pot belly and needed a shave. "This is supposed to be a quiet zone! What the hell is going on out here?"

The interrogation room in the Marshals Office was a bright, cheerful place, with a large table surrounded by comfortable chairs. Michael Flynn sat in one, flanked by Jack Adamly on his left and Peter Chow on his right. Flynn's computer—which, with its legal software, was acting as his attorney—was open on the table in front of him. Across the table sat Marshal Hathaway and her chief deputy, Herb Rustin. Rustin looked bored. Hathaway was bristling.

"There are serious discrepancies between your written statements and what Lavalle's been telling us," the marshal said.

Flynn tried to look as bored as the deputy. "You'd expect a man with a felony conviction for assault and too many arrests to count to tell the truth?"

Hathaway drummed the eraser of her pencil on the table. "You claim they started the fight by assaulting you, but Lavalle's got a strained arm and DiGeorgio's in the hospital with a badly broken nose and a concussion, while the three of you sit here none the worse for wear."

Adamly's mustache quivered. He pulled up his shirt, revealing the dark bruises on his abdomen. "What the hell do you call this?" he growled.

Hathaway looked at the bruises and changed her argument. "The evidence report does not list the twenty thousand dollars you claim they were trying to steal."

Flynn rolled his eyes. "I didn't say I had twenty thousand on me. I said that they *thought* I had twenty thousand with me."

"Yes, yes, because you claim you were going to buy from them the name of Leron Cross's murderer."

"No," Flynn corrected, "I was going to buy from Bill Gorkov the name of Cross's murderer."

"Gorkov wasn't there," the marshal said.

"No, he wasn't," Flynn admitted. "The bastard lied to me."

Rustin chuckled. Hathaway gave him a warning glance. "DiGeorgio's fingerprints aren't on that hammer you gave us," she continued.

"The Company security guards will vouch for the fact that he was wearing gloves. He's a professional thug. He knows better than to leave fingerprints on a murder weapon."

"We have only your word that DiGeorgio was trying to kill you."

Flynn glanced from side to side. "Actually, you have Jack's and Pete's word that he was trying to kill me. I didn't actually see the attempt—Knuckles was behind me."

"Adamly has five arrests for brawling," Hathaway said, as though that made him a liar.

Jack leaned forward, giving Hathaway a close look at his moustache. "Those were fair fights! And I was only convicted twice—both misdemeanors!"

"Convicted because you threw the first punch," Hathaway pointed out.

Flynn sighed. "Marshal, do you think Knuckles could have left those bruises on Jack's stomach *after* Jack improved the appearance of his face?"

Hathaway scowled. Rustin barely suppressed a smile.

"Lavalle claims you tried to dump him down a recycling chute," the marshal said.

Flynn was running out of patience. "We came here to press

charges against the people who assaulted *us,* and you charge us with assaulting *them.*"

"It's Lavalle's voice calling for help on the Security recording!"

"He was losing the fight," Chow chimed in, trying to contribute to the conversation. "What would you say if you were losing a fight?"

Hathaway rested her elbows on the table. She smiled. "Why would a mugger call the cops for help?"

The door opened and U.S. Attorney Kyle Pierce entered the room. Wendy Chadwick was right behind him.

"We don't need you yet," Hathaway said. "We're not quite ready to charge these bozos."

Flynn raised an eyebrow. "Charge us with what? Self-defense in the first degree?" He looked at his wife. "Thanks, Wendy, but I don't need you." He nodded at his computer. "I have my usual attorney."

Wendy looked sadly at the computer. "I know. I'm not here to represent you. I'm here to represent him." She looked at Adamly.

Jack frowned. "Where's Mr. Habruch? He always defended me before."

"I'm Mr. Habruch's boss. I pulled rank on him." Wendy looked at the marshal. "Since you haven't charged my client, he and I will leave now."

Hathaway stood up. She was shorter than Wendy but had a much more powerful build. Her jaw jutted out. "Push me like that and I will charge him!"

U.S. Attorney Pierce looked amused. "Self-defense in the first degree isn't listed in the U.S. Criminal Code."

Hathaway stabbed her finger at the three men sitting on the other side of the table. "They held Lavalle head first down a recycling chute!"

"None of them has a felony record," Pierce said. "Lavalle does. DiGeorgio isn't up to talking yet, but the doctors say he was only hit once, so he must have hit Adamly before Adamly hit him. You still haven't found Hector Rivera, so we can't get his version of the event, but he also has a felony record and a psych evaluation as a pathological liar. I'd believe him even less than I believe Lavalle. You have three honest citizens with one version of events, and you choose to believe a convicted felon."

"They were trying to get him to confess to murder! How would Lavalle have concocted a story like that? He didn't kill Cross!"

Flynn slouched in his chair. "Yeah, yeah, because Washington says Gorkov wasn't involved. When did Washington get telescopes that can see what's going on all the way out here, right through the steel walls of the Station?" He shook his head. "Forget what Washington says. I shouldn't have to point out the obvious to you, but Manstein was struck three times with a tool—a wrench—in a location where there was no security camera, and his body was chucked down a recycling chute. Leron Cross was stabbed three times with a tool—a screwdriver—also where there was no security camera, and his body was found right next to a recycling chute. Tonight, Knuckles DiGeorgio was about to hit me over the head with a tool—a hammer—right next to a recycling chute where there is no security camera. When Jack interrupted him, Knuckles hit him three times in the stomach. Knuckles is a creature of habit—he always hits his victims three times. And Manstein's name still hasn't been released to the press, but when I mentioned him Lavalle didn't say, 'Who?' Finally, Knuckles, Lavalle, and Weasel were all wearing Company coveralls tonight. Three men in Company coveralls and carrying tools are not going to attract attention anywhere on the Station. They're your killers. You have Lavalle and Knuckles in custody—make them an offer they can't refuse and they'll rat on their boss."

Pierce blinked. "I don't have the evidence to charge Lavalle with anything at all, not even conspiracy. I can't get DiGeorgio for attempted murder—we have no idea how hard he was intending to hit you. But I can get him for aggravated assault."

Flynn clenched his teeth and slammed the palm of his right hand onto the table, bouncing his computer into the air. "Assault, hell! You can get all three of them—four, counting Gorkov—for murder!"

Pierce shook his head. "I'll look like an idiot when an FBI agent comes forward to testify in their defense."

Flynn took a deep breath, unsuccessfully trying to calm himself. "At the very least you can charge them with attempted armed robbery!"

Pierce's black eyebrows rose. "For trying to steal twenty thousand dollars that you didn't have?"

"Weasel said he thought I had it with me!" But that didn't make Pierce change his mind. Flynn slumped in his chair in disgust. "What about the coveralls they were wearing? The Company *gives* those to its employees; they aren't sold to anybody. Those thugs probably stole 'em. And I'm willing to bet that Knuckles didn't get that hammer at Jeffrey's True Value."

Pierce nodded. "Okay, if it will make you happy, I'll charge all three of them with misdemeanor theft." He turned to Hathaway. "Unless you can get a believable witness against these guys, kick them loose before Ms. Chadwick decides to sue you for false arrest."

Hathaway put her hands on her hips. "There *is* a witness—a man who lives on Fifteenth Street! I'll get him in here!"

Pierce didn't think that was a good idea. "I'll also look like an idiot if I prosecute these three—one of whom is at the top of the Station's list of heroes—for assaulting a convicted felon who the jury will wish *had* been dropped down the recycling chute.

We can't impanel a jury on the Station that will convict them. So kick them loose. We'll get DiGeorgio for assault and Gorkov will be down to two thugs. Maybe he'll take the hint and leave."

The marshal gave Pierce an icy stare. "Fat lot of help you are! No wonder law enforcement is such an uphill battle out here!" She looked at her three suspects. "What I wouldn't give to get the three of you on a thought-pattern analyzer!"

Flynn flashed a smile. "But you don't have a thought-pattern analyzer." He folded his computer and stood up. "Probably just as well—some scientists now think that they aren't nearly as accurate as originally claimed." Michael slipped the computer into his pocket and headed for the door.

"I'm going to talk to that witness, Flynn! We'll see who's smiling then!"

Michael held the door open for Adamly, Chow, and his wife. Right outside Hathaway's office stood Missy Adamly, wearing a Company tee shirt and shorts brief enough to display almost all of her legs. She hurried to her husband. "Are you okay?"

"I'm fine." Jack lifted his shirt. "Just a few bruises."

Missy stepped back and looked at the bruises, which were turning from red to purple. Then she glared at Flynn. "When you said you were going to get together with Jack tonight, I didn't know you were going to get him into a fight!"

Flynn shrugged. "I didn't know, either. I only suspected that there *might* be one."

Missy gingerly touched her husband's bruises. "Come on, hon. I'll get you to the ER."

Jack scowled. "I don't need to go to the ER for a couple of little bruises!"

"They are not 'little' bruises!" Missy was the only person on the Station who could control Jack no matter what mood he was in or how drunk he was. She took Jack's hand and led him into the street.

"You need me anymore tonight, Mike?" Chow asked. Flynn shook his head, and Chow followed the Adamlys through the door.

Michael looked at his wife, who was deliberately not looking at him. "What?"

Wendy scowled at her husband. "I thought you were going to meet Gorkov to buy from him the name of the killer. But you suspected he might try to kill you and you went to meet him *alone?*"

"I wasn't alone! I invited Jack and Pete to the party!"

"I read your statements! Jack got there half a second before you got your skull caved in!"

"I told him to wait till the last moment, and it still wasn't enough to convince these Keystone Kops that Gorkov and company are the murderers they're looking for."

Flynn stepped up to the counter, where Deputy Marshal Sid Feldstein, in charge of the night shift, was sitting at a desk. Michael retrieved his stun pistol. Feldstein looked sourly at him. "They didn't do it, Mike."

Flynn studied Feldstein's expression. "What's going on tonight? I break two murder cases wide open and everybody's upset with me!"

"Thanks to you, I spent this afternoon climbing up and down the inside of a recycling chute. There wasn't a scrap of evidence—no marks, no rope fibers, no footprints on the walls—to indicate that anyone had used that chute to get into the area where Cross was stabbed."

Flynn shrugged. "That's not the only way to get in there."

Wendy was in a hurry. She took Flynn by the arm and led him out of the Marshals Office. They turned right on the Government Plaza. "They're not the murderers," she said.

Flynn looked at his wife, who was looking straight ahead as they walked. "Wendy, my love, weren't you listening? The similarities between the two murders and the assault on me—"

"They didn't do it!"

Flynn stopped walking. Wendy took three steps before she stopped and turned around.

"And how do you know this?"

Wendy blinked. "I can't tell you that, Michael. I'm sorry, but it involves attorney-client privilege."

Wendy worked for the Company, so she was talking about something she had learned from her employer, something about an illegal act committed by a Company employee. "Did Silvanus Drake have a security-camera watch on Gorkov and his pets?"

Wendy opened her mouth, thought better of it, and stayed silent. Flynn knew he was right. "Wendy, they were careful to commit the murders in places where there were no security cameras."

"But there are security cameras in most other public places on the Station. If a Company employee had broken the law by programming the cameras to track Gorkov's thugs—and I'm not saying that one did—there'd be video records of them leaving Gorkov's office before the murders. There aren't."

"What do the video records show Lavalle, Weasel, and Knuckles doing tonight?"

Wendy hesitated. "One of my jobs as Company legal director on the Station is to make sure that the Company complies with all applicable laws, including privacy laws."

"Gee, thanks, Wendy—" Flynn suddenly remembered his earlier conversation with Missy Adamly. Drake must have thought Gorkov was behind the killings, and couldn't believe that his cameras didn't track Gorkov's thugs to the scenes of the crimes. "Is there anything wrong with Security's computer system?"

Wendy shook her head. "Drake just had it checked. The

software and database got a clean bill of health."

Flynn resumed walking. "But they must be the killers! They knew Manstein's name! Both murders and the attack on me—"

"Gorkov is smart enough to have his thugs copy the *modus operandi*. That way the killer of Manstein and Cross would get blamed for your murder. By the way, Cross's killer didn't come in through the hatch we inspected this afternoon—the Security records show that hatch wasn't opened for five hours before the time of death."

Flynn shrugged. "Well, since the killer didn't climb in through the recycling chute or come through the hatch from the outside, he must have used the third possible entrance—which is the most likely entrance in any case, if my hypothesis about the motive for Leron's murder is correct."

"Why do you think he was killed?"

Flynn ran his tongue around the inside of his mouth. "For something he didn't do."

Wendy waited for elaboration. None was forthcoming. "Which was . . . ?"

It was payback time. "Sorry, Wendy. Can't tell you. Professional ethics—you hired me to investigate the Manstein killing, not the Cross murder."

Wendy glared at her husband out of the corner of her eye. "I don't know what you did to make Gorkov want to kill you, but you're starting to give me a motive!"

"Gorkov wants to kill me because I'm working on the Cross killing, something he learned when I asked him about it. If he didn't do it, he has no reason at all to want to kill me."

"The murderer of Manstein and Cross could have hired him."

Wendy could be immune to logic when she had made up her mind. "Wendy, if you'd already killed two people, would you bother hiring a hit man to kill a third?"

"Michael, Manstein and Cross were ordinary people, not

trained to take care of themselves. You have a gun permit and a reputation for marksmanship. The murderer might have thought that you were out of his league, and hired professionals to kill you."

"Well, if you're right, then Francine Cross definitely didn't kill her husband—something the marshals haven't gotten around to proving yet. If she wanted me dead, she wouldn't have put me on guard by having Gorkov offer to sell me the name of the killer. She would have suckered me to someplace quiet where Lavalle, DiGeorgio, and Weasel would have been waiting."

Wendy smiled. "We're making progress, then. Now you can quit wasting time and find out who really did it—and it wasn't Gorkov and Company."

"They figured out a way to beat the security cameras!" Flynn walked silently for a few steps before he added, "I just haven't figured out how to prove it." Figuring out something that Silvanus Drake and the Station's computer experts couldn't wasn't going to be easy. "Come on, we'll take the twenty thousand in cash back to Francine Cross."

Wendy glanced reflexively at Michael's empty hands. "Where is Francine's twenty thousand?"

"Near Gorkov's chosen meeting place, of course."

Flynn led Wendy to one of the elevators on Government Plaza. They rode it to level ten, and walked up Station to Sixteenth Street, five blocks from the scene of the fight. Flynn opened a recycling hatch. He reached into the chute and pulled out a string, which ended in a package wrapped in white paper and sealed with tape. Flynn untied the string from its anchor point on the hatch hinge.

Wendy peeked over Michael's shoulder and down the empty blackness of the chute. "That's not a safe place to hide money.

There are two levels above us. Falling garbage could have knocked that package loose."

Flynn glanced upward. "There's nothing above us but Meditech Hospital. Didn't think they'd be recycling a lot tonight, so it was unlikely that anything would hit the package and knock it loose."

Wendy's nose wrinkled. "Why didn't you have Jack or Chow hold on to it?"

"Because I thought they might need their hands for other purposes."

Francine Cross was waiting hopefully in her apartment. Her look of anticipation changed to one of disappointment when she saw the package.

"Didn't the informant show up?"

"He wasn't really an informant, Ms. Cross," Flynn explained. "He was trying to obtain money under false pretenses."

"You mean, he . . . he didn't really know who killed Leron?"

Flynn glanced at Wendy. "Oh, he knew. But he had no intention of telling me."

Francine squeezed the package between her hands. "Maybe, if I posted a reward . . ."

"You'd get a lot of people trying to obtain money under false pretenses. Get that," Flynn pointed to the package, "back to the credit union."

Francine looked at Wendy, who didn't contradict her husband. "You'll keep investigating?"

Flynn nodded. "First thing in the morning."

Francine closed her door.

"She really had her hopes up," Wendy said.

Flynn didn't respond. Francine's high hopes had been his fault—he had painted a very optimistic picture to get her to borrow the twenty grand.

Wendy wrapped her arm around Michael's. "I know it's late, but we don't get out as much as we used to. Why don't we stop for a drink?"

Chapter 10

Wendy stood with arms akimbo, head cocked to the side, and stared at the glowing sign above the door of the Gold Dollar Casino. "This is Big Bill Gorkov's headquarters! There are better places to get a drink on Government Plaza than this dive!"

"Not if you want a side order of information." Flynn opened the door for his wife.

Wendy stood in the doorway and surveyed the predominantly male clientele. Someone hit a number at the roulette wheel and brought loud cheers and groans from other players. A cocktail waitress hustled past with a tray of drinks. Wendy looked at the bare skin on the waitress and frowned.

The same blonde was tending bar. She seemed happy to see Flynn until she noticed that Wendy was with him. Flynn took out his wallet and laid a hundred-dollar bill on the bar. The blonde rested her fingertips on it but didn't pick it up. "The lady must have quite a thirst."

"White wine and seltzer for my wife," Flynn ordered. "I'll have a beer. You can keep the change."

The blonde's fingers twitched on the bill. "You have something kinky in mind?"

Flynn could feel his wife's temperature rising. He was in for a severe cross examination. "Did you see Lavalle, Knuckles, and Weasel leave just before twenty tonight?"

The blonde picked up the bill. "The marshals were asking about them an hour or so ago. What did they do?"

"Attempted murder."

The bartender's eyes opened wide. They were very blue. "Really? Who'd they try to kill?"

"Someone who fought back."

"But he survived? He can testify against them? I'd love to see them locked up!" The blonde's expression changed and she sighed. "But I can't help you. Lavalle and DiGeorgio came in before dinner, Weasel right after. But I didn't see 'em leave. As far as I know they're still in Gorkov's office."

The door at the end of the bar opened and a man in a brown business suit came out. He had light brown hair and a broad nose that spoiled what otherwise would have been a handsome face. He walked directly to the door to the Plaza and left the casino.

"Donovan McAllister," Wendy said. "That might be a good sign."

The name sounded familiar to Flynn. "Hmm?"

The bartender put the drinks on the bar. Wendy took a sip of hers. "If you're on Jupiter Station and you want to spend a lot of money for legal advice, you hire Donovan McAllister."

Flynn nodded, remembering where he had heard the name. "I didn't know he was that good."

Wendy shook her head. "He's not. He's just expensive. And, since Sharon Bonin went back to Earth last year, he's also the president of the Jupiter Station Bar Association. I'm surprised you didn't recognize him—he's on the Bar Association's airball team."

Flynn sipped his beer. It was the Company brew and was never going to win an award. "And he was talking with either Bill Gorkov or Jorge Allesandro."

"It couldn't have been my boss," the bartender said. She nodded toward the gaming tables. "He's at the crap table at the moment."

Flynn took out his computer, called up the photograph of Helmuth Manstein, and showed it to the bartender. "Recognize him?"

The blonde stared at the photo, then tilted her head to view it from a different angle. "He looks familiar. I think he's been in here." She looked at Flynn. "What's his name?"

"That," Flynn said, "is what I'm trying to find out." He put his computer in his pocket and emptied his glass. "I'll be right back."

Wendy gulped her drink. "Hold on. I'm coming with you."

"Wendy, the drink is socializing. Gorkov is business."

Wendy grimaced. "Paying her a hundred bucks for a Company beer and a really cheap wine is socializing?"

"Why would you want to meet a mobster?"

"Curiosity." Wendy fingered the lapels of her coat. "Besides, this business suit is out of place in here." She glanced at the bartender. "I feel conspicuously overdressed."

Flynn guessed he was in enough domestic trouble and relented. "Come on." He led the way through the door at the end of the bar.

"The bartender doesn't like me," Wendy said quietly.

"Probably because when she saw you she realized that I wasn't about to get a divorce and marry her."

Wendy looked at her husband as though the bartender's mistaken impression was his fault. "Whatever gave her that idea?"

"In severe cases of desperation, unfounded wishful thinking can occur."

"She's attractive enough. She shouldn't be desperate."

"I don't think she has enough money to go back to Earth, and the men on Jupiter Station didn't turn out to be what she expected."

From Wendy's point of view, most of the unattached men on

Jupiter Station left something to be desired. But many women on Earth imagined the Station to be crawling with big, hunky, sex-starved adventurers, and came a billion kilometers to catch one. Somebody, a women's magazine perhaps, needed to warn them that the average man on Jupiter Station preferred girlfriends who accepted debit cards. "Well, what does she expect to attract if she walks around in public in a minuscule loin cloth?"

"Grope guard," Flynn corrected.

Wendy was familiar with the term but considered it to be suggestive and inappropriate for polite conversation. "Well, if you want to make my case for me . . ."

"Wendy, I remember a redhead in a bar—"

"I'd had too much to drink! And I only took my blouse off!" Flynn didn't reply, so Wendy said, "You *told* me I only took my blouse off!"

Flynn stood in front of the door to Gorkov's office. "And you frequent our swimming pool in your birthday suit."

"A private swimming pool, for residents of our apartment complex, with other women—and men—" Wendy glanced at her husband, "similarly attired. Swimming naked in such circumstances is socially acceptable—there are lots of nude beaches back on Earth." She looked back at the door to the casino. "How could she not see Gorkov's men come out of that door?"

Flynn knocked on the door to Big Bill's office. "She could have been distracted—customers demanding refills, somebody hitting a jackpot at the tables . . ." Flynn knocked again, then tried the doorknob. It wasn't locked. He guided his wife to the side, out of the line of fire, and opened the door enough to see inside the room.

"I'm not in!" Gorkov growled.

"Too bad." Flynn opened the door the rest of the way and

stepped into the office. Wendy was right behind him. "I'll have to settle for talking with the man who looks like you."

Gorkov's demeanor changed when he saw Wendy. "Ah! You brought a guest!" He got up from behind the desk. "Drinks?"

Flynn opened his mouth to respond, but his wife was standing next to him. He glanced at her.

"Do you have anything better than what the bartender calls white wine?" Wendy asked.

Gorkov smiled. "I do indeed." He walked to his liquor cabinet. "I have an excellent sherry here. Mr. Flynn, I assume you'll have another scotch?"

Flynn was looking at his surprisingly thirsty wife. She didn't return the stare. "Sure."

Gorkov nodded at the chairs in front of his desk. "Please, sit down." He brought the drinks. "What can I do for you that doesn't involve answering questions about what some acquaintances of mine allegedly were doing this evening?"

"You can explain what's obviously a gross misunderstanding on my part," Flynn replied. "I thought I was going to meet you tonight, and get the name of the person who shut off Leron Cross. But when I get to the meeting place that you suggested, you're not there. Instead, I find your 'acquaintances.' One of them tries to cave in the back of my skull with a hammer. If some passersby hadn't come along at that moment and stopped him, I'd be resting peacefully in a recycling bin right now."

Gorkov had poured himself a scotch. He fingered the glass while staring at Flynn. He shook his head. "I don't know what gave you the idea that we were supposed to meet tonight—"

"Bill, it's late, and we're alone, and your fancy sensors—the same ones that spotted my stun pistol last night—have already informed you that neither one of us is wired for sound or video and that our computers are off. Anything you say here is deniable. So stop spewing manure and tell me what I did to make you so upset."

Gorkov leaned back in his chair. He gazed at his guests for fifteen seconds. "When I told a friend on Mars that I was coming out here, he said there were only two people I'd have to worry about. One was the head of Company security, an efficient and amoral man named Drake, who followed no rules except his own and changed those whenever he felt like it. The other was a private detective named Michael Flynn."

"Does that mean you're going to try to rub out Drake, too?"

"I didn't even try to rub out you."

"Then what were Lavalle, Weasel, and Knuckles doing at what was supposed to be our meeting tonight?"

Gorkov tilted his glass and looked at the liquid within. "I asked them to collect the twenty thousand dollars you promised me. I don't like to carry around that much cash."

"And then they were going to give me the name?" Gorkov nodded. Flynn shook his head. "No way. You give me the name first."

Gorkov grunted and made a face. "I couldn't stay in business if I worked like that!"

"You can't stay in business without your thugs, and at the moment one's in the hospital, another's in jail, and the third will be in jail as soon as the marshals find him."

"They'll be out of jail as soon as my attorney posts bond, and Knuckles will heal in time." Gorkov finished his scotch.

"Just give me the name you promised. In exchange, we'll drop the charges against your 'associates.' And we'll give you the twenty thousand."

Gorkov stared at his guests. "As you said, Mr. Flynn: It's late. I'm going to close my office and go home. I suggest you do the same."

Normally, Flynn didn't take suggestions from mobsters, but the only way he would get more information out of Gorkov would be to dangle him head down in a recycling chute. He finished his scotch and stood up. "Thanks for the drink."

Wendy put her unfinished glass of sherry on the desk and rose from her chair. Flynn led her from the room without looking back.

"I thought you didn't like sherry," Flynn said.

"I don't, really. I can't believe he didn't take the deal you just offered. Why didn't he give you the name of Cross's killer?"

"Because *he* is Cross's killer. Instead, he told me why he wants to kill me: I'm one of the two people on this station that he worries about. He wouldn't be worried if I was investigating something he didn't do."

"If you're so certain he's the killer, why did you agree to meet him tonight? What did you expect to get? Besides killed, I mean."

"There was a small chance that he'd give me the name of some innocent person, somebody he wanted to get into trouble." Flynn paused. "And a smaller chance that he really didn't do it but knew who did. But, if I was right, I thought he'd try to kill me, and we'd get the goods on his thugs, who would rat him out in a plea bargain." He shook his head once. "That part didn't go as planned."

Michael turned to the right, away from the door that led to the casino. Wendy followed him down the corridor. "Where are you going?"

At the end of the corridor was another door. It was unlocked, and behind it was a janitorial closet. "No back door in here, either." Flynn backtracked down the corridor to the door marked *Proprietor.* He knocked, but there was no response; Allesandro must still have been on the casino floor. Flynn tried the door knob and found it unlocked. "Humph. Trusting soul." He opened the door. Allesandro's office was less ornate than Gorkov's. The walls were unpanelled and the desk looked like the same model that Flynn had in his office.

"Even though the door is unlocked, that's still breaking and entering," Wendy warned.

"I'm not entering. See anything that looks like another exit?"

Wendy stuck her head into the room and looked around carefully. "No. Not even in the ceiling."

"Neither do I." Flynn closed the door. "Gorkov's office has that nice, new panelling, which Company workers must have installed. They wouldn't have covered up a back door."

"I can check that." Wendy took out her computer and called up a Station diagram. "Let's see. We're here . . ." She indicated their location on the diagram and shook her head. "There's no hatch in the back wall, although the other side of the wall is a utility tunnel." She looked at her husband with a smile. "*Our* utility tunnel!"

"And the bartender saw Gorkov's thugs come in here tonight but didn't see them leave."

"Maybe she was in the john," Wendy suggested.

"Or maybe Gorkov's paying her more than I am. Come on. Let's go home. Like you said, you're conspicuously overdressed for this place, and, although it's late, I would dearly like to get you—and your birthday suit—into the swimming pool tonight."

Chapter 11

The toast, warm and fragrant, had been made from bread baked the previous day. Wendy held the slice halfway to her mouth, which was open—not for the toast, but in astonishment.

"Have you lost your mind?" she asked her husband, who was spooning corn bisquettes into his mouth on the other side of the table. Wendy put the toast back on her plate. "Let me guess: You lied in your statement to the police. Knuckles actually hit you with that hammer and you suffered serious brain damage."

"Wendy, it's fifty thousand dollars—per year."

"They are trying to manipulate you!"

Flynn finished the bisquettes. The milk he had poured on them, reconstituted from powder shipped from Earth, left something to be desired. He pushed the bowl aside. "Into doing—or not doing—what?"

"I don't know!"

"Neither do I. But if Drake's life is really in danger, I want to know as much as I can about the situation."

Furrball jumped onto the table and sniffed at the milk remaining in the bottom of Flynn's bowl. He started to lap it up.

Wendy scowled. "They won't tell you anything about the situation until after Drake is dead."

Flynn shook his head. "That would be too late. If Drake wants me to succeed him he'll have to tell me something right away—that's my condition for accepting the retainer."

"Okay, okay! Take their retainer! I'll tell them Monday morning."

"We might not have that long. Tell them today."

"It's Friday. Nobody's working today."

Flynn sighed. "If only that were true! We could spend the day together."

"In bed?" Wendy suggested, attempting to dissuade her husband from the course of action he had selected.

Michael smiled. "Ah, Wendy, my love." He reached across the table and patted her hand. "Turning down that offer is *prima facie* evidence of a serious brain injury. But Warshovsky and Drake work all the time. Tell them today." He got up from the table. "Unfortunately, I have to work all the time, too."

Flynn found only one request for a background check waiting for him in his office. There were three reports on investigations he had subcontracted, two of which were embarrassingly bad and one that was almost written in English. He was editing the reports when Dr. Liao Chu darkened the office doorway.

"Gumshoe! I hear you solved the Manstein murder!"

Liao was smiling. Tobacco-stained teeth stretched from ear to ear. Smoking was not allowed on the Station. He had to be on nicotine-replacement therapy.

"I proved who did it to my satisfaction but not, alas, to the satisfaction of the marshals or the U.S. attorney."

Liao nodded in understanding. "They are understaffed. Your government is broke."

"For the same reason yours is: too many retired people and not enough working people paying taxes."

Liao frowned. "There would be enough if capitalists wouldn't steal so much for themselves."

Flynn didn't know if Liao was serious or if he was speaking for the benefit of his bodyguards, who were standing in the street and watching the traffic. Michael leaned back in his chair.

"Capitalists actually create wealth, but ours can't create enough wealth to support the thirty percent of the U.S. adult population that is retired. Only raising the retirement age will solve that problem." Flynn crossed his arms. "Manstein's name hasn't been released by the police yet. Where did you get it?"

Liao blinked. "Ah, people are talking; word gets around. This gangster, Gorkov: Why did he do it?"

Flynn shrugged. "Someone probably hired him."

"Do you know who that someone is?"

Flynn shook his head. "Not a clue. If the marshals and the U.S. attorney weren't convinced of his innocence, they'd arrest him and offer a deal in exchange for that name. I, however, will have to dig it out the hard way. Are you going back to the Asian station soon?"

Liao nodded. "This afternoon. I have checked out of the hotel. I have much work to do to get the project back on schedule." He shook his head slowly. "It is going to cost a lot of money."

"They won't like that—it will reduce their profits."

Liao grinned. "My humble contribution to the class struggle—separating capitalists from as much of their profits as possible." The grin vanished. "Of course, they might not have any more money. Would you let me know if you find out who paid Gorkov to kill Manstein?"

"I won't have to. It will be on the news."

"Gumshoe, it's been a pleasure knowing you. Goodbye."

"Goodbye, Dr. Liao."

Flynn returned to his reports. The results of the investigations looked reasonable; he wouldn't have to check them before forwarding the reports to planet three. At least, he hoped he didn't have to. He didn't have the time.

Flynn's computer beeped. Missy Adamly's face glowered at him from the display.

"Morning, Missy." Flynn peered at the display. "The wall behind you looks like the one in your office. Why are you working this weekend?"

"Doing you a favor, although I don't know why I should, after what you did to Jack last night!"

Flynn tried to look puzzled. "I didn't do anything to Jack last night. It was that gorilla, Knuckles."

Missy's dark blue eyes flashed. "Jack would have been drinking in one of his favorite bars if you hadn't invited him to your ambush! I did this favor for you on the condition that you leave Jack out of your future fight plans!"

Flynn sat erect in his chair. "You found the name Manstein was using for his e-mail?"

Missy moistened her lips. "I think so. After checking e-mail traffic patterns and correlating with movements of guests to and from the Station, the most likely name that Manstein was using was George Smiley."

Flynn slowly leaned back in his chair. He had seen that name before. "Who's been e-mailing him?"

"In the two weeks—that's how long we save the e-mail logs—before he died, nobody."

"Nobody? Then how could you . . . oh. Who'd he e-mail?"

"Twelve days before he died, he sent one to Hamburg. It bounced back a day later—invalid address. The day after that he e-mailed Helsinki—"

"*The* Helsinki? The one in Finland?"

"Yeah. Two days later he got a response from the same address. Over the next six days he sent four e-mails to very similar addresses—just one or two characters different from one to the next, like he couldn't quite remember the address, and was trying to get it right. They all bounced. Invalid addresses again."

Flynn tapped his fingers on the desk. "Can you send me the e-mail address Manstein used that didn't bounce?"

Missy reached for something outside the range of her camera. "Your wish is my command."

"Missy, when this is over, I am taking you and Jack out for the evening, and everything will be on me."

"I'll tell Jack. We'll fast for a week so we both have enormous appetites and unquenchable thirsts."

"Well, if you're going to cost me that much, I'm going to have to ask for another favor."

Missy looked like she was going to tell Flynn what he should do to himself, but she said, "And what would that be?"

"I need to know whom Bill Gorkov e-mailed between last Wednesday and the time Manstein was shut off. More importantly, I need to know who e-mailed him."

Missy pursed her lips, then shook her head vigorously. "No can do, Michael."

Flynn squinted. "Why not?"

"E-mail logs are private information. Gorkov isn't the victim of a crime, like Manstein was. And he hasn't been charged with anything. I can't go poking into his e-mail logs without a court order."

Flynn wondered why the women in his life were suddenly finding legal reasons not to do him favors. "Missy, you're a computer system analyst. You look at people's private files all the time."

Missy waved her finger at Flynn. "Only in the performance of my duties, while troubleshooting system problems."

Flynn smiled. "There you go! Troubleshoot the e-mail server!"

"There's nothing wrong with the e-mail server! They're highly reliable! We haven't had a server problem in . . . two years!"

"But a brilliant systems analyst like you could create one this afternoon." Michael pointed at Missy's image on his display. "*Two* evenings on me for you and Jack."

Flynn switched off his computer and pushed his chair back

from his desk. He needed to finish his reports, but his mind was on overdrive and he couldn't concentrate on them. Helmuth Manstein had been murdered the night before Dr. Liao had reached the Station. Flynn had to find out if Manstein had been killed to protect Liao.

Michael locked his office door behind him and headed for Second Street. He climbed one level to the Main Plaza and took the moving sidewalk around to the other side of the Station. The paramedics had found Knuckles DiGeorgio in Company coveralls so they had taken him to the Company hospital. He was still there, guarded by Company goons—the marshals were too busy to do it. The arrangement suited Flynn, who was on much better terms with Company Security than with the Marshals Service. The goon at the door of Knuckles's room was happy to let Flynn enter.

"His lawyer says that we shouldn't let anyone but medical people in," the guard said, "but, what the hell, I don't work for him."

DiGeorgio was sitting up in bed, watching a pornographic video. He glowered at Flynn through a pair of black eyes, collateral damage from when Jack Adamly broke his nose. "What the hell are you doing here?" His voice was more guttural than usual due to the bandages over the nose, which the doctors had reconstructed.

"Doing my Christian duty, visiting the sick. How are you feeling?"

Knuckles scowled. "How the hell do you think I'm feeling? I had a concussion! Damn doctors won't let me outta here until they're sure I'm okay." He turned from Flynn to the video display. "My lawyer says I shouldn't talk to anybody unless he's here."

"You always do what lawyers tell you to do?"

"I do when my boss is paying 'em large green to defend me."

"And you always do what your boss says. Look where that got you."

"Get out of here, Flynn. I'm an injured man. I need my rest."

"You need to get out from under a murder charge."

"I'm not charged with murder. I'm charged with aggravated assault and petty theft."

"That's only because the FBI told the marshals that you didn't switch off Cross. The marshals aren't going to believe that forever." Flynn paused, unsure of how fast DiGeorgio's brain could process information. "When they can't find anyone else, you'll be their prime suspect. Now, are you going to be smart and turn in your boss, or are you going to let him keep drinking his expensive booze while you spend the rest of your life as a guest of the Federal government?"

Knuckles stared at his video display. "I didn't kill nobody."

"That might be true, but I'm not investigating the murder of nobody. I'm investigating the murders of Manstein and Cross. And I don't even care that you did it. Neither do the marshals. All we want to know is why your boss had you knock them off."

Knuckles still didn't look at Flynn. "I didn't kill nobody."

Flynn sighed. Knuckles wasn't smart enough to get himself out of the situation. He would blindly follow Gorkov to a prison cell. Michael looked at the video display. "That position looks almost as painful as your nose. Why is she smiling?"

Knuckles grunted.

Flynn rode the moving sidewalk on the Main Plaza back to Denver Avenue. He took Denver's moving sidewalk to Fourth Street. Betty's Bar was busy with the people who liked to drink their lunches. Betty saw him come in and was waiting with a smile on her face as he stepped up to the bar.

"Well it's about time, stranger! I was beginning to think you'd gone on the wagon!"

"Wendy doesn't like me drinking," Flynn explained.

Betty cocked her head. "You sure? You drank plenty when you used to take her here."

"And I got lectured for it. Say, Betty, have you heard anybody mention the name Manstein recently?"

"Helmuth Manstein? Guy about this tall with a round face?" Betty held her hand level with the bridge of Flynn's nose. She shook her head. "I don't think he has many friends. I rarely see him talk to anyone when he comes in here."

"You knew—you know him?"

Betty's eyes narrowed. "What do you mean, knew? Did something happen to him?"

Flynn glanced from side to side. No one seemed to be paying attention, but he leaned across the bar and lowered his voice. "He was the first murder victim."

The look on Betty's face almost made Flynn sad. "Oh, no! He was such a nice, polite man."

"Keep it quiet—the authorities haven't managed to notify his next of kin yet. How well did you know him?"

Betty shrugged. "He drank vodka, mostly. We'd talk sometimes. He was a sales rep. Had been here . . . oh, about four or five years, I think. He said his job here was really important—stayed a couple of years longer than he'd originally planned. Expected to get a nice promotion." Betty's eyes lost focus. "He seemed kind of depressed the last time he was here. Maybe he didn't get it."

Flynn cocked his head. "When was that?"

"Oh, a couple of weeks ago."

Michael tried to fit that information into his crime scenario. "Did he ever talk about his home?"

"Ah, he said he was from someplace in Germany. Munich?" Betty nodded. "Yeah, Munich."

"Ever see him associate with anyone?"

Betty shook her head. "He was very polite, but . . . introverted. The kind of person who didn't make friends easily."

"If he was here four or five years he must have made some."

"Not in here." Betty paused. "He was always polite, but . . . if he didn't get that promotion, I'd bet he lost it to a Chinese guy."

"Hmm?"

"Well, you know what the Station's been like ever since construction of the Asian station started—Orientals all over the place. Never bothered him. But the last time he was here, I'd just refilled his glass when some Asian workers stepped up to the bar next to him. He paid for his drink, belted it down, said, 'I'm fed up with Chinese,' and walked out."

Flynn's focus gradually shifted from Betty to the bottles behind the bar and then to the mirror behind them. "And he'd never seemed bigoted before that?"

Betty shook her head firmly. "I thought it was only robots he didn't like."

Several seconds elapsed before that remark registered in Flynn's brain. "Robots?"

Betty nodded. "He said he liked my tavern because I didn't have 'one of those damned machines' tending bar."

If Helmuth Manstein didn't like machines, he had picked the wrong place to spend four or five years—Jupiter Station was one of the most automated places in the solar system. "Thanks, Betty." Flynn turned to leave.

"You should take that wife of yours out more. You'll bore her to death if you stay home every night."

Flynn turned back to the bar. "Wendy's not like that. She's . . . intellectual."

Betty glanced at one of the tables next to the window. "Are we talking about the same Wendy Chadwick who was dancing on that table right there a week before your wedding?"

Wendy couldn't remember that night. Until she had met Michael, she had limited her alcohol consumption to a glass or two of wine with dinner. Her body was not inured to the amount of alcohol she consumed in a night of partying with Flynn, and when Wendy got drunk she lost all her inhibitions. Fortunately, Michael had reached her before she unhooked her bra, which had brought boos from the mostly male bar patrons. "She'd had too much to drink that night."

"Maybe she should have too much to drink more often. She was in here the other day. Alone. Looked bored." Betty shook her head. "She never looked bored when she was here with you."

Flynn's computer beeped, interrupting the conversation. Flynn stepped through the doorway onto Fourth Street and opened his computer. Edwin Warshovsky's face appeared on the display.

"Mr. Flynn, your wife informed me that you've conditionally accepted our offer."

Flynn nodded. "That's right."

Warshovsky was wearing a conservative gray suit. With his somber expression, he looked like a funeral director. "Mr. Drake has convinced me that your condition is . . . reasonable." Warshovsky obviously didn't agree with his security chief. "Can you meet us at the main shuttle dock in an hour?"

The shuttle dock? Flynn's curiosity, already aroused, nearly went off the scale. "Where are we going?"

Warshovsky took a deep breath. "You'll see in an hour."

Chapter 12

No passenger vessels were visiting Jupiter Station that Friday. Flynn found the shuttle-arrival area deserted except for Ed Warshovsky, Silvanus Drake, and Wendy Chadwick. Flynn's wife was dressed in a bright green coat, tights, and miniskirt. Wendy, who usually wore little or no makeup, had polished her nails green to match her outfit. She had dressed to express her displeasure with her boss for hiring her husband, and with her husband for accepting the offer. Flynn was in for an interesting meeting.

The shuttle-arrival area was on the Station axis; there was no effective gravity. Flynn launched himself upward from the ramp in front of the elevators, toward the airlock where the other four were waiting. He was out of practice, and missed the airlock hatch as well as the rod that extended from it along the Station axis. Flynn grabbed a conduit on the bulkhead above the airlock to keep from ricocheting back into the arrival area. Drake extended his hand and helped Flynn to the hatch.

"Let's get the paperwork out of the way," Warshovsky said.

Flynn looked from the Station's manager to his wife. Wendy handed him her computer. "It's the Company's standard nondisclosure agreement. You can sign it."

Flynn put on an artificial smile. "And just whose attorney are you at the moment?"

Wendy wasn't in the mood for bantering. "Okay, then download it into your computer and let your damned software tell you it's okay to sign!"

Michael took the proffered contract. Warshovsky handed him a pen.

"As a licensed private investigator, I'm required to report any crimes I uncover to the authorities," Flynn reminded him.

"You won't be uncovering any crimes on this trip," Warshovsky said.

Flynn "signed" the holographic display; the computer transcribed the signature. He handed it to Wendy and gave the pen back to Warshovsky. "Where are we going?" he asked cheerfully.

Warshovsky looked at Wendy, and Flynn surmised that his wife had already asked that question at least once. "You'll see when we get there." Warshovsky opened the hatch and led the party into the airlock.

A small work boat was docked to the other end of the lock. Its pilot was chewing gum, and was wearing the bright orange coveralls of a security guard instead of the red worn by every other Company pilot Flynn had ever seen. The work boat had only six seats. Drake took the seat next to the pilot. Warshovsky sat behind Drake. Flynn led Wendy to the back row of seats.

"Everybody strapped in?" the pilot asked. He undocked without waiting for an answer. The boat backed away from the Station, then turned and headed retrograde to the Station's orbit. The thrusters kept firing, so the work boat accelerated instead of coasting toward its destination like on every other shuttle ride Flynn had ever taken. Flynn and Wendy were pressed back in their seats. Nothing but distant stars showed through the forward ports; the satellites were all on the other side of the Station.

"Ah, excuse me," Flynn said, "but does the pilot know where he's going?"

Drake didn't turn around. "Yes."

Wendy had also realized that the boat was going the wrong way. "Where are we going?" she asked quietly.

Flynn said, "Wherever it is, we're all going there together." This couldn't be an attempt by Warshovsky and Drake to get rid of him—and Wendy too, since she had invited herself along—no one in the boat was wearing a pressure suit. "I suspect this is part of the Grand Tour that Dr. Liao didn't get."

"We just put him on an Asian shuttle at the other end of the Station."

"The two of you share a love of old mystery novels."

Wendy turned from the viewports and looked at her husband. "Hmm?"

"When we met at his reception, he asked if I was carrying a 'gat.' That's a very old expression for a firearm. And he calls me 'Gumshoe,' an equally old term for a private investigator."

"You don't carry 'gats' anymore?"

Flynn continued to peer through the viewports. "Now we 'pack pieces.' And 'gumshoe' reflects a time when private investigators had a sleazy reputation and would do whatever it took—breaking and entering, wiretapping, peeking through windows—to make a case. But now job-protection laws have induced employers to check out every job applicant, our services are in demand by polite society, and we have licensing boards that don't cut us any slack and a code of ethics that puts the ABA's to shame.

"Speaking of old mystery novels, I was reading one of yours a couple of months ago. Hero was a guy named George Smiley."

Wendy had watched him read it. Michael had been sitting in their living room and waiting for the live telecast—actually delayed an hour due to the light lag from Earth—of a Bruins hockey game to begin. Wendy had thought at the time that her husband was becoming more interested in her books and her music than he was in her. "George Smiley wasn't a private investigator. He was a spy."

"Yes. And Manstein was sending and receiving e-mails under that name."

Wendy glanced toward the bow of the boat. She lowered her voice even more. "Do they . . ."

Flynn shrugged. "Drake usually knows everything."

Wendy stared through the viewports in the bow. "It would be pretty stupid for a spy to choose a cover name of 'George Smiley.' "

"Maybe it was Liao Chu's idea," Flynn suggested. Wendy stared at him. "Manstein's name hasn't been released yet, because the authorities haven't been able to find his next of kin. But Liao knew it. Said that people have been talking, and that he'd overheard it. But people talk in bars, and the bartenders haven't heard that Manstein was the murder victim." If Liao read old mystery novels, maybe he read old spy novels, too. Michael looked at Warshovsky and Drake. They didn't seem to be listening, but he leaned toward his wife and said quietly, "Drake told you that Manstein had been seen in bars. Do you happen to know which ones?"

"He didn't say which ones at the time, but I think it was in a security report . . ." Wendy took her computer from the pocket of her coat and opened it. "I can't access the Station network . . . must be too far away. Maybe I downloaded it . . . yes. Here it is." She handed the computer to Michael.

Flynn was familiar with the listed taverns. He nodded, and handed the computer back to his wife. "Thanks."

"Was that important?"

"Maybe."

The pilot finally shut off the aft thrusters, but immediately turned on the forward ones, slowing the vessel. Wendy turned and looked behind her, but there were no viewports in the aft end of the work boat. "We are getting a long way from the Station."

"Getting bored?"

"No."

Flynn rubbed his chin; he hadn't shaved closely that morning. "Wendy, would you, ah, like to go out more often? In the evenings, I mean."

Wendy didn't look at her husband. She wiped her moist palms against her tights.

"I know you're educated, intellectual, cultured," Michael continued, "and most of the nightlife on the Station is none of those. At least, my kind of nightlife isn't. But you did seem to have a party streak in you when we were dating."

Wendy looked toward the bow of the boat. Before she had left Earth, she had gone out frequently. To the opera, to the ballet, to upscale clubs—intellectual, cultured places appropriate to her education and social status. When she had met Michael, she was still in social shock from a disastrous love affair, which was how she rationalized her willingness to frequent bars and low-priced restaurants with him. The only other possible explanation was that she really did have a Mike Flynn–style party streak in her. Memories of dates with the man who would become her husband made her smile. "We did have a lot of fun before we got married. I wouldn't mind going out more often." She paused. "I wouldn't drink as much, though. I didn't take my bra off in Betty's, did I?"

Flynn stared out the forward viewports of the work boat. "No. Are you not having a lot of fun now?"

Wendy hesitated. She wasn't embarrassing herself now. "Do you hear me complaining?"

Flynn chose his words carefully. "Not all communication is verbal." He looked toward the bow. Warshovsky was leaning forward, whispering something to Drake. "You told me that

Drake's goons were harvesting all sorts of contraband from the Asian workers who visit the Station."

Wendy nodded. "Illegal drugs, knives . . . even some guns."

"Would Drake get suspicious if it stopped suddenly?"

Wendy looked puzzled. "It hasn't stopped! According to the security reports, they find something nearly every day!"

"Could Gorkov be smuggling anything onto the Station that way?"

"Of course not." Wendy glanced toward the bow. "Nothing gets past Drake."

"Did they find anything yesterday?"

"Ah . . . no, according to this morning's security report. The sensors found nothing yesterday. You're not still thinking that Gorkov is the murderer, are you?"

"I *know* that Gorkov is the murderer." Flynn nodded toward the bow. "I think we're here."

Wendy looked through the viewports. A bright dot that was too big to be a star was directly ahead. The pilot shut off the bow thrusters. Wendy squinted. "It's too small to be a satellite. Must be another work boat, or a shuttle."

It was neither. It was cylindrical, with the off-white, anodized finish that the Company applied to the exterior surfaces of all its Jupiter property, and stabilized, since it wasn't tumbling. It was also very small, no bigger than a large work boat, because its image grew too rapidly to be a large structure at a long distance. The pilot fired the braking jets again. Wendy could see no identifying marks on the object, but it had a standard docking hatch on the end closest to the boat and a dish antenna pointing toward the Station.

"What is that?" Wendy asked.

Drake remained silent. Warshovsky said, "An artificial satellite of Jupiter." He leaned back in his seat and looked over his shoulder. "You might consider it to be the astronautical equivalent of a storage shed."

To Wendy, the answer was evasive. "Why are we storing stuff way the hell out here?"

Warshovsky was still looking over his shoulder. "*We* aren't."

Wendy frowned. "There's nobody else out here but the Asians!"

Warshovsky looked at the object again. "At the moment, that's true."

The pilot might have been out of practice; while docking, he hit the object hard enough to destabilize it. The object's attitude-control jets fired. The pilot took his hands off of the controls and let the object stabilize itself and the attached work boat. He pressurized the coupling and nodded at Drake. "All set."

Drake unstrapped and opened the work boat hatch. There was an electronic lock on the storage shed's outer hatch. Drake let it scan his retinal patterns, then pushed the door inward. The space beyond was as black as the space outside and lacked the star field. Drake reached into the blackness. Flynn heard the click of a switch. Lights glowed, revealing a small airlock. Drake entered. "Follow me," he said.

They followed, Warshovsky first, then Wendy and Flynn. The air in the lock was stale and cool.

"We won't be staying long," Drake said. "The radiation shielding of this structure is inadequate." A status panel on the bulkhead showed that interior was properly pressurized. Drake opened the inner hatch and revealed another black void. He reached around the edge of the hatch and flipped a switch, lighting the interior.

There was no gravity. The four drifted through the inner hatch. Drake closed the hatch behind them so the boat's pilot would not overhear their conversation.

The interior of the structure consisted of just one room. The bulkheads looked like unpainted steel adorned with electrical conduits and plumbing for the air supply. In the center of the room was a partially disassembled cylinder about a meter long, suspended by taut cables stretched to the bulkheads. The cables were fastened in place with combination padlocks.

Drake and Warshovsky drifted weightlessly to the object. Wendy was right behind them. Flynn hastened to put himself between the object and his wife, but then he saw that the explosive segments were still in place and that the only radiation danger came from the Jovian environment. Wendy hadn't recognized the object or the possible danger. Flynn, however, had been a lieutenant in the Marine Corps. He knew exactly what the object was.

Drake and Warshovsky were looking at Michael. Warshovsky had not been in favor of giving Flynn additional information. The detective looked at Drake and asked, "Where did you get the A-bomb?"

Chapter 13

It had been during the Station's first expansion. A supervisor, verifying work logs, had discovered *more* work finished—a sealed compartment completed rather than half done—than the log showed. He had mentioned this unprecedented anomaly to Security. The perpetually suspicious Silvanus Drake had ordered the compartment cut open. Inside, connected through a computer to the Station's control network, had been the bomb. Drake had summoned Company engineers to replace the bomb with an electronic circuit that would make the computer think that the bomb was still there and in working order. The supervisor who had started the investigation, the worker who had cut into the compartment, and the engineers who had replaced the bomb had been retired to Earth on fat pensions, the usual Company way of keeping secrets. Since the bomb's computer still thought it was connected to the bomb, the people who had planted the device didn't know it had been discovered, so they had no reason to sabotage the Station by some other, undetected, means.

"It was an ideal location," Drake said, "in a sealed compartment just below the new reactor. The only reason anyone would have gone in there would have been to repair structural damage."

Flynn took advantage of the lack of gravity to float beneath the bomb. The outer surface was painted flat gray. "Any idea where it came from?"

"There are no identifying marks or serial numbers on any piece of the bomb or its controlling computer," Drake said. "All of the electronics are commercial components available to anyone. But Dr. Devereaux in R and D, who used to work in the nonproliferation group at Los Alamos, says it looks like a southern or southwest Asian design from the latter part of the twentieth century. He can't be more specific: Except for India, all of the nuclear powers in that part of the world had Chinese input—official or unofficial—in their weapons programs, so their nuclear devices all share the same basic design characteristics."

Flynn gingerly slid his hand along the bomb's featureless casing. The device was well-made, like it had been built in an ordnance facility, but an official, government-manufactured weapon would have been covered with part numbers for inventory control. Some of the most violent terrorist organizations in the solar system made their homes in southern and southwest Asia. Their supporters in the host governments could have provided components from an old device that was being dismantled, components with the official serial numbers stripped off. "Did Devereaux estimate the yield?"

"About ten kilotons," Drake answered. "He says it's fairly easy to put together a critical mass of plutonium two thirty-nine—eight kilograms, in this case—and get a yield of around ten kilotons. To get an order of magnitude more—or less, for that matter—you really have to know what you're doing."

A ten-kiloton explosion next to the hub would destroy the Station. "Unless the bomber was on a kamikaze mission he would want to detonate it from a long way off," Flynn said. "I supposed it was tied into the Station's control system so it could be set off from anyplace on the Internet."

"No," Drake said. Flynn looked at him sharply. "The Station's control system has a hardware firewall between it and the regular computer network—there is no electronic connection between the two. The bomb's computer can only be accessed from inside the Station."

"But, the control system has lots of wireless access points. I've seen technicians use them. Whoever planted the bomb could have connected a transmitter to the regular computer network and used that to access the bomb's controller."

The firewall's designers had anticipated Flynn's argument. Drake said, "The wireless interconnects have very short range—two meters, maximum—and at no point are the regular computer network and the Station's control network that close together. No, the people who planted the bomb needed a babysitter on the Station to monitor and control it."

Flynn's eyes lost focus, but the image in his mind became crystal clear. "Manstein."

Drake glanced at Warshovsky, who deliberately avoided looking at his security chief. "The bomb's computer could be set to delay detonation for seconds, days, or even months, giving time for the babysitter to leave safely."

Flynn patted the bomb. "The people who planted this thing had to have access to the Station's control system, to assign it an IP address."

Drake nodded. "When the Station was first expanded, the Company didn't have enough employees—or the expertise—out here to do the job. Most of the work—design, transportation, construction, and programming—was performed by contractor personnel. Several people could have been involved in planting the bomb; at least one of them had computer expertise. He gave the bomb an IP address so high that the Station would have to grow to ten times its present size before that address would be assigned to something else. And the bomb's computer will not respond to a message more than once every ten days, so if anybody ever noticed a message to an IP address much higher than any on the assigned list and polled it to see what it was, there would be no response and it would be put down to a glitch. One of the conspirators took advantage of the commotion when the contract employees were shipped back to Earth to remain on the Station as the first babysitter, living unnoticed in the apartment rented anonymously from Earth and most recently occupied by Manstein. When his tour of duty expired, someone—perhaps Manstein—came from planet three under an assumed name and the first babysitter used that name to return to Earth."

"So there would be no record of Manstein's arrival—no unaccounted for arrivals or departures." Flynn gingerly touched one of the bomb's high-explosive segments. "I assume the Station's control system has been watching for messages to and from the bomb's computer."

Drake nodded. "It has been accessed at random intervals, never exceeding three months, ever since it was planted. The messages were to make sure the bomb was still there and functioning—we reverse engineered the bomb's computer so we could decode messages to it. We were unable to determine how the control system was being accessed until Manstein turned up dead and we found a hardware interconnect—which didn't appear on our wiring diagrams—in his apartment."

"When was the last time the bomb was accessed?"

"The last successful access was on the Wednesday before Manstein was killed. There was an attempt to access the bomb six days later, on the Tuesday after the murder, through a wireless port not covered by security cameras, but the bomb would not respond because less than ten days had elapsed since the preceding access."

Flynn was looking at the bomb but was thinking of the timeline. "Where was Dr. Liao last Tuesday when the access was attempted?"

"At a reception in his honor at the hotel."

Wendy poked at the bomb's innards. Flynn brusquely grabbed her shoulder and pulled her away. "Don't mess with that. Plutonium's a hot alpha emitter."

Wendy made a face. "But the plutonium's been removed, right? This isn't a complete nuclear weapon anymore." She looked at Warshovsky for confirmation.

"We disconnected the fire set," Drake said.

That was not what Wendy wanted to hear. She looked at her husband, not trusting either Warshovsky or Drake. "This is a *functioning* nuclear weapon? It can still go off?" She pointed so vigorously at the device that she started a slow zero-gee tumble. Flynn grabbed her by the ankle, but she kicked free. She glared at her supervisor. "There are *laws* prohibiting individuals and corporations from possessing weapons of mass destruction!"

"American laws," Drake answered. "They don't apply here."

Kicking free from Flynn had set Wendy tumbling again. She grabbed one of the lines securing the bomb. "The hell they don't! The Congress of the United States made all of these satellites U.S. territory when Jupiter Station was annexed five years ago!"

"This . . . storage shed is not one of the Station's satellites," Warshovsky explained. "It is not the property of the Conglomerated Mining and Manufacturing Corporation. It belongs to Mr. Wilmer de Birk and its contents are therefore in his possession."

Wendy managed to stabilize herself by wrapping her legs around the line she had grabbed. "The de Birk who's on the Company's Board of Directors?"

Warshovsky nodded once. Drake said, "He's not a U.S. citizen. He's from Namibia, a country which currently has no laws prohibiting its citizens from possessing nuclear weapons."

Wendy's anger was not assuaged. "It looks like we have possession of it now!"

"Mr. de Birk is on planet three," Drake said. "He asked me, as a personal favor, to keep an eye on his property." He looked at the combination locks securing the stabilizing cables. "I don't know the combinations to those locks."

Wendy gripped her rope so tightly that her knuckles turned white. "You can cut those cables any time you want! You're doing it again—observing the letter of the law while violating its intention! Why wasn't the bomb promptly turned over to the government?"

"We don't know that the government didn't plant it," Drake replied with his usual blank face.

Wendy's lips trembled. "Don't you believe Dr. Devereaux's assessment?"

Drake said nothing. Warshovsky sighed in exasperation.

Flynn knew that his wife's thought processes short-circuited when she lost her temper. "Wendy, if our intelligence agencies know enough about foreign nuke designs to identify one, then they obviously know enough to counterfeit one—although in that case I would expect to find part numbers of a foreign nation on all the components, to complete the forgery."

Wendy's expression changed from angry to disbelieving. "Why would our government want to plant a nuclear device in Jupiter Station? They made it American territory—"

"Perhaps to keep it out of the hands of potential enemies," Drake suggested. "Destroying the Station if it was captured would be much cheaper than maintaining the armed forces necessary to keep it from being captured—and the government is deeply in debt. In such an event it would be politically desirable to make someone else appear responsible."

Warshovsky looked at Flynn. "Do you have any other questions? We should head back. As Mr. Drake said, the radiation levels are rather high in here."

"Who knows you found the bomb?"

Warshovsky glanced around. "The four of us, the welding supervisor who started the investigation, the workman who cut open the bomb compartment . . . the two engineers who designed its dummy replacement . . . Dr. Devereaux . . . and the nine people on the Board of Directors when the device was discovered."

Flynn turned to Silvanus Drake. "Are you sure there aren't any other nukes planted on the Station or its satellites?"

"A team of technicians checks every compartment every month for structural damage. Unknown to them, their equipment includes sensors tuned to the neutrons and gamma rays given off by plutonium two thirty-nine and uranium two thirty-five. In ten years, they haven't detected anything but normal Jovian radiation."

Flynn looked at the bomb. "Has the Asian station been equipped with one of these?"

Drake's black eyes were as empty as those of a doll. "I don't know. The Consortium hasn't given me access to their facilities."

"Have you at least *warned* them?" Wendy asked.

"I told Mr. Takimoto that that there had been attempts to sabotage the Station with bombs—I couldn't be more explicit without revealing that this nuke isn't in place and active like its computer says it is. But he seems to be primarily concerned with keeping secret the details of his station's construction. He hasn't even tried to curb the flow of weapons and illegal drugs into his bailiwick."

Flynn had more questions, all concerning what Company Security knew about the deaths of Manstein and Cross, and all of which Drake refused to answer. The party returned to the work boat, where the discussion stopped—the pilot wasn't in on the secret. Michael sat in the back with his seething wife, calmly considering his latest information. "Drake thinks that Manstein's death means that someone is trying to get the bomb," he said quietly. "No computer was found in Manstein's apartment, even though he must have had one to contact the bomb. That means Manstein's killers have the computer and probably the interface codes." The codes should have been memorized, but people often stored security codes in computer files in the mistaken belief that no one could find them there.

"Which means Gorkov didn't kill Manstein," Wendy pointed out. "He has no reason to blow up the Station."

"He was probably *hired* to kill Manstein and steal the computer. The people after the bomb wouldn't have told a gangster what he could do with that computer. In fact, *they* might not want to blow up the Station. They might want to move the bomb elsewhere . . ." That started Flynn thinking. "They'll have to cut into the compartment where the bomb was planted. That would attract the attention of Security, unless Security has something more important to deal with—like the murder of the Security chief. Drake showed me the bomb so I'd know what to watch if I had to take over from him."

Wendy grunted. "Dettweiler could do that."

Flynn was still thinking out loud. "Drake must also consider the possibility that the people who planted the bomb will think that Manstein's death means the bomb has been discovered. They would have to cut into the compartment to make sure the bomb is still there. We catch them doing that and we'll know who planted the device, and why—which, I'm willing to bet, are the only things that Drake hasn't figured out yet, or he would have already taken action against the guilty parties."

Wendy glared toward the front of the boat. She spoke through clenched teeth. "Only Silvanus Drake could think that our own government would plant a nuclear device on the Station."

"He said 'government.' You should have understood, 'people

in the government.' "

Wendy looked sharply at her husband. "There are people in our government who'd plant a nuke on the Station?"

"For years presidents have been raiding the defense budget to keep Social Security solvent. A lot of people think national security has been seriously compromised. If this Station was nuked, reductions in the defense budget would be political suicide. In fact, it would probably be increased." Flynn paused. "There are other people who think this highly automated station is costing too many people on Earth their jobs."

Wendy was still glaring. "And they'd kill twenty-four thousand people to get their way?"

"If they think they're defending the entire nation, from either military attack or economic ruin."

The work boat docked at the Station. Drake's telephone beeped as the party passed through the airlock. "Yes? I'm on the scene. It's my gun . . . and Mr. Flynn's gun." He put his telephone away. "Security sensors in the airlock," he explained.

No one spoke on the elevator to level three. Warshovsky and Drake crossed the Plaza to Company Headquarters. Wendy watched them disappear into the lobby.

"We'll have to put my piano in storage," she said. "Or some of my books. Everything won't fit in a smaller apartment."

There was only one reason why Wendy would be talking about moving to a smaller apartment. "Wendy—"

"Our apartment is a perquisite of my position. I'm . . . resigning that position."

"Again?"

"This is not funny, Michael! They have an A-bomb that they didn't tell me about!" Wendy glanced over her shoulder to make sure she hadn't been overheard. "After what happened last year, I asked them if there was anything else going on around here that their lawyer should know about, and Ed Warshovsky looked me right in the eye and said, 'Absolutely not.' Hah!"

"Wendy, Warshovsky could have fired you last year. Then you couldn't have found out anything that Warshovsky didn't want you to know. Since you're still legal director, he wants *you* to be his chief attorney."

"Then why doesn't he trust me? Why doesn't he tell me things?"

Wendy had once been Warshovsky's favorite executive. The Station manager had mentored her, promoted her, made her his corporate attorney. And now she despised him. She was angry enough to do something stupid. Flynn needed to calm her down. "Because he's afraid you'd do exactly what you're threatening to do—quit. Then he'd have to find a new legal director and he probably couldn't find one as good as you. Not on the Station, certainly."

Wendy was staring at the front of Company headquarters instead of looking at her husband. "Well, he's going to have to."

"Are you just going to quit, or are you going to turn them in this time?"

Wendy glanced at the overhead, with its imitation skylights, far above. "I . . . I wish I could. The attorney-client privilege doesn't apply if the attorney knows about ongoing or planned illegal activities by the client, but, as far as the legal system is concerned, they aren't in possession of the bomb now—back in the twenties an appellate court ruled that even a flimsy lock is sufficient to keep someone from 'being in possession' of something he isn't supposed to have." Flynn had suspected something like that—Warshovsky and Drake would never have shown him the bomb if they were illegally in possession of it. "If I turn them in, the Ethics Board would rule that I had betrayed my client's confidentiality and recommend that I be disbarred." She took a deep breath. "Can you see me tending bar in the Gold Dollar?"

Flynn put his arm around his wife. "Will you do me a favor? Postpone your resignation until this is over. I need someone who has access to the daily security reports. In particular, I'd like to see what the marshals found when they searched Manstein's apartment."

Wendy pulled away. "Okay." She took out her computer, punched a few keys, and handed it to her husband. "My copies of the security reports are in that file. But when this is over, I'm resigning. The Company is effectively, if not legally, in possession of a nuclear weapon."

"When this is over they won't even be effectively in possession of a nuclear weapon." Wendy looked at her husband, who was reading the computer display. "Drake thinks that Manstein's death means that the situation is coming to a head. Once the bombers are revealed, there will be no need to conceal the fact that the Company found the bomb. Wilmer de Birk and Namibia will no longer be nuclear powers . . . Huh. Not a single book in Manstein's apartment." Flynn gave the computer back to Wendy. "I doubt his killers stole his books. Were those Smiley novels ever published in digital format?"

Wendy wasn't in the mood to give a polite answer. "Would I have packed a crate full of books all the way out here if they were?"

Or Manstein *could* have read one of those spy novels before he came to Jupiter Station. Flynn bit his lip. "I'd love to know who chose the cover name 'George Smiley.' "

"Why were you interested in the saloons he frequented?"

"None of them have bartending robots. In fact, Manstein patronized every tavern on the Station that *didn't* have a robot."

"You mean, he didn't like robots? Like those neoluddite terrorists who blow up automated factories?" The revelation distracted Wendy from her anger and she was able to think. "Michael, I read someplace that dedicated neoluds have had computer chips surgically removed from their brains . . . A neoluddite group bribed someone to delete their DNA and fingerprints from the European-Union's database. And we're living in the most automated production facility in the solar system." Wendy considered the implications. "Its original designer is visiting it for the first time! If the Chinese had known that Manstein was a terrorist, they could have killed him to protect Liao!"

Michael shook his head. "If the Chinese had killed Manstein, Liao wouldn't be trying to find out who did it. He would know already."

"But he knew Manstein's name . . . maybe he's trying to figure out who beat him to it!"

"That would be my guess."

"It can't be us. Our government could have had Manstein arrested."

Obviously, Wendy wasn't referring to "people in the government." "Right. It would have to be somebody who doesn't want our government to know about the bomb. Manstein's employers . . . no, can't be them. Manstein's death cost them access to his apartment and to the computer system through which they controlled the bomb. It must be an as-of-yet unidentified third party that wants to get its hands on that nuke. A third party that Drake thinks might 'take him out of the picture.' Let me see that report again." Flynn took back the computer. "Manstein didn't have a radiation detector. At least, the marshals didn't find one in his apartment."

"Big deal. We don't have a radiation detector, either."

"Wendy, Manstein babysat that bomb for years. Don't you think that he would have wanted to get close to his baby once in a while?"

Wendy shrugged. "Maybe he was afraid of it." She shivered. "It gives me the willies."

"Wendy, a bartender told me that Manstein had extended his stay out here. He wouldn't have done that if he was afraid of the bomb."

The elevator doors opened, unleashing a load of passengers onto the Main Plaza. Wendy waited for them to move out of earshot. "The closest Manstein could get to the compartment where the bomb was planted would be the new reactor. He could have taken the tour—" Her eyes opened wide. "But the security cameras image everyone who tours sensitive areas of the Station! Drake described the system to Liao just the other day!"

Flynn smiled as he nodded. "Exactly. If Manstein had toured the reactor to get close to his bomb, Drake's computer system would have noticed that Manstein wasn't in the database. Since that didn't happen, Manstein never took the tour."

"So, Manstein didn't know where the bomb was?"

"Good security would prevent his superiors from giving him that piece of information, like it kept the bomb from being right in Manstein's apartment. But he didn't have a radiation detector—and he could have bought one at Jeffrey's True Value—so he didn't try to find it himself. Which probably means he thought he knew where it was, but his superiors had lied to him about its location."

Wendy pondered her husband's reasoning. "So where did he think it was?"

Michael shrugged. "Did Liao have his computer with him when he toured the Station and the satellites?"

Wendy shrugged. "I wasn't with him all the time, but he had his computer whenever I saw him."

"The Chinese are negotiating with us to improve relations. If a nuke with Chinese characteristics destroyed the Station, no amount of negotiating would do any good. The Chinese might have learned that a neoluddite terrorist group had planted that

A-bomb. Liao might have been sent here to find and deactivate it. The business of getting construction of the Asian station back on schedule might be a cover story. Liao's computer might contain a radiation detector."

Wendy's pale-blue eyes opened wide. "So he could find the bomb!"

"Or bombs."

Wendy paused. "Drake said there were no more bombs."

"No. He said he hadn't *found* any more bombs. And after ten years, he's still looking."

Wendy had pale skin, the genetic complement to her bright red hair. But Flynn had never seen her face turn so white. "You mean, there might still be a live nuke on the Station?"

Chapter 14

Wendy was no longer thinking about resigning. She was thinking about being incinerated. "Why don't they just take this station apart? Look in every compartment, the radiation shield, the—"

"Why don't they just tell everybody to keep their eyes open for an A-bomb?"

Wendy looked around the Plaza, imagining it filled with a panic-stricken mob. "I suppose." She looked at her husband. "I'm not going to be able to sleep tonight."

Flynn put his arm around his wife. "You've worked enough hours for a Friday. I don't feel like cooking. Why don't we eat out?"

"I . . . I'm not hungry, Michael." Wendy couldn't imagine when she would ever be hungry. "What I need is a drink."

Betty's Bar was only two blocks up Denver Avenue from the Main Plaza. The time was not yet eighteen o'clock and the bar was barely half full. The video display in the corner behind the bar was tuned to the Solar System News channel. The announcer was saying:

> ". . . a neoluddite group has claimed responsibility for last week's explosion at a diamond mine on the south slope of Olympus Mons. The explosion, which was apparently intended to entomb five automated excavators, killed two

maintenance engineers who were performing a safety inspection . . ."

A man at the bar said, "They're as far as Mars. They'll be out here next. Why don't those wackos just leave us alone?"

The man next to him replied, "Hey, it's your job they're trying to save."

"Yeah, well, if I'm dead, I won't need a job."

Someone else at the bar interjected, "Don't worry about neoluds. Not here. Drake wouldn't let one get within an AU of the Jovian system."

The first man grunted. "He doesn't run Security at the Asian station."

Wendy leaned close to her husband. "They have no idea how right they are."

There was an empty table against the far wall. Betty came out from behind the bar before Michael and Wendy could sit down.

"Well, if it isn't my favorite couple! Been a long time since I've seen the two of you together!"

"Hi, Betty. Beer for me. White wine for Wendy."

White wine was too tame for Wendy's mood. "Make it a champagne cocktail."

Betty left to get the drinks. Flynn said, "Oh, I'll send you my bill in the morning."

"Huh?"

"You hired me because you thought your employers were covering up something in Manstein's death. They just showed you what that was."

"Oh, right . . . then I'd like to hire you to find out who killed him."

"Wendy, if you were on planet three and you wanted to kill someone on Jupiter Station, whom would you hire to do it?"

Wendy opened her mouth, then closed it. She leaned back in

her seat. "Michael, Gorkov couldn't have done it!"

"I only asked you whom you would hire."

Betty brought the drinks. "Are you two celebrating tonight?"

"Recuperating," Flynn said. Before Betty could reply, she was summoned to refill glasses at the bar.

"Michael, there's one thing that doesn't make sense. Why did neoluddites go through the trouble to acquire a nuclear weapon, plant it on the Station, and just let it sit here for ten years? Why didn't they blow up the Station years ago?"

"Mmm, waiting for the optimum time, maybe. With only one nuke, they'd want to get maximum effect from it. Ten years ago, hardly anybody thought this station would be a success. If it failed, they wouldn't have had to blow it up, and they could have moved their bomb to a better target."

"But this station has been a resounding success for over five years. An *automated* success. And now another one is under construction and a third's in the planning stage."

"Yes, but the Asian station won't be nearly as automated as this one. Many neoluds are also environmental activists—they like to see factories moved off of Earth. By destroying the most automated station at Jupiter, they strike a blow against automation without driving all this mining and manufacturing back to planet three."

A shadow fell across the table. "Is this what you call, 'Buying me a drink'?" Sid Feldstein asked.

The deputy was in his marshal's uniform. Flynn assumed he had been working overtime. "No, this is what I call buying my wife a drink. It's kind of fun. You should try it sometime."

Feldstein grunted. "*Time!* I worked nine hours of overtime today! We have two murders, and there's a brawl nearly every night. I have aggravation, headaches, and a p.o.'d supervisor, but I don't have *time.*"

Flynn slid over. "Okay, you're in a hurry. Sit down." He got

Betty's attention, pointed to Sid, and mouthed the word "scotch." Betty nodded. Michael smiled at Feldstein and said, "FBI still insisting that Gorkov is innocent?"

"Yes."

"Have they told you how they know?"

Feldstein glanced from left to right without moving his head. "They can't. They say it involves national security. And don't breathe a word of that to anyone!"

Flynn and Wendy avoided looking at each other. Wendy said, "Ah . . . you mean, um, Big Bill Gorkov is . . . some kind of secret agent?"

Flynn didn't want the conversation to go in that direction. " 'National security' means that someone high up in the government doesn't want anyone on the Station poking into Gorkov's affairs, probably because he's been supplying the Feds with information on the Mars underworld."

"That 'someone high up' might be right," Feldstein said. "There was no forensic evidence at the crime scenes—no hair follicles, no DNA residue, no nothing—implicating Gorkov or his thugs."

Betty appeared with a scotch for Feldstein. "Who's buying?" Flynn raised his hand. "Okay, I'll put it on your tab."

Sid quaffed the entire shot and slammed his glass on the table. "I needed that."

"Gorkov's pets were wearing Company coveralls when they accosted me," Flynn said, "and Knuckles—the one with the hammer—was wearing gloves. Coveralls and gloves would keep them from leaving forensic evidence at the crime scenes—if they didn't drool."

"True, but with no evidence, we can't get a warrant." Sid looked coldly at Flynn. "But if you keep interfering with suspects in Federal custody, Hathaway will have no trouble getting an arrest warrant for you!"

Flynn squinted. "With whom am I supposed to have interfered?"

"That innocent routine won't work this time, Michael. I saw the security videos showing you entering DiGeorgio's hospital room."

"With the permission of the guard!"

"He wasn't supposed to give you permission!"

Flynn shrugged. "How am I to know that?"

"You have enough experience to know it! DiGeorgio's not supposed to see anyone except medical personnel unless his attorney is present! Why did you see him, anyway?"

"I tried to keep him from going to jail with his boss. And since when have Federal prisoners been allowed to watch porn?"

The counterattack caught Feldstein by surprise. "What . . . where the hell did he . . ." Sid slumped in his chair. "His lawyer probably brought it to him."

"Well, it's nice to know that the Marshals Service can figure out *some* things." Flynn tried to get Betty's attention. "Let me get you another drink."

Feldstein stood up. "I'll take a rain check. I've been home so little this week, if I don't get there right away my wife will forget who I am. And if she smells scotch on my breath, she'll forget anyway."

Feldstein left. Wendy was looking at the bar. The tavern had become crowded with Friday-night regulars, and Betty was busy. "Does she always work this place alone?"

"Hmm?" Flynn followed his wife's gaze. "Oh, sure. She's a sole proprietor."

"Can't her husband help out once in awhile? Or is that ring on her finger just to dissuade lonely men?"

"Does the ring on *your* finger dissuade lonely men?"

Wendy glanced at her wedding ring. "No. So why doesn't Mr. O'Brien help his wife?"

"It would be a long commute. He's a New York Transit Authority cop."

Wendy gave her husband a questioning look. "What has she been doing out here all these years if she's married to a man back on planet three?"

"Because, although she is married to him, he is not married to anyone."

Wendy needed a moment to digest that. "Ah! He's one of those!"

"In spades. I, ah, did an investigation for a New York firm in exchange for having them watch Mr. O'Brien for a couple of weeks." Michael shook his head sadly.

"Did Betty hire you? If she didn't, you didn't have an investigatible interest. You had no right to commission that New York firm."

Flynn gestured at the room. "This is—was my favorite bar. I didn't have an investigatible interest in the stability of its sole proprietor?"

Wendy considered Flynn's argument. "That is stretching the statute on investigatible interest beyond the breaking point. Why doesn't she divorce him?"

Michael could only guess. "She's a very traditional Catholic—believes in the 'better or worse' part of the marriage vows." He shrugged. "And maybe she's still in love with the bum."

Wendy finished her cocktail. "Do you believe in the 'or worse' part?"

Flynn's phone beeped. Michael took the instrument from his coat pocket and opened it. "Yes?"

"Michael," Missy Adamly said, "Jack's under arrest!"

Flynn put down his beer. "Why? He was saving my life!"

"No, not for that! He . . . he got in a fight." When speaking about Jack Adamly, that was not news. "He . . . he hit a guy. Mike . . . he might have killed him."

Chapter 15

Michael and Wendy found Missy Adamly in the emergency room of the Company hospital. She was wearing shorts, as usual, dark yellow this time, under a matching tee shirt and over sandals. She stood facing a trauma-room door, chewing the nails on her left hand and oblivious to anyone else in the ER.

"How's Jack?" Flynn asked.

Missy didn't look at Michael. "Oh, he's fine. He just hurt his hand. He hit him so hard . . . he broke a bone in his hand."

"Whom did he hit?"

Missy shrugged. "A guy. I don't know him. Didn't know him. Somebody said his name was Colin . . . something. Colin . . . Brennerman. Something like that."

"What happened?"

Missy bit her fingernail again. "We were in Joey's Joint. At the bar. Jack went to the other end of the room to talk to a friend of his, and this guy Colin comes up beside me and grabs my butt." She sighed. "I was handling it, and suddenly Jack was there, and he grabs this guy's shoulder, and tells him to keep his hands off of me . . . and then he hit him." She sniffled. "I've seen him hit people before, but this was different. It *sounded* different, like . . . like he'd hit bag of popcorn or something, instead of a man's face. And the guy fell backward . . . and he just lay there. He didn't even twitch. And then they said he wasn't breathing . . ." Missy took her fingernails out of her mouth. "He's not a Company employee; they took him to Meditech." She turned away from the trauma room, put her arms around Flynn, and pressed her face against his chest. "The marshals arrested Jack. They're using words like 'manslaughter' and 'homicide.' Oh, Michael, what am I going to do?"

Flynn glanced at his wife, then gingerly placed his hands on Missy's shoulder blades. "You're not going to do anything. Wendy's going to defend him. She'll talk to the marshals—"

Blue lights flashed through the transparent outer door as an ambulance pulled up. The door slid open to admit a gurney, pushed by two paramedics. Tubes and cables ran from the motionless human figure on the gurney to the life-support apparatus beneath it. A white-coated doctor followed behind.

Missy stared at the figure, its face black and purple and distorted into a caricature. "That's him! That's Colin Whatsisname!"

The Station morgue was beneath the hospital, but if Colin Brennerman had been dead he wouldn't have been connected to life-support equipment. The door to the second trauma room opened, as though it had been waiting for Brennerman, and the gurney was wheeled through it. Flynn saw what looked like a surgical team waiting inside. He grabbed the doctor who had accompanied the victim. "How is he?"

The doctor had been on Jupiter Station only six months. She hesitated. On Earth, explicit medical information could be shared only with the patient's immediate family. But Jupiter Station had a lot of single men for whom friends would have to substitute for families. The doctor pulled away, heading after the gurney. "Stable, but very comatose," she said. "His jaw is broken in four places, and a piece of his jawbone was driven into his brain. His PET scan looks like nothing I've ever seen before. The EKG shows only autonomic processes, and even those are distorted." She shook her head and her hair, tinted white to match her coat, rippled. "We don't have the equipment or the personnel at Meditech to make him a functioning human being again." She looked into the trauma room. "I'm not sure they do here, either. He should be at Johns Hopkins." She stepped through the door, which slid shut behind her dazzling white hair.

Johns Hopkins was eight hundred million kilometers away. That's why the Company paid a fortune to have top-flight medical personnel and equipment on the Station.

Flynn glanced at Missy. "A charge of homicide would seem to be a bit premature."

The door to the first trauma room opened and two deputy marshals led Jack Adamly through it. Jack's wrists were handcuffed in front of him and his right hand was wrapped in gauze. Marshal Hathaway, looking happier than she had been since arriving on the Station, was right behind Jack.

Jack showed off his bandaged hand. "Think they'll let me play airball with this?"

"There's no airball cage in the Station jail," Hathaway said.

Jack glared at her for interrupting. "The Company'll bail me out!"

Hathaway shook her head. "There won't be any bail if the doctors can't get Brennerman breathing on his own again."

Jack was thirty-five centimeters taller than the marshal. He bent forward to stick his face in front of hers. "I was defending my wife! The bastard was pawing her! And I only hit him once! Is it my fault that he's got a glass jaw?"

"No, but it's your fault that he's almost dead." Hathaway noticed the ambulance at the door. She looked toward the second trauma room. "Is he here yet?"

Flynn glanced at the other trauma room. "Just arrived."

The marshal looked at the deputies. "Lock him up. But be careful! I can't afford to have him do to you what he did to

Brennerman." She smiled at Flynn. "Your friend won't get out of this mess. I have witnesses that even Kyle Pierce will believe." She turned to the front desk, pointed at the door through which Brennerman had been wheeled, and said, "I want to be informed immediately of any changes in his condition." Then she followed her deputies through the front door.

Wendy took her computer from her purse and opened it. "Mitch Habruch," she said, and waited for her colleague to answer the call. "Mitch, we have a problem."

"Are you talking about the fight in Joey's?"

Wendy nodded. "The victim is not a Company employee and he's on life support."

"I'm at the Marshals Office. The victim's name is Colin Brennerman. Works for the Second National Bank. They've arrested Jack Adamly, but he's not here yet."

"He just left the hospital—he broke his hand."

The image on Wendy's computer display squinted. "Adamly broke his hand? Just how hard did he hit him?"

"He shattered Brennerman's jaw. Drove pieces of it into his brain. The Meditech doctor didn't sound optimistic."

Habruch grimaced. "As long as Brennerman isn't dead I might be able to get Adamly out on bail, although with his record for brawling Pierce is likely to make a strong argument to keep him locked up to protect the public." He pursed his lips. "At least he didn't resist arrest."

"Do what you can, and keep me informed. Jack—" Wendy glanced at Flynn. "Jack is a friend of my husband."

Wendy put her computer away. "Habruch is our expert on criminal law. He's Jack's best chance."

Missy looked desperately at Flynn.

"Go home, Missy," Michael said. "This isn't just another fight; the marshals will have to wait for the magistrate to set bail, and that won't be until morning at the earliest. Maybe not before Monday."

"Can you do anything?"

Flynn took a deep breath. "I can find witnesses, see if there are extenuating circumstances . . . was Jack drunk?"

Missy shook her head. "He hadn't finished his third beer."

"I can check out Brennerman, too," Flynn continued. "He might have a reputation for molesting women." Missy just stood there, as helpless as a lost puppy. "Come on. We'll take you home."

The door to the second trauma room opened. The paramedics pushed the gurney bearing Brennerman through the door and toward the elevator. Doctors and nurses followed. Wendy stopped Dr. Jasniak, the Station's medical director.

"Will he make it?"

Jasniak was wearing green surgical scrubs. Dark brown hair peeked out from beneath her cap. She was shorter than Wendy and so thin that she appeared malnourished. "It's an interesting case. This is our first chance to do state-of-the-art medicine out here. We have the latest equipment; we just haven't had any experience with it." She glanced at the gurney as it was wheeled onto the elevator. "We can keep him alive. Whether we can restore his higher brain functions . . ." She shrugged. "We'll see." Jasniak hurried onto the elevator.

Flynn summoned a cab and the three rode to Missy's apartment in silence. Wendy stayed in the cab while Michael walked Missy to the door.

"I . . . we have some money saved. We can pay you for your work."

Flynn made a face. "After all the favors you've done for me? I owe you this one."

Missy hesitated. "Thanks. Oh, about that last favor: Bill Gorkov sent an e-mail to the FBI—the IP address from their Web page where people can report crimes—last Friday."

Flynn's eyebrows rose. "Gorkov ratted someone to the Feds?"

Missy shrugged. "The FBI has a different e-mail address for people who just want to sound off."

Michael had been right: Gorkov had been supplying the Feds with information. No wonder the FBI didn't want him arrested for the murders. "When did they get back to him?"

Missy hesitated, as though she had to think about her answer. "They didn't."

"Missy, the FBI always acknowledges e-mails."

"They didn't acknowledge this one. At least, not from a known FBI server. Since last Friday, Gorkov has exchanged four messages with an IP address that I can't identify. As far as I can determine, the originating server doesn't exist. I can't find it in any IP directory anywhere. The best I can say is that it's in the Washington area."

"Washington, DC?"

Missy nodded.

"Government agency? Important mobster?"

Missy shrugged. "Don't know. Can't tell."

Without thinking, Flynn said, "Thanks, Missy. I owe you one."

Despite her mood, Missy said, "Again?"

Flynn returned to his waiting wife. "You might as well take the cab home," he said. "I need to track down those witnesses before they talk to each other too much and get their stories confused."

Wendy felt safer with her husband, even though he couldn't protect her from a nuclear explosion. "I don't want to be alone right now, Michael. I'll help you investigate."

"All you're going to get out of following me around is sore feet."

Wendy slid over to make room for Flynn. "Not if we take the cab."

Joey's Joint was more crowded than normal for a Friday night—bar business usually increased after a fight as people came from other taverns to get the story from eyewitnesses. The fight seemed to be the principal topic of conversation—no one was paying attention to the video displays at each end of the bar, both of which were showing the airball game taking place in the Station's central core. Flynn took Wendy by the hand and led her though the crowd toward the bar.

"Wait a minute! Flynn's been to college! Hey, Flynn!" Michael turned toward a table where four men in Company coveralls clustered around empty glasses, a half-empty pitcher of beer, and an open computer. "How does this sound to you?" The speaker pushed his glass aside and turned the computer so that Flynn could see the display.

Michael bent over to read it. "What is this?"

"We're putting Brennerman in for a Darwin award. What do you think?"

Flynn read the document. The writer hadn't been to college. Flynn wasn't sure he had finished high school. "You need to get Jack's name in here sooner. And in this sentence, it's unclear if 'he' refers to Jack or the victim. I'd use 'derriere' or 'bottom' or 'tush' instead of 'ass'—you don't want to offend anyone. And fix the grammatical errors the computer has indicated—you have some dangling participles and misspelled words in there."

"Thanks. If Brennerman gets the award, we get ten thousand bucks for nominating him."

"Don't spend it before you get it. Brennerman's not dead yet."

The writer brushed aside Flynn's concern. "A temporary situation, believe me. I *saw* Jack hit him. An elephant couldn't have survived that punch. I'm surprised his head remained attached to the rest of him."

Flynn took out his computer. "Can you elaborate on what

happened?"

The man squinted. "You're investigating *this?* Why? Everybody knows what happened! You should investigate the murders of Leron Cross and that guy the marshals won't identify!"

"First, I'm going to get Jack out of jail. What happened?"

The man patted his computer. "Just what I wrote. Brennerman was at the table back there in the corner, drinking with those guys. Jack leaves that curvaceous wife of his alone for two seconds, and Brennerman walks up and pinches her ass. Then he looks over at Jack and grins." The man chuckled. He turned back to his computer. "Hey, I should put that in here."

"Boy, did Jack wipe that grin off his face!" another man at the table said. The last two nodded.

"You all saw it?"

"My back was turned," said a man dressed in yellow Maintenance coveralls. "I saw Jerry stare at the bar, his eyes got this big, and he says, 'Oh, my God!' and I turned around just in time to see Brennerman's face get caved in. You could actually see it deform. We heard that they took Jack to the hospital instead of the jail. Do you know if he's okay?"

"He broke a bone in his hand. It couldn't have been a serious break; the medics put a splint on it instead of a cast. Whom did you say Brennerman was drinking with?"

The first speaker nodded at the back corner of the bar. "Those guys in the corner. See 'em? One black guy and two white guys?"

Flynn ordered a pitcher of beer for the informants and got their names. Then he headed for the table in the corner.

Wendy leaned close to Michael's ear. "If they're to be believed, it sounds like Brennerman was deliberately trying to provoke Jack. That's mitigating."

Wendy rarely handled criminal cases; she had missed the most important revelation. Michael let it slide.

Flynn didn't know the three men at the table in the corner. He pulled out the empty chair and said, "Mind if I join you?"

The three men looked at him. The black guy leaned back in his chair and said, "You're Flynn, the private detective. The one who married the Company's top shyster out here."

Michael flashed a smile. "That's me." He glanced around, but there wasn't another vacant chair in reach. He gestured with his head for Wendy to take the empty seat. "My associate, Wendy Chadwick."

Wendy settled into the chair and placed her purse on the table, clutching it in her hands. "The Company's top shyster out here," she added.

The black man winced.

Flynn opened his computer again. "I hear that you guys know Colin Brennerman."

"Is he still alive?"

"Mmm, depends on your definition of 'alive.' "

"Yeah, we know him. Knew him. Whatever."

"Did he say anything tonight before he tried to commit suicide?"

The man seated next to Wendy nodded vigorously. "That's just what it was, suicide! He was sitting where Norm is now, back to the wall, looking toward the bar. He points out Adamly and his wife, and when he leaves her alone Colin says, 'Bet you a hundred bucks he's not as tough as they say he is.' " The speaker pointed to himself with his thumb. "He expected us to take that dumb bet! Then he walks over there and stands right next to Adamly's wife. We couldn't see from here, but people over there said he actually grabbed her butt, right where Adamly could see him! Adamly strides back there—seemed like he crossed the room in only two or three steps—and pow!" The speaker slammed his right fist into the palm of his left hand. "That was the end of Brennerman." He took a sip from his glass of beer.

"Had he drunk a lot?"

The three men looked at each other. "I think he was on his first beer," the black guy said. "He'd been nursing it for an hour."

Norm, who had taken over Brennerman's chair, shook his head and said, "Brennerman and his dumb bets."

The black man nodded. "He had a serious gambling problem. If he was trapped in a leaking airlock with another guy, he'd bet on who'd croak first."

The third man at the table drained his glass and tried to get the attention of the bartender. "Oh, hell, he's too busy to come over here." He got up. "You guys ready for another?" He looked at Flynn. "What are you drinking?"

Flynn lifted his hand. "Thanks, but we can't stay. Did Brennerman lose a lot of money gambling?"

The three men glanced at each other. "He was always trying to borrow money. We knew better than to loan him any."

Flynn got the men's names and he and Wendy left the table. Wendy said, "If Brennerman borrowed money from Gorkov to pay his gambling debts, Big Bill might have offered to write off the debt if Brennerman would take a couple of punches."

Flynn nodded. "To get Jack Adamly out of the way before he went after me again. Or maybe he wanted to discredit Jack as a witness against Knuckles. And now Gorkov doesn't even have to worry about Brennerman changing his mind and talking to the marshals."

They stopped at the bar. Flynn pointed to the security camera in the corner and asked the bartender, "Did that catch the fight?"

"Not really," the bartender said while continuing to pour drinks. "I checked. It was panned to the other side of the room. It started to swing back when Adamly yelled at Brennerman, but all it caught was Brennerman hitting the floor." He handed Flynn a glass of scotch. "On the house, Mr. Flynn. I've been waiting almost a year for the privilege of buying you one."

Flynn hesitated. He glanced at Wendy. She was looking at him out of the corner of her eye. "Ah . . ." He took the glass. It was a generously stiff drink. Add it to the beer he had downed in Betty's and his blood alcohol level had to be pushing the legal limit for a man carrying a concealed weapon. "Get my wife a champagne cocktail."

"Make it one of those instead," Wendy said. Flynn looked at her, surprised. "Lawyers drink champagne cocktails," she explained. "Detectives drink whiskey."

"You're not a detective! And you don't like whiskey!"

The bartender handed Wendy a glass. "On the house as well," he said.

Wendy took the glass, poured the shot down her throat, and slammed the glass onto the bar. She poked Michael with her elbow and croaked, "Let's go."

Flynn paid the bartender to deliver another pitcher to the three men at the back table, then hurried to catch up with Wendy. She was waiting for him on the street. Her eyes were watering. "Is there something in the private investigator's code of ethics that keeps you from drinking champagne instead of whiskey?"

"It's part of our image. Our clients expect it of us, just like they expect their lawyers to drink wine and champagne."

"Don't ever let me do something that stupid again."

"What made you do something that stupid the first time?"

Wendy swallowed, trying to ease the burning in her throat. She blinked to clear her eyes. "Where to now? Gorkov's?"

Flynn shook his head. "He wouldn't say anything truthful. No, we know what happened here tonight, and I have the names of enough witnesses to make Habruch's case for him." Flynn gestured with his computer. "As soon as I contact Peter Chow and warn him that Gorkov might be trying to take him out, too, we can go home."

Wendy took Flynn's arm. She needed to feel normal. In her husband's embrace, she would forget all the worrisome things she had learned that day. "Let's not linger long before bedtime."

Chow answered his computer as soon as Flynn accessed it. Pete wanted to know about the fight in Joey's. Flynn didn't have to explain the significance of the witnesses' statements. "Gorkov's trying to get rid of us! We'd better get that bastard before he gets us!"

"That's what I was thinking," Flynn replied. "Until then, be careful. You don't know whom Gorkov will get to go after you."

Flynn slipped his hand into his coat pocket where he kept his stun pistol. He ejected the energy cell and put it in his other pocket, just in case Marshal Hathaway was keeping tabs on him. He kept a close watch on his surroundings as he and Wendy walked home. Michael halted Wendy in front of their apartment door. "Permit me to be ungentlemanly for a moment." The security camera on the balcony wasn't watching him; he took his stun pistol from his pocket and inserted the energy cell. He guided Wendy out of the doorway and slid the door open. The lights came on automatically. Furrball was just inside the door. The cat wouldn't have been waiting for his support staff if strangers were in the apartment. Flynn put his pistol back into his pocket, but kept his hand on the grip.

Wendy frowned. "Are you *trying* to frighten me? Gorkov doesn't have access to our apartment!"

"No, but Security does, and goons don't get paid very much." Flynn quickly checked the bedroom and bathroom to confirm that no one was hiding there. "The door locks can be programmed to record whenever the door is opened. Then your computer can tell you if anyone's opened the door while you were out."

"Thanks, but Gorkov's not after me."

"I wouldn't bet on that." Furrball rubbed against Flynn's leg. Michael picked him up. "Gorkov has someone in Washington keeping the marshals off his back, and the marshals are keeping Drake from investigating the murders. That leaves only me."

"And he thinks I could make you drop the case?"

Flynn nodded. "Which is why, if you're not with me, I don't want you out of sight of a security camera until Gorkov and his thugs are locked up."

It wasn't enough that Wendy could be incinerated by a nuclear explosion at any moment; she had to worry about Gorkov and his gangsters, too. She hated feeling vulnerable. She needed to be hugged, to feel that she would be safe. She tossed her handbag onto the couch and removed her coat. "Would you like to make love to me in here or in the bedroom?"

Michael gave Furrball a final hug and put the cat on the floor. "Bedroom. The last time we made love on the couch, Furrball jumped on my back. I'll just program the door lock first."

Wendy pulled her blouse off as she passed her husband. "Don't take too long or I'll start without you."

Michael took the hint. He checked the food supply in the cat feeder and shut off the living room light. Wendy was sliding under the bed covers when he entered the bedroom. Her clothes were scattered on the floor instead of hanging in the closet. Flynn put his stun pistol on the bedside table and began to undress.

Wendy's eyes lit on the gun. "Can you teach me to shoot?"

Of all the things Wendy might have said at that moment, that was the one Flynn had least expected. "Ah, sure. I can teach almost anyone to shoot. Why?"

"I can't do anything about a nuke planted somewhere in the radiation shield. I just have to live with that. But I'll be damned if I have to start hiding from Gorkov and his thugs."

Flynn made a face. "You don't have a permit to carry a concealed weapon."

"I can get one."

"Fat chance! This is a Federal jurisdiction! Hathaway has to approve it!"

Wendy smiled. "I married you, but Kyle Pierce will still do any personal favor I ask of him—especially if he thinks I'm in danger. Pierce will endorse my application, so Hathaway will issue the permit, and I won't have to go to the magistrate and have her overruled."

Wendy's legal brain had overlooked something. "Wendy, I only have the one pistol. Or do you expect me to take on Gorkov, Lavalle, Weasel, and Knuckles—especially Knuckles—unarmed?"

"I'll get a gun from Drake. He has an armory full of them."

Flynn needed a better argument. "Wendy, there's more to defending yourself with a gun than shooting skill. There's judgment, combat tactics—"

"You were a Marine Corps officer. You can teach me combat tactics, too. Drake has a shooting range and tactical course in the basement for training his goons. We can use that."

"Wendy—"

"Michael, I was helpless once last year. I don't *ever* want to feel like that again! If you don't agree to teach me to shoot, I am going to get up right now and *put on a nightgown!*"

"Wendy, you are a heartless and cruel woman."

Wendy lifted the covers so that Flynn could join her. "But—if you haven't been lying to me for the past year—one who is very good in bed."

Chapter 16

On Saturday morning, the doctors at the Company hospital removed the bone fragments from the brain of Colin Brennerman. His autonomic neural functions returned to normal and he was disconnected from life-support equipment. Thus encouraged, the doctors took the time to restore his face to one that would pass for human. As the tired doctors headed home, John "Knuckles" DiGeorgio, his reconstructed nose on the mend, all symptoms of his concussion gone, and released on bail from charges of aggravated assault and petty theft, walked out of the hospital right behind them. On the Government Plaza at the other end of the Station, the Federal magistrate listened to U.S. Attorney Kyle Pierce's request to keep Jack Adamly in jail for the protection of the residents of Jupiter Station, heard Mitch Habruch's argument that Brennerman's improved condition justified releasing Jack into the custody of his wife (who promised to keep Jack sober), and, after a somber pause to show that his decision was reached with judicial wisdom, set Jack's bail at two hundred and fifty thousand dollars. And as Jack Adamly was led back to his cell to wait for the Company to post his bail, the memorial service for Leron Cross was held in the Station's Protestant church, the Reverend Jimmy Meems officiating.

Leron had had a lot of friends, but the circumstances of his death and the tragedy of leaving a widow less than a year after the wedding had prompted many people who hardly knew Leron to come to the ceremony. The church overflowed and many people were turned away. Flynn and Wendy arrived in time to squeeze into seats at the back of the church. Wendy wore a somber black dress, plucked from the deepest reaches of her closet, that concealed the upper half of her legs and made her look properly mournful. Michael owned only one suit—the blue one he had purchased for his wedding—but it was dark enough for funeral attire. Reverend Meems, an old-school Southern Baptist with a voice that could make the deck plates jump up and shout hallelujah, gave a eulogy that left the congregation with tears in their eyes and the conviction that Leron should be held in the same esteem as the twelve apostles.

Michael and Wendy let most of the congregation file out of the church ahead of them. It was a slow procession, as Francine Cross stood at the door of the church to receive the condolences of the mourners. Francine, wearing a black dress, still looked ravishing and would not be taken for a mourning widow except for the tears in her eyes. She looked at Flynn and said, "Thanks for coming," for the five hundredth time that morning. "You know, at least a dozen people here today told me that the smartest thing I've done since marrying Leron is hiring you to find his killer."

"I found Leron's killer. I just can't prove it."

"Marshal Hathaway says she's out of leads. How can she be out of leads? I heard about that thug Gorkov, who tried to kill you and steal my money."

"The FBI has convinced her that Gorkov didn't kill Leron."

Francine blinked. "Well, who convinced the FBI? And who convinced Company Security?"

Flynn couldn't tell Francine about Gorkov's e-mail to the FBI. "Drake trusts his security cameras, and the cameras don't show anything."

Francine looked into the now empty church. "I'm shipping

Leron's body to Earth, to his parents. They want to bury him—in the ground, not in Jupiter's atmosphere. I like the idea; I can visit him, when I go back."

Reverend Meems came through the door of the church and approached Francine. Flynn took his wife's arm and they turned to leave. The church was on Sacramento Avenue, only a block from the Main Plaza. Flynn headed up station. Wendy pulled her arm free.

"I need to go to the office."

Flynn hadn't expected Wendy to have her own plans for the day. "On a Saturday? You're not going to help me investigate anymore?"

"It's safe—security cameras all the way. I'll catch up with you later."

Wendy didn't go to her office. She went to Silvanus Drake's office and, as she expected, found the security director at his desk.

Drake looked up from his computer, his dark eyes expressionless. "Ms. Chadwick, what can I do for you on a Saturday morning?"

Wendy took a deep breath. "I want you to add my name to your Security roster." She tried to make it sound like she wasn't requesting a very big favor.

Drake never looked surprised. He gently rubbed his chin. "Your friend Kyle Pierce couldn't persuade Marshal Hathaway to give you a gun permit?"

Wendy started to ask Drake how he had known what she wanted, but realized that she wouldn't believe his answer—if he bothered to give one. "I haven't applied. There's a seventy-two-hour waiting period after application before the permit can be issued. Gorkov might not wait that long."

Drake's empty black eyes stared at Wendy. "Mr. Warshovsky has instructed me to keep Gorkov and his associates at least a block away from you."

Wendy snorted. "Gorkov knows I won't let them get near me. He got Colin Brennerman to go after Adamly."

"It looks that way. However, our security agreement with the government requires me to train all Security personnel in the safe and proper use of firearms before issuing them deadly weapons."

"You didn't train Mr. Warshovsky before putting him on the list!"

"Mr. Warshovsky served in the Army," Drake explained. "I accepted his military training in lieu of training him myself."

Wendy changed her argument. "What if the Company attorney gave you a memo affirming that I already know the proper use of deadly force due to my legal training, and that my husband—who was an officer in the Marine Corps—will provide the safety and marksmanship training?"

"Your husband will really train you?"

"He's not keen on the idea, but I can get him to do anything I want." Wendy smiled.

For a moment Drake's eyes dropped from Wendy's face to her figure. "I believe you can." He stood up. "Follow me."

Drake led Wendy past Security Control to the back of Security Headquarters. The electronic lock on the Armory recognized Drake's retinal patterns but there was a mechanical combination lock as well. Wendy had never seen the Armory and was surprised by how big it was. She had expected something like a gun cabinet, but it was an entire room, lined with racks of laser carbines, pistols, and weapons that Wendy didn't recognize but which she guessed were grenade and rocket launchers.

Drake walked to the back wall. "You want something small that won't print under your coat," he said. He took a computer from his pocket, unfolded it, and studied its display. He opened a cabinet beneath a rack of laser pistols and removed a pair of rings. "These will fit you." He selected a pistol from the rack, stared at its serial number, put it back in the rack and took the pistol next to it. From the cabinet below the rack he took two energy cells. "These cells will fit in your husband's charger." He handed them to Wendy, then showed her the pistol. "Ruger thirty-five twenty pulsed laser, with stun. This is the selector knob on the back. It's in the stun position. To make the pistol kill, pull out the knob and rotate it one hundred and eighty degrees so that the red indicator faces up." Drake demonstrated the action, then put the pistol back into the stun mode. He handed Wendy the rings. "Since the pistol has a lethal mode it will not fire—even on stun—unless held in a hand wearing an activation ring, as required by Federal law."

Wendy took the rings from Drake's outstretched palm. They were smaller than the activation rings worn by Drake's goons and actually looked like women's jewelry. She held one so that the light reflected from the jewel set into it. "Are these stones real?"

"Semiprecious."

Wendy slipped one onto the ring finger of her right hand. She had trouble getting it over the knuckle. "Tight fit."

"Also as required by Federal law. That's to keep a bad guy who gets hold of your gun from easily getting a ring he needs to make it function."

"Lucky you had rings in my size."

"I try to be prepared."

Wendy gave Drake a sharp glance, then took the gun. It was smaller than the sidearms carried by the uniformed Security personnel and fit easily in her hand.

"One more thing—" Drake opened another cabinet and took out a black holster. "This will clip onto the waistband of your skirt or slacks."

Wendy shook her head. "No thanks." She put the pistol, the energy cells, and the ring for her left hand in her purse. "I'll carry it in my purse."

Drake decided to let Wendy's husband argue that point. "Take the holster; you might change your mind. When can I expect that memo from the Legal Department?"

"Would ten minutes be soon enough?"

Ten minutes would have been enough if a message from Mitch Habruch hadn't been waiting for Wendy in her office. The magistrate had set Jack Adamly's bail at two hundred and fifty thousand dollars, the highest bail ever set on Jupiter Station. Habruch lacked the authority to spend that much Company money. Wendy had the authority but not the money—less than ninety thousand dollars remained in her bail budget and she didn't have another account she could raid for that much cash. She would have to get Ed Warshovsky to transfer funds from another department, but her boss didn't answer his computer or his telephone.

Flynn had fallen behind on his paperwork. Reports from investigations he had subcontracted earlier in the week were in his computer, reports that had to be checked, rewritten to his standards (which were almost as high as those of Ms. Hammond, his high-school English teacher), and transmitted to the contracting agencies on planet three. Fortunately, no new investigations had been forwarded to him overnight. He finished his paperwork before noon, and turned his attention to the murder investigations.

Flynn needed evidence that would make the marshals stop believing what the FBI was telling them. He needed something that would get Drake to overlook what his security cameras weren't telling him. He needed witnesses who had seen Lavalle, DiGeorgio, and Rivera outside of Gorkov's office at the times of murders, witnesses who could put them at, or at least near, the scenes of the crimes. But Gorkov's thugs had chosen their disguises well. Company maintenance technicians in yellow coveralls were ubiquitous on the Station. Nobody gave them a second glance, so nobody—at least, nobody that Flynn could find that Saturday—had noticed the three bill collectors dressed as technicians either Monday or Tuesday night. In fact, most of the people Flynn talked to couldn't remember the last time they had seen a Company technician. Michael was frustrated enough to want a drink.

Wendy called him on his computer. "I got a part-time job."

That news gave Flynn a moment of anxiety. "Please don't tell me you quit your full-time job."

Wendy shook her head. "It's in addition to my full-time job. I got Drake to put me on his Security roster."

Flynn winced. "So you can carry a concealed weapon. A gun won't protect you, Wendy. It's just a tool you can use to protect yourself. And you don't know how to use one."

"But you promised to train me. Remember last night, just before you got on top of me?"

Flynn took a deep breath. "Okay, okay. As soon as Drake issues you a gun—"

Wendy held her gun so that it would show on Michael's display. "This gun?"

Michael looked closely at his display and confirmed that the energy cell wasn't inserted in the grip. "Ah, yeah. That gun."

"Drake's training facility is right below the basement access hatch on Fourteenth Street, just off San Diego. I'll meet you there."

Flynn was closer to the access hatch, so he got there before Wendy did, even though she took a taxi. "Any progress on the investigation?" she asked cheerfully.

"No. It's those damned yellow coveralls—they're all over the place, and nobody notices them. They made Gorkov's gorillas invisible."

"Drake's security cameras would have noticed."

"Wendy, we can focus the security camera outside our apartment on whoever rings our doorbell. The businesses on the Government Plaza have the same control over the cameras there. Gorkov could have paid someone down the block to pan the camera away from the door to the Gold Dollar long enough for those thugs to slip out."

Wendy reluctantly conceded the point. "What are you going to do now?"

"They couldn't have worn those coveralls when leaving Gorkov's office. Three technicians in the Gold Dollar Casino would not have been invisible. So they put them on someplace else. I have to find that someplace."

"One of their apartments?"

Flynn shook his head. "Drake would have been watching those, too."

Wendy nodded. She turned to the hatch protruding from the deck. "Executive lock override: Wendy Chadwick." The red light on the lock turned to green.

"I'll get it." Flynn spun the handle to undog the hatch. The light in the airlock came on automatically. The airlock extended all the way to the basement deck. Michael let Wendy climb in first. He pulled the hatch closed as he joined her. They had to wait ten seconds for the lock pressure to be reduced to the basement level. Wendy opened the hatch in the side of the airlock.

One dim lamp lit the basement. Wendy stared into the shadows and said, "They can't train in this. There must be a light switch."

"Lights!" Flynn commanded, and the Security training area was flooded with light. He grinned at Wendy. She wrinkled her nose in response.

Wendy marched directly to the firing range. Michael hurried to keep up. "Okay, lover, let's see that gun."

Wendy took the gun from her purse. "I think it needs these, too." She fished out the energy cells and handed them to her husband.

"Those cells won't be worth more than ten shots each. Maybe twenty each—all of Drake's lasers have had their energy reduced so they won't penetrate the Station bulkheads." Flynn looked around and spotted a rack of energy cells recharging next to the firing range. "Ah! Just what we need!" He grabbed a handful and returned to his wife. She was wearing a ring he hadn't seen before on her right hand. "Is that the activation ring? It looks like real jewelry."

Wendy nodded. "Semiprecious stone. He gave me one for my left hand, too, but I'm right-handed."

"Well, we'll get you on target with your right hand first, then switch to the weak hand." Flynn took the gun. "Ruger model thirty-five twenty." He shook his head once. "Probably underbid Smith and Wesson. Too bad—Smith's have smoother triggers." He held the gun in front of Wendy's face. "Is this loaded or unloaded?"

Wendy stared at the gun. She hadn't seen Michael insert an energy cell. She stooped until she could see the empty slot in the grip. "Ah, empty."

"Wrong. There's no such thing as an empty gun. They're all loaded and must be treated as such."

Wendy cocked her head. "This is a safety lesson, right?"

"Right. This is a pulsed laser, Wendy—a lethal weapon. Make a mistake with it and you could be in the market for a new husband—right after you serve your sentence for reckless homicide. Second lesson." Flynn tapped the muzzle with his finger. "This is called the muzzle. That's where the energy pulses come out. Always point it in a direction in which you're willing to shoot. That's known as muzzle control."

"Even if it's empty?"

Flynn took a deep breath. "Wendy, repeat lesson number one."

Wendy sighed. "There's no such thing as an empty gun."

"Good." Flynn tapped the muzzle again. "What's this called?"

"The muzzle. Always point it in a direction in which I'm willing to shoot."

"Lesson number three: This is the trigger guard." Flynn traced it with his finger. "It's called that because it guards the trigger from accidental activation. Never put your finger inside the trigger guard until you're ready to shoot."

"Will I be ready to shoot sometime today?"

Flynn handed her the gun. "Didn't Drake give you a holster?"

"Yes, but I don't need it. I'll carry it in my purse."

"No, you'll carry it in a holster. You might need it in a hurry, and you can draw it from a holster much faster than you can get it from your purse."

"You carry yours in your pocket!"

"Mine is smaller than yours but my pockets are bigger. This won't fit in the outside pockets of any of your coats. Use the holster. Then you won't have to think about where you're pointing your purse."

"I left it in my office."

Flynn shut his eyes. "Okay, we'll do the holster next time." He nodded at the target range. "Step up to this firing bench." The targets were cheap paper ones and not the expensive models that would record stun pulses. He showed Wendy how to attach a target to the slide and send it down range. "We'll start at ten meters. Did Drake show you how to switch from stun to kill?"

Wendy nodded. "Pull out this knob on the back and rotate it

a hundred and eighty degrees."

"Do it. Stun pulses won't make holes in paper. Then aim the gun at the target. Use two hands."

"Ah, I know guns are always loaded, but this one isn't."

"It's called dry firing. The sight is holographic; there's no parallax. Just put the orange dot on the sight on the center of the target and hold it there."

Wendy did as she was told, but the target wouldn't stand still. At least, the orange dot wouldn't stay on it. "Now what?"

"Hold the gun with the last three fingers of your right hand and wrap your left hand around them. Put your finger on the trigger. Concentrate on holding steady while you press the trigger."

Wendy squinted at the gun. "Don't I have to release the safety catch?"

"It doesn't have one." Wendy turned her head from the pistol and stared at her husband. "It has a trigger stroke of at least one and a half centimeters and a trigger force of at least twenty-five newtons," Flynn explained. "It takes a very deliberate action to pull the trigger, so Federal regulations do not require a safety catch. Now, press."

Wendy looked back through the sight and pressed. The target seemed to hop to the left.

"You jerked it."

"I did not! I pressed it!"

"Try again. Concentrate on holding the gun steady."

Wendy tried again. The target didn't move as far to the left.

"You jerked it again."

"I did not! I pressed it!"

"Wendy, I could see the muzzle move."

"Well, how can I make it keep still?"

"Practice, practice, practice. Here, insert an energy cell. Repeat the safety lessons."

Wendy inserted an energy cell into the grip and pressed it home until it clicked into place. "Guns are always loaded. Always point the muzzle in a direction I'm willing to shoot. Never put my finger inside the trigger guard until I'm ready to shoot."

Flynn nodded. "This one's for real. Concentrate. Press the trigger, don't jerk it."

Wendy aimed and pressed the trigger. There was a red flash on the target.

"You jerked it."

Wendy clenched her teeth. "I did not jerk it!"

"You hit low and to the right." Flynn nodded toward the target. "Keep shooting. And keep count. We'll see how many shots one cell is good for."

Wendy fired fourteen more shots before the trigger locked up. She stared at the gun. "It's broken!"

"No, the energy cell's depleted. That button next to the trigger guard will eject it. Don't put in a new cell yet." Flynn ran the target back up to the bench. There were only nine holes in it; eight of them were below and to the right of the black dot in the center. Flynn tapped the target with his finger. "Low and right. You jerked every shot but the third one. That's this hole here, five centimeters left of the bullseye."

"I didn't jerk the trigger! The sight must be off!"

Flynn looked at the gun. "Let's see. Where's that other activation ring?" Wendy took the ring from her purse and handed it to him. Flynn sent the target down range to the twenty-five-meter mark. He clenched the ring in his left fist, inserted a new energy cell in the gun, held the pistol with both hands, aimed, and fired five quick shots. He ejected the energy cell and retrieved the target. There was a ragged hole, three centimeters in diameter, two centimeters to the left of the bullseye and slightly above it. "How about that! The sight is off!" He looked around for a screwdriver and found a small one in a drawer in the shooting bench. He adjusted the sight, sent the target back down range, reinserted the energy cell, and fired five more shots. When he retrieved the target the black bull's-eye was gone, shot out. He nodded. "That's more like it." He ejected the energy cell, handed the gun to his wife, and said, "Safety lesson number four: Always remove the energy cell before handing a weapon to another person. Load a fresh cell and try again."

Wendy snatched the gun and slammed an energy cell into place. "Show off," she muttered.

They used all of the spare energy cells on the shooting range. When they finished, Wendy was consistently getting all fifteen shots from each cell on paper.

Wendy put the gun in her purse and smiled at her husband. "Do I qualify?"

"No." Wendy's smile vanished. "You need to score fifty points with ten shots at twenty-five meters," Flynn explained. "Left-handed as well as right-handed. The best you did was forty-two points with fifteen shots at ten meters. And then we move over to the tactical range, where you start learning how to defend yourself instead of just killing defenseless targets."

"If Drake's goons are that good, why do you claim that they can't hit a shower stall from the inside?"

"Drake's budget isn't big enough for him to train his goons that well. Force Recon Marines have to be that good. It's your life we're trying to protect. You have to be that good."

"If Drake trusts his goons—"

"Wendy, when you fire a gun, you always hit *something,* even if you miss your target. Drake's goons are insensitive thugs in orange Company coveralls. If they shoot a kid by mistake, they'll get over it. Will you?"

Wendy looked unhappily down the shooting range. "Practice, practice, practice." Learning to shoot was going to be much harder than she had anticipated. "Come on—I'll buy you dinner at the Martian Nugget."

"On a Saturday evening? We don't have a reservation! We'll never get in!"

Wendy's eyes twinkled. "Sure we will. I'll show you a trick."

Wendy's "trick" was a pair of hundred-dollar bills slipped to the maitre d', who led Michael and Wendy to a small table in the front corner of the restaurant. Wendy waited until they were alone to explain, "They always keep a table or two available in case important people show up without reservations."

"It's nice to be married to an important person—especially one who can afford to spend two hundred bucks just to get into a restaurant, although I hear that she intends to quit her high-paying job. Menu!" The menu was displayed on the tablecloth. "Mmm, tenderloin! I'll have a big one!"

"You should try the lemon chicken."

Chickens had been raised on Satellite Delta for over a year, and were now raised on the new Satellite Kilo, but steaks had to be shipped from Earth and were very expensive. "So you keep telling me. But I feel like steak tonight. Will you pick the wine?" Beer, whiskey, and vodka were produced on the Station, but wine, like steak, was shipped from planet three at considerable expense.

"White wine with fowl, red with steak. You don't really like wine anyway, so we'll have a white." Wendy jabbed her finger onto the projected list. "From California."

They sipped wine until a robot brought their orders. "The magistrate set Jack's bail at two hundred fifty thousand dollars," Wendy said.

Michael stopped with a piece of steak halfway from the plate to his mouth. "A quarter of a million? To where does he think Jack will run?"

"It's not to insure that he'll appear at trial. Since there's no question that he threw the punch, the court is allowed to keep him in jail for the protection of the public. The magistrate is effectively telling the Company—which he expects to pay the bail—to keep Jack under control."

"So, did you pay the bail?"

"I can't. I don't have that much in my budget. I left a message for Warshovsky to get me more funds, but he hasn't responded yet." Wendy shook her head once. "I don't know why he hasn't. Maybe he's trying to send a message to Jack."

"Probably. He knows the case won't go to court."

"This one will. Brennerman doesn't work for the Company. We've no leverage to get him to drop the charges—if he lives. If he doesn't, Kyle Pierce is certain to charge Jack with manslaughter."

"And the jury will be selected from the residents of Jupiter Station, all of whom have heard the details of the fight. Remember those guys in the bar last night, submitting Brennerman's name for a Darwin award? I'm sure their opinion of Brennerman is shared by every guy on the Station who knows Jack's reputation. And how many women out here would vote to convict a man who rushed to the defense of his wife while she was being pawed by a stranger?"

Wendy put down her fork. "You heard what Marshal Hathaway said last night! She's still angry that Pierce wouldn't let her charge the three of you when Gorkov's goons assaulted you!"

"Hathaway's new. Pierce, Warshovsky, and the magistrate know the score out here. The only way Jack will go to trial is if Brennerman has politically powerful friends on planet three—and even they won't be able to stop Jack from being acquitted. The only time Jack's going to spend in jail is the time he waits for Warshovsky to post bail."

Wendy picked up her fork. "Maybe I should get myself disbarred. This is a weird place to practice law."

It was a dangerous place to practice law, too. There didn't have to be another A-bomb hidden somewhere on the Station. The one in Wilmer de Birk's storage shed was less than twenty minutes away by shuttle. Flynn had thought that Leron Cross had been murdered because he had refused to smuggle contraband for Bill Gorkov. But what if he had been killed because he had refused to take Gorkov—or whoever was paying Gorkov—to the storage shed?

Chapter 17

The energy cells for Wendy's pistol were discharged, so Michael knew his wife couldn't accidentally shoot anyone that evening. He promised to meet her at Betty's, and entrusted her safety to the crowd and the security camera on the street in front of the Martian Nugget. He took out his computer, displayed a map of the Station, and tried to figure out where Gorkov's enforcers could have donned yellow Company coveralls. They would have needed a private apartment, someplace where Maintenance personnel wouldn't accidentally discover the garments. Flynn ruled out Gorkov's friends—the gangster didn't have many, and their apartments would be too easy to keep under surveillance. Lavalle, DiGeorgio, and Rivera had probably used the apartment of somebody who owed the gangster money. Flynn could spend weeks chasing rumors, trying to find Gorkov's customers. He decided to pursue a different line of investigation.

Michael took the moving sidewalk to the new end of the Station, walked down two levels to the Government Plaza, and followed the circumference of the Station until he stood in front of the Gold Dollar Casino. He looked up at the camera closest to the casino's door. Any of the nearby businesses could have commandeered it to view their front doors; Lavalle, DiGeorgio, and Weasel would then have had ten seconds to make it from the Casino's door to Phoenix Avenue. That was where the puzzle began. Phoenix Avenue was a major thoroughfare, well-covered by security cameras. Gorkov couldn't have controlled enough of them for his thugs to evade detection.

But security cameras didn't cover every meter of every street. Children on Jupiter Station played a game: going as far as they could without being spotted by a camera. If nine-year-olds could get across the Station undetected, Gorkov's thugs could, too—if Lavalle was leading them, since Weasel and Knuckles weren't as smart as a typical nine-year-old.

Not twenty meters away on the Government Plaza were the very experts Flynn needed to consult: two boys, aged about ten, were looking at him. One had black hair, the other light brown.

The boys were delighted to be noticed. "You're Michael Flynn, the detective, aren't you?"

"That was the name on my official government ID card, the last time I looked."

The boys looked at each and grinned. "My dad says you're going to solve the murders. You know, the cowboy and the guy the marshals won't identify. Is that what you're doing here?"

"Umm, I'm trying to discover how someone left the Government Plaza without showing up on the security cameras."

The boys' eyes opened wide. The black-haired one said, "Only by wearing somebody else's face or by bribing the goons in Security Control! There are no gaps in the camera coverage on Government Plaza." He wrinkled his nose. "My dad says it's because the government is parend . . . par . . ."

"Paranoid," his pal said.

"Yeah, that too." The boy shook his black hair from side to side. "The only way you can get past Government Plaza without being spotted is to go up to level five."

"Six," the brown-haired boy corrected.

"Krissie says she did it on five."

"Krissie lies like a politician."

Flynn glanced upward. Gorkov's thugs hadn't been on level five, let alone six. They had been on level three, in a back room of the Gold Dollar Casino, with no exit other than the front door. Silvanus Drake would have ruled out the possibility that his goons had been bribed.

Flynn took out his wallet and gave each boy twenty dollars. "Thanks, guys. You saved me a lot of work." The two delighted children skipped away.

Flynn looked at his watch. Saturday night was party time, and the only place on Jupiter Station where Gorkov's thugs could have purchased new faces was still open.

Phoenix Avenue had a moving sidewalk. Flynn rode it to the Main Plaza, where he switched to the Plaza's sidewalk and travelled around the Station to Tucson Avenue. He climbed the ramps to level five and walked toward Fifth Street. The Station's fanciest night spots were on that stretch of Tucson Avenue. Their signs, interspersed with electronic billboards, bathed pedestrians in conflicting and unsynchronized colors. On Saturday evening there were a lot of people on the street. A dozen assailants could have been hiding in the bright, confusing lighting, but Tucson was well covered by security cameras. Flynn expected no trouble there.

Flynn's destination was a shop called The Party Prep. Its door was open. The lighting inside was continuous and white, giving Flynn's eyes a much-needed rest. Except for the attendant, a young man in a dazzling yellow shirt and tight black slacks, the shop was empty.

The attendant wore a music pod in his right ear and was playing a video game. He didn't see Flynn until the detective stepped up to the counter.

The attendant paused the video game. "Ah, can I help you?"

"I hope so," Flynn said. He wasn't making polite conversation; if the attendant couldn't help him, probably no one could.

The attendant touched the music pod in his ear, quieting it. "What do you need? Decorations?" He gestured at the racks along the far wall. "Costume? Mask?"

"Information," Flynn said. He took out his computer and placed it on the counter where the attendant could see the display. "These guys bought masks here—the lifelike ones that let you impersonate celebrities. I'd like to know which masks they bought."

The attendant was younger than Flynn's first impression of him, probably a teenager. He looked at Flynn, then at the computer display. "Tonight?" he asked.

Flynn shook his head. "At least a week ago. Might have been several months."

"These guys weren't in here tonight."

"Do you remember when they were?"

The boy looked at the photos again and shook his head. "I don't think I've ever seen 'em before . . . but I only work evenings. Maybe they came in during the day . . ." He pointed at one of the photos. "That guy looks like that gangster that was on the news last year . . . Gorky, I think his name is."

"Gorkov."

"Hmm?"

"His name is Gorkov. Are you sure you never saw him in here?"

The boy stared at Gorkov's image. He shook his head. "I don't think so, and I'm pretty good with faces."

Flynn chewed his lip. Gorkov probably would have paid cash for disguises, but . . . "Could you check your records and see if Gorkov ever bought a mask here?"

"Ah, I don't know if I'm allowed do that. Are you the police or something?"

"Or something." Flynn took a business card from his coat and handed it to the boy. "I'm a private investigator."

The boy took the card and stared at it. His eyes grew large. "You're Michael Flynn? I heard you were investigating the murders!" He looked at Flynn's computer display. "You think one of these guys was involved?"

"I think at least one of these guys bought a mask in here. I'm trying to prove it."

The boy turned toward his computer, then stopped. "I don't know . . . I'll get into trouble. Privacy laws, you know. You're not a cop."

"How can you possibly violate someone's privacy by telling me that he *didn't* buy anything here?" The boy glanced toward his computer, but his feet didn't move. Flynn opened his wallet, took out a hundred-dollar bill, and placed it on the counter.

The boy's fingers flexed. He picked up the bill and tucked it into his shirt pocket. "I guess there can't be a law against that." He stepped to his computer. "The Gorkov account." His expression changed. "Uh-oh." He swallowed, looked at Flynn, then at the display, then to the money in his pocket. To help him make up his mind, Flynn took out another hundred-dollar bill.

"You didn't hear this from me, right?"

"Hey, I don't even know your name."

The boy looked impressed. "That's right!" He took the second hundred. "He bought five masks. Five different sizes, so they weren't all for him. Put 'em on his debit card."

"Masks of whom?"

The boy threw up his hands. "That I can't tell you, except that they were stock images—we charge extra if we have to make an image for a customer."

Flynn squinted at the boy. "How do you control inventory if you don't know what you sold?"

"The masks we get are all blank. You specify the face, and the computer vacuum forms and colors the mask." The boy could see the disappointment in Flynn's eyes. "The person who sold the masks might remember."

"Who was that?"

The attendant looked at his display. "Oh. Mr. Donescu, the owner . . . Yeah. Fourteen ten. Middle of the afternoon. Mr. Donescu would have been here then."

"What day?"

"Ahh . . . twenty-eight October. That's Halloween, isn't it? They were probably going to a party."

The party Gorkov had in mind was unlike any the boy had ever attended—or would ever want to attend. "Do you know if your boss is home tonight?"

"Um, no, he's not. He said he was going to the Ionosphere Club." The boy gestured at the wall behind him. "It's only a block down the street."

Flynn nodded. "I know the place." He smiled at his informant. "Thanks."

The sign above the Ionosphere Club had simple black letters outlined by bright white lights, an attempt to imply sophistication and good taste compared to the kaleidoscopic signs above the other businesses on Tucson Avenue. It wasn't surrounded by electronic billboards. The club was too upscale for Flynn's taste and too expensive—at that time of the evening there was a fifty-dollar cover charge. The woman at the door had Oriental features and wore a shiny black minidress over black tights. She slapped the hundred-dollar bill that Flynn gave her into her cash register and took out a fifty.

"How would you like to keep the change?" Flynn offered.

The woman studied his face, and a trace of a smile appeared on hers. "Normally, fifty bucks wouldn't get you to first base, but you're so cute that I'll give you your change. I get off at two."

Flynn didn't call the woman's attention to his wedding ring. "Do you know a guy named Donescu?"

The smile faded from the woman's face. She palmed the fifty and slammed the cash drawer closed. "He's over there at the bar, hitting on that Hispanic girl . . . Oops, he must've struck out. Now he's talking to that blonde."

"Thanks."

There was an empty stool on the other side of Donescu from the blonde. Flynn slipped into it, opened his computer and put it on the bar. "Mr. Donescu?"

The man turned around. He had a round face under straight black hair. "What?" He looked annoyed, but his expression quickly changed. "Hey, aren't you Mike Flynn, the detective?" Before Flynn could deny it, Donescu said, "Let me have the honor of buying you a drink!" He raised his hand. "Bartender!" He looked back at Flynn. "It's whiskey, right?"

Flynn started to protest, but the bartender was on the scene too quickly. "Get Mr. Flynn here a whiskey, neat," Donescu said.

The bartender looked at Flynn. Michael hadn't come to the club to drink, but Donescu was being friendly, and it was easier—and cheaper—to get information from friendly people. "Scotch. Or Irish, if you have it."

The barkeep shook his head. "It will have to be scotch."

"That'll be fine."

Donescu said, "I don't think I've ever seen you in here."

"It's been a while." Flynn drew Donescu's attention to the computer display. "Did these guys ever buy party masks at your shop?"

Donescu looked at the display and frowned. "Do you know who they are? That's Bill Gorkov, the gangster, and some of his bill collectors." He shook his head. "They won't like having you ask questions about 'em."

"I know." Flynn indicated Knuckles's photo. "That one tried to hit me over the head with a hammer a few nights ago."

Donescu glanced around, lowered his voice, and said, "I

heard a rumor that they're the ones who killed that cowboy last Tuesday."

"I heard that rumor, too. Were they ever in your shop? I asked the kid who's working there tonight, but he started quoting privacy laws."

"Really? Huh. I didn't think he was that smart." Donescu thoughtfully rubbed his chin. "Maybe I'm not paying him as much as I should."

The bartender brought the whiskey. "Next one's on the house, Mr. Flynn."

"Thanks, but I'll probably have to take a rain check tonight." Michael turned back to Donescu. "Did you ever see them in your store?"

Donescu hesitated while he tried to figure out how angry he would make Gorkov if he admitted they had bought party masks from him. But Donescu had the mask monopoly on Jupiter Station, so everyone who had seen the gangsters in their party attire would know where they had obtained the masks. "Yeah. Those four, and another guy: midsized—bigger than the runt, but not as tall as the handsome one." That would be the thug currently in the Station jail for using a prostitute as a punching bag. "Last Halloween, I think it was. Gorkov was throwing a party."

"Do you remember whom they impersonated?"

Donescu stared at the display. He pointed at Gorkov. "George Washington. Huh. Must have made him roll over in his grave." He indicated Weasel's photo. "President Mendez." Donescu looked at Flynn. "We had a little trouble with that mask—Mendez doesn't have mustache, and we couldn't have his upper lip bulging." He looked at the computer again. "These other two . . . the one who tried to hit you in the head doesn't have a sense of humor. I joked that he looked like he didn't need a Halloween mask. He got real upset." He shook his head. "But for the life of me I can't remember what he got. Or the handsome one." Donescu looked up at Flynn. "Sorry."

DiGeorgio and Lavalle were the two who were most likely to have committed the murders. Flynn tried not to be disappointed. "What about the fifth man?"

"The midsized guy? Um . . . Cliff Siddig, the actor. Made him look a hell of a lot better." Donescu chuckled. "Might have got him kissed for free for the first time since he moved here."

The blonde on the other side of Donescu looked bored with the conversation. She was wearing a glaring white outfit that was cut to emphasize her two principal assets, but her face would never launch a thousand ships—probably not even a toy boat in a bathtub.

Flynn drained his glass and picked up his computer. "Thanks for the help." He returned to the crowds and the garish lights of Tucson Avenue. On a weeknight he could have found Sid Feldstein in the Marshals Office, running the evening shift, but on a Saturday night Sid could have been anyplace. Flynn looked for a quiet spot. Compared to Tucson Avenue, Sixth Street was almost deserted. Flynn stepped into a doorway and opened his computer.

Feldstein was not happy to see Flynn's image on his display. "I can't talk now, Mike. I'm investigating."

"And I'm helping you. Last Halloween, Gorkov bought lifelike masks for the four thugs he had at that time. When those masks fit well, they're hard to spot. Those FBI agents who have supposedly been watching Gorkov and Company might not have recognized them."

Whatever Feldstein was investigating was suddenly less interesting than what Flynn was saying. "Oo! Hathaway would be delighted if we could prove the FBI screwed up! What masks did they get?"

"Weasel would have looked like President Mendez. The guy

you have locked up—What's his name? Belinguer?—went as Cliff Siddig. I haven't been able to determine who DiGeorgio and Lavalle were impersonating. But there's a security camera right in front of the Gold Dollar, and its record from the forty-eight hours before Manstein's body was discovered was saved on Hathaway's orders. All you have to do is check the record for people who left the casino but who never entered it."

Feldstein nodded. "Thanks, buddy. This pays back a bunch of favors."

Betty's Bar was as crowded as usual on a Saturday night. All the tables were occupied, and Wendy could see only two openings at the bar. She started for them, then stopped. The openings were on either side of Missy Adamly. Even with her husband in jail, the male patrons gave her elbow room, not wanting accidental contact to be reported to Jack and misconstrued as sexual assault. Wendy took another look around Betty's but there was nowhere else to sit or stand. She sighed, and headed for the bar. Unlike the male customers, Wendy could brush against Missy without arousing Jack's ire.

Wendy put her purse down on the bar in front of her. Purses were rare enough in Betty's for Missy to turn and look at its owner. She immediately looked away.

"I hope you're here to tell me that the Company paid Jack's bail."

Wendy took a deep breath. "No, I'm not. I just spoke with Ed Warshovsky in his apartment. He's making an example of Jack in the hope of reducing the brawling on the Station. He intends to let Jack sit in that cell for a week or so."

Missy had a half-full glass of beer on the bar in front of her. She tilted the glass and looked at its contents without noticing that the beer had gone flat. "But he will pay the bail?"

Wendy nodded. "He has to. It's in the standard employment

contract. He's just not required to pay it promptly."

Missy continued to play with her glass. "Betty told me to keep bail money handy. She didn't tell me I'd need a quarter of a million." She put the glass down. "When I married Jack I knew he had a temper. I'd seen him fight. But I never thought . . . I never thought he might kill someone." She closed her eyes. "What if Brennerman dies? Jack could spend the rest of his life in prison!"

Wendy hesitated, but Missy, like Jack, was a Company employee; Missy was her client, too. Chadwick decided to do her good deed for the day and cheer up Jack's wife. "I called Dr. Jasniak before I talked with Mr. Warshovsky. Brennerman's in no danger of dying. They're going to try restarting his higher brain functions tomorrow morning. Jasniak sounded upbeat." Wendy didn't know if that was because the doctor was optimistic or because she was getting a rare chance to practice state-of-the-art medicine. "And even if they can't get him functioning again, or even if he dies, no jury on this station is going to convict Jack of a felony when all he did was punch out a man who was molesting his wife. That's why Mr. Warshovsky is letting him sit in jail—he thinks it's the only time Jack will serve for this incident."

Betty O'Brien made her way along the bar. She stopped across from Wendy. "White wine?"

"Ah, yes."

"Where's Michael tonight?"

"Investigating homicides."

Betty put a glass down on the bar and filled it with wine. "I heard that Big Bill Gorkov did in Leron Cross."

"Did you hear of anybody who saw him do it?"

Betty shook her head. "That I haven't heard." She indicated Missy's glass. "You okay?" Missy nodded, and Betty moved on.

Missy looked at her half-empty glass. "You really think Jack won't be convicted?"

Wendy sipped her wine. "Criminal law is not my specialty." She put her glass back on the bar. "But Michael thinks Jack won't be convicted of anything more than a misdemeanor."

Missy continued to stare at her beer. "Jack didn't have to punch Brennerman. Mike wouldn't have." She looked up. She didn't notice her reflection in the mirror behind the bar. "And Mike's the only person I know of who fought Jack and won."

Wendy looked at her sharply. "When was this?"

"Last year. Around the time he met you. Jack was drunk, but that never saved anyone else. Michael taught unarmed combat in the Marine Corps, but I suppose you know that."

Wendy picked up her glass. "He mentioned it."

"Their fight was about me. Someone had told Jack that Michael was still hitting on me."

"Was he?"

Missy gripped her beer glass so fiercely that Wendy thought it might shatter. "No!"

"You sound like you regret he wasn't."

Missy put her glass down hard. "Jack's an almost perfect husband. He loves me to a fault. Brings me flowers every week, which he can scarcely afford on his contract. He puts me on a pedestal and worships me. If he caught me in bed with another man . . . well, first he'd beat him to death, then he'd take me gently in his arms and ask if the man had hurt me."

Wendy wanted to leave her wine on the bar and walk away. It would have been the intelligent thing to do. But Missy was the only serious competition for Michael's affection. Wendy had to know. "Do you love Jack?"

A man stepped up to the bar on the other side of Missy, then recognized her and hastily stepped back. Missy never noticed him.

"I . . . I . . . I don't love him the way I love . . . the way I *loved* Michael." Missy swirled the beer in her glass. "He was mine, you know. All I had to do was be patient. But I started talking about marriage, just when that damned Barbara Olsen with her long legs came along . . . and you know what Michael thinks about long legs."

Wendy wanted to smile, but thought better of it. "I once asked Michael what had first attracted him to you. He said you had cute legs."

Missy looked at Wendy. "He did?" She couldn't stop her eyes from glancing downward. "What does he say about yours?"

Wendy took a drink of wine. "Lots of very flattering things."

"And yours are longer than mine—almost as long as Barbara's. So, just to show him how mad I was, I married Jack." Missy sipped her stale beer without tasting it. "How did you do it? Get him to marry you, I mean."

Wendy spun her engagement ring around her finger to hide its diamond, which was noticeably bigger than the one on Missy's ring, while her mind went back to the previous year. She had needed weeks to decide to ask Michael to move in with her, an arrangement requiring no long-term commitment, an arrangement that could have been easily discontinued if it proved to be a mistake. It had taken her only seconds—most of that to get over the surprise—to say yes to Michael's proposal. "It wasn't my idea. I suggested he move into my apartment . . . and he proposed."

Missy had never asked Michael to move in with her, or offered to move in with him. Their apartments had been too small, and she valued her space. "What's it like, being married to Michael?"

Wendy studied her reflection in her glass of wine. "Challenging. Every woman we meet wants to bear his children."

"Besides that."

Wendy chose her words carefully. "He treats me the way Jack

treats you. He's quieter now than when we were dating. Almost boring, sometimes. Stays home a lot."

"He says you're intellectual." Missy wasn't sure about that—she'd heard about the table-dancing incident. "Probably thinks that's what you want in a husband."

"So I've been told. But he does most of the cooking and gives me flowers every week."

Missy made a face. "He never gave me flowers!"

Wendy noticed a reflection in the mirror and did not reply. Michael stepped up to the bar between the women. "Betty!" he demanded. "Irish whiskey! A double!" He remembered the stun pistol in his pocket. "Ah, just make it a single."

Wendy looked at her husband. "Is this a celebration or are you frustrated?"

"Celebration." Flynn turned to Missy. "You're not answering your phone or your computer."

Missy didn't look at Flynn. "Jack's friends keep calling, asking if he's been bailed yet. I think they're planning a party to celebrate his release."

"From what distance can a security camera scan someone's retinals?"

The question surprised Missy. She turned toward Flynn. "Oh, ah, depends. The ones covering the Station entrances can read retinals as soon as you step through the hatch. I don't think the others have that capability. I'm not sure they could get a retinal image even if you stuck your nose against the lens. Why do you ask?"

"Because Gorkov's thugs got out of the Gold Dollar without being spotted by wearing those lifelike masks you can get for parties or stage plays. And if the camera in front of the Gold Dollar can read retinals, they wore contact lenses with false retinal patterns, too. I don't know what those masks looked like, but those disguises will be their undoing: The security videos will show people who left the Gold Dollar but had never gone in."

"They weren't wearing disguises when they assaulted you," Wendy pointed out.

"They took them off when they put those yellow coveralls on—they knew I was expecting *them,* not three celebrities who have never set foot on Jupiter Station."

Betty brought Flynn's whiskey. Michael pointed at Missy's glass. "Freshen that beer." He glanced at Wendy's glass. "Is the wine paid for? Put 'em all on my tab."

"I'll present your theory to Drake on Monday," Wendy said.

Flynn shook his head. "Don't bother. I already told Sid Feldstein tonight."

Chapter 18

Sunday promised to be a good day. In the morning the doctors at the Company hospital managed to restart Colin Brennerman's higher brain functions. They were confident that it would be a matter of days, at most, before he came out of the coma. Jack Adamly was nearly free; the magistrate would certainly reduce his bail to something that Wendy could pay from her budget. In the afternoon the Red Sox were playing the hated Yankees. Carver, who had won ten games in a row, was pitching for the Sox. Right after the baseball game the Bruins were playing Moscow in the Stanley Cup finals. Flynn decided that the murder investigations could wait until Monday. He made a big bowl of popcorn, added enough butter and salt to make Wendy wince, took a six-pack of German beer from the refrigerator, and sat down in front of his video display to enjoy the afternoon. Furrball jumped into his lap and curled up.

The door chime sounded. "I'll get it," Wendy offered.

Outside the door stood Deputy Marshal Juan Salazar and his partner. Wendy sensed bad news, but she tried to be pleasant. "Can I help you, deputies?"

Salazar nodded toward Flynn. "We gotta take you in, Mike. We have a warrant for your arrest."

Flynn suppressed the urge to throw the popcorn bowl against the wall. "The Red Sox game is about to start!"

"On what charge?" Wendy asked.

Salazar handed the warrant to Wendy. "Obstruction of

justice—interfering with a police investigation."

"What?" Wendy exclaimed.

"I tried to warn you, Mike," Salazar said, "but you just had to piss off Hathaway."

"Pissing off a U.S. marshal is not obstruction of justice!" Wendy protested.

"Well, Hathaway convinced the magistrate that it was." Salazar stepped into the apartment. He took the handcuffs from his belt.

Flynn sighed. He could argue with the deputies, but he couldn't argue with a warrant. He put the popcorn and Furrball on the floor and got to his feet. "Let me get my coat." He turned to his video display. "Computer: record the Red Sox and Bruins games."

"Got your pistol on you?" Salazar asked.

Flynn put on his coat. He shook his head. "It's in the bedroom." He took his computer and slipped it into his pocket.

Wendy finished reading the warrant. "This is a crock!" She looked at her husband. "Just keep your mouth shut. I'll have this quashed before you get to the Marshals Office."

"Put the beer back in the refrigerator first."

No release order awaited Flynn when he was bundled through the door of the Marshals Office. Salazar escorted Flynn directly to Hathaway instead of the interrogation room and removed the handcuffs. The marshal was sitting behind her desk, smiling. She nodded at an empty chair. "Sit down, Flynn." She glanced at Salazar, then at the door to her office. The deputy took the hint, carefully closing the door on his way out.

Flynn sat down and crossed his right leg over his left. He took his computer from his pocket, opened it, placed it ceremoniously on the desk, and started his legal software. "You're keeping me from the Red Sox game. Can we get this nonsense over with?"

"Oh, it's not nonsense, Flynn." Hathaway leaned back in her chair. In the wall behind her was an artificial window, showing a sunlit view of New York City as seen from a skyscraper. "I have only twenty-four deputies out here. There are almost that many bars and casinos on this station, and I have to cover them during all three shifts while patrolling the public areas of the Station and investigating two homicides. Last night I found out why we were making so little progress: My deputies were investigating red herrings that *you* had suggested to them."

"Red herrings?"

"The suggestion that Manstein was a federally protected witness. The suggestion that Cross's killer had gained access to the murder scene by climbing through a recycling chute. And the suggestion that kept Deputy Feldstein from his family last night: that Bill Gorkov's thugs had worn lifelike masks so they could slip out of the Gold Dollar Casino unobserved."

"They did. But don't take my word for it. Talk to the owner of Party Prep, where they bought the masks."

Hathaway's eyes sparkled. "This mask idea could only occur to you, and not to Silvanus Drake?"

Flynn got a sinking feeling in his stomach. It was bad enough that his theory had been wrong, but Drake had beaten him to the punch *again.*

The marshal savored the moment of triumph. "Feldstein should have checked with Company Security before getting eyestrain studying video records. Drake investigated that theory last week. Everyone who left the Gold Dollar Casino on the days of the murders had entered the casino earlier the same day."

And Gorkov's muscle men hadn't been wearing disguises when they entered the Gold Dollar—the bartender had seen them come in.

The marshal leaned across her desk. "Helmuth Manstein had

no plastic. He paid for everything in cash. During the five years he lived here, somebody noticed that. That somebody got to know Manstein, got himself invited to Manstein's apartment, and killed him for his cash. He stole Manstein's computer, too. Leron Cross was killed in a secured Company work area that Gorkov's enforcers don't have access to. Gorkov and his thugs didn't commit either murder, and we don't need the FBI to tell us so. But you've been giving us these silly ideas to investigate so that you can solve the cases before we can. *That's* obstruction of justice."

Flynn had to phrase his arguments carefully—he didn't want to say anything that would get one of his informants in trouble. "Then why can't the Munich police give you an address or family contacts for Helmuth Manstein?" He leaned forward, putting himself nose to nose with the marshal. "Why did a 'manufacturer's sales representative' not have a credit card to which he could charge his expenses? Why was a 'sales rep' on this station for five years without once trying to sell anything to anybody? Why do you have no leads and no suspects? And it's *not* because you've spent all your time checking out the leads I gave you. Why was Leron Cross, a well-liked man with no enemies you can find, killed just a couple of weeks after being seen talking to Gorkov? Big Bill's such an obvious suspect you didn't even bother clearing Cross's wife. You've wasted plenty of time proving that nobody *but* Gorkov and his pals could have committed the murders. All of the people with authorized access to the area where Cross was murdered have alibis, except for the night-shift manager, and he has no motive."

"We'll find someone with a motive, now that you won't be distracting us anymore. And with your partners Jack Adamly and Peter Chow in jail—"

Flynn sat upright in his chair. "Chow's in jail? Since when?"

"Since an hour ago, when he beat the stuffing out of two

perfectly ordinary people who he claimed attacked him—conveniently out of sight of any security cameras."

"These two 'perfectly ordinary people' wouldn't happen to owe money to the Gold Dollar Casino, would they?"

Hathaway hesitated, then her expression changed. "Oh, no! You're not getting me to chase a red herring like that!" She placed her hands flat on the desk. "You're going to jail, Flynn. And while you're there, and not distracting my deputies, we'll have the time to investigate your altercation with DiGeorgio and Lavalle the other night." She sat back in her chair. "The witness—the man living in the apartment at the scene—doesn't confirm your version of the event."

"I bet he doesn't confirm Lavalle's version, either, or you'd be charging me with that, too."

The marshal gave Flynn an icy stare. She keyed her intercom and summoned Deputy Salazar. "Put this joker in a cell."

Flynn picked up his computer—its legal software was acting as his attorney; the marshal couldn't take it from him. Salazar escorted Flynn through the lobby of the Marshals Office and down the corridor to the cells.

Chow, wearing his usual turtleneck shirt but without his usual leather coat, was in the cell next to Jack Adamly, watching a golf tournament on his computer. Jack was scratching his ear with the splint on his right hand. He stood up when he saw Flynn.

"Hey, Mike! Did you hear about Brennerman? The doctors got him breathing on his own again! The magistrate'll have to reduce my bail now!" Jack stopped smiling when Salazar put Flynn in the adjoining cell. "What's going on?"

"Marshal Hathaway likes new experiences. She's never been sued for false arrest, so she trumped up some charges and had Deputy Salazar pick me up."

Chow said, "*We* get assaulted, and *we* get arrested. Is this a wonderful country, or what?"

"Gorkov got to Pete," Jack said.

"I heard. What happened?"

Chow had been to the hotel for the Sunday champagne brunch. His way home took him through a two-block stretch of Eleventh Street that had no security cameras. A man Chow didn't recognize had stepped out in front of him. His retreat had been blocked by another stranger behind him. Both had pieces of stainless-steel pipe hidden in their coat sleeves. Neither, however, had any experience with physical altercations. Chow had sent one to the hospital with a roundhouse kick to the ear and had forcibly disarmed the other. The assailants had claimed that Chow had attacked them, so the goons had arrested Pete. "I took your advice and got the same legal software you have—great deal, by the way. It says I can press charges and make the marshals arrest 'em. So I filed a complaint. But do you see those two guys in here?"

"Since they weren't arrested at the scene, the marshals will have to get a warrant," Flynn said. "Maybe the magistrate doesn't do warrants on Sundays." Maybe he didn't do anything on Sundays, which would explain why Wendy had not yet arranged Michael's release.

Flynn sat on the cell bunk. It was comfortable, so that it couldn't be construed as "cruel and unusual punishment." He opened his computer and tried to call Wendy. But his computer said it couldn't upload to the network. "What the hell . . . Hey, Pete! My computer can't get the network!"

"Uplink or downlink?"

"I tried to call my wife. She's supposed to be getting me out of here."

"Uplinks don't work in here," Chow explained. "They can't take your computer away if it's acting as your attorney, but they don't have to let you call outside."

So Flynn couldn't call Wendy. He stared at the locked cell

door. After thirty seconds he got bored. His computer had no trouble getting the downlink of the Red Sox game. Carver was pitching a no-hitter and the Red Sox were leading the Yankees two to zip, but Flynn was too worried about what was delaying his wife to enjoy the game. Gorkov had been busy: first Adamly, then Chow . . . That left only Flynn, one way or another. Michael imagined his wife kidnapped by hoodlums, to be held until Flynn agreed to drop the charges against Gorkov's enforcers. He called up a map of the Station on his computer and tried to figure out the route Wendy had taken from their apartment to the judge's, and where along that route she had been waylaid. By the sixth inning he wondered if he should yell for the watch commander and report Wendy missing. In the eighth inning Carver lost his no hitter when a ground ball leaked under the second-baseman's glove. It would be the Yankees' only hit; the Red Sox won, four to nothing.

The Bruins hockey game wasn't due to begin for another half hour. Flynn folded his computer. The cell door was still locked.

What had happened to Wendy?

The door at the end of corridor opened. Wendy, followed by the watch commander and U.S. Attorney Kyle Pierce, entered the cell area. Wendy was obviously unharmed.

Flynn's concern for his wife was replaced by irritation at having to spend the afternoon in jail. "You said you were going to have the warrant quashed before I got to the Marshals Office."

"Lucky for you, I called Judge Avila's clerk instead of the judge himself," Wendy said. "She warned me that Avila is a Yankees fan. If I had interrupted him while he was watching the game, he might have let you sit in here all night. But then I checked the score and saw that the Yankees were losing, and I figured he might not be in the mood to let you out even when the game was over. So I enlisted Kyle's help. We went over to Avila's apartment and got the warrant rescinded."

Flynn nodded at Pierce. "Thanks."

The deputy opened the cell just as Marshal Hathaway reached the scene. "What the hell's going on here?"

The watch commander brandished a folded piece of paper. "The magistrate has cancelled the arrest warrant."

"It took me all of two minutes to explain the reasoning behind the hypotheses my husband presented to Deputy Marshal Feldstein," Wendy said.

While Hathaway read the judicial order, Pierce said, "Next time you want the magistrate to issue a warrant, please go through me. I can save you a lot of time and embarrassment."

Hathaway looked up at Pierce. "You would have given me a load of horse dung about insufficient grounds for a warrant—"

Pierce pointed at the document in the marshal's hand. "Which is what the magistrate says. Obstruction of justice requires *evidence* that Flynn knew the suggestions he gave your deputies were false. You don't have any."

"Well, I have him on video interfering with a suspect in Federal custody. Can you get me a warrant to bust him for that?"

Pierce tried to be patient. "I told you yesterday: The guard at DiGeorgio's hospital room gave him permission. That's all Flynn would need to talk to one of the prisoners in the cells here. You have, at most, a case against the guard, because he wasn't supposed to let just anybody in to see DiGeorgio."

Hathaway was getting desperate. "Hector Rivera backs up Lavalle's version of the events the other night!"

Pierce was losing his struggle to be patient. "The witness who lives on Fifteenth Street says Rivera wasn't there."

"So he ran off! Even Flynn says he ran off!"

"In which case he couldn't have seen Flynn and Adamly stick Lavalle's head in the recycling chute!"

Flynn stepped past the marshal. "I'll be going now. Next time

I get a good idea, I'll leave the Marshals Office off the distribution list." He turned to his wife. "Let's go."

But Wendy didn't move. She was staring at Chow's cell. "What's Peter Chow doing in here?"

"Self-defense," Michael explained. He looked at the marshal. "A couple of 'perfectly ordinary people' assaulted him."

"Oh, really?"

Pete repeated his story to Wendy. "But my computer says I can file a complaint, so I did. As soon as the marshals get a warrant, those guys will be in here with me."

Wendy thought Pete should be trying to get *out* of jail instead of waiting to be joined by his attackers. "If you want me to represent you, I'll get a copy of the arrest report. If you want that," Wendy glared at Chow's computer, "as your attorney, you should get a copy of the report. They have to give you one if you ask for it. Find out what happened to those pipes. If they were impounded as evidence, petition the Federal magistrate for an immediate evidentiary hearing." She looked at Hathaway, who was standing with her hands on her hips. "As soon as he sees the pipes he'll dismiss the charges."

Chow looked at his computer. "You must be a pretty good attorney, Ms. Chadwick! That's *exactly* what my software advises!"

Wendy closed her eyes and gritted her teeth. "Well then, your software can represent you."

Michael had to hurry after his wife. Wendy would let Chow sit in his jail cell until he learned that a computer program could not expedite warrants or threaten jailers the way an attorney could. She wished the ABA would do something useful for its members: buy the company that wrote the damned software and take the program off the market.

"Want to bet that Chow's assailants owed money to the Gold Dollar?"

Flynn's question brought Wendy's mind back from planning a war against legal software. "Only if I can bet with your money."

"I'm back to square one. Hathaway says that Drake beat me to my theory about the masks last week. Drake claims that the security videos show that everyone who left the Gold Dollar on the days of the murders had entered the casino earlier."

Wendy patted her husband's shoulder. "Maybe it's time to admit that Gorkov didn't do it."

"If Gorkov didn't do it he wouldn't have tried to kill me!" Flynn squinted while he tried to think of an explanation. "Maybe Drake is lying."

"Drake never needs a reason to lie, but this case involves the death of a Company employee. Warshovsky's pressuring him for results."

"Ah, but what results? Does Warshovsky want Gorkov convicted or protected?"

Wendy gave her husband a sour look. "Why would Warshovsky want to protect Gorkov?"

"Gorkov's a loan shark. Company employees borrow money from him at usurious rates, then have to renew their contracts to pay him off. Saves Warshovsky the expense of shipping them home when their contracts expire, and bringing replacements out here."

"The best way to get into debt out here is to lose money gambling, and we have a program to help people with gambling problems. Their credit at the Company casino is cut off and they're given counseling. It's required by Federal law and I made certain we're in compliance."

"Wendy, those thugs got out of the Gold Dollar Casino while Drake had a security-camera watch on them! Something smells fishy here!"

Wendy hesitated. "All I can smell is plutonium."

Wendy had a better sense of smell than Flynn did, and the

plutonium wasn't far away, following the Station in its orbit.

They rode the moving sidewalk on Denver Avenue to Eighth Street, walked the ramps up to level five, and cut over to the ramp to their apartment on Ninth Street. Flynn's popcorn was cold but so was the refrigerated beer. Michael switched on the computer just as the videocast of the Bruins game began. Timchenko, Moscow's seventeen-year-old rookie phenom, blocked forty-two shots on goal—four in thirty seconds during a Bruins power play while the Icemen had two players in the penalty box—and the Bruins were shut out two to nothing. Flynn shut off the display in disgust.

Wendy looked up from the Cold-War spy novel she was reading. "Did they lose?" she asked.

"Yes, they lost."

"They're still in the playoff, though, aren't they?"

"Moscow's up three games to one, with only one game remaining in Boston. The Bruins are going to lose the Stanley Cup for the third year in a row." Flynn glanced at the floor next to his chair. Two bottles of beer remained. He'd had enough to drink for one day. He stood up. "What would you like for dinner?"

Flynn's computer beeped. Ed Warshovsky's face appeared on the display. "Good evening, Mr. Warshovsky." Flynn looked at his wife. "It's for you."

"No, Mr. Flynn," Warshovsky interrupted, "it's for you." Flynn turned back to the display. "At fourteen fifty-eight this afternoon Mr. Drake called his wife from his office and told her he was on his way home. It is now eighteen fifty and he still isn't there. We can't find him anyplace."

CHAPTER 19

Warshovsky opened the door to Drake's office and gestured for Flynn to take the lead. "You are now security director, so this office is yours."

Flynn hesitated in the door. "We don't know that Drake's dead."

Warshovsky wasn't in the mood to argue. "He's not answering his phone or his computer. We can't detect his locator. He's not only dead; he's destroyed." He took Flynn by the shoulder and directed him into the room.

Warshovsky and Wendy followed Flynn through the door. The desktop was bare except for a holographic projector and a picture of Drake's wife, the only personal touch in office. The carpeting was industrial-strength light gray. Inexpensive Company-issue paintings hung on two of the pale-green walls. In a window in the back wall Flynn could see the satellites that preceded Jupiter Station in its orbit. The window was artificial—it was several bulkheads removed from the end of the Station and the view wasn't rotating. Next to the window was an open door that led to a private bathroom. The wall behind the desk was of one-way glass; on the other side of the glass was Security Control.

Werner Dettweiler, the deputy director of security, appeared in the doorway. He had a bull neck and broad shoulders that had served him well when he had played college football and had kept order at the Company's Martian mines. "We've completed the corridor sweep," he announced. He had a high-pitched voice that didn't match his physique. "Nothin'."

Flynn raised an eyebrow. "What about the recycling bins?"

"We checked those first. We also investigated every instance an exterior hatch was opened since he disappeared: Everyone who left the Station has been accounted for, and radar shows no unidentified objects nearby."

"Did the security cameras catch anything?"

"We have security video of Mr. Drake leaving Company Headquarters and walking along the Main Plaza to Sacramento Avenue," Warshovsky said. "He turned right on Sacramento, toward First Street. That's the last video we have of him."

Wendy's brow furrowed. "You said he told his wife he was coming home."

"After he had checked on some things," Warshovsky corrected.

"What things?" Flynn asked.

"He wasn't specific. He just said, 'some things.' "

"Any idea what 'things' would need checking at that end of Sacramento Avenue?" Flynn looked from Warshovsky to Dettweiler but neither answered.

"Maybe there's something in his computer," Dettweiler suggested.

Creases wrinkled Flynn's forehead. "Haven't you checked?"

"It's secured by his retinal patterns."

"Your ITs can get you around that." Flynn stepped behind the desk and switched on the holographic display. He squinted, then pulled out the keyboard and began tapping keys. "It's responding to me."

Dettweiler looked surprised. "Well, it didn't respond to me!"

Flynn gestured to his wife. "Wendy, you try it."

Wendy walked around the desk to her husband's side and put her purse on the desktop. She gingerly "touched' some of the icons on the holographic display, then tapped some keys at random. She shook her head. "It's not working for me, either."

Flynn pulled up Drake's chair and sat in front of the computer. He had no trouble accessing files. "It likes me." He looked at Warshovsky.

"Mr. Drake might have entered your retinal patterns into the computer's security system," Warshovsky suggested. "It was his idea to hire you if anything happened to him."

"Wonderful foresight on his part." Flynn looked at Dettweiler. "How many people do you have looking for Drake?"

"Everybody. I called in both off-duty shifts. They would have come in anyway, as soon as word got around."

Flynn nodded. "Send the day shift home. We're going to need them wide awake tomorrow morning."

"They won't go. One of our own has been killed. We won't rest until we find who did it, at least until we find his body."

Flynn stared at his new subordinate. He drummed his fingers on the desktop. "Do you know why Drake wanted me to be security director if anything happened to him?"

Dettweiler shifted his weight from one foot to the other. "He, ah, said that if, ah, anything happened to him, ah, the Station would need someone with military experience to direct its security."

"And from my military experience, I know we'll need alert guards tomorrow. Send the day shift home. E-mail the status of the investigation to the off-duty guards every hour." Flynn shifted in his chair and crossed his legs. "Drake once told me that he had two specially trained tactical squads."

Dettweiler nodded. "Ten men each. But they're not full-time squads. The guards involved have regular duties."

"Take those guards off their regular duties. I want one of those squads on duty at all times—six-hour shifts, starting now. And I want you to station the on-duty squad . . ." Flynn turned to the computer, hesitated with his fingers over the keyboard, and said, "Computer, display a schematic diagram of the Station." Flynn smiled at the immediate response. He motioned with his finger for Dettweiler to come over and look at the display. "Right there," Flynn pointed. "In the hub, next to the new reactor."

Dettweiler squinted at the display. "That's . . . right where Mr. Drake usually put 'em during drills." He looked at Flynn with new respect in his eyes. "Right. I'll get your Company phone, computer, and gun." He turned to leave.

"Something small," Flynn called after him. "I won't need to take out any armored vehicles." He looked at Warshovsky. "Close the door." When the three were alone, Flynn said, "Now, is there anything else you'd like to tell me?"

"We told you everything we know the other day."

"Tell me everything you suspect."

"We told you all of that, too."

Flynn rubbed his forehead. "What's the security for Wilmer de Birk's storage shed?"

"Ahh . . . there's an alarm, linked to Drake's computer—er, your computer, just in case. It doesn't really need any. Nobody knows it exists, or what's in it."

Flynn was shocked. Flynn was flabbergasted. Flynn was speechless. No one was *supposed* to know the bomb's present location, but Drake would never have taken that for granted. Not the old Drake, who had discovered the nuke and acted quickly and efficiently to protect the Station. "All it takes to get there is a shuttle and a pilot, and one of your pilots was murdered last week, probably by the same person or persons who killed Manstein!"

Warshovsky's cheeks quivered. "I told you, nobody knows—"

"Lots of people know! You told me their names on Friday! Maybe *you* never told anyone and *Drake* never told anyone, but if only one of the other people told someone else, dozens of people might know where that bomb is now! A hydrogen torch could cut into that shed in a minute! It would take twenty minutes for us to respond from the Station!"

Warshovsky didn't seem to share Flynn's concern. "We track every shuttle and work boat with radar. We'd know—"

"Mr. Warshovsky, the people behind this might have failed to recruit a pilot on this station last Tuesday. Maybe they went to the Asian station, where security is quite lax. Do you track all the Asian shuttles? Do you track shuttles from ships that come from the inner solar system?"

"There are no ships due from planet three or four—"

"Somebody coming to steal the bomb might not inform you of his ETA! We need to protect that storage shed! Are any of our shuttles—or the Station itself—equipped with lasers or missiles?" International law prohibited arming civilian spacecraft, but that wouldn't have stopped Drake. The only thing that stopped Drake was the budget limitations Warshovsky imposed on him.

Warshovsky frowned. "I think your concern is misplaced, but Drake wanted you to succeed him . . . what do you think we should do?"

"How many pilots work for Security?"

"Just the man who took us to the bomb on Friday. I forget his name. Dettweiler would know."

"Does Security have immediate access to a shuttle or work boat?"

Warshovsky nodded. "There are two, permanently assigned . . . you're not planning to put Security personnel in the storage shed, are you?"

"Ah, yeah."

"Ah, no!" Warshovsky waved his finger in Flynn's face. "You run Security, but I run this Station, and I'm not letting another dozen people know what's stored out there!" Warshovsky looked Flynn right in the eye to make his point. "You can leave 'em here, on standby. They can get there in twenty minutes if the shed alarm goes off."

Flynn stared at his new boss. Wendy had told him more than once that no one on the Executive Staff had any doubt as to who ran Jupiter Station. Still, he wondered what Warshovsky would have said if Drake had wanted to put guards in the storage shed. "Okay. That might work." Flynn took a deep breath. "What do you want me to tell the press?"

"Let me deal with the press."

"Then you'd better go do that, Mr. Warshovsky. With every security guard called to duty, people will be talking."

"I'll get you executive authority over our systems." Warshovsky closed the door behind himself as he left.

Wendy wasn't looking at her husband. Not only was Drake dead, but the bomb was unguarded! Wendy felt physically vulnerable. And helpless. She clenched her fists and wished she had her gun. "What's going on?"

"That's what I have to figure out, and quickly. If Drake's removal is the first step in someone's attempt to get hold of that A-bomb, the second step should happen very soon, while the bad guys think Security is in disarray."

There was a knock on the door and Dettweiler returned. He placed a Company telephone and pocket computer on the desk and handed Flynn a clip-on holster containing a pulsed-laser pistol. It was a Ruger 3520, the same model as Wendy's. Dettweiler extended his hand, palm upward. "These activation rings were in an envelope with your name on it."

Flynn slipped a ring onto each hand. They fit perfectly. Michael grunted. "The things you can do with computer-enhanced imaging these days."

"The phone contains a locator," Dettweiler said. "Security

personnel keep their locators with them at all times so we know where they are if there's an emergency."

"Fat lot of good that did Drake." Flynn checked the pistol. It was set to stun and the energy cell that came with it was fully charged. He inserted the energy cell into the grip, put the pistol into its holster, and clipped the holster onto his belt. He started to put the Company phone into his inside coat pocket, but his own phone was there. He looked at Dettweiler. "Is that first tactical squad in position yet?"

"I'll check." Dettweiler took his pocket computer, pressed a few keys, and stared at the display. "They just reached the elevator to the hub."

"Good. Change in plans: That squad will have to guard that location around the clock, no more than half the men sleeping at any time. The other squad, along with Security's pilot, is to report immediately to Security's shuttle and don pressure suits."

"Where are they going?"

"Nowhere, until I say so. Then the pilot is to take the squad as fast as possible to the same place he took Mr. Warshovsky and Mr. Drake on Friday."

Dettweiler looked puzzled. "Where did they go?"

"The pilot will remember."

Dettweiler ran his tongue around the inside of his mouth. "Okay."

"What's the next step in the search for Drake?"

"Basement search, starting from the two basement hatches that aren't covered by security cameras and working outward from there."

Flynn looked at his watch. "That should take us through the twenty-two-o'clock news. By then everyone on the Station will know that Drake is missing. Perhaps someone will report seeing him after he left his office."

"I hope so." Dettweiler gestured toward the glass wall behind

Flynn's desk. "I'll be next door."

"Ah, Werner, have any shuttles left for the Asian station since Drake disappeared?"

"Um . . ." Dettweiler looked at his watch. "Yeah. At sixteen. They run every four hours. The next one departs in thirty minutes."

"Stop it. Nobody leaves this station for the Asian station until they've been interrogated."

"You can't do that, Michael," Wendy said. "You can't keep Asian workers here against their will unless you can connect them to Drake's disappearance."

"Oh, yes I can. Police are allowed to detain and investigate persons found at a crime scene."

Wendy would have expected that kind of response from Silvanus Drake. She was surprised to hear it from her husband. "Drake disappeared at this end of the Station! The shuttles leave from the other end!"

"Drake was last *seen* at this end of the Station. We don't know where he was actually assaulted. As far as I'm concerned, this whole Station is a crime scene, and nobody's leaving without being checked out."

Wendy opened her mouth to respond, then stopped. She wasn't an expert on criminal law, and she didn't want to lose a legal argument with her husband. She wished Mitch Habruch was there.

Flynn didn't wait for his wife to think of a response. He turned to Dettweiler. "The shuttle that departed at sixteen: Has it reached the Asian station yet?"

Dettweiler shrugged. "It might have. Trip time depends on relative positions of the stations in their orbits."

"If that shuttle is one of ours and hasn't reached the Asian station, recall it. Have everyone on board interrogated."

Werner nodded. He hadn't thought of stopping the Asian

shuttles. Maybe Drake had been right when he had selected Flynn as his successor. "I'll see to it."

"Oh, and Werner: Nobody gets on a shuttle to any of the satellites unless he's going to his regular work location. And no joyriders."

"Okay, boss."

Flynn didn't watch Dettweiler leave. "Wendy, the Company's security agreement with the government: Does it specify a maximum blood-alcohol level for armed guards?"

"Ah, yesss. The same as the Company policy for all workers—point oh eight."

Twice the level permitted civilians with concealed-weapons permits. "Four beers in three hours . . . I'm probably pretty close to that. Hope I don't have to shoot anybody for awhile." He turned his attention to his computer. "Let's see: How do I access the security cameras?"

Wendy stepped behind the desk so she could see the display. "The computer's voice activated; you could probably just ask for it. Or touch that icon, there."

The icon led to a command menu. One of the menu items displayed a diagram of the Station with the locations of all the security cameras. There were thousands of them, covering the major thoroughfares, many side streets, all work areas, utility tunnels, and parts of the basement. The camera symbols on the schematic were color coded for camera capability. Flynn could view what any camera was monitoring just by touching its symbol on his display. One camera piqued his interest and he pointed it out to Wendy. "Would you look at that one? In the elevator shaft closest to the sealed compartment where Drake found the bomb. Low-light and thermal imaging capability." Flynn touched the camera icon and the Station schematic was replaced by a thermal image of the elevator shaft. The shaft was empty. Its walls were intact. Flynn switched back to the Station schematic. “And this one: in the hub, just above the bomb compartment.” It also revealed no attempt to get to the bomb.

“There’s a camera at the end of Sacramento where Drake disappeared,” Wendy noted. “It must have been looking in the wrong direction.”

Flynn returned to the command menu. He could access the security cameras on all the satellites, but there was no hint of a camera in Wilmer de Birk’s storage shed. There had to be one, but its access was as carefully concealed as the storage shed itself. Flynn started to instruct the cameras outside the compartment where the bomb had been found to sound an alarm if anyone appeared there, but someone—probably Drake—had already done so. “Let’s see what else I can do: Security camera watches . . . he’s still tracking Gorkov and his thugs!”

Wendy leaned over Flynn’s shoulder to get a better look. “He told me he’d suspended that!”

“Well, they are suspects in two homicides. He now has a right to keep them under video surveillance. They’ve been in Gorkov’s office or the Gold Dollar Casino all afternoon and evening.”

Wendy’s stare moved from the display to her husband. “You think they did in Drake?”

Flynn shook his head. “They’re not good enough, even if they were armed, which they aren’t. Drake had a gun and knew how to use it.”

“So, who took him out?”

“Whoever’s trying to get to the bomb.” Flynn leaned back in his chair. It was very comfortable. “This looks like the same type of chair you have in your office.”

Wendy nodded. “All executive-staff members have one. Premium model. They automatically adjust themselves to provide ideal lumbar and thigh support. The only thing you have to set yourself is the arm height and the height of the seat above the floor. You do that by voice command—just tell the chair how you want it to configure itself."

"I don't have to. It fits me perfectly." Flynn nodded toward the computer display. "I think I'll check Drake's files to see if he left me any more information or hunches."

"Want me to help?"

Flynn hesitated, knowing his wife wouldn't like his answer. "You might hinder me." Wendy frowned, so Flynn explained, "Drake might have programmed his computer to suppress certain sensitive files if he—and now I—wasn't alone in the room."

Wendy sighed. "Yes, that sounds like Drake." That left nothing for her to do. "I might as well go back to our apartment." It had been her apartment before it was theirs. Her gun was there. If she couldn't be with Michael, she would feel safer there than anywhere else on the Station. "When will you be home?"

"Late. Maybe not before morning. I'll keep you informed. I'll leave a message on your computer if I'm very late, so I don't awaken you."

"You think I'm going to be able to *sleep?*"

Flynn rolled his chair back to the computer display and contacted Dettweiler. "Please send a couple of guards to escort my wife home and remain with her until she dismisses them."

"Right away, sir."

The display went blank. Flynn rubbed his chin. "I don't think anyone's called me 'sir' since my last day in the Marines."

Wendy put her hands on her hips. "I wouldn't need an escort if you let me carry my gun."

"Oh, yes you would. The danger right now isn't Gorkov; it's whoever hit Drake. And if Drake couldn't defend himself from them, you can't, either." And neither could two run-of-the-mill goons, but Flynn doubted that Wendy was in danger. The escort was only to make her feel safe.

Flynn was left alone with Drake's computer. Michael found no note from Drake with more information concerning the bomb. There were files on the Manstein and Cross murders—under the security agreement between the Company and the government, Hathaway had been supplying Drake with daily reports on the investigations. The Manstein investigation was at a standstill; neither Hathaway nor Drake had been able to determine the dead man's real name. The marshal hadn't come up with any suspects. No wonder Hathaway had been in such a bad mood.

Leron Cross had had the good sense to get killed in a secured Company work area. The computer system had recorded the names of the employees who had used their retinal patterns to unlock—from the outside—the doors to the work area and the times at which they had done so. Security-camera videos from other parts of the Station had been used to determine who had exited the area and when. The evening-shift technicians had entered the work area at fifteen fifty-five and fifteen fifty-eight. They had been tasked to other duties and both had departed by sixteen oh eight. Traffic Control records showed round-up ships docking at fifteen-minute intervals; Security files showed airlock openings that corresponded. Russ Murrow had entered the work area at sixteen thirty-three; the airlock to his ship had been opened ten minutes later. Andy Deltoro had docked at sixteen fifty-four. Leron Cross had entered through the front door at sixteen fifty-nine. Deltoro had seen him receive a phone call; records showed a call had been placed to Leron from a public phone, out of sight of any security camera, on Twelfth Street at seventeen oh three; the phone had been cleaned of fingerprints and DNA. Cross had left the locker room to take the call in private before Deltoro had left through the main door. That left only Jerry Paloukis, the evening-shift manager, in the work area, and he claimed he had not entered the corridor where Cross had been murdered. The marshals had found no motive for Paloukis to have killed Cross. Neither had Drake. The security chief had suspected Gorkov, but Drake had generated a map showing possible routes along the Station's streets that avoided security cameras, and none of the routes led to the Gold Dollar Casino. Drake had even sent Security personnel to check the utility tunnel that ran along the back wall of Gorkov's office, to make sure that the gangster hadn't cut himself a back door. Drake was aware of Gorkov's e-mails to planet three; he was trying to identify the unknown server in Washington, DC. He also knew that Manstein had been using the alias George Smiley for his e-mails—the microcam that he had placed in Missy Adamly's office had yielded another dividend.

In Drake's computer were the daily security reports dating back fifteen years, to the day when construction had started on the Station. Flynn started with Saturday's report and worked backward. Since the reports were circulated to all members of the executive committee they contained nothing about the bomb. Mostly they documented the barroom brawls that were almost a daily occurrence, but they also listed the contraband confiscated from the visiting workers from the Asian station. Hardly a day went by when the scanners didn't detect weapons—usually knives, but there had been some guns—and illegal drugs. Flynn confirmed that the scanners' unsleeping watch on every entrance to Jupiter Station hadn't found anything the day that he and Wendy had had their harrowing ride with Russ Murrow.

Then Flynn found another file on Manstein. Drake had compiled a video record of every appearance of Manstein in a security video during the forty-eight hours—the length of time that security videos were stored—before his murder was discovered. The cameras hadn't been programmed to keep him under observation, so the coverage of Manstein consisted of bits and snatches of Manstein's face on the streets, in bars, and in restaurants. But all Station elevators had security cameras, and on the night he died, as well as the night before that, Manstein had ridden elevator number three by himself all the way to the hub and then immediately back down to level eight, where his apartment was. On both elevator rides, Manstein had smiled.

Flynn replayed the recording several times. Elevators one through four all reached the hub in the arrival lounge, but no ships had visited Jupiter Station at the times of Manstein's elevator rides, so the terrorist couldn't have been meeting a new arrival. He had been the only passenger above level twelve on both nights. The elevators were in the old section of the Station, not the new section where the bomb had been secreted. Perhaps Manstein had enjoyed riding elevators. But elevator number three was on the opposite side of the Station from Manstein's apartment. Manstein could have taken the same ride more conveniently on elevator number one.

There was a knock on the door. Flynn looked up. "Enter."

The door opened and a man with a square face and black skin stepped into the office. He had the build of a security guard but was too short, not more than a couple of centimeters taller than the diminutive Missy Adamly.

"I apologize for the interruption, Mr. Flynn. I'm Jake Jefferson, the office manager."

Flynn glanced at his watch. "The office manager works at twenty-two oh five on a Sunday evening?"

Jefferson nodded. "He does when the boss—er, former boss—has just been eliminated."

"We don't know what happened to Mr. Drake."

"Well, maybe not, but everybody I've talked to thinks we'll find his body before morning. Thought you should know: Drake's . . . disappearance just made the nightly news. And Mr. Warshovsky has announced that you've been hired to replace him and find out who did it. I'd guess that you're about to receive a lot of calls."

"Can you block everything except calls from my wife and official business?"

Jefferson nodded. "Your wish is my command, er, boss."

Unfortunately for Flynn, Marshal Devon Hathaway qualified as official business. Jefferson had barely left the room before a call from the marshal came through Flynn's computer.

The marshal was wearing the expression she used when giving suspects the third degree. She skipped the social niceties. "How the hell did you get to be Company security director?"

"You know the Company: they always want the best."

Hathaway was in no mood for humor. She jabbed her finger at Flynn. "Let me warn you, Flynn: I didn't like working with Drake and I'm going to like working with you even less. I suggest you study the security agreement between the Company and the government until you understand everything in it. Get that lawyer wife of yours to help you with the multisyllable words. Pay special attention to the paragraphs that specify where Company Security is subordinate to the marshals. Just because you're security director doesn't mean you can't be charged with obstructing an official investigation."

Flynn took a deep breath. "I have enough to do without interfering with your investigations. I'll send you an e-mail address in Helsinki. Helmuth Manstein sent a message to it. Might help you identify him. Good night, Marshal."

Flynn found the Helsinki address in Drake's computer—the security chief had tracked the deceased's communications. Drake had already requested the Helsinki police to investigate the address. Flynn sent the address to the marshal anyway—it would give her something to do and keep her out of his hair.

Michael spun his chair around and looked through the one-way glass into Security Control. Dettweiler was sitting at the desk behind the main console. The deputy director only had to find Drake's body. He didn't have to deal with small-minded government bureaucrats or figure out why Drake had disappeared. Maybe Drake had picked Flynn to be his successor as a favor to Dettweiler.

Drake's computer also held personnel files, lots of them. There appeared to be one on every Station employee and everyone else who had piqued Drake's interest. At Flynn's fingertips was all the information he would need to do most requested background investigations. Michael could download the files to his own computer and his regular job would become trivial. But Wendy would strongly disapprove. Flynn resisted the temptation, and tried to convince himself that he would have done so even if it wouldn't have led to a long exile from the bedroom.

The thought of his regular job reminded Michael that requests for background checks were piling up in his computer. He accessed his account and posted the prepared message that Michael Flynn was on vacation and that prospective clients should contact one of the other private detectives on Jupiter Station, e-mail addresses for whom were given. He subcontracted the four requests for background checks that were already there to other investigators.

Flynn couldn't resist the urge to see what Drake had on him. All of it—and it was a big file—was accurate. Comparing the file size to that of other personnel records, Drake must have been much more curious about Flynn than about the average Station resident. There were also thick files on Big Bill Gorkov and his pets. Flynn started to peruse the files on the members of the Station's executive committee, and immediately noticed that there were no files on Edwin Warshovsky and his wife or on Wendy Chadwick.

Flynn commanded the computer to find the Warshovsky and

Chadwick files but the search returned a null result. He spent ten minutes searching manually, just in case Drake had programmed his computer to refuse commands for those files, but was no more successful than the machine had been. There was a small probability that Drake hadn't compiled information on the Warshovskys, but Flynn couldn't believe that Wendy had been so favored. Drake disliked lawyers, and Wendy had been in his face, trying to rein in his not-so-legal tactics, ever since she had become legal director. Drake would have investigated her background to find a weakness he could exploit. If her file wasn't on Drake's computer now it must have been recently erased. Flynn searched for the link to the concealed microcam in Missy Adamly's office. He couldn't find it. He couldn't find links to any concealed microcams. Drake had covered his footprints thoroughly.

Flynn's computer beeped and his office manager's face appeared on the display. "Mr. Flynn, Brenda Stahl, the SSN correspondent, is outside of Company headquarters with a camera operator. You're the only director here at the moment, so she's probably waiting for you."

"Or any member of the security force she can pump for information. Instruct all security personnel not to talk to the press. Thanks, Mr. Jefferson. I'll sneak out the back way."

Jefferson looked impressed. "You already know about the other exits?"

"I'm a professional investigator. I'll find them."

Flynn leaned back in his perfectly fitting executive chair, wondering how much information had disappeared with Drake, while the night progressed and Sunday turned into Monday. Behind him, in Security Control, Dettweiler learned that the guards had found no trace of Drake in the basement, and sent them to sweep the utility tunnels. The shuttle to Asian station that had been recalled was searched and found to contain nothing but puzzled and irritated Asian workers. And the Station itself, unconcerned with trials and tribulations of the living organisms within it, plodded unthinkingly in its orbit and passed into Jupiter's shadow.

Chapter 20

At oh five-thirty Monday morning the lights on Jupiter Station's streets began to brighten, simulating dawn. Shuttle pilots headed for their vessels to take day-shift workers to jobs on the satellites and to bring night-shift workers home. Restaurant employees switched on griddles, preparing for the breakfast rush. The Station passed out of Jupiter's shadow and into the light of the distant sun. And in his new office next to Security Control, Michael Flynn stared with glazed eyes at his computer display. The night had passed quietly. That had to be a clue as to what had happened to Drake.

There was a knock on the door and Dettweiler stepped into the room. He shook his head. "Nothin' in the utility tunnels. Not even a hint that he'd been there—we did radiometric resonance scans for hemoglobin, and all the blood traces we found were at known accident sites."

Flynn rubbed his eyes, trying to make the image of Dettweiler sharp and clear. "Any tips from the public?"

"A couple o' dozen. Maybe thirty. We've checked out half of 'em so far. Nothin'."

"He might be in an apartment or hotel room," Flynn said. "We'll need warrants to search those."

"We won't get 'em without probable cause. Besides, how the hell could they have gotten the boss—er, Mr. Drake—to an apartment or the hotel without showing up on security videos?"

"On the floor of a taxi?"

Dettweiler hadn't thought of that. "I'll check the cab records." He turned to leave.

"Oh, Werner." Dettweiler paused in the doorway. "Ask Operations if there are any known anomalies in the shaft of elevator number three."

Rapid thinking was not Dettweiler's forte. "You think the boss is in that shaft?"

"No, I don't. What's the usual morning routine around here?"

Dettweiler glanced at his watch. "The shift commander should be writing his report about now. As soon as I get in—I usually start at seven—I compile all three shift reports from the previous day into the daily security report, which I transmit to you. You review it, add any pertinent info you get from the marshals, summarize what you think is important, and circulate the report and your summary to the executive committee."

"Can the usual paperwork be postponed during emergencies?"

Dettweiler nodded. "It did when Mr. Drake was in charge."

"Well, it will be this morning, too. You've been up for twenty-four hours. Get a few hours sleep."

Dettweiler hesitated. "I need to check those cab records first."

"Let the shift supervisor do that. I need you alert. Get some sleep."

"You've been up for a full day."

"Don't remind me. But I expect Warshovsky any minute; I'll have to brief him. You sleep now, I'll sleep later. I'll call you if we find anything."

Dettweiler scarcely heard Flynn's last two sentences—in the four years he had worked for Drake, he had never heard his boss refer to the Station's general manager as anything but *Mr.* Warshovsky. He was so stunned by Flynn's lack of respect that he left without further protest.

Warshovsky did not appear in Flynn's office; he called Flynn on his computer. Even before six in the morning he was clean-shaven and wearing a suit. "Well?" he growled.

"Nothing." Flynn briefed the station manager on the investigation.

Warshovsky's exasperation showed in his scowl. "This is a space station! We know Drake didn't leave through any of the hatches! We have security cameras everywhere! How the hell can he just disappear?"

"It's a very large station. There are lots of places to hide Drake that we haven't even thought of, let alone searched. If one of our shuttle pilots is involved, Drake might have been smuggled to a satellite. We haven't searched those yet." And if Flynn's assessment of the situation was correct, they wouldn't have to. "People will shortly be reporting to their jobs. If he's in a work location that was closed over the weekend, we'll know in an hour or so."

Warshovsky wasn't a happy man. "Members of the Executive Staff were calling me all night, asking what's going on. Chalmisiak called me at four a.m. Four a.m.!" He made the unwanted wake-up call sound like it was Flynn's fault. He lowered his voice. "And why haven't his assailants done anything else?"

Flynn hesitated, wondering how much of what he suspected he should tell his boss. Drake hadn't told Warshovsky anything, so Flynn decided to do the same. "When I figure that out, you'll be the first to know." He switched off.

Michael was more alert than he had been during the wee hours—it was the time of the morning when he normally got up, and his body was awakening. A quick check of his computer confirmed that nobody was showing interest in the bomb's original location. No alarms had been tripped anywhere, so the storage shed was safe. The lack of defenses there still bothered Flynn. Big shuttles could carry two hundred passengers. An assault by that many people on the storage shed would overwhelm his ten-man security squad. Flynn wished he could send more guards if necessary, but Security had just one pilot. The only pilot Flynn knew was Russ Murrow, but the computer showed that he had switched with another pilot and would be working the day shift on Monday. He would be in a round-up ship and unavailable until sixteen-thirty. Flynn tried to convince himself that Drake had known what he was doing and that more security for the storage shed wasn't necessary.

Flynn couldn't think of anything else to do. He returned to Drake's computer. As a member of the Station's executive committee, he had access to nearly every Company file. Drake knew all about Kevin McSheridan's affair with Clarisse Jackson. He even had a file on Marshal Hathaway—an affair with a subordinate had gotten her moved to the top of the list for transfer to Jupiter. Dr. Jasniak reported improvement in Colin Brennerman's condition. Flynn could access the radar displays in Traffic Control; nothing was moving in the direction of the storage shed, which was so far away and so small that it didn't show on the radar.

Flynn's search of Company files was interrupted by a call from Wendy. She was sitting at the dining table in the apartment and, from what showed on the display, appeared to be wearing nothing but a towel. Flynn smiled. "Morning, Wendy."

"Morning, lover. Anything important happening?"

Flynn shook his head. "Suspiciously quiet."

Wendy took that as an invitation to have a normal conversation. "I think I've been on the Station too long—our shower stall seems enormous without you in it with me. Did you get any sleep last night?"

"I don't think so, but I had to read some paragraphs for five or ten minutes before they made sense, so I might have dozed briefly a few times. How about you?"

"Would you think I didn't love you if I admitted to falling

asleep in the wee hours, even though I had nothing to cuddle but Furrball?" She didn't mention cuddling her gun, which she had loaded and placed under her pillow.

"What did you do until the wee hours?"

"Sat in bed. Read a book. Read some e-mails—my mother wanted to know if I'd talked with Jon Duprey lately."

"The divorce attorney?"

When Wendy's father had learned of the wedding plans, he had asked to see the prenuptial agreement. His horror at learning that his daughter and obviously gold-digging son-in-law had no prenup had prompted him to e-mail Wendy the entire text of the Federal Spouse Protection Act. Her mother had blamed herself for the news, wishing she had spent more time with Wendy when she had been a child. "My parents still haven't accepted the fact that I married a private investigator."

"We're even, then. Mine haven't forgiven me for marrying a lawyer." Flynn's father, however, had allowed that she was good-looking, and had asked for a photo of Wendy in a swimsuit.

"You've found no sign of Drake?"

"I haven't, but I've been sitting here all night," Flynn quipped. "Unfortunately, the goons haven't found a sign of him, either, and they've swept every corridor, the basement, and the utility tunnels."

Wendy's pretty nose wrinkled. "Then where the hell is he?"

"Damn good question."

"Are you alone?"

Flynn nodded. "At the moment. Why?"

Wendy wiggled her shoulders and the top edge of the towel, which was all that Flynn could see of it, disappeared off the bottom of the display. "Because this is a video link and this towel's wet and cold."

"Are *you* alone? What happened to those goons I sent home with you last night?"

"I sent them away. Before midnight. They couldn't protect me from an A-bomb. Haven't you made *any* progress?"

"A lot of stuff I expected Drake to have isn't in his computer, but no deletions are recorded in the log file. As soon as Security's system analysts get here, I'll have them check this computer."

To Flynn's dismay, his system analysts didn't come in until nine. Michael glared at his computer display, trying to make Jake Jefferson feel as though his office management was deficient. "You never have computer problems except between nine and six?" Flynn growled.

"If we need them at other times, they're on call. Nobody on the Station is ever very far from the office."

"Then call. I want somebody here in fifteen minutes."

It was closer to twenty minutes before Emilio Romero appeared in the doorway. He was shorter than Flynn, with square shoulders and a thin, black moustache. Flynn glanced at his watch. "You're four minutes late."

"I was asleep when Jake called!"

"And you've just wasted another twenty seconds with an excuse I don't want to hear." Flynn pointed at his computer. "I want to know what's been deleted from this machine in the last twenty-four hours."

Romero was used to dealing with computer-ignorant people. Feeling in control, he said, "That would be in the log file."

Flynn shook his head. "I checked the log. It shows no file deletions. But lots of stuff that should be in this computer isn't here."

Romero had thick black hair but thin eyebrows. The eyebrows almost disappeared into the wrinkles on his forehead as he said, "You think that the guys who did in Mr. Drake deleted . . . but that's not possible. Every computer in Security is secured by retinal patterns and voice print. Only Mr. Drake—oh, and Mr.

Warshovsky, too; he has access to everything—could have deleted anything, and that would show in the log file."

Flynn turned toward his desk. "Computer, display the log file for Mr. Romero."

"People around here call me Leo." Romero stepped behind the desk. "Ah, scroll that back up . . . when did Mr. Drake disappear?"

"Shortly after fifteen yesterday."

Leo nodded at the display. "In the four hours between fifteen and nineteen, the only process spawned was the security routine. Some unauthorized person must have—"

"Werner Dettweiler tried to see if there was any useful information on the computer. It wouldn't let him in."

Romero was still eyeing the display. "The security routine was spawned again at nineteen eleven, which must have been when you started—" Romero looked at his new boss. "How the hell did you get access to this machine?"

"Maybe you'll be able to figure that out when you find what happened to the missing files."

"Mr. Flynn, there is no way this computer should have responded to you . . . unless Mr. Drake gave you access," Romero added thoughtfully.

"That's not bad for someone who was sound asleep twenty minutes ago. Now, about the missing files?"

Romero looked at the display again. "Huh. The last process listed before the gap is a text editor. Spawned from the keyboard. Mr. Drake insisted on having system-manager privileges on our system; he could have edited the log file."

"To remove evidence of having deleted files. So, is there any way to get those files back?"

Romero shook his head. "All file modifications and deletions on Security's computers are permanent—the deleted data are overwritten with random ones and zeroes. For security reasons, and confidentiality of personnel records."

Flynn rubbed his chin without noticing the stubble thereon. "And if he had made copies of those files before deleting them?"

Romero hesitated. "That would be in the log file."

"The *edited* log file."

Leo nodded. "But, if he sent the copies to another computer over the network, that would show in the server's log."

Flynn almost got excited before he realized that Drake wouldn't have made such a mistake. Still, Romero didn't have anything better to do with his time. "Track down all the files Drake sent over the network yesterday afternoon—hell, make it the last forty-eight hours before he disappeared—and get them back on this computer."

Romero nodded. "Right, Mr. Flynn. Ah, any news about the boss—er, Mr. Drake?"

Flynn smiled. "Leo, with what you just told me, I think I'll know by noon exactly what happened to Mr. Drake."

There was one more person Flynn wanted to talk to, but that interview would have to be conducted in person. Flynn got the address from his computer and headed for the door.

Wendy was standing on the other side of it.

She was dressed in shiny pale yellow, all the way from her boxy coat, to her tights, to her shoes. She didn't look like she had been awake most of the night. Wendy studied Flynn's face. "I expected as much. You look like you haven't slept, showered, or shaved." She handed Michael a plastic bag. "I brought you a fresh shirt and your razor."

Flynn hadn't given a thought to his personal appearance. He felt his chin; he knew what he looked like if he hadn't shaved in twenty-four hours. "Thanks, Wendy. I have to go and talk to a witness right now, but I'll change as soon as I get back."

"Whoa! Slow down, lover! You don't know what it's like out there. People are *worried.* Everyone's wondering what happened to Drake. They're glad you took his place, but they want to know that the situation's under control. You have to look professional."

"I look like a professional investigator."

"You need to look like the person in charge. Now, before things start happening."

Drake had a shower in his bathroom—all department directors had that perk. Wendy took Flynn by the arm and turned him around. Flynn pretended to resist as Wendy pushed him back into the office. "Are you going to join me?"

"Thanks for the offer, but I already showered this morning. Besides, someone might come looking for you."

"I'll tell my office manager that I don't want to be disturbed. A squad of armed Marines couldn't get past Jake Jefferson."

"What if it's Mr. Warshovsky that's looking for you?"

Flynn took a deep breath. "I knew there was a good reason I married you. You just showed me another one."

The shower stall in the bathroom behind Drake's office was as small as the one in the Flynns' apartment. Wendy leaned against the jamb of the open bathroom door and pumped her husband for information.

"Drake gave more credence to my theories of the Cross and Manstein murders than the marshals did," Michael said over the sound of the shower. "But he couldn't get over the lack of confirming videos from his precious security cameras. He has several security-camera watches going: Gorkov and his pets; Jorge Allesandro—"

"The owner of the Gold Dollar. You have to cancel that one—he's not a suspect in a criminal investigation so he can't be kept under a security-camera watch without his consent."

"Everyone who was known to be in the cowboys' locker-room area around the time Leron Cross was killed, and Liao Chu and his four bodyguards."

"Those can remain. The people in the locker room are suspects in a homicide investigation. And Dr. Liao and his party are target risks; they require extra security. But at this moment they're on the Asian station."

Flynn shut off the water. He opened the shower door and grabbed a towel from the wall. "Hand me my clothes."

Wendy feigned a sad expression. "Do I have to? You look so cute in your birthday suit. Oh! I made a rhyme!"

"Clothes," Flynn repeated. "I'm supposed to look like the man in charge, remember. People are really happy that I'm Drake's successor?"

"Surprised, too." Wendy paused as a thought hit her. "Do you suppose that Drake wanted you to succeed him because that would be unexpected? Maybe that's why nothing else has happened. Drake's assailants thought they'd be dealing with Dettweiler; now they're afraid their plan won't work because you're in charge."

Flynn buttoned the shirt Wendy had brought him. "That's possible." But if it was true, then Flynn was wrong about everything. "Station residents must not think much of Werner Dettweiler."

"Dettweiler is a faceless functionary. Most residents probably don't know his name. They know yours and they knew Drake's. Anyone capable of eliminating Drake is a very serious threat, and they don't think Marshal Hathaway can deal with it. Where were you headed when I intercepted you?"

"Mrs. Drake."

Wendy looked surprised. "Didn't Warshovsky and Dettweiler talk to her yesterday?"

"Yep." Flynn stepped into his shoes. "And I'm going to talk to her today."

Wendy hesitated. "Why?"

"Because getting her statement secondhand isn't good enough."

"That reporter from SSN is camped out in front of the main entrance. She's dressed all in white—white hair, white jumpsuit, white shoes. Even white eyebrows." Wendy winced. "That can't look good on video."

"SSN can dub in any color they want digitally. They could make her a brunette if they so desire."

"She says she's not leaving until she's interviewed you."

Flynn clipped his Company gun onto his waistband, under his coat. "So I'll leave through another exit. There's one on every level. Want to come along?"

Chapter 21

The Drakes lived on Second Street on level nine, on the opposite side of the Station from Company headquarters and almost directly below the apartment of Edwin and Mary Warshovsky. The street was barely wide enough for an electric vehicle but was devoid of traffic in the middle of the morning. A security guard, ordered by Dettweiler to protect Mrs. Drake, stood next to the apartment door, leaning with his back against the wall. He wiped the bored expression from his face and stood upright when he recognized his new boss and the Company's top attorney coming down the curve of the Station.

"Mr. Flynn! Did you find—"

Flynn shook his head. "Not yet. I'm here only to ask Mrs. Drake a few questions."

The guard made himself useful by ringing the doorbell. Mrs. Drake was slow to answer; the guard was reaching for the button again when the door slid open.

Megan Drake was wearing a vee-necked blue sweater and blue jeans. She looked surprised. "Mr. Flynn! Can I help you?"

Mrs. Drake had already helped him, but Flynn said, "I just need to confirm a few things you said yesterday. May we come in?"

Megan stood aside so that Flynn and Wendy could enter. The apartment was as small as most of the living quarters on the Station. The Drakes had lived there since arriving at Jupiter, before Warshovsky had been placed in charge and had made his security chief a member of the Executive Staff. Drake wasn't interested in the external trappings of power and had seen no reason to move to the larger apartment to which the security director was entitled. The coffee table in front of the couch was bare, as was the dining table. Megan gestured at the empty couch. "Have a seat."

"No thanks," Flynn said. "We'll only take a second. I need to know exactly what Mr. Drake said in his last phone call to you yesterday."

"I told Mr. Dettweiler and—"

"I need to know his exact words, if you can remember them."

Megan's eyes were almost as expressionless as her husband's. "He said . . . 'I'm done here. I have a few things to check, then I'll be home.' "

"That's all he said, 'a few things'? Not what or where?" Megan shook her head. "Why would he have visited this end of Sacramento Avenue on level three on a Sunday afternoon?"

Megan's eyes involuntarily darted toward the empty couch, as though she wanted to sit down. "He just said, 'I have a few things to check.' "

Flynn consulted his Company computer. "That was just before fifteen yesterday. Almost exactly one hour later, you called Security Control and reported him missing."

"I tried to call him first. His phone and his computer. I got computerized messages that the calls could not be completed."

Flynn was still looking at his computer display. "Yes, the communication records show two calls to valid contact codes that were not acknowledged. His phone and computer must have been switched off."

Or destroyed, Wendy thought.

Flynn looked at his host. "Well, thanks for the info. That's all I needed to know."

"I'm sorry I couldn't be of more help."

Wendy and Flynn retraced their steps along Second Street. "I've been on the Station over three years and that interview probably doubles the time I've spent with Megan Drake," Wendy said. "I wondered, when I learned that Drake was married, what kind of woman could live with him. Now I know: She's a mirror image of her husband! Did you see her eyes? Just like his—blank and expressionless. She hasn't been crying. Her husband just disappeared, is probably lying dead someplace, and she doesn't shed a single tear."

Flynn, whose thoughts were elsewhere, was slow to respond. "Yeah, they're a matched set, all right."

Wendy glanced at her husband. "We just wasted half an hour. Why aren't you annoyed?"

"Because Mrs. Drake told me exactly what I thought she would."

When her husband didn't elaborate, Wendy stopped walking. "Did she say something that I didn't hear?"

Flynn forced himself not to smile. "Wendy, you are a great corporate attorney. The Company is lucky to have you. But you'd never earn a living examining witnesses in court. It's not what she said, it's how she said it." As an afterthought, he added, "And what she didn't say."

Wendy put her hands on her hips. "And because of how she said nothing you didn't already know, you now know where Drake is?"

Flynn chose his words carefully. "Now I know what he was planning."

Wendy waited for her husband to elaborate. She waited in vain. "You're not going to tell me, are you!" She clenched her fists. "I don't believe it! You've become one of them!"

"Wendy—"

"I hired you to investigate Manstein's murder because they wouldn't tell me what was going on! You take Drake's place and now *you* won't tell me what's happening!"

Flynn searched for an argument that would mollify his wife without telling her anything. "Wendy . . . your face reveals what you're thinking. If Drake's carefully laid plan is going to work, I can't have you—or anybody else—inadvertently revealing it to the wrong person."

"Michael, I'm going to my office! My office manager is not going to be able to deduce Drake's secret plan by reading my face!"

Wendy's office manager was not the person Drake's plan was designed to uncover. Flynn's job had collided head-on with his marriage. Michael did a quick assessment—not a smart move when marriage was concerned, especially since Flynn was not an expert on the subject—and decided the marriage would be easier and cheaper to repair. He was going to have to anger his wife and accept the consequences. "Wendy, my love, I'm sorry, but you'll have to trust me. I'm not covering up any Company wrongdoing."

Wendy's eyes narrowed. "You are so lucky that we have a big couch, because you are going to be sleeping on it until you are too old to care."

Flynn took youth drugs; that could be sixty years.

Wendy was too angry at her husband to worry about nuclear weapons. Besides, she had work to do. Three days of legal paperwork had piled up in her computer files. In her anger she pounded her keyboard hard enough to hurt her fingers.

One of the items flagged for attention was a garnishment order from a court in Maryland for a Company employee who had stopped making child-support payments. Wendy had to confirm that it was legal and that the Company would incur no liability by sending part of the earnings of the employee—a master welder named Carl Wiesen—to Earth. The court order was complete and correct, but Wiesen might—probably would—still raise a fuss. He could get the order lifted if he paid what he owed; Wendy investigated his finances.

Wiesen banked at the First National. The Company owned the First National. Wendy's executive privileges gave her access to its records. Wiesen's bank balance was almost zero. It hadn't been much better than that for two years, when he had first overdrawn his account. Then it had increased slowly, but after a year had vanished again. Six months later it had showed a positive spike, but that too had quickly evaporated. Since then his biweekly pay deposits had been withdrawn—in cash—on the same days they had been received.

A master welder could make a third of a million dollars a year on the Station, and according to his bank records Wiesen hadn't been transferring his money elsewhere. Wendy found the explanation for his poverty in his human-resources file. When he had first overdrawn his account he had been declared *persona non grata* in the Company casino and had been ordered by his supervisor to seek counseling for his gambling habit. A year later the Gold Dollar Casino had opened, and Wiesen had put the counseling to use by taking advantage of a new place to lose his money. After six months of bad luck in the Gold Dollar, someone or something seemed to have arrested his gaming losses, because his account had shown a balance of over ten thousand dollars for two weeks. Wendy guessed that he had either had a lucky streak at the tables or had been working overtime . . . it had to be a lucky streak—no overtime showed in his work record. Besides, the deposit had been in cash.

That made Wendy pause. Company craftsmen had been known to do off-the-books jobs for Station residents.

Wendy located the records of the remodelling of the Gold Dollar Casino. Bill Gorkov's office had been panelled and re-carpeted at the same time that Carl Wiesen, a big loser at the

Gold Dollar's tables, had suddenly shown a positive bank balance.

It was probably a coincidence, but Wendy couldn't shake the thought of the expensive panelling in Gorkov's office covering the steel wall that separated the office from a utility tunnel.

Was Michael right? Had Gorkov's thugs killed Manstein and Cross? Had they used a secret exit from Gorkov's office—created by Carl Wiesen, master welder—to avoid the security cameras?

Wendy desperately, petulantly, wanted her husband to be wrong. She wanted him to fail. At *something.* She had graduated sixth in her class from Yale Law School, but her husband, with his crummy master's degree from Boston College, was the Station's hero. He thought he could keep her in the dark about what was going on. And she was so . . . so . . . *frustrated* because he might be right—about what had happened to Drake, what Drake had been planning, about Gorkov and the murders.

Wendy couldn't do anything about what had happened to Drake, but maybe she could prove Michael had been wrong about the gangster.

And if she couldn't, maybe she could discover the evidence that her husband had failed to find.

Wendy didn't know that Drake, as usual, had beaten everyone to the punch, that his security guards had already looked for a secret exit. She didn't know that she was wasting her time.

She was too angry to care, anyway.

According to Wiesen's work schedule, the welder was helping to assemble the ESA ship. Riding the shuttle there would take too long, and Wiesen was too likely to lie about an off-the-record job he'd done for Bill Gorkov. But Wendy didn't need to question Wiesen; she could investigate Gorkov's back wall. She shut off her computer. Her phone was already in her coat pocket. She slipped her portable computer into her purse.

Susan DuJong, Wendy's office manager, was in a blue mood: shiny, dark-blue coat, blouse, tights, shoes, and hair. Her lips and eyebrows matched her ensemble. Wendy knew that dark clothing on Monday was a sign that Susan had had a lousy weekend. "I'll be out of the office for an hour or so," Wendy said. "Call me if anything important comes up."

Susan nodded. "Ah, did they . . . did your husband . . . is there any word of Drake?"

Wendy was not in the mood to say anything nice about her husband. "Mr. Flynn is optimistic that something will develop soon."

Susan studied Wendy's face, then turned back to her computer. "That sounds like a 'no.' "

Just because Wendy was angry with Michael didn't mean other people could be critical of him. "Did that miner you've been seeing dump you?" She left before Susan could respond.

Wendy stopped at her apartment on her way to the other end of the Station. The housecleaning robot was vacuuming the floors; Furrball was watching it from atop the refrigerator. Wendy went into the bedroom and took her pistol from the drawer in the bedside table. She was a member of the security force, and she could shoot as well as most of the goons, so she was legally entitled to carry a concealed weapon, no matter what her husband said. She made sure the pistol was set to stun, checked its energy cell, and slipped it into her purse. If any members of the Gorkov gang were running around that utility tunnel, she was going to be able to take care of herself. Wendy wasn't worried about the people who had eliminated Drake—they probably didn't know that she was married to the new, unanticipated security director.

The moving sidewalk on Phoenix Avenue took Wendy to within one block of the Government Plaza. The door to the utility tunnel blended into the wall. Most of the Station's residents didn't know it was there. Wendy glanced quickly up and down the avenue. No member of Gorkov's gang was watching. Neither was the nearest security camera. She opened the door, stepped into the tunnel, and closed the door behind her. She made sure it was locked.

The walls of the utility tunnel extended upward several levels. Lamps on the walls provided dim light. The tunnel was narrow and crowded with pipes and electrical conduits. The walls and floor, like most of the Station, were of steel, and were coated with flat gray paint to prevent rust. But that very utility tunnel—on the opposite side of the Station—had been the scene of one of the most romantic moments in Wendy's life, when she and Michael had stopped pretending that they hated each other. For a moment Wendy's mood softened, but she couldn't back down. She would use their tunnel to demonstrate to her husband that he couldn't treat her the way Drake and Warshovsky did. She took her computer out of her purse and displayed a diagram of the Station. The Gold Dollar Casino was fifty meters along the Government Plaza from Phoenix Avenue. Wendy paced off the distance, her heart pounding with increasing excitement as she counted past thirty . . . forty . . .

There was no portal cut into the flat, gray steel, no hatch neatly welded into the wall. Wendy looked both ways and up and down, but there was nothing but black vertical pipes, and, two meters above the deck, horizontal conduits. Wendy explored farther, in case she had underestimated the distance, but there was no sign of a door. The steel walls were unbroken except for the painted-over seams where the steel panels had been welded together.

A pipe next to the wall was wrapped in insulation; Wendy could hear water flowing through it. She squinted: The insulation looked scuffed.

Wendy was nearly blinded by bright, white light as the wall

seam in front of her suddenly parted. With a creak an entire steel panel slid to the side, and Wendy found herself staring at Pierre Lavalle. Lavalle stared back.

The thug recovered first. Lavalle reached out, grabbed Wendy's arms, and pulled her into Gorkov's office. DiGeorgio and Weasel were there, looking as surprised as Wendy.

"What the hell . . ." DiGeorgio said.

Lavalle ripped Wendy's purse from her hands and tossed it onto Gorkov's desk. He pushed her at DiGeorgio. "Search her!" he growled.

Weasel was glad to oblige. While DiGeorgio pinned Wendy's arms to her sides, Weasel started with her ankles and worked his way up her legs.

"Just her pockets, you idiot!" Lavalle said. "She's not concealing anything under those tights!"

Weasel reluctantly stood up and patted Wendy's coat, spending more time than necessary on the part that draped her hips. He found her phone and tossed it to Lavalle.

Wendy tried to squirm away. Knuckles tightened his grip.

Lavalle dropped Wendy's phone on the desk next to the purse, took his own phone out of his coat pocket, flipped it open, and said, "Gorkov." He eyed Wendy as the call was completed. "Boss, we got a problem."

Wendy took a deep breath and, trying to reach the audio input to a security camera, shouted, *"Help!"* But the office was soundproof, and there was no one in the tunnel to hear her.

Chapter 22

Big Bill Gorkov wore a perfectly fitted light-blue suit and a gray vest. They were traditionally styled, with none of the shiny fabric that Ed Warshovsky and Michael Flynn found so distasteful. The gangster leaned back in his chair, turning Wendy's phone over and over in his hands, then looked at Lavalle out of the corner of his eye. "I distinctly remember ordering that the hatch was not to be opened without checking the video monitor."

Lavalle eyed Hector Rivera. "I watched Weasel check the monitor," Pierre said wearily. "He said it was clear."

"It *was* clear!" Weasel insisted.

Gorkov's eyes turned to Wendy. "Hector, the only thing on her that isn't shiny yellow is her hair, which is bright red. The microcam is a low-light model; even if the lamps in the tunnel had failed she would have glowed like a plasma display."

Weasel shifted his weight from one foot to the other. "But Boss, I checked the monitor!"

Gorkov looked at Weasel. "And panned it both ways?"

Weasel opened his mouth to respond, but thought better of it.

Gorkov turned his attention back to Wendy. "What were you doing in the utility tunnel behind my office?"

Wendy carefully avoided drawing attention to her purse, with her gun in it, which was on the desk in front of Gorkov and just out of her reach. She could feel Knuckles DiGeorgio standing behind her, leaning against the door, blocking her escape. She gripped the arms of her chair. Her palms were sweating. She needed to get Gorkov away from her purse. Failing that, she needed to convince Gorkov that the jig was up and that killing her would do him no good. She needed to look and sound confident. "My husband is very busy at the moment, discovering what happened to Silvanus Drake—he doesn't think you did it, by the way—so I thought I'd do him a favor and investigate the lead we got from Carl Wiesen. You really got your money's worth from him—those welds look perfect. There's no way to tell that the entire steel panel lifts out."

"We should have taken care of Wiesen," Lavalle said.

"Pierre, if a welder with a gambling habit had died a suspicious death, do you really think that Drake would have overlooked our back door?"

"Instead, the Company lawyer didn't overlook our back door."

Gorkov chuckled. "We *can* take care of the lawyer." He looked at Wendy. "If Carl Wiesen told anybody about the job he did for us, Jorge Allesandro would cut off his credit and he wouldn't be able to gamble. *Ergo,* he didn't come forward—not to the marshals, not to Company Security, and certainly not to you. So how did you learn about him?"

"His ex got his wages garnished because he stopped making child-support payments." Wendy forced herself to smile. "The garnishment order is in my computer, waiting for my return."

Rivera squirmed like a rodent caught in a trap. "Now what are we going to do?" he wailed.

"We're not going to panic," Gorkov said. "Right now the Company is primarily concerned with finding out what happened to the late, unlamented Silvanus Drake. Ms. Chadwick's disappearance might distract her husband so much that he will be completely ineffective. Washington will keep the marshals off our backs. Without Ms. Chadwick, the Legal Department will be shorthanded; by the time someone else gets around to Wiesen's garnishment order, no one will associate it with her demise."

"My office manager knows I'm here!" Wendy blurted.

Gorkov stared at Wendy, at the look on her face. "If that were true, you would have mentioned it earlier. Nice try, though." He brandished Wendy's telephone at Lavalle. "This probably contains a locator. Sanitize it and leave it somewhere on this side of the Station—there will be security video showing her coming this way. You handled her purse, I suppose? Rifle it, then clean it thoroughly and chuck it down a recycling chute. Wear gloves, a hair net, and a mask—the authorities will go over it with a microscope. They will be able to determine the time of her disappearance, so give me, oh, forty-five minutes to establish an alibi. You won't have to sanitize this office: She was in here with her husband last week, which will explain any DNA that might be discovered. Just make sure she isn't found for several days."

Lavalle crossed his arms. "We won't be able to dump her down a recycling chute. They check the garbage bins first thing now."

Gorkov reached to his desk and switched on his computer display. "Let's see . . . Bart Jannigan. Yes. Has an apartment to himself. He won't object to having his interest payments held in abeyance while he stores a large parcel for us." He looked at Lavalle. "Make sure the parcel is well sealed. I don't want any funny odors drawing attention to it." He had seen the way Weasel was looking at Wendy. "And don't let Hector leave any evidence on the body." Gorkov stood up. "Ms. Chadwick, I must be going. It's been a pleasure knowing you. At least, it was until this morning. And please forgive my lack of manners. I'd offer you a glass of sherry, but I can't have it showing up during your autopsy."

"I don't like sherry!"

Gorkov smiled. "Perfect."

Michael Flynn glanced at his wristwatch—almost noon. He looked through the one-way glass at Security Control. The three guards there moved like robots—no smiles, no banter. They had been badly shaken by Drake's disappearance, and frustrated by their inability to find him.

Flynn turned his chair around and faced his computer display. There was no news there, either.

Michael looked again at the log file, searching for something of interest that Drake hadn't deleted. His eyes stopped on the investigation that Drake had done on the party masks. Drake had taken no chances. Unlike Deputy Feldstein, he hadn't strained his eyes studying video records. He had had the computer compare the faces of the people who had entered and left the Gold Dollar Casino on the days of the murders, and the computer had found no one leaving the casino who had not entered earlier—

Flynn's heart skipped a beat. Drake had made *another* mistake! Michael should have caught it immediately, but he had not slept for thirty hours and his brain wasn't sharp. He looked over the file again to make sure. The computer had only compared faces leaving to faces that had entered earlier. *It had not checked the faces against Drake's database!*

Anyone could buy celebrity masks at Party Prep. Flynn wondered which of Gorkov's customers had had their loan payments reduced in exchange for buying masks identical to those worn by Gorkov's thugs, and then wearing those masks when they entered the Gold Dollar. Gorkov's hoodlums could then be seen to enter the casino. No one would have recognized them when they left wearing their masks, and Drake's computer search would confirm that everyone who left the casino had entered it earlier that day.

Flynn forgot he was tired. He only had to redo the search, comparing the faces of everyone entering and leaving to the Station's database. Three celebrities who had never visited the Station would stand out like Jupiter's Great Red Spot.

The computer beeped. One of Drake's security-camera watches had triggered an alarm.

Michael forgot about his database search. His heart was racing as reached for the key to call Dettweiler and send the tactical team to the storage shed. But the alarm hadn't come from the shed. The shuttle disembarkation area at the new end of the Station was displayed. Flynn's heart rate began to recover.

Then Flynn recognized the people in the disembarkation area. He called Ed Warshovsky.

The Station manager's face appeared in the upper half of the computer display. "Mr. Flynn! Have you found Drake?"

Flynn ignored the question. "What's Liao Chu doing on the Station today?"

Warshovsky was obviously surprised. "Liao? Today? I invited him to come back any time he wanted to, but he didn't tell me he was coming today."

"He and his four bodyguards just got off the shuttle from the Asian station. They're dressed informally—look like Asian workers on R and R."

"But . . . we've made no preparations, no security arrangements! You'll have to move fast—"

"You bet I will. Since this isn't an official visit, he's probably here for the bomb."

Warshovsky blinked. "Liao? Dr. Liao?" He got to his feet. "I'm coming down! Wait for me!"

Flynn didn't wait. He didn't know if he had time to waste. He called Dettweiler and got him out of bed. "Werner, put both tactical squads on high alert."

Dettweiler was still trying to wake up. "What's happening?"

"Dr. Liao, our honored guest last week, has returned. Incognito."

Dettweiler wasn't a fast thinker even when he was wide awake. "Liao? What's he doing on the Station today?"

"That's what I'm trying to find out. Get moving."

Flynn poked his head into Jake Jefferson's office and told him that he was leaving Company headquarters. As he stepped back into the corridor he almost bumped into Ed Warshovsky. The Station manager's office was at the end of the Station one level above Flynn's; Michael was surprised that he had arrived so quickly.

"You're going to intercept Liao?" Warshovsky asked.

"I'm going to *shadow* Liao," Flynn replied. "We have to find out if he's here to save us from the bomb or to set it off."

Flynn had surprised Warshovsky for the second time that morning. "Liao? A terrorist?"

"No, a communist. This might be his ultimate contribution to the class struggle."

Warshovsky, unlike Dettweiler, could think quickly. "Taking your car?"

Flynn raised an eyebrow. "Didn't know I had one."

"Follow me."

Warshovsky moved very rapidly for an out-of-condition man of fifty-nine who had been too old to benefit much when youth drugs had been invented. He led Flynn down two levels to the garage and to an electric vehicle next to the door. "This was Drake's. It will respond to you now."

"You want to drive? I'll navigate."

Warshovsky got behind the wheel. "Garage door, open!" Every Company-owned controller on the Station would obey his voice, and the door rolled upward. He drove out of the garage and turned left on Denver Avenue. "You want lights and siren?"

"Just the lights. If Liao gets a hint that we're coming he'll put on an innocent act and we'll never find out why he's here."

"Where's he going?"

Flynn checked his computer. "He's on the elevator with his bodyguards. They just left level six, going *down*. That means he's mistaken about where it was planted . . . or he's not trying to remove it." He looked at Warshovsky. "He could be trying to access its controller. It's been more than ten days since Manstein did that; the controller will respond to him today."

"How the hell would Liao know the control codes?"

"Maybe from the same source that told him about the bomb."

Flynn used his computer to check the traffic-control radar—Liao's visit could have been a diversion. But there were no radar targets in the direction of the storage shed. Michael called Dettweiler. "Tell the tactical squad near the reactor to follow me. I have my locator."

"Where are you going?"

"I don't know yet."

Warshovsky slowed the car to maneuver around a cluster of pedestrians who didn't respect the flashing lights. "As I recall, there is a code to deactivate the bomb—he could render it harmless without knowing where it is."

Flynn didn't reply. It was unlikely that Liao would know everything about the bomb except its location.

"He's probably headed for the Government Plaza," Warshovsky surmised. "From there they can take a moving sidewalk to this end of the Station."

"Probably." Liao had designed the old end of the Station. He knew where its control-system access points were. "Their elevator's on the opposite side of the Station. Cut over on Eighth Street."

Liao and his bodyguards left the elevator at the Government Plaza on level three. They walked to Phoenix Avenue and got on the moving sidewalk.

"They're coming this way," Flynn said.

"There must be fifty or sixty access points in this end of the Station. Which one is he headed for?"

Flynn consulted his computer. "There are actually a hundred and twenty-five in this end of the Station. He'll want one that isn't covered by a security camera . . . and there are sixteen of those. That's interesting: Liao's bodyguards have spread out. They were always close to their boss when he was here on official business. Whoa! They've left Phoenix! They're taking the ramp down to level two!"

"Damn!" Warshovsky hit the brake and caught Flynn, who wasn't strapped in, by surprise. "I just missed a ramp!" Eighth Street was wide enough for Warshovsky to make a U-turn. He doubled back to the ramp.

"Hold it! They're going all the way down to level one! Every system-access point on that level is within sight of a security camera!"

Warshovsky shook his head. "No. Only the wireless ones are. I know where he's going."

"Enlighten me."

"We're remodelling a machine shop on level one. The wiring's being rerouted and the security camera in that area is temporarily disconnected. We showed Liao the remodelling when he toured the Station. He knows the security camera there isn't functioning, and he'll be able to get a hardwire connection to the control system."

Flynn furiously punched the keys on his computer. "Okay, I've found it." He called Dettweiler. "Werner, Liao and his troops are on level one, headed for Fourth Street between Phoenix and Chicago."

Werner's image on the display grimaced. "There's construction in that area. I don't think we have any guards close by."

"Good. Guards would scare him off. Get the tactical team there. Are you tracking Liao's bodyguards? Make sure they don't spot anybody in orange coveralls."

Dettweiler nodded. "Right."

"We'll beat them to the construction site," Warshovsky said.

"Don't park anywhere near it," Flynn warned.

Warshovsky parked the car on Fourth Street. He led Flynn three blocks to the construction site, which was deserted.

Flynn stood in the open doorway to what had been a machine shop and surveyed the remodelling clutter. Power tools were scattered on the floor and scaffolding gave access to the ceiling, but there were no construction workers. "Lunch time," Flynn said. "He planned it for lunch time."

Warshovsky looked at the wiring hanging down through missing ceiling panels. "That's where the security camera used to be. All Company work areas are covered by security cameras, in case of on-the-job accidents." He looked at Flynn like a teacher about to reveal the secret of the universe. "One of those optical cables up there is for the Station control system."

Flynn looked at his computer. "They're coming. At least, Liao is. His bodyguards have surrounded the area, I think—two of them are out of sight of security cameras." He nodded toward a row of packing cases. "Let's hide behind there."

There was less than a meter of space between the packing cases and the wall, but that was enough room for Flynn to draw his pistol.

"Put that away!" Warshovsky ordered. "Liao's a Chinese big shot!"

"Ah-hah. Perhaps a very dangerous one."

"He can't do any harm, even if he has the code to detonate the bomb!"

"Unless there's a second bomb we haven't found. Quiet!"

Flynn couldn't see the door from his hiding place, but he heard footsteps as someone entered the room. "Smith?" The voice sounded like Liao's. "Joe Smith?" The footsteps crossed from the door to the center of the room. Michael peeked around the corner of his packing case. Liao had added a tee-connector to the control cable and was connecting a cable from his computer to the connector. He tapped a sequence of keys and smiled.

Flynn carefully placed his computer on top of the packing case so that it could record what was about to happen, then stepped from his hiding place. He glanced at the doorway to make sure that none of Liao's bodyguards had followed their boss into the room. "Dr. Liao! This is a pleasant surprise!"

For Liao, the surprise was anything but pleasant. His smile vanished. He looked from Flynn to Warshovsky and back to Flynn. "Gumshoe! I hear you are now a Company employee!"

"It's a step down from my previous position, but the fringe benefits are first rate." Flynn gestured at Liao's computer. "Looks like you're plugged into the Station's control system."

Liao looked from Flynn to Warshovsky. "I . . . I was going to check on something I built into the Station years ago . . ." He looked at the cables dangling from the ceiling. His expression hardened. He clenched his jaw. "I . . ." His Adam's apple quivered. "I am putting an end to your plundering!" Liao thrust his chest forward. "You capitalists are never satisfied! Stealing the resources of Earth wasn't enough for you! You had to steal the resources of the entire solar system! But it ends now!"

It was Warshovsky's turn to be surprised. "Dr. Liao, our governments are negotiating to improve relations!"

Liao's eyes shown brightly. "My government is run by tired old men, who want only to live out their lives in peace! But I have not abandoned the class struggle!"

"You designed the original Station!" Warshovsky said. "You helped the Company get started out here!"

"I never thought you would succeed! I was delighted to take your money! And when you expanded the Station, increasing your folly, you paid me even more! But, to be safe, I had some of my comrades take precautions, which are now paying off!"

"You're building the station for the Asian consortium," Warshovsky pointed out.

"Yes, and I have ensured their failure! I made the new station too small and too expensive! They will never make a profit and will go bankrupt! We will be able to buy it for a song, and then the riches of the Jovian system will belong to the people!"

And never again would Liao's career be stymied by a lack of resources.

Flynn shook his head. "I don't think the Consortium will keep you on after this incident. Capitalists hate it when people try to drive them to bankruptcy."

Liao stared at the detective. "They will never know. I have a bomb planted next to your new reactor. I had planned to program its detonation for when I was at a safe distance, but you will trace the command I'm about to send and you might find it in time. Unfortunately for you, I am willing to die for my beliefs. Goodbye, gentlemen."

Liao looked down at his computer and punched a sequence of keys. He seemed puzzled when nothing happened. He was punching the keys again when a small black hole appeared in his forehead. Another hole appeared right next to the first. Liao still looked puzzled as his legs collapsed under him and he slumped to the floor.

Flynn looked at the doorway. There stood Silvanus Drake, laser pistol in hand.

"It's about time you got here!" Michael said.

Warshovsky looked dumbfounded. "Drake! You're alive!"

Drake's eyes were expressionless. "Why shouldn't I be?"

"But . . . where have you been?"

"In an empty apartment, awaiting developments."

Warshovsky opened his mouth, closed it, and looked at Flynn, who was checking the body for signs of life.

"No pulse." Flynn shook his head. "Two in the head. Might not be enough brain matter left for the medics to save him." He stood up and holstered his pistol. He took his computer from the top of the packing case and called Dettweiler. "Werner, there's been a shooting at this location involving a member of the security force. Respond paramedics and the other appropriate people."

"Who got shot?"

"Dr. Liao. Arrest his bodyguards. But stun them first! Don't get close to them until they're unconscious! You can't imagine the damage those guys can do with their hands!"

"Right, chief."

"Oh, Werner, you don't have to call me 'chief' anymore."

Warshovsky waited for Flynn to put away his computer before he said, "Did you have to kill him? His death will cause us no end of trouble! The diplomatic flap will have the politicos all over us!"

"If he had planted a second bomb that we never found, we wouldn't be having this conversation," Drake explained. "Besides, his arrest would have the politicians—Chinese as well as American—all over us. Now the Chinese will be able to claim that Liao was out of his mind, and there won't be a living Liao to say otherwise. And when we turn over the Chinese A-bomb that we are about to discover on the Station—an obsolete design, but a real Chinese bomb nonetheless—we won't get too much flak from Washington."

Flynn slipped his holster off of his belt and handed his gun to Drake. "Since I'm not actually the security director, I'm not authorized to carry a lethal weapon."

Drake dropped the gun into his coat pocket. "You asked Operations if there were any anomalies in elevator shaft number three. Why?"

"Because Helmuth Manstein showed inordinate pleasure in riding that elevator."

Drake's eyes looked even more expressionless than usual as the security chief considered Flynn's response. "According to Operations, the radiation level is higher than average just above level twelve—loose fill in the radiation shield."

"Really?" Flynn said. He glanced at Liao's body. "I'd better let Wendy know what's happened. She'll be steamed if she learns the details from someone else." He opened his computer and frowned at the display. "Huh. She's not answering her computer." He switched to an audio link to her phone and got her voice mail. "That's funny. She's not answering her phone, either." He looked up. To no one in particular he said, "Where the hell's my wife?"

Chapter 23

Weasel paced back and forth in front of Gorkov's liquor cabinet. Lavalle, leaning against the back wall of the office, cleaned his fingernails with a pocket knife. Gorkov's empty chair was right in front of him, but if he sat in it he knew that Weasel would try to regain Big Bill's favor by ratting him. Knuckles stood impassively in front of the office door, his arms folded. His black eyes had nearly healed and the doctors had straightened his broken nose. He didn't have enough imagination to get bored.

"Isn't it time already?" Hector complained.

Lavalle glanced at his wristwatch. "Close enough." He folded his knife and put it in his pocket, then stepped to the desk and activated the computer monitor. Wendy couldn't see the display from her chair, but guessed that Lavalle was checking the microcam that the gangsters had installed in the utility tunnel. Pierre tapped a couple of computer keys. "It's clear." He looked at Weasel. "Come on. Help me open it."

Weasel winced. "That's Knuckles's job! I'm not big enough!"

"Yeah, but I don't trust you to keep her from bolting through the door. Let's go."

Pierre grabbed one end of a bookshelf mounted on the back wall. Weasel took the other end. Muscles bulged on their necks and cracks appeared in the wall. They slid the movable section to the side, forming a narrow door. Weasel breathed a sigh of exhaustion.

"There are too many cameras on this level," Lavalle said.

"We'll take her up to five. I'll check it out." He stepped through the gap in the wall and started climbing the drain pipe next to the gangsters' back door.

Weasel stood behind the desk, facing Wendy. He set his feet apart and put his hands on his hips. "You're one lucky girl. If we could put you someplace you'd never be found, we could have a lot of fun with you in your last hour alive." He grinned.

Wendy tried to sound nonchalant. "Knuckles and Pierre would have to go first, so you could learn what to do."

Knuckles laughed. Weasel scowled. He stuck his head through the back door and looked upward. "How's it look?"

"Hector, you know the boss doesn't like us talking in the tunnel!" Knuckles said.

Weasel pulled his head back into the office. "It's okay. Pierre's waving to us to bring the girl."

Knuckles left the office door and walked to the back of Wendy's chair. "Let's go, lady." He grabbed Wendy's left arm so firmly that it hurt, and led her around the desk to the wall opening.

"You'll carry her up the pipe, won't you?" Weasel asked.

Knuckles snorted. "I thought you wanted to get your hands on her."

Wendy had only one chance left. She turned and tried to return to the desk. "My purse."

Knuckles dragged her back. "You don't need your damned purse."

"My makeup's in my purse," Wendy said weakly.

"Oh, by all means let the girl have her makeup!" Weasel said. "We want her to look her best when they find her decaying carcass!"

Knuckles released his grip. The desk was only two steps from the back wall. Wendy stood between DiGeorgio and her purse as she picked it up. Her hands were trembling and she fumbled with the clasp.

Lavalle climbed down the pipe and looked into the office. He knew that no one had checked the contents of the purse. "Hey!"

Wendy tore open the clasp and turned around, reaching into the purse for her gun. Lavalle was sweeping back his coat, reaching for something behind his right hip. Wendy's hand closed on the grip of her pistol. She let her purse drop. Lavalle's hand reappeared. Wendy nearly froze: Clutched in his hand was a gun. It was a primitive, cartridge weapon—a revolver—but it was a gun nonetheless and Lavalle shouldn't have had one. Drake's ironclad security kept all unlicensed firearms off the Station.

Wendy brought her pistol to eye level. She put the red aiming dot on Lavalle's chest. Pierre was raising his revolver. Wendy jerked the trigger, but her target was only two meters away.

"Oo!" Lavalle grimaced. To Wendy's surprise, he didn't fall.

Wendy jerked the trigger again, hitting the gangster on the right edge of his abdomen. He winced, and seemed to be unable to raise his gun. Wendy rushed another shot and missed. She fired a fourth time and managed to hit Lavalle in the solar plexus. The revolver fell from his hand and he fell slowly backward into the utility tunnel.

Knuckles looked as stunned as Lavalle, but he recovered and dove for the revolver. Wendy aimed her pistol at his broad back. "Go ahead, Knuckles! Pick it up!"

Knuckles froze, his hand over the gun lying on the carpet where Lavalle had dropped it. Wendy was holding a pulsed laser. For all he knew, she might have reset it from stun to kill. He flexed his fingers, then withdrew his hand.

Weasel did what he could do best. He bolted into the utility tunnel and disappeared.

"Okay, Knuckles. You've been through this drill before. Stand up—slowly!—and grab that wall."

Wendy kept one eye on the gangster as she picked her purse

off the floor. She took out her computer, opened it, and called Security. "I need a security force in Bill Gorkov's office right now!"

The panel in Gorkov's back wall had been placed in the closed position. Flynn and Drake stood in the utility tunnel and studied the seams. Drake carefully ran his fingers over one of them.

"I thought you had this wall checked for an escape hatch," Flynn said.

"If I had known that Gorkov could have purchased this kind of workmanship, I would have checked it myself. Still, they should have found it—they had test instruments." Drake looked up and down the utility tunnel. "They probably examined the wrong section of wall." He turned around. "Or the wrong side." His investigators didn't know it yet, but they had volunteered for the graveyard shift.

Flynn pressed his hand against the removable panel. He shook his head. "I thought they used party masks to beat the cameras."

"So did I, for awhile," Drake said, "so I had the computer check faces leaving the casino against faces entering."

Michael almost smiled. "But you didn't have the computer check those faces against your database."

Drake stared at Flynn with his usual blank expression. Michael guessed that the security director didn't like having his mistakes—even those that proved to be harmless—discovered by others. Drake nodded at the goon standing to his left, who raised his phone to his lips and said, "Okay, open it."

The panel slid aside and Drake led Flynn into the office. DiGeorgio was seated in the chair Wendy had occupied, with his hands manacled behind his back. A deputy marshal stood next to him. Lavalle, in the custody of another deputy, was sitting on a chair in the corner. His hands were out of sight behind his back and his shirt was off. A paramedic was treating the bruises that the stun pulses had left.

"Where's my wife?" Flynn asked.

The deputy at the door opened it and stuck his head into the corridor. "Ms. Chadwick!" He held the door open for her.

Wendy took one step into the office and stopped, her mouth open. "Drake! You're alive!"

"I must be. People keep saying so."

Flynn couldn't stop himself from grinning. "Careful, Drake. If you keep talking like that, people might think you have a sense of humor."

Wendy glared at her husband. "You knew he was alive all along, didn't you!"

"I deduced that he—"

"And you didn't tell me!"

"Wendy, I—"

"What else didn't you tell me?"

Flynn counterattacked. "Why didn't you tell me that you were coming here?"

Wendy put her hands on her hips. "Because you wouldn't tell me what you were doing!"

"You could have been killed!"

Wendy lifted her nose in the air. "I was armed!"

"They still managed to take you prisoner and hold you for over an hour!"

Wendy moistened her lips. "I was . . ." She drew herself erect. "Trying to find out as much as I could about their criminal activities!"

Drake had heard enough. "I trust that you'll send Security a report on your investigation." Lavalle's gun was in a plastic evidence bag on the desk. Another bag held the six cartridges. Drake picked up the gun. "Colt Python. These things haven't been made in almost a century." He held it up for Flynn to see.

"Just look at that workmanship." He picked up the bag containing the cartridges. "Hollow points. Shouldn't make holes in the hull and let the air out." He turned to the deputy guarding Lavalle. "Did he say where he got the gun?"

The deputy shook his head. "They're not talking until their lawyer gets here, and apparently that won't happen until Gorkov calls him."

Drake consulted his computer. "We just picked up Gorkov. We're taking him to the Marshals Office. We haven't found Rivera yet." He switched his computer to another display. "The doctors have given up trying to revive Liao."

Drake eyed another plastic bag on the desk. He picked it up. "Inexpensive radiation detector. These things will respond to anything."

One of the security guards said, "We found it in Lavalle's pocket."

Drake looked at Lavalle. "Why would you need a radiation detector?"

Lavalle looked straight ahead. He said nothing.

The office door opened and Marshal Hathaway entered the room. She stared at Drake. "It's true. You're not dead."

Drake looked blankly at the marshal. "You sound disappointed."

Hathaway frowned. "I want to know what the hell's going on!"

Drake gestured at Wendy. "Ms. Chadwick here was taken prisoner by these—"

"I know all that! I was here before you were! I want to know why everyone thought you were dead for the last twenty-four hours! I want to know why there's a dead Chinese big shot—a man *you're* supposed to have killed—in the emergency room of the Company hospital! I want to know where Lavalle got that gun! I want to know what Big Bill Gorkov has to do with all of this!"

Drake considered his answer carefully. "It's complicated."

Hathaway was out of patience. She turned to the closest deputy and ordered, "Take 'em all in!"

"Oh?" Flynn interjected. "Are we under arrest?"

"Yes!"

"On what charge?"

Hathaway pointed at Drake. "Him: murder. You: accessory to murder. Her: carrying a concealed weapon."

Wendy took a sharp breath. "I'm a member of the Security Force! I'm legally entitled to—"

"Marshals Office!" Hathaway ordered, and stormed out of the room.

The interrogation room in the Marshals Office overflowed with Gorkov, two of his thugs, Wendy Chadwick, Silvanus Drake, Michael Flynn, Marshal Hathaway, and U.S. Attorney Kyle Pierce. Pierce tried to bring order out of chaos, but Hathaway refused to believe that Drake had merely "tried to make whoever had killed Manstein and Cross think they had a window of opportunity" and bring them into the open. Gorkov refused to say anything without his attorney present, and his attorney was in court. The back door in Gorkov's wall puzzled Hathaway; she still believed the FBI's assertion that Gorkov was not involved in the murders. She found the killing of Liao Chu to be completely incomprehensible, even after viewing the recording that Flynn had made of the event.

"Why would he plant a bomb on the Station? He was the original designer! His government is negotiating with our government to reduce tensions!"

"He planted the bomb a decade ago," Drake pointed out. "The hard-liners weren't in power then."

Hathaway frowned. "There's been a bomb on this station for ten years and you didn't know about it?"

"I hate to appear inept, Marshal, but there probably have been lots of things on this station for ten years that I don't know about."

Hathaway found the answer flippant and unresponsive. "You had no need to use deadly force on Liao. You could have stunned him." She looked at U.S. Attorney Pierce. "That's manslaughter, at least. Maybe second-degree murder."

Drake was not flustered. "Liao said he was detonating a bomb. Regulations permit the use of deadly force in that circumstance."

Pierce was leaning back in his chair, his computer on his lap. "Marshal, I can present the evidence to a grand jury, but I'd bet my pension that they won't indict."

Hathaway stared at the attorney. "Maybe you should consider impanelling a grand jury someplace other than on this God-forsaken outpost!"

"The magistrate would have to grant a change of venue," Pierce said. "He's never done that for a trial. It costs too much to transport the witnesses. That's why we have a magistrate here."

Drake's computer beeped.

"Shut that damn thing off or I'll take it away from you!" Hathaway said.

Drake read the message on his display. "Dr. Liao's bomb has been found. It was in a sealed compartment, which explains why it went undetected for ten years. Would you care to see it?"

Hathaway insisted on seeing it. She had Gorkov, Lavalle, and DiGeorgio locked up, then let Drake lead her to the Station hub. Kyle Pierce came along. So did Wendy and Flynn.

A hole had been crudely cut into the compartment wall. Two orange-suited security guards stood on either side of it. Portable lights had been installed. There sat Wilmer de Birk's bomb, casing intact, attached to its controller as though it had been there all along. A cable from the controller was spliced into the wiring that ran through the compartment.

"That's the bomb?" Hathaway asked.

"Don't spend too much time in there," Drake warned. "The radiation level is above normal."

Hathaway's forehead wrinkled. "Why? Isn't this compartment shielded from the outside?"

"Nothing's shielding you from the bomb."

Hathaway needed a moment for that to sink in, and then she looked like she was going to melt into her shoes. She opened her mouth, but no words came out. She swallowed. "It's a . . . a . . . a nuclear bomb?"

"Where did Liao get a nuclear device?" Pierce asked.

"I assume the inevitable government investigation will answer that question," Drake replied.

Pierce looked at the marshal. "The FBI has to be informed immediately."

Hathaway stared at the bomb. "Ah, yeah." Jailing Flynn and Drake wasn't important anymore. "Has that been deactivated?"

"We shut off its controller," Drake said. "Other than the neutron flux it's emitting, it's harmless."

"Are you sure this is the only one?"

"We're checking the rest of the Station with radiation detectors." It was a lie, but Drake didn't want to appear incompetent. "The satellites, too. But one nuke would be enough to destroy the Station. Liao would have had no need for another one."

Hathaway bit her lip. "Who knows about this?"

"Mr. Warshovsky. The technicians who found it. These guards."

"What about the people searching for another one?"

"They're looking for unexplained radiation. They don't know why."

Hathaway turned away, nearly losing her footing in the light gravity near the hub. "I'm going to inform Washington. I want this compartment guarded round the clock. Nobody touches that thing until Washington tells us what to do! And this discovery is top secret—I don't need twenty-four thousand panicked residents running amok!"

Flynn guessed that he, his wife, and Drake were no longer under arrest. "Marshal Hathaway, come to the cowboys' locker room at sixteen-thirty. You'll be able to see for yourself where Lavalle got that gun."

"Why sixteen-thirty?"

"That's when the evidence arrives."

Little things like smuggled firearms and murders weren't high on the marshal's priority list at that moment. "Flynn, this had better be good!"

Michael glanced at the bomb. "Well, nukes are a tough act to follow, but I'll do my best."

Drake waited for the marshal to leave before he said, "They had Wiesen make a secret door into that murder scene, too?"

"No."

Hathaway, still looking like she wanted to take the first ship leaving ground zero, didn't get to the cowboys' locker room until sixteen thirty-five. It was just as well: Russell Murrow didn't dock his ship until sixteen thirty-eight. Four more minutes elapsed before he appeared in the locker room and was surprised to find Flynn, Wendy, Drake, Marshal Hathaway, and two security guards waiting for him.

"What's going on?" Murrow said.

"Take off the pressure suit," Drake ordered.

Murrow took one step backward, then noticed two more

security guards standing on either side of the door through which he had entered. They stepped sideways, toward each other, blocking the door. "You don't have probable cause to search me. You need a warrant."

Wendy shook her head. "You're wearing Company property in a Company work area during your work shift. We can ask for our property back any time we want."

Murrow hesitated. He looked at the marshal. "What's she doing here?"

"She's my guest," Flynn explained.

Murrow scowled. "Now that *he's* back," he nodded at Drake, "you don't have authority to be here!"

"He's *my* guest," Drake said. "The pressure suit: Remove it yourself or I'll have my men do it for you. Now."

Murrow pursed his lips. He slowly pulled down the front zipper and carefully extracted his arms from the suit. He held the top half of the suit so that it wouldn't slump, but Flynn spotted something and reached into the suit for it.

"Hey! That's my personal property!"

The package was wrapped in white, air-tight plastic and sealed with tape. "What is it?" Flynn asked. "Your lunch?" He took his pocket knife and began to cut through the tape.

"You have no right to do that! That's my property!"

"Check your employment contract," Wendy said. "The Company has the right to inspect personal property brought into work areas."

Murrow's "personal property" proved to be a classic, government-model automatic pistol, a box of ammunition for it, a Heckler and Koch pulsed-laser pistol, and an electronic device that Flynn assumed was a transponder that would enable Murrow to home in on the package. In the other side of the suit Michael found another package that contained a transponder, a bag of white powder, and vials of clear liquid. He handed them to the marshal. "Looks like synthetic heroin and polymethyl two four. And we heard him say this was his property." Flynn shrugged. "My mistake—I thought he was smuggling it for Gorkov. He got paid extra for letting Knuckles in the back door to stab Leron Cross."

"I want a lawyer!" Murrow looked at Wendy. "The Company has to get me a lawyer if I'm in legal trouble! It's in the contract!"

"You're going to need one," Hathaway said. "You're under arrest for possession of controlled substances with intent to sell and unlicensed possession of concealed weapons. We'll add the charge of accessory to murder as soon as the U.S. attorney can do the paperwork." She nodded at the two goons behind Murrow. "Put cuffs on him and take him to the Marshals Office."

Drake waited for Murrow to be led from the room before he asked Flynn, "Have you figured out who helped him? He doesn't have the training to get around our security sensors. Gorkov and his thugs don't, either."

"He didn't need training." Flynn picked up Murrow's discarded pressure suit. "Murrow gave Wendy and me a ride last Wednesday. I was wearing one of these. Went through the airlocks four times with my stun pistol in my pocket and, according to your own security report, the sensors never beeped." He demonstrated the thickness of the suit with his right thumb and forefinger. "These suits are designed to block serious radiation. They're opaque to your sensors."

Everyone who worked outside wore the suits, but they couldn't open them in vacuum to stuff contraband inside. Only pilots could pick up packages dropped off by Asian shuttles, depressurize their ships, take the packages aboard, repressurize the ships, then open their suits and put the packages inside, where the sensors wouldn't see them. Drake nodded. "Gorkov has probably been supplying the Asian station with drugs and weapons from his contacts on Earth and Mars. How did you know it was Murrow?"

"The day I met him, his ship was squawked for repair. Didn't bother him at all—gave him more time for drinking. But his ship malfunctioned the day he gave us a ride and he threw a fit, so he probably had a pickup to make that day. Today he switched shifts with another pilot, so I figured the contraband was arriving before his usual shift started, and that he'd have it on him when he docked."

"Was Cross involved?"

Flynn hesitated. "I don't know if Cross actually did anything illegal, although Gorkov certainly tried to recruit him—in exchange for the money he needed to buy himself out of his contract and go back to planet three with his wife—either to smuggle contraband or to give Gorkov and friends an unofficial and unrecorded lift to . . ." He glanced at the marshal. "Someplace. Whichever it was, the thought of doing something wrong bothered him—Francine said he wasn't sleeping well—and Gorkov started worrying that he might go to the marshals. So last Tuesday, Murrow made sure the maintenance labs were empty and then let Lavalle and DiGeorgio in here through the side door—he opened it from the inside so its lock wouldn't inform Security Control. After Murrow undocked and had an ironclad alibi, Gorkov or Weasel called Cross. Leron wanted privacy so he left the locker room and stepped into that corridor there, where Lavalle and DiGeorgio were waiting. The recycling chute was filled all the way to the top of the hatch, so they left Cross's body on the floor and departed the way they'd come in."

"He'll talk," Hathaway said. "We'll get Gorkov for murder, in addition to kidnapping and conspiracy to commit murder. He'll spend the rest of his life in custody." A smile flickered across her face. "Even the FBI couldn't nail Gorkov."

"You'll be the hero of the Marshals Service," Flynn said.

Chapter 24

The crowd in Betty's Bar was celebrating. The killers of Manstein and Cross were in custody and a plan to sabotage the Station had been thwarted in the nick of time. Two of the people responsible for the favorable outcomes were in Betty's, sitting at a table in the back corner, and the crowd could express its appreciation to Michael Flynn and Wendy Chadwick by buying them drinks. Round after round of drinks.

Jack and Missy Adamly sat across the table from Michael and Wendy. Betty appeared with yet another tray of beverages and placed a Coke ceremoniously in front of Jack, who grimaced.

"These are on Jason," Betty announced. She was wearing tight black slacks that revealed how well youth drugs had helped her keep her figure.

"Who's Jason?" Flynn asked.

Wendy gestured toward the bar with a nod over her shoulder. A man who looked vaguely familiar to Flynn saluted with a raised beer glass. Flynn returned the salute with the Irish whiskey that Jason had provided. He set the glass on the table next to another full glass and the half empty one he was nursing.

"Coca-Cola," Jack muttered. "If I drink any more of this gunk my guts will rot! I have to play airball in less than an hour! How will I be able to play if I'm sick to my stomach?"

"You told me that Marines don't get sick to their stomachs," Missy said. To emphasize the point, she drank from her glass of beer. "And the magistrate wouldn't reduce your bail until Mr. Habruch pointed out that you only get into fights when you've been drinking."

Jack glowered at his soda. "Yeah, and then the damn magistrate makes abstaining from alcohol a condition for reduced bail! I should've punched that idiot Habruch in the face instead of Brennerman!"

Missy set her glass on the table and put her hands on her husband's arm. "Gee, honey, I didn't know you enjoyed sleeping in jail so much. I thought you wanted to come home and sleep with me."

Jack drank his Coke.

Wendy finished a glass of champagne and picked up the one Jason had bought for her. "I like being the object of all this hero worship."

"You won't in the morning," Flynn warned. "Remember the weekly Executive-Staff meeting? You have to work."

Wendy sipped more champagne. "And you don't?"

Adamly frowned. "I can't believe Murrow was working for that bastard Gorkov. And I can't believe Dr. Liao would try to blow up the Station. He was the original designer! This is his baby!"

Flynn tasted his whiskey. He was too tired and too drunk to appreciate it. "He never intended for this station to be a success. He tried to do the same thing to the Company that he was doing to the Asian consortium—drive it into bankruptcy—and when that didn't work . . . He was an old-line communist, a century past his time, trying to accomplish what Lenin, Stalin, and Mao couldn't do—bring down capitalism."

Wendy was two drinks ahead of her husband and was in a very good mood. She took a long sip of champagne and poked Flynn with her elbow. "Drink up! Or are you starting a collection?"

Flynn fingered his glass. “I don’t live right down the block from this place anymore, and I haven’t slept for almost—” He looked at his watch. “Thirty-eight hours. I have to stay sober enough to stagger home.”

“I’ll spring for a cab.”

“How big was the bomb?” Jack asked.

Flynn didn’t look up from his whiskey. “Big enough to hold two hundred, maybe two hundred and fifty kilos of explosive.”

“And it was right below the new reactor?” Jack had spent seven years in the Marine Corps and could envision the effect of a high-explosive blast in a confined space. “We lose the new reactor, the Station’s uninhabitable. The old reactor’s much too small to carry the load.”

“Probably why Liao had the bomb planted there,” Missy guessed.

Jack unconsciously took a drink of his soda as though he was holding a glass of beer. “The first guy who was killed: Are they ever going to release his name?”

Flynn hesitated. “The authorities still haven’t found his next of kin.” Maybe they never would. Liao no doubt had known Manstein’s real name, but Liao was dead. The Helsinki police had traced the IP address of the e-mail that hadn’t bounced to an apartment on the city’s north side. The tenants had claimed no knowledge of Manstein. The next day the apartment was vacant. The tenants had left no forwarding address and had been living under false identities. Anyone else who knew Manstein’s real name was probably beyond the reach of American justice.

“He was Liao’s man?” Adamly asked.

Michael nodded. “He was here to make sure nothing happened to the bomb before Liao decided to use it.”

Jack grunted. “Must have really knocked Liao for a loop—comes all the way out here, and learns his man on the spot was murdered the day before he arrived. Why did Gorkov kill him?"

Flynn shrugged. "Big Bill's not talking. The deceased visited the casinos; maybe he borrowed money from Gorkov, lost it gambling, and couldn't pay him back." It was the official story, and would have to do until Gorkov or one of his thugs confessed.

Adamly looked at his watch. "We'd better go, hon. We play in less than an hour, and we gotta stop by the apartment for my gear." He looked at Flynn. The bottom of his mustache was stained with Coke. "I won't be seeing you in a bar any time soon. Maybe Missy and I can have you over for dinner some night."

Missy patted her husband on the back. "Nice try, Jack, but you won't be drinking at home, either. Not until the doctors get Brennerman functioning again and Pierce accepts a plea of misdemeanor assault. Besides, Michael owes *us* dinner. Two dinners, in fact."

Jack stood up. Missy poured down the last of her beer and followed him.

"Set a scoring record," Flynn called after them.

Missy made an excuse to her husband and stepped back to the table. She bent over so she could whisper. "That server I couldn't locate? The one that Gorkov was exchanging e-mails with?" She looked at Wendy out of the corner of her eye, but Flynn didn't stop her. "I told Howie Ng about it. He thought he could track down any Internet server anywhere in the solar system, but he had to call in favors from some old college classmates to find it. It's in the White House!" Missy glanced from side to side to make sure no one had overheard. "Physically inside the White House! Who the hell inside the White House was talking with that gangster?"

"There are lots of Federal offices in the White House," Flynn said soothingly.

"We don't know everything about this case," Missy said, then turned and followed her husband.

When Wendy was drunk, her mood could change in a heartbeat. "That's the understatement of the year." She played with her glass. The champagne was inexpensive but Wendy had drunk too much to care. "You're security director for less than a day and you become just like Drake. You can feed your friends the Company manure without batting an eye. They believed every word you said. You can even keep your own wife in the dark."

Flynn pushed his glass away. "Wendy, you now know as much about this case as I do. I'm sorry I couldn't tell you what I suspected this morning, but Liao was Drake's prime suspect—that's why he kept the security-camera watch running when Liao went to the Asian station. Liao might have made another official visit and talked to you, and I couldn't take the chance that he'd detect something in your attitude that would make him suspicious—for a lawyer, you lie very badly. Hell, Drake didn't even trust Warshovsky to keep the secret."

"I'm not married to Drake! And I didn't hire him to find out for me what was going on! I hired you!"

Deputy Marshal Sid Feldstein pushed his way through the crowd toward Flynn's table. He was in his marshal's uniform and was in a hurry.

Flynn indicated that Sid should take the chair that Jack Adamly had vacated. "Why aren't you running the evening shift?"

"I am. I'm on my break." Sid leaned across the table and lowered his voice. "National security again! Hathaway can't tell us anything. We're not allowed to talk about it, even with each other."

Flynn looked at his whiskey. "Figures."

"Yeah, well, whatever they're keeping secret, it's big," Feldstein said. "I've seen Hathaway angry. I've seen her puzzled. I've seen her frustrated. But I've never seen her . . . *frightened.*

She's been exchanging messages with Headquarters and the FBI as fast as the light lag will allow. What the hell's going on?"

"Dr. Liao had close ties with the Chinese government," Flynn said. "Beijing might be real upset with the United States right now. And President Mendez is trying to improve relations with the Chinese. If he can't convince the public and certain powerful congressmen that Liao wasn't operating under government orders, relations with the Chinese stay sour—probably get worse. Then Mendez can't cut the defense budget. And he has to come up with money from someplace to keep Social Security from going bankrupt, or tens of millions of angry retired people will vote against him in the next election."

Feldstein shook his head. "That's not it." He tapped his chest. "*We* didn't kill Liao. We can't be blamed for this mess. But Hathaway's *frightened.* Like they're going to send her head to the Chinese to atone for Liao's death."

Betty appeared at the table. She pointed at the bar while addressing Feldstein. "That group in the middle there would like to know what you're drinking."

Feldstein looked over his shoulder at the bar, then turned to Betty and sighed. "I'm on duty. Tell 'em I'll take a rain check."

Betty shrugged. "As you wish, but tomorrow those guys will have forgotten that they offered to buy you a drink."

"It won't be tomorrow. It will be shortly after midnight, and they'll still be here." Sid got to his feet and turned to Flynn. "Let me know if you learn anything."

Flynn held up his hands. "Sorry, Sid. The national-security blanket applies to us, too. We've been ordered not to talk about it. Why do you think I spent half the afternoon saying 'no comment' to reporters?"

"But you don't work for the government! You don't have to follow their orders!"

"No, I don't. I can choose to piss off people who can stuff

my investigator's license up my nose."

Feldstein lowered his eyebrows and put his hands on his hips. "After all the favors I did for you last week, you owe me!"

Flynn raised a finger. "Can you do me one more favor? Can you get my license back after the government takes it away? And before you say 'yes,' remember that if I tell you anything you're not supposed to know—which, in this case, seems to be everything—you'll be transferred to Pluto or maybe just assassinated."

"Thanks, buddy. I'll remember this the next time you want some info from the Marshals Office." Feldstein stalked out.

Wendy gulped more champagne. She looked at her husband out of the corner of her eye. "Just when did you figure out that Drake was still alive?"

"Last night. All sorts of sensitive files had been deleted from his computer—files that he wouldn't want me to see, like the one he certainly has on you and the ones he has on the Warshovskys. And Drake's chair fit me perfectly, although his legs are shorter than mine. He must have raised the seat before he left his office, which meant he knew I'd be using the chair before he would. But if Drake had been about to enter a dangerous situation, he would have covered himself with security-camera surveillance and well-armed goons. He didn't. So I guessed that Drake had faked his disappearance. This morning, one of Security's computer experts confirmed that the missing files had been deleted from the keyboard by Drake, so I knew I was right. I tested my hypothesis by interviewing Mrs. Drake, and she confirmed it."

"When?" Wendy demanded. "I was there! She didn't say anything you didn't already know!"

"When she opened the door." Wendy did not appear enlightened, so Flynn explained, "Bad news should be delivered in person. When we appeared in Mrs. Drake's doorway, she should have assumed that we were there to tell her that we'd found her husband's body—that's what the guard thought, remember? Instead, she politely asked if she could help us. She knew her husband wasn't dead."

Wendy stared into space while she digested the revelation. "That's going to take a lot of getting used to."

"Hmm?"

"The thought of Drake as a human being. He didn't tell Warshovsky, he didn't tell Dettweiler, he didn't even tell his handpicked successor, but he briefed his wife so she wouldn't worry about him." Wendy leaned back in her chair. "That's more than you did for your wife."

"Drake didn't have to keep the secret from his wife. She isn't a Station executive and she doesn't go out much. She wasn't going to be talking to whoever planted the bomb and inadvertently give the game away. Besides, you said yourself she was a mirror image of her husband—expressionless eyes."

It was so obvious when Michael explained it. Wendy wanted to kick herself. She was the one with the expensive Yale education; she should have been able to figure it out herself. "Drake's entire plan was to draw out Liao?"

"Liao and anyone else who knew about the bomb. The untimely death of the bomb's babysitter made him think that something was about to happen, but Drake didn't know what and he didn't know when. He wasn't going to let someone else determine the course of events. Liao was Drake's prime suspect—he had cast suspicion on himself by showing concern about Manstein's death, and had designed the section of the Station where the bomb was found—but he obviously hadn't killed Manstein. So Drake didn't know how many factions were trying to get their hands on the device. He figured that if he disappeared, at least one of those factions would think that someone else was about to make a move, and would be forced to move first and possibly move carelessly—which is exactly what Liao did."

"And this would be Drake's one and only chance to get the goods on Liao, so he couldn't take any chances." Wendy looked at her husband. "You thought Liao was the bad guy because he was so concerned about Manstein's murder?"

"I thought he was *involved* with Manstein because he was so interested in his murder. But I didn't know he was the bad guy until he told us he was about to detonate the device."

"*One* of the bad guys. We still don't know who hired Gorkov to kill Manstein."

A shadow fell across the table. Flynn looked up. A blonde—a very attractive one—was standing there. She looked familiar.

"You didn't tell me you were Mike Flynn!"

Michael finally recognized the bartender from the Gold Dollar Casino. She was wearing tight tan slacks and a short white top. "It was a top-secret investigation. You didn't have a need to know."

"Are you still looking for that guy? The one you showed me the picture of? I remembered where I'd seen him before. He came into the Gold Dollar a couple o' weeks ago and went in back."

The fog of alcohol in Flynn's brain thinned. "To see Gorkov?"

The blonde shrugged. "Probably. Hey, I'm glad you caught Gorkov and his gorillas. They gave me the creeps."

Flynn looked at his wife. "I had help. You're not working tonight?"

"My night off. I've never been in here before. Is this place always this busy?"

"Sometimes." Flynn nodded at the bar. "The owner's tending bar. She's a friend of mine. Why don't you ask her if she could use another bartender?"

The blonde looked toward Betty. "You mean, the one . . ."

"With her clothes on," Wendy completed the thought.

"Ah, thanks. I might do that."

Flynn didn't know if he'd done the blonde a favor. Betty couldn't pay as much as the Gold Dollar.

"If Manstein was borrowing money from Gorkov . . ."

Flynn shook his head. "Drake's investigation showed he never lost more than five hundred dollars at one time gambling. He didn't need money."

"Then, why did Manstein see Gorkov? And why did Gorkov kill him?"

Now Flynn could figure out the entire story. "Three weeks ago, when Liao and his entourage started appearing on the Station news, Manstein was in here and made a disparaging remark about Chinese. I'd guess that Manstein had recognized whoever had recruited him, and discovered that he'd been lied to—when he was recruited, they'd told him they were neoluddites. He was willing to blow up the Station in a glorious protest against industrial automation, but he wasn't going to blow it up just so that the Asian station—of which the Chinese are minority owners—would have a monopoly out here. So, to get even with the people who'd lied to him, he decided to give the bomb to some real neoluddites. He sent several e-mails to invalid addresses—probably neoluds he knew before he came out here—trying to contact someone who would use the bomb for a purpose of which Manstein approved. In the meantime, he needed to find somebody who could smuggle a nuclear weapon back to planet three. To whom on Jupiter Station would you go for help in a criminal enterprise?"

"And Gorkov killed him in a sudden attack of patriotism?"

Flynn shook his head. "Liao had lied to Manstein about the bomb's location—better security that way. He'd told Helmuth that the bomb was adjacent to elevator number three, maybe because he knew the radiation level was high there. Manstein liked to visit his baby—he rode that elevator every night before going to bed, just to be close to it. But Gorkov double-crossed him. A neoluddite group couldn't pay as much for the bomb as the Feds could. Big Bill checked out Manstein's story with a crude instrument—the radiation detector they found in Gorkov's office today—that couldn't differentiate between Jovian radiation and the neutron flux from a nuke. When it showed higher than normal radiation in elevator shaft number three, he concluded that Manstein hadn't made up the nuke story. Since he thought he knew where the bomb was, he didn't need Manstein anymore. To keep him from having a suicidal change of mind, he had Knuckles cave in his head with a wrench. Lavalle and Weasel couldn't control their criminal impulses and stole the cash that Liao had given Manstein to live on—plus everything else of value they could find." It was all supposition but it all fit.

"So, *nobody* hired Gorkov to kill Manstein!" Wendy paused while she tried to figure out the rest. "But if Big Bill was about to get a fortune from the Feds, why did he kill Leron Cross? He could certainly get the government to overlook his drug and arms dealing as part of the deal for the bomb—they were keeping the marshals from investigating him."

"The government could keep him from being indicted, but it couldn't stop Drake from plugging the hole in his security and cutting off Gorkov's main source of income. No, Leron had to be silenced, if for no other reason than that's what gangsters always do with rats."

Wendy stared at her champagne glass like it was a crystal ball. "You don't suppose Drake is past his prime, do you? Telling his wife about his top-secret plan, going to such extremes to keep it secret and then leaving so many clues behind that you were able to figure it out . . ."

"He left the clues on purpose. He wanted me to figure it

out." Wendy stared at her husband, so Michael explained, "He couldn't tell me outright—he couldn't tell anybody, not even Dettweiler—because he hadn't told Warshovsky."

Wendy considered the Company politics involved and nodded slowly. "Yeah, I could tell, this afternoon, that Warshovsky was unhappy about being kept in the dark . . . and Dettweiler isn't bright enough to figure it out from the clues."

"That's right. Dettweiler might have overreacted, might have sealed off the Station from the rest of the solar system, might have prevented the prime suspect from revealing himself."

Cheers and shouts of "Good job!" made Flynn look up. Silvanus Drake, his arm around the waist of his wife, was approaching Flynn's table. Drake nodded at the chairs that the Adamlys had vacated. "Are these seats taken?"

"Only if you're sitting there," Flynn said.

Drake stood aside to let his wife take the chair closest to the wall. He slipped into the seat next to her.

"If I had known that you frequented this establishment, I'd have gone elsewhere," Wendy said.

"We can go elsewhere, too." Drake looked over his shoulder for the bartender, but Betty was already approaching. He took out his wallet and put twenty-five dollars on the table. "I'll have a beer. The Company brew is fine. My wife will have a vodka and tonic."

Betty nodded. "You can put your money away. It's on those guys at the middle of the bar."

Drake nodded in appreciation at his benefactors. He put his money back in his wallet. Betty left to get the drinks.

"We found Hector Rivera in an apartment belonging to a couple of prostitutes," Drake said. "Also in the apartment was a computer secured by Manstein's retinal patterns. Some of the fingerprints on it were Manstein's, too. The others belonged to Rivera."

Drake was speaking freely in front of his wife; she obviously knew everything. "Is Weasel cooperating?" Flynn asked.

"He's following his boss's orders and not talking, either."

Betty returned with the Drakes' beverages. Flynn watched her return to the bar, then raised his glass in a toast. "Very well done."

Drake disagreed. "I didn't foresee that you'd question my wife. I failed to brief her on what to say to you."

Flynn had done everything Drake had hoped he would, and then some—and by interviewing Drake's wife, he had put the plan in jeopardy. If there had been witnesses to that conversation, they too might have figured out that Drake was still alive, and might have inadvertently revealed the plan to the bad guys. Flynn looked at Megan and she averted her eyes.

"Well, the rest of the operation was very well done," Flynn said. "I'm especially impressed with how quickly you got the bomb back to the Station. Just when did you order its return?"

Drake sipped his beer. "I couldn't. It wasn't Company property."

Wendy gave Drake an acid stare. "Well, what would you have done if Wilmer de Birk had decided to keep it?"

"Let him. We could build a much better nuke ourselves."

Flynn wondered if the device had been in its original compartment for the entire ten years except for the one day when Warshovsky and Drake showed it to him. That would explain the lack of security at Wilmer de Birk's storage shed. But Drake would never confirm that suspicion.

Drake said, "The government wants the bomb returned to Earth on the next fast ship. A couple of marshals will probably accompany it—can't have bombs like that lying around unattended. That will leave Hathaway even more short-handed. Fewer marshals means additional work for my security force. I don't need that, not with Liao's sabotage of the construction of the Asian station becoming public knowledge. We're certain to get the contract to complete it. I'll have to provide security over there while we're working on it. And just today I learned that the security scanners at the entrances to this station—and the satellites—are inadequate, and that there could be dozens of unlicensed firearms in the hands of untrustworthy individuals."

Wendy seemed amused. "Chalmisiak will have a conniption if you ask Warshovsky for more resources."

"We'll be short a master welder, too," Drake said. "Pierce isn't charging Carl Wiesen with anything, but Ed Warshovsky has decided to make an example of him for doing unauthorized work and loaning Company equipment to people who aren't Company employees. His contract's being cancelled."

Wiesen had no connection to Manstein, so that meant . . . "He loaned equipment to Gorkov?" Michael asked.

Drake nodded. "A hydrogen torch."

Flynn squinted. "When?"

"This morning. We found it hidden in the utility tunnel."

It was the final piece to the puzzle. For a moment Flynn thought he could see a glimmer in Drake's empty eyes.

"Warshovsky wanted to cancel your retainer," Drake continued, "but I persuaded him that we might need your services again some day."

"Planning to die again anytime soon? Or do you anticipate legal problems over shooting Liao?"

Drake chose his words carefully. "The government will do whatever is necessary to keep the details of the bomb from being made public." Almost as an afterthought, he added, "You've already signed a nondisclosure agreement, so there's nothing you have to do to keep earning your retainer."

Flynn looked at Drake, at his blank, mannequin's face. If Drake had deleted one more file, the security director might have let Warshovsky cancel the retainer.

Drake looked at Wendy. "Mr. Warshovsky ordered me to take your name off the Security roster."

Wendy inhaled sharply. "Doesn't he trust—"

"I managed to convince him that you—that all the members of the Executive Staff—are target risks, and should be trained and equipped to defend themselves."

Wendy's brain, slowed by alcohol, needed a second to digest that. "Oh." Drake seemed to have done her a favor. She couldn't figure out why.

Drake finished his beer. "We have to be going. Thanks for holding down the fort today. I knew you were the only one on the Station who could do it."

Flynn shrugged. "The way you set it up, it wasn't hard."

Wendy didn't watch Drake and his wife leave. "You sound like you admire him!"

"I admire the way he keeps this station secure. So should you. He saved you from nuclear incineration."

Wendy clenched her teeth. "You're even starting to think like Drake! That's just how he would excuse his behavior! And the way you two were looking at each other? Nonverbal communication, if I ever saw it!"

"Drake was confirming our supposition that Manstein had hired Gorkov to smuggle the bomb."

Wendy's expression didn't change. "Are you going to keep me in the dark about that, too?"

"The hydrogen torch—Gorkov was going to use it to get to the bomb. When you discovered their secret exit today, they were probably on their way to elevator shaft number three with it."

Wendy relaxed in her chair. "We should drink a toast to the murder victims. Manstein figured out he'd been lied to, and set in motion the chain of events that led us to Liao. Cross was killed because he wouldn't be a criminal, and led us to a weakness in Drake's security." Wendy raised her glass. "Is it a social *faux pas* to propose a toast with an empty glass?"

"Not if you're too . . . celebratory to notice. And while you're complimenting the victims, don't forget that Drake said someone had tried to access the bomb during the reception for Liao. Must have been somebody who came out with Liao on the *Californian.* He was probably going to program the bomb to go off after Liao had finished his business and gone home. But Manstein had accessed the bomb's controller the week before, just so that it wouldn't respond to Liao before it was moved off the Station. If it had responded to Liao's associate, Liao wouldn't have had to come back here and we never would have caught him."

Wendy wasn't too drunk to think beyond that. "Why *did* Liao come back here? Why didn't he send the same person who tried to access the bomb during his reception last week?"

Michael shrugged. "Maybe because Liao didn't *know* that the bomb hadn't been discovered and disconnected. He was the engineer. He was probably the only one in his party who knew enough control codes to see if the lack of response last Tuesday was due to a malfunction or to a recent access by Manstein."

Wendy wished someone would buy her another glass of champagne. "Oh, the Administration must be upset. They thought they were getting a terrorist nuke in secret, but now the negotiations with the Chinese are endangered and the entire solar system knows about the bomb."

"But they don't know it was a nuke. This incident is a major embarrassment to Liao's hard-liner friends in Beijing. It might weaken them enough to give the market socialists the upper hand. That makes it easier for Mendez to improve Sino-American relations and cut the defense budget. The Administration won't be upset about that." Flynn almost chuckled. The market socialists, with their undisguised capitalist tendencies, were the darlings of Western politicians, but under their rule China could be an economic powerhouse, which would lead inevitably to better military capability. That, however, was a long-term problem. The U.S. government's immediate concern was funding Social Security, something that was less impossible if there was no need to stand up to the Chinese. "When Warshovsky goes back to Earth next year to become the Company CEO, he will remind the Administration of the Company's role in improved Sino-American relations at every opportunity."

Wendy peeked at her husband from the corner of her eye. "You make this affair sound like a Machiavellian Company plot."

"Drake always plans for the future. He's had ten years to work this out. He arranged the conclusion to benefit the Company as much as possible."

Wendy started to take a sip of champagne, then remembered that her glass was empty. "He didn't have to kill Liao. He knew Liao couldn't set off the bomb. He could have let him walk away. There would have been no publicity, no need for the Chinese to disown him . . ."

But Liao had planted a nuclear device on Drake's station, a serious sin, and Liao had to be seriously punished for it. Flynn considered his wife's mood and decided not to share that opinion with her. "Liao tried to detonate the bomb before Drake shot him. If he had survived, how long do you think it would take an engineering genius like him to figure out that his bomb hadn't exploded on command because the Company had disconnected it?"

Wendy's shoulders sagged. "And Drake couldn't have Liao spreading that theory around—our government would wonder why we hadn't told them we'd found a nuke on the Station." Once again, Drake had acted in the Company's best interest. "But legally, he still committed murder." She sighed. "And since I'm his lawyer, I can't turn him in."

But Flynn wasn't Drake's lawyer. Like any citizen, he was required by law to report felonies to the authorities. His wife had, in a legalistically deniable way, just told him what he should do. "Wendy, no matter how much Hathaway dislikes Drake, and how much she'd like to nail him for something, the government won't let her investigate him—they'll do anything necessary to keep the fact that the bomb was nuclear from becoming public knowledge. Why do you think the government ordered us not to talk about it? A secret presidential pardon for Drake isn't out of the question." Gorkov and his flunkies were going to walk, too—they knew about the bomb, and it was the only way the government could buy their silence.

Wendy clenched her fists. Drake would get away with it *again,* this time with the help of the government. She surveyed the noisy crowd. "They could have been vaporized today and they haven't a clue. The people they elected won't tell them of the danger they were in. Whatever happened to government of, by, and for the people?"

"It disappeared during the Great Depression. Didn't that expensive Yale education of yours include reading Puerifoy's *Descent into Socialism*?"

Wendy pushed her glass away. She looked at the two full whiskey glasses in front of her husband and said, "Are you going to drink that whiskey or just admire your reflection in its surface?"

"Wendy, you don't like whiskey."

Wendy grabbed one of the glasses. She gulped its contents.

"Wendy, you told me not to let you—"

Wendy was too intoxicated to be bothered by the booze. She smiled, and a trickle of scotch escaped from the corner of her mouth and ran down her chin. "Private investigators don't drink champagne. They drink whiskey. I know—I've read enough detective novels."

"You're not a private investigator. You're an attorney."

"Being an investigator is more fun. And I'm good at it." Wendy tapped the center of her shiny yellow blouse, unnecessarily calling Flynn's attention to what was concealed beneath it. "I'm the one who got the goods on Gorkov. Silvanus Drake couldn't do that." She jabbed her index finger into Flynn's chest. "And neither could you!"

"You nearly got killed in the process! If you had carried your gun in its holster, like I told you to do, instead of in your purse, you might have been able to draw it before they captured you!"

Wendy smirked. "They would have found it when they searched me. Instead, I shot Lavalle and dropped him in his tracks—"

"You needed three shots from two meters, plus one that missed!" Flynn wished he had used his brief tenure as security director to take his wife's name off the Security roster. "If you had called me and told me your plans . . ."

Wendy rolled her eyes. "You would have told me that Drake had already checked that utility tunnel. And we never would have caught Gorkov. I make a pretty good investigator."

Flynn shut his eyes. "Wendy, my love, you're not still contemplating resigning from the Company, are you?"

"Being a lawyer's no fun. Nobody ever bought me drinks all night because I graduated sixth in my class from Yale Law." Wendy had never gotten so intoxicated while graduating sixth in her class from Yale law, either. In fact, as far as Flynn knew, she had never gotten really drunk until she had started dating him. "But I catch one bad guy, and I'm a hero—er, heroine." Wendy tried to drain more whiskey from the empty glass. "Besides, my clients never listen to me."

"They will now. We know something Drake wants to keep private." Wendy looked at him. "He told his wife his plans so she wouldn't worry about him. People think of him as an emotionless robot, and he likes it that way."

Wendy sat up straight in her chair. "You're right! I've got him by the short hairs!" Understanding penetrated her besotted neurons. "*That's* why he talked Warshovsky into keeping me on the Security roster!" She scowled. "The bastard's trying to bribe me!"

Drake had also neglected to check the faces of people entering and leaving the Gold Dollar Casino against his database—a flaw in his image as the perfect security director—and Flynn knew it. Michael, however, had been working under a nondisclosure agreement when he had made the discovery. Drake had come to Betty's bar to remind him of that. "And me—he arranged for me to keep getting the fifty-thou-a-year retainer. But when Warshovsky gets promoted and his replacement comes out from Earth, you might be able to get between him and Drake and become his principal advisor. Then Drake won't be able to do everything in secret."

Wendy's mood had reversed again. "I knew there was some reason I married you!"

"I thought you married me for my wit, my good looks, and my incredible charm."

Wendy's eyes focused on the remaining whiskey glass in front of Flynn. Michael's hand barely beat hers to the glass. "Okay, be that way." Wendy looked around the bar and called out, "Doesn't anybody in this place want to buy a lady a drink?"

Wendy had reached the level of intoxication at which she was capable of doing something that would embarrass her to death when she sobered up. Some partying soul in Betty's Bar might even record it on his computer and post it on the Web. Michael belted down his whiskey and stood up. "You don't need a drink. We're leaving."

"Why? The night is young!"

"Because I want to ravish you right now and I don't want to do it here."

Wendy hesitated. "Oh. Yeah. Our apartment would be better." She tried to stand up but nearly stumbled. Flynn picked her up and slung her over his shoulder, bringing hoots of laughter from the crowd. "Can we come back here when you're done ravishing me?"

Flynn shook his head. "I intend to ravish you all night." It was an empty boast; he had been too long without sleep and had had too much to drink. He wouldn't be able to ravish her even once. But Wendy was too intoxicated to notice his condition.

"I love youth drugs," she said.

ABOUT THE AUTHOR

David Michael Drury grew up in Casco, Wisconsin, twenty miles east of Green Bay. He earned a BSEE degree from the Milwaukee School of Engineering in 1972 and a Ph.D. from Marquette University in 1978. He spent three years with Motorola in Schaumburg, Illinois, and for nine years was a Member of the Technical Staff in the Radar Department of Sandia National Laboratories in Albuquerque, New Mexico. Since 1987 Dr. Drury has been a member of the faculty of the University of Wisconsin—Platteville, where he is a professor of electrical engineering. Dr. Drury enjoys hunting, fishing, and target shooting, plays golf and the guitar, and used to play a fairly good game of chess. He flies his own plane, a Grumman Tiger N53GT. Dr. Drury is single and lives with Midnight Sky and TC, his little pet cats.